THE PROGENITOR SAGA

SPARK RISING

KATE CORCINO

Spark Rising: The Progenitor Saga
Contact Information: www.katecorcino.com

First paperback edition December 2014
All Rights Reserved.

Publishing History
First Edition, December, 2014
Print ISBN: 978-0990732808

Published in the United States of America

Dedicated to all the girls
who struggle to believe.
Whatever the dream may be,
you can.

And for my Oso,
who always believed in me,
even when I did not.

Un mil besos
no son bastante
para expresar mi amor para ti.

THE PROGENITOR SAGA

SPARK RISING

KATE CORCINO

 ONE

"Nothing says 'Home, Sweet Home' like an abandoned gas station."

The words came with a muffled snort from one of the two men following Lena. He probably hadn't meant for her to hear them—probably—but the rich, husky tone of his voice carried them to her.

Lena rolled her eyes, her back still to the client and his assistant. "Does my home offend you, Mr. Reyes?" She kept her tone even and pleasant. It took effort. A lot of effort.

"No, no," he answered from behind her. "I'm just trying to understand what would make someone see this place and say, 'Now this...this is the place I want to call home.'" He paused. "Miss Gracey," he added, mimicking her formality.

She could hear his amusement. It was nothing she hadn't heard from other clients before. As far as she was concerned, he could keep trying. She highly doubted he'd get it.

When she'd arrived at the ancient gas station nine years before, she'd been fifteen and full of rage, fear, and pride over making her escape from a life of hiding in the city. The empty building still stood firm against the onslaught of the world. Buckled, collapsed pavement at the far end of the lot showed where the tanks below ground had ignited during the cataclysm two centuries before. The void was filled with sand pushed by the wind—a shifting, fatal trap for the unwary. A tumbleweed bounced across the rubble of the road, smashing against teetering pump fourteen, shedding thorns and seeds as it rolled off again.

The desolation was a reflection of Lena's grief. She'd staked her claim on the station and carved her home out of drifted sand and weeds. She didn't expect those who lived in the comfort of a relo-city—surrounded by people and walls to keep the world at bay—to understand why it mattered to claim a corner of the wild as hers alone. The cities that had grown out of the post-disaster relocation centers were the last hope of those clinging to the old ways. They were willing to give up a lot to live in safety. She knew safety was relative.

Now her client, and the assistant who'd powered the electric vehicle to get him out here, sized her home up as they followed her inside. The visual examination of the home she'd built for herself, the life alone, was typical of every client, every time.

This time the examination, and the judgment it implied, rankled. She spun around, mouth opened to snap at them.

She stopped. Alejandro Reyes had removed his antique sunglasses, and his dark eyes were focused on her. She tried to escape the intensity of them by looking down, but that was a mistake. Instead of a heated gaze, she caught his wide-chested, lean-hipped body as he slid closer to her like one of the big cats of the desert, stalking prey.

He's not a hunter, Lena. Just another indolent client looking for a black market charge to make his easy life easier.

She cleared her throat, turning to his assistant. The other man, Lucas, was busy inspecting every detail of her home. She doubted Reyes's attention had ever left her back. It certainly didn't leave her face now that she had turned to the other man. She could feel his focus still, the itch of attention that always made her self-conscious. He wasn't interested in the room.

"Where'd you get the light bulbs?"

They were a luxury item, rarely seen outside of Council buildings, but she wasn't fooled. He was studying her, not her fixtures.

She shrugged. "I barter for everything." She considered him for a moment, gauging the risk he presented. He didn't seem threatening, merely interested, and Lena didn't sleep with her clients, no matter how hot they were. She held out her hand. "May I have the item, please?"

Reyes had to snap his fingers at Lucas to get his attention. She'd dismissed the Spark assistant as soon as she'd seen his energy bloom, the faint displacement like a heat shimmer that other Sparks could see. The brightness indicated the inherent power of a Spark and showed up the moment the mental power was accessed. Typically, the bloom would grow as a Spark worked with the Dust to create the electrical energy that was otherwise dead to the world.

The assistant's bloom was unimpressive, probably the reason his boss had to seek out black market charges from people like her. It was also the likely reason for his slack jaw as he noted the energy signature on all of the modifications she and the Dust had made to nearly every item in her home.

Lucas crossed to Reyes and handed him a small, cloth-wrapped package. Reyes held it up, delaying giving it to her.

"Now, I was assured you're a strong Spark. You can get the Dust to make anything work, whether you've seen it before or not," he said.

Like so many others, obviously Reyes thought that the power to create or store energy was due to a Spark's ability to force the Dust to do one's will. They didn't understand the truth of the Dust, any more than any of them understood what it really was. Everyone had a theory—a virus to which Sparks alone were immune, invisible aliens working to keep humanity weak, even that Dust was the final ruse of the old government meant to hide an evolutionary shift. The Tribulationists believed Dust, and the Sparks themselves, were a sign of their god's displeasure.

They were all wrong. The Dust was alive. It wanted to help. She wasn't special because she could force it to do what she wanted; she was special because she knew how to ask. She knew how to listen.

"You're assuming I haven't seen whatever you found." She wiggled her outstretched fingers at him for the item. She hadn't been told what the object was, but her brother's contact had assured her that if she made Reyes happy, she'd earn a regular client.

"I am. Yeah." Barely contained laughter danced behind the words. He settled it onto her palm.

Why all the mystery, gentlemen?

Whatever it was, it was illegal as hell. But then, so was she. Females as powerful as she was didn't exist, and the Council scoured what was left of the world to make sure of it. Lena made a noncommittal noise and turned away as she began unwrapping the package.

From his behavior, she could tell he'd brought her an antique object to charge. Most of her business was in batteries and capacitors. City people often ran out of the rations of electrical charges earned through work before they got through the month. The unsympathetic Council of Nine didn't promise the people in its walled cities an easy life, just protection and an opportunity to work hard to earn a taste of electrical luxury.

People scavenged or bought black market copper and aluminum. Once they added some salt water—even lime juice would work in a pinch—they could build a battery. But the things weren't all that strong. What they really needed was a homemade capacitor. And, of course, a Spark willing to break the law to charge it. Enter Lena, and her black market talents. Demand was high.

"Is this a straight charge of a refurbished item, or will you need me to custom fit a capacitor into it and charge that?" Before he could answer, she finished unwrapping the object. A shock of recognition flashed through, and she spun around, arm extended stiffly to thrust the item back at him.

"Danny's rep would have explained the rules to you," she bit out, referring to her brother. "No powder weapons of any kind."

There was risky, and then there was stupid. She didn't do stupid. And Reyes wasn't nearly as beautiful now that she knew he was a dumbass who was perfectly willing to give stupid a try.

"Take it and go."

He grinned as he shook his head. "It's not a powder weapon."

"Do you think I'm an idiot? It's a gun."

"No, it isn't."

She glowered at him. "Take. It. Back."

He sighed and tilted his head. "It's not a gun."

She closed her hand around the weapon and cocked her arm back. He spoke rapidly then, hands up to forestall the throw.

"It's not. It doesn't shoot bullets. It shoots little barbs that are attached by wires. It isn't long-range. And it doesn't even hold bullets. It uses electricity. No powder." He licked his lips. "Look at it. Look at it."

She did, not sure what to look for outside of general shape. Powder weapons were rare and forbidden by the Council. Only the Council's agents, those who policed each of the nine zones, had use of the old weapons. It took a strong Spark to overcome the Dust's effect on powder. While no one knew exactly what Dust was, they did know what it did. Inhibiting combustive reactions was one those things. Agents, the men who'd been sent to the Ward School as boys and gave their youth up to train their native gifts, could get the Dust to fire powder. They were the strongest of the Sparks.

Her lips twisted. *Yeah. Right.* She was the exception. But her father had made it clear any girl strong enough for the Ward School wouldn't go there for training. She'd go and disappear.

She examined the weapon. Guns fired bullets out a hollow barrel. The front of this thing had two flaps, one atop the other, and beneath them, small twin holes with tiny tips perched within. She flicked a fingernail over the top of one.

"If you open the handle, you'll see there aren't any bullets. There's a battery pack," he said. "Electricity. Not combustion."

She turned it over again, found the small latch, and pried apart the handle. Nestled inside was an ancient, corroded battery pack.

"See? I told you. It's not a gun. It's called a Taser." The laughter was back in his voice. It was light, almost a chuckle.

The sound of it could soothe any raised hackles, except for hers.

"Can you make a capacitor that'll fit in there?"

Now that he'd said the name, she recognized the weapon. Electrical current could disrupt a Spark's ability to generate a charge, one current disrupting another. The Council's agents used Tasers to control Sparks who went rogue.

She didn't know how often it happened. From the time a child demonstrated any Spark at all, they were immersed in the Council's propaganda: It was an honor to be a Spark. The gift of control over the Dust meant you were privileged to help support the recovery of the human race. What could be a more worthwhile pursuit for a human life?

Lena could think of a few things, but she was smart enough to live quietly. Those who didn't... Well, those who refused had led the Council to research ways to ensure their cooperation.

And now I have an opportunity to play with one and figure it out.

She met Reyes's eyes again, risking the intensity of his dark brown gaze. Instead, she found amusement. He raised his brows, a grin curving his lips, as if daring her to try.

Well, shit.

A dare was a lure she couldn't resist. She responded with an answering smile, easing the tension.

Decision made, she turned away. "The question isn't whether or not I can fit a capacitor, but whether or not it will work anyway. This compartment is in bad shape."

She carried the weapon over to her work area and sat at her stool. She could ignore them now. The work end of being a black market Spark was easy. Trusting people long enough to take their C-notes or barter in exchange for a charge was the hard part. If it didn't give her a vengeful thrill every time she broke the Council's laws by charging an illicit item for a client, she'd never do it. She'd live as a happy hermit deep in her desert instead. Infrequent trips to the city would be reserved for sex and the few items she couldn't make or scavenge for herself.

Lena tucked her hair back behind her ears and leaned over the weapon. Wrapping a soft bit of cotton around the tip of a thin bone pick, she used her gentlest touch to rub away the worst of the bright orange and brown corrosion to assess the damage. She'd have the Dust check the leads when she was done.

"Where'd you find this thing anyway? Not in Relo-Azcon,

that's for sure."

"*Relo*-Azcon?" Reyes's challenging tone made her turn her head. He threw a knowing smile at Lucas. "She's one of those."

She turned fully to him. "One of what?"

Reyes smiled lazily. "One of those who uses 'relo' to remind herself what a big, bad place she managed to escape." He wandered closer, his casual tone belied by dark eyes that held her own. Intense Reyes was back with a vengeance. "C'mon. It's Azcon. It's not a relocation center anymore. It's a city. It has been for more than a hundred years. It's a safe place, a good life, for everyone who lives there. You should come back."

Of course, *he* thought so. He was one of the wealthy who lived in charged comfort.

What do you know about what life is really like for the people who make your life comfortable, you big jerk?

Most Sparks didn't live in charged extravagance. They used as little electricity as possible, because they knew someone like them had paid the price for it in pain. Each week, every Spark in every city took their scheduled turn on the grounding platforms or risked overloading their brains and stroking out. The huge open-air stages were built above the cities, for the safety of the unpowered, so the Sparks could discharge the feedback energy that accumulated within their bodies.

It was hard for Lena to believe now, but when she had been very small, she'd thought the groundings on the platform were beautiful. The crash of the lightning discharge was scary, sure, but the constant flashes of light made the days sparkle and chased the dark from the night.

And then she'd gone for her first grounding. She had been four, and had started working with a Spark tutor often enough that she'd built up her own feedback. She clutched her mother's hand, staring at her brother's profile as he climbed up to the platform ahead of her. He was sweating as they climbed the open, winding stairs, despite the chilled winter air on their cheeks. Those in line before them went first, removing clothes, standing shivering on the platform for a moment before being encased in blinding electric light. Their bodies were rigid, corded with agony, and the crash wasn't merely loud up that close. It deafened Lena, froze her in place while the vibrations shook through the platform to her bare feet and up her small body.

When it was over, the Sparks fell, collapsed from the pain to the heated floor of the platform. Council employees scooted forward, lifting them and moving them inside to spend their hour in recovery before heading back to family, job, or school. It was an efficient system, a machine that ran smoothly so long as the cogs were well-oiled by obedient citizens.

She blinked the memory away. "This is a safe place. Nobody but me makes the rules. I like it here just fine."

"Are you sure about that?" His tone dropped as he leaned in and smiled, voice turning low and persuasive. His proximity, coupled with her awareness of their chemistry, set off alarm bells in her head. "I'm a man in a position to be good to the right woman."

Heat flooded her face, but it wasn't embarrassment. It was anger. The man was a head and half taller than her tiny self, so more than six feet tall. He was older, perhaps early thirties, and dark, with olive skin and black hair trimmed close to his head. He moved with a sinuous grace that reminded her of how long it had been since she'd made her way back to find a boy in the city. The whole package was wrapped in a perfectly preserved, black, relic-silk shirt.

Everything about him screamed C-notes and sex. He expected her to believe he was this interested in *her*—a skinny, short, reclusive Spark? Oh, she wouldn't deny the sexual spark between them. As far as the physical? Her dark red hair and blue-green eyes were unusual, but so were the galaxies of dark freckles spinning across her skin. And she was *fragrant* today. The damn water heater she'd scavenged and dragged across the desert was broken again—it never worked more than a week or two before it burned out every circuit she attached to it.

In spite of her self-conscious anger, she could feel the pull as her body tried to respond to Reyes's lure, heat swirling low and slow in her belly. It pissed her off even more. Plus, a bit of chemistry between strangers didn't explain this level of attention.

Whatever he wanted, it wasn't her.

Please don't be stupid enough that you came out here to prey on me. It wouldn't go the way they planned.

"I'm not the right woman." She stood, keeping the stool between her and the man in front of her. "And I'm not interested."

She shook her head. It wasn't just figurative alarms going off in her head. She could hear the Dust at the back of her mind, a sibilance, not quite a whisper. The Dust liked to help. Lena let it. Reyes spoke again, a pleasant drone she ignored. She focused on the images the Dust flashed in her mind.

Six intruders made their way across the desert, moving through the blanket of Dust and sand. They encircled her home in pairs. Teams of two? Council agents.

And two more were here inside with her. The Council had found her. Her father hadn't been wrong.

Rage ticked her eyelid. With every step the agents took across the desert, everything she had built went up like so much tinder. Unlike the mid-range Sparks who tried to flee the Council, she could keep them from dragging her back to be a power plant slave. All she had to do was everything her parents had warned her against. She'd have to reveal her true abilities.

She focused on the Dust within their bodies.

Wake up, little friends. Wake up. I have work for you. Listen....

Reyes stopped speaking the moment she went still. He exchanged a look with Lucas before looking back at her. It was all the time she needed.

Lungs and muscles. Lungs and muscles. No breath. No movement.

She could see the shift behind his eyes as he realized he had underestimated her, and then he gasped. His windpipe and lungs constricted then he grabbed at his chest. His muscles locked.

Beside him, Lucas made a wet, wheezing sound as he toppled to the floor, body rigid.

She stepped away from behind the stool and moved sideways across the room.

"Your friends are coming." She had no idea why she spoke.

"I'm sorry it hurts, but you should have left me alone. I wasn't bothering anyone." Lena didn't even know if he could hear her.

Reyes's face purpled and veins stood out in his neck and forehead. He shouldn't still be standing.

She hated that she felt guilty. "The Dust will stop once I'm gone. If you make it, don't look for me. I won't hold back next time."

TWO

She ducked into her room, silently ordering the Dust covering her escape route to wake. Alarms shrieked in her head. She'd cut it too close. Lena pushed the wooden bed frame out of the way and wiggled on hands and knees toward the corner. She'd have to come back later for her things, after the agents were gone.

A heavy thump sounded behind her. Reyes wasn't going to make it.

She hesitated, then snarled at herself for giving a damn about the agent who'd masqueraded as a new client and invaded her home. She slid headfirst, arms extended, into the hole the Dust opened for her.

It was his own fault, anyway.

He had no way to know you could hit back.

She growled at herself. Simple rule. People who don't want to get hit shouldn't go looking for trouble.

The Dust left after the Great Disaster was everywhere, including in food, water, and air and the people who ate, drank, and breathed it. They didn't know what it was, but other Sparks used it as a catalyst to help spark, or flame, or charge objects. She had played with the Dust every day as a child, during those long hours spent alone, locked away for her own safety. The Dust was alive, and it liked the attention she gave it. It would pretty much do whatever she wanted, including keeping her escape route safe.

She wiggled forward, urging her body down the slope. As soon as her feet cleared the opening behind her, the Dust resealed the floor. They'd see that the bed had been moved, but the floor would be nothing more than what you'd expect to see in a former gas station: worn, ancient, and coated with Dust.

She slid down the smooth tube for about fifteen sloped feet. When she reached the bottom, she pulled herself up onto her elbows, placing her hands flat against the walls.

"Glow," she breathed, visualizing the dim light she wanted the Dust to make for her.

The tube lit up around her. Running footsteps thumped across the floors behind her. Voices shouted about men down. The bed groaned as it was pulled to the middle of the room.

She didn't wait for them to start pounding on the floor. The Dust would keep the floor knit together for a long time, and when forced, would collapse the head of the tunnel behind her. Still, she scooted, elbow crawling through the tube as fast as she could.

Her tunnel ran two hundred and fifty feet diagonally away from the house to end in a hidden exit on the side of a dried streambed. She couldn't hear anything from behind her now; her own breath rasping in and out of her throat eclipsed every other sound. She had no idea how far she'd come, or how far she still had to go.

Don't panic. Don't panic. Don't panic.

The silent chant did little good. The memory of her father's warning echoed in her head.

She had been five on her first day of Testing Year. Her father had come into the room as her mother finished braiding her hair. He'd squatted in front of her, somber, voice soft but emphatic. As a girl, she'd mistaken his fear for anger.

He'd placed his wide hands on either side of her round, freckled face, the girlish mirror of his own, and told her, "You *must* remember, Magdalena. Remind yourself every day, every moment that you must not do well. The Council has been watching for a girl like you. You *must* fail, or they will take you away from us and we will never, ever see you again."

She'd looked at her mother, who leaned against the closed bedroom door to keep out her brother and sister. No one was allowed to know she was different, not even them.

Her father had gently tugged one braid to pull her attention back to him. "We love you, Magdalena. Please remember."

She'd nodded, terrified.

She was terrified again. She'd gotten so used to being authentically herself here in the desert that she'd forgotten how to hide, just as she had only days after starting her Testing Year. She'd wanted to win. Now, as then, she had to disappear.

Her elbow hit solid wall—the end of her tunnel. She slapped her shaking hand against the hatch, and it fell away into its component Dust and whispered down to the dry, orange earth of the stream bed three feet below. Lena clawed at the edge, pulling her way out.

Sudden sunlight blinded her. She tumbled face-first to the ground. Her head shrieked at her to stop, listen, and watch for agents. She didn't. She ran as soon as she gathered her feet under her.

The Pueblo of Santo Domingo offered shelter only four miles away. The arroyo she'd chosen as her escape route cut shallow through the red earth by the seasonal rains. The edge wasn't above her head, but scrubby juniper and mesquite trees were thick around the edges. She hoped it would be enough to protect her from any eyes searching her out.

Less than two days after she had staked her claim on the gas station, the Kewa had appeared. They'd known she was a Spark, of course, just as they'd known she had moved into the abandoned station. Natives could spot the energy bloom practicing Sparks gave off like a heat signature. They were happy to barter in exchange for charges that didn't come from a Council Spark. Over time, they'd come to trust each other. Now, they would be her safe haven.

The agents wouldn't pursue her into occupied Kewa territory. As a friend of the Nations, she could only be taken if there were no tribal witnesses. The Council of Nine had long since begged peace with the Native Nations.

Her feet pounded on the arroyo bottom, carrying her closer to sanctuary. Every impact sent a spike up her spine and into her head, a reminder of how close she was to burn out. She risked a pause to turn back, looking for signs of pursuit. The twisted trees protected her from discovery, but they limited her vision. And she couldn't hear anything over the sound of her own heartbeat and panting breath. She turned back from the direction of home to run on.

Movement flickered through the branches to her side.

Lena snapped her head around, breath caught in her throat. A young agent paced through the desert a hundred yards away. His head swung as he searched for her. She bent at the knees, intending to sink below the arroyo edge. Her movement caught his attention. Their gazes locked.

She spun and exploded up the shallow arroyo wall behind her. The compacted sand crumbled beneath her scrabbling fingers and feet. When she made the top, she clawed through the tearing thorns of the scrubby trees and bushes to reach the desert on the other side. She flew then, running flat out, desperate. He crashed through the brush only moments later as he made it down and then up the arroyo again. His footsteps pounded behind her as the ground rose ahead.

A drop-off loomed on the other side, leading down to the remnants of a cracked and pitted caliche road. A quarter mile to the west and just across the road, Santo Domingo rose from the desert.

Except the sound of breath sawing loud in her ears wasn't only her own. He caught her at the crest of the rise, yanking at her shirt to pull her back. The momentum of her leap pulled him down with her, and they tumbled together down the steep, eroded, red sand.

She hit the hard caliche, and her breath exploded out of her. Even as she gasped, she rolled to her side. She'd pull herself across the road if she had to. His hand caught her ankle, fingers like an iron band, and he dragged her back toward himself. She tried to pull away, her fingertips clawing in vain at the dry top of the road.

She flipped and looked down her body. He held tight to her ankle, pinning it to the road as he reached for a weapon at his side with his other hand. A gun? Or a Taser?

She kicked out with her free foot, desperate and vicious. Her heel made contact with his nose, and she was free. She rolled back over, scrambling to her knees and then her feet. If she could catch her breath, she could run the last stretch to safety.

Wheezing, she made it ten unsteady steps before she blinked the sand from her eyes. She froze.

Across the road from the single turn into Santo Domingo, Reyes leaned against the hood of the Volt, ankles crossed in front of him, hands in pockets. He'd lost the sunglasses, and his dark glare burned across the distance. The heat of it belied his relaxed slouch. Sometime in the hour it must have been since she'd run from him, Reyes had recovered. He wasn't happy.

Lena's breath hissed out of her. She started to reach out to the Dust in his body again before remembering her overloaded brain might well stroke out. She was on her own.

She side-stepped away from the agent scraping the ground behind her. The town was right there, on the other side of a thick earth wall. If she started running now, would either of them catch her before she made it?

Reyes might be slouched against the car, weakened and in pain from her attack. Maybe he wasn't able to run.

Doesn't seem hurt. Seems like a coiled rattler.

Where he'd positioned himself, he'd only have to intercept her.

The agent behind her coughed and got to his feet, spitting blood.

"Enough," Reyes called out as the younger man made to reach for her. He jerked his head in a sharp gesture for the man to head back through the desert. "It's done."

She could feel them now—the Natives gathering in the town. Reyes was right. The Kewa wouldn't allow these Councilmen to lay hands on her now.

Lena let her head fall back for a moment. Gooseflesh rose as a breeze sighed across her skin and cooled the rivulets of sweat. Her hands went up to her hair, smoothing the damp, dark red strands back behind her ears. She crossed her arms tight over her chest and walked right up the middle of the crumbled road. She could see a faint energy bloom hazing the air around him.

Reyes is a Spark, too?

He must have grounded and then abstained in order to fool her with the employer/employee act they'd used to gain access to her. For some irrational reason, that pissed her off even more.

She didn't stop until she was in front of him. If he'd wanted to, he could reach out and grab her. She didn't say anything, just stared right back into those dark, angry eyes. She'd be damned if she'd apologize for hurting him. It wasn't she who had come to his house looking for trouble.

Reyes shook his head, unclenched his jaw, and laughed softly. His gaze flicked to movement in the town behind her. When he looked at her again, he'd managed to dampen the worst of the heat.

"That was a pretty neat trick you pulled back there," he said. His voice was low and rasping raw.

She would not feel bad about this. She shrugged.

Reyes cleared his throat. "Don't suppose you'd consider telling me how to do it?" He managed an amused snort at the look on her face. "No? Not even if I promised not to turn around and use it on you?"

It was her turn to bark a laugh.

As if you could.

She said nothing, but didn't bother to hide her scorn. Her father had made sure she understood no one could do what she did. It was why they wanted her.

Reyes's smile faded. He gave her another sharp look, considering. He pursed his lips. "Okay, Lena." He nodded. "So, here's the thing. Council's been waiting for a girl like you, but they're not the only ones interested. What do I have to do to get you to come with me? What reassurances can I give you—?"

She shook her head. "There is nothing you can say or do to ever make me go with you." She paused to be sure she had his attention. "Not ever. I have zero interest in being one of Peller's Pistons." Her mouth twisted at speaking the title. It was an affectionate term coined by the man who had figured out how to use Spark abilities to rebuild civilization. They were all just parts of his machine.

Mark Peller had died long ago, but the term was still in use. Peller had been that important. He had become their First Councilor, faraway in Zone Two, starting the restoration among those left alive in the relocation center there.

"C'mon." Reyes uncrossed his legs and stood, shrugging his shoulders. "There has to be something you want. I'm not really a useless rich boy, but I do have influence with a certain group—"

"I already told you. I want to be left alone," she said. "I want to be myself without constantly looking over my shoulder. I want what everyone who hasn't been mind-fucked by living in a Relocity wants, Reyes. I want to live for me and not the Council."

He chuckled. She didn't think he was all that amused.

"Do I look like the kind of guy who is easily mind-fucked?"

"Easily? No. Not easily. But they had plenty of time, didn't they, with their Testing Year, and their special programs for talented children? Tell me, Reyes, did you go to the regular gifted school with the mid-range Sparklets and work your way up, or were you one of the special kids? Did they snatch little Alejandro away from Mommy and Daddy and make him a Ward?" She could feel the heat in her cheeks and felt her eyes go glassy with moisture.

Keep it together, Lena.

When she was a girl, she'd wanted the chance to show she was as good as those boys, but it was forbidden. Her father had made it clear: the Council would never allow a girl like her to show she was stronger than the Ward boys. They'd take her away from her family, yes, but not to teach her. They'd use her. Or they'd kill her.

Reyes's impassive face gave her nothing. The mere thought of what her parents had worked so hard to shield her from upset her, but clearly he'd come to terms with his stolen childhood long before. His face was such a mask she didn't think she'd even gotten through.

But then he asked with a soft note of pity in his voice, "What happened to you?"

She laughed and shoved her hair behind her ears in a quick,

defiant motion. "Bad childhood, I guess. So I'm an antisocial misfit, and I have attachment issues, and I—"

"Is that an official diagnosis or did it come from an over-eager program leader?"

"I—what?" She shook her head. "No, Reyes. It came from me. I made it up right now." It wasn't true. Her sister had spat those words at her the last time she'd visited.

She threw her hands up in the air. "Why are we even having this conversation?"

"I'm trying to figure you out."

"Why?"

"I like you, Lena. That much of today wasn't an act." A sly smile pulled his lips up, and he held her gaze. "And I am in a unique position to make sure you are safe and happy."

She felt her skin prickle, almost an electric response. She shifted away from him, took a step back, and shook her head. "I'm never going back. Not even if you ask nicely."

She waited a beat, but he just put his hands on his hips and shrugged again.

"So unless you plan on trying to force me into your car…?"

Reyes rolled his eyes. He cocked his head to the side and leaned out to look past her at the Pueblo, and then leaned back in again. His tongue slid across his lower lip. "That probably wouldn't be a good idea, considering."

"Probably wouldn't. Considering." She took a step backward then stopped. "Reyes? How did you know I would come here? You know, instead of haring out and holing up in some abandoned wreck somewhere?"

He shrugged. "You live four miles from Santo Domingo. The Kewa belong to one of the biggest Nations. It made sense for you to come here, knowing we wouldn't go in after you. And it's what I would have done."

Lena nodded. *So much for not being predictable. Better get to work on that, chica.*

She backed away across the road to the Pueblo. She hated being predictable. "Goodbye. Have a good life, Reyes."

He smiled and shook his head, calling after her, "This isn't good-bye. In fact, you should call me Alex. We'll see each other again."

She turned away and strode into Santo Domingo. "Not going to happen," she shouted back over her shoulder.

"Yes," Reyes said, the certainty carrying to her with his voice. "It will."

THREE

A lex leaned back into the corner where the bar and the wall met, watching the young people circulating in the long room. The far end held a tiny dance floor and a small corner stage where a trio of young men worked setting up a homemade drum set. Tables hugged each other in the space between the bar and the dance floor. The whole place was dim, lit by tallow lamps hung on short chains well out of reach of customers in their twenties flitting around each other. His gaze moved with the crowd. Was one of these people the key to bringing Lena back to the city?

"We might've had her if we'd approached her differently," he told himself under his breath. He couldn't believe how thoroughly the op had been screwed.

Lucas had been after him for months, telling Alex he was ready to lead and implying Alex was holding him back. A rumor had come in about a powered girl living in the desert—yet another nonexistent ghost girl. Alex had given the entire file to Lucas to shut him up. He remained hands-off, letting Lucas build his own op and handle his own research and contacts. Alex had assumed she was a Neo-barb, or at best a mid-range runaway they'd drag back to the city and put to work in the power grid. He had encountered both before. From the moment they'd driven up and he'd seen her up on her roof making repairs and glowing like the sun, he'd known she was the real deal. So had Lucas. What a clusterfuck.

Once they'd returned to Azcon, Alex had sent Lucas to both

Council and city offices to research all official employees named Danny. Lucas had tried to fight him, of course. Alex had been forced to coach him through the process, yet again.

"Listen, we already have all the information we need. We have her name, Lena. We know her brother is her contact, which means she has family in Azcon. We know her brother's name is Danny. And we know from your contact that he uses a messenger to bring her client lists when he can't get away—the messenger who put our names on the list."

Lucas stared at him, wheels finally turning. "And if he has access to a runner he trusts and the ability to get out here regularly—"

"Well to the south of the fields and the range land—"

"Then he probably works for the city or the Council."

"Exactly. Now, go find him."

Lucas would follow any leads he found. Alex had conflicting loyalties, which meant he saw the problem of Little Miss Lena from a different angle, and he didn't need Lucas peering over his shoulder.

Back at her place, tucked up next to the wall on her work table, had been a small stack of old books from the Azcon library. He'd grabbed one off the top and fanned through the pages. A slip of paper fluttered free from Orwell's *1984*.

Someone had written on the scrap in loopy, classical writing, "Piece of Asp. Saturday. Drinks are on me, girlie." It was signed "Ace."

Alex had no way of knowing which Saturday the note referred to, but the note told him either Lena or the mysterious Ace might be a frequent visitor to the Piece of Asp. He'd hoped to find someone who knew her to take her a message.

But he'd have to wait for that someone to find him. He had come in earlier than the usual post-shift crowd to chat up the bartender. He'd described Lena. The bartender's eye twitched as he glanced out at the growing crowd. He shook his head and told Alex she didn't sound familiar. Alex dropped her name, then, and her friend's, too. The bartender's shifting gaze told Alex he was lying when he said he'd never met a Lena; he didn't know any

Ace, either. The man had moved off to serve other customers.
And, Alex believed, to find Ace.

Alex waited, sipping an excellent, house-made tequila, and
focused on tasting it instead of frustration. He leaned his head
down to rub his eyes. He was tired. Tired enough that he found his
usual discipline slipping in little hitches. It was just flashes of
Lena's freckled face or that energy bloom, unlike any he'd seen
before. But those flashes were intrusive signs that he needed to
focus. That on-target dig she'd made about him being snatched
from his parents didn't help any. It had taken everything he had to
not respond, to focus on her pain instead of his own old wound.
Now, with her no longer in front of him, he could allow some of it
to leak out. Not much. Not enough to make him weak. Just
enough to fuel him through the rest of his work.

He needed to be on his way, first back to the office to write
up his Council report, and then to Fort Nevada to make his real
report. It was already an hour past dark, and it had been a long
day with no sign of rest in the immediate future. If it weren't
critical to make some kind of contact with someone Lena trusted,
he'd leave now.

A pair of hard arms, heavily muscled and burnished deep
brown, appeared on either side of him. One hand came to rest on
the bar to his right, the other on the wall to his left. The breath
Alex had just taken whispered out as his body subtly tensed,
easing into position for quick, deadly movement.

"Hey there, stranger." The voice in his ear was deep and too
close. "I don't know you. Is there a reason you're dropping my
name?"

Alex took a last sip as he turned his head. He cupped the
small glass, and as he took the measure of the man leaning in, he
recognized what a shame it would be to splinter the glass into the
perfect skin of the face before him. The dim light gave his dark
skin a bronze and gold glow over a clean-shaven jaw and pate.
Pale whiskey-brown eyes shone out from his dark skin and fed the
illusion of the glow.

"Depends, Ace," Alex kept his voice low, "on whether you're
interested in ensuring the continued safety of a mutual friend—the

one living in the middle of nowhere?"

Ace's eyes darkened. He didn't so much as twitch an eyelid, but Alex could feel the shift from curious to menacing.

Oh, yeah, Ace and Lena are close.

He had the man's attention. He leaned in, putting his head next to the other man's. "When did you last see her?" Alex kept his voice low and friendly. "I saw her this afternoon. Four Council teams threw her a party at her place."

Now he had a reaction. The man's jaw muscle jumped in time to the rapid pulse at his temple.

"But she left early and took off to stay with her friends in Santo Domingo," Alex said.

"Good for her." Ace's voice was nonchalant, but he took a quick breath, and his eyelids dipped in relief.

"No, Ace, bad for her." He made his voice hard. "If she had come quietly, if she'd cooperated, even if she'd been dragged back kicking and screaming, I could have arranged something."

"Could have arranged something? And who the Dust are you?"

"Alejandro Reyes. Senior Council Agent. And the only man in Azcon, other than you, interested in keeping her *out* of the hands of the Council. But that doesn't matter now." He leaned back into the bar and slid the glass away in a quick, angry motion. "Now she'll have the Council's attention. Having their attention is bad. It's worse than either of you think." He let that sink in. "I'm not talking about giving up her freedom outside for a spot in a power plant line-up, I'm talking about real danger and being shipped away and forced to—"

A hand dropped onto Ace's shoulder, pulling him away from Alex. A young man, blond hair cut into a shaggy frame for his long face, glared at Alex. He turned to Ace, eyes wide and indignant. "What the hell is this?"

Ace reached out and ran a placating hand across the young man's lower chest. "It's business, Jimmy. It's just work."

Jimmy's gaze flicked over to Alex and ran over him. "He doesn't look like work to me."

Ace's hand closed around Jimmy's shirt, and he pulled the

younger man in close to get his attention. "It's work. Go on back, and I'll—"

Alex tossed back the last of his tequila and shook his head. "No worries. We're done. Get her to come to you. Send word to me at work. *Quietly*. I'll get her somewhere safe."

He turned to push through the crowd, but Ace's hand left his boyfriend's chest to shoot out and grab Alex's arm.

"Wait." Ace had been leaning against the bar. He stood now, towering over Alex and Jimmy both. "Why are you doing this? Telling me—it's a little dangerous, isn't it?"

The implied threat hung there for a moment, amusing Alex.

He met Ace's dark expression. "You don't get anything without giving a little. I'm giving you trust. So trust me. Convince her to trust me before it's too damn late. Once she's in custody, my hands may be tied. She'll be on her own." He pulled his arm free. "I can buy her a few days. Move fast."

Alex slid off into the crowd. He didn't look back. He didn't have to. He'd planted the seed. Now to wait for it to bear fruit.

—m—

Alex dropped his pen into its holder, leaned back, and rubbed his eyes. They ached, and it wasn't simply the tedium of the paperwork waiting when he'd returned from the Piece of Asp. His office was dim. He could have flipped a switch and turned on the artificial lights, as the Zone Three Council offices were well-powered by Azcon Sparks, but he knew what it took to provide the energy. He preferred to conserve. He also genuinely liked the light of the beeswax candles that were the alternative. He liked the rhythm and elegance of the dip pens everyone else bitterly complained about, too.

He should go. Full dark had fallen hours before. He still had to report in to Fort Nevada about what had happened, and the Fort was a long way away. He rarely risked a written report outside of regularly scheduled message drops. When something worthy of the attention of his partner, Thomas, occurred, Alex disappeared from his life here in Council Zone Three and made the report in person. It would be a long night before Alex got any rest. Lena was worthy of Thomas's attention.

She was worthy of attention, period. Alex kept turning her around in his head like a living puzzle box. His fascination wasn't solely because they had been searching for her, believing in her existence, for so long. He admired what she had built. She lived life on her own terms, without any safety net.

The revolution Alex and Thomas were quietly stoking was dangerous and could be fatal. But they'd built a network to support their efforts. And if all else failed, they had a friendship spanning decades. They had each other. Lena was alone.

If he had been in her position—if his parents had held onto him like a treasure instead of handing him over to the Council in exchange for prestige and a bump in their monthly allotment of charge—could he have made his way, as she had, with no training, simply independence and that ass-kicking attitude?

Alex leaned back in his chair, a grin spreading at the memory of her clawing and kicking for freedom as she'd come down that slope with a Council agent doing everything he could to restrain her. She'd pulled free, and then when she'd seen Alex waiting for her, she hadn't panicked. She hadn't given up. She'd marched up that road to get in his face.

They needed her.

He turned to look out the wide-ledged window his rank afforded him. Azcon was dark. It was one of the largest of the relocation centers turned cities, and a little more than twenty thousand people lived here, though few of those citizens wandered the streets now. They were safe at home or, if they were night shift, tucked in to work. The Council touted the comfort it offered citizens during this time of "new prosperity." Were they comfortable? Or were they resentful but complacent in the aftermath of two centuries of hunger and fighting and uncertainty? Perhaps they didn't even care who ruled them.

And what about the men and women in Councilor Three's offices, the bureaucrats and peace officers and agents? Did any of them care? Lucas did. He was a Council man. Alex's lip curled. After spending the last year and half dealing with the ambitious little prick, when the time came, Lucas would be one of the first to die.

As if the thought of him was a beacon, a quick double knock sounded at Alex's office door. Lucas entered, reaching over and flicking the lights on as he did. Alex squinted. He continued looking out the now reflective glass for a moment, enjoying that last thought, before he turned to the younger man.

"Hey," he said mildly. "I thought you were done for the day. What's up?"

Lucas showed his teeth and slapped a file on Alex's lap. He kept some papers in reserve, a few thin, faded sheets. "I got her."

Alex arched a brow. "You got her? How's that?" He sat forward and lifted the file to inspect. He'd seen it before, the last time about a decade before. Family name, Gracey. He flipped open the family file and read aloud the Citizen Contact Sheet from the top. "Daniel Joseph Gracey. Son of Joseph Michael Gracey and Mercedes Solano Gracey. Home address: 235 Ochoa Street, Unit 9A. Status: Mid-level Spark. Occupation: Junior Assistant Councilor Aide to Councilor Three." None of this was news to him. He paused, arching his brows. "Is this brother Danny?"

It damn well better not be. He'd been grooming the young Mr. Gracey as an informer for close to a decade. If the kid had been hiding a high-powered sister the whole time, there'd be hell to pay.

He looked over the top of the paper at Lucas, who gestured for him to continue with the next page.

Alex flipped to the next page and read, "Teresa Maria Gracey Luevano. Daughter of Joseph Michael Gracey and Mercedes Solano Gracey; Widow of Roberto Luevano; Mother of Joseph Gracey Luevano. Home address: 18 Martin Circle. Status: Mid-level Spark. Occupation: Electrical Source Level Two, Water Resources, Day Shift." He flipped through the rest of the papers, reading the names. Mama Gracey, another mid-level Spark, assigned to work the electrical plant here at the Council building. Gracey Senior, former Senior Councilor Aide to Councilor Three, deceased. All of the birth and education records, and the one death certificate, were in order. He frowned, searching his memory. The papers for the little sister who had died as a child were missing.

"I'm tired, Lucas. Councilor's aide named Danny. Well-placed family—not the kind you go throwing accusations at, and I'm not in the mood for games. You're holding back his dead sister's papers. If you think they're relevant, give them to me."

Lucas allowed a smirk to stretch across his thin face, pulling the skin around his eyes down. He produced the folded papers with a flourish. Alex took them.

He dimly remembered seeing them before. The first was a Certificate of Live Birth. Same parents. Daughter, Magdalena Elizabeth Gracey. He checked the date. Almost twenty-five years ago. Magdalena. Lena. He unfolded the death certificate dated five years after her birth, shortly after she'd started her Testing Year. His eyes narrowed.

Alex had seen the file twice before. Once, ten years before, he had done a check on Junior Aide Daniel Gracey when he'd signaled his intention to follow his father's footsteps in service to the Councilor. And before that, as a young agent brimming with suspicion, he'd pulled this file shortly after the child's death. He and Thomas had been investigating every girl who had died or disappeared during the Testing Year. They both suspected the Council abducted highly powered little girls. Alex remembered he'd found nothing amiss, just the grieving family of a Councilor's Aide.

Her parents hadn't just held onto Lena, they had buried her. Somehow, they had managed to fake her death and hide her away from the Council. Alex had missed it. He'd screwed up.

And now Lucas had information on her family, information he'd use to draw her to the Council. Alex couldn't allow that to happen. He and Thomas hadn't been able to find any of the missing girls over decades, couldn't prove the Council had them, let alone what they were doing with them. This time, it would be different. The Council couldn't have Lena.

Alex nodded at the younger agent, thinking fast. He had to buy time. He turned back to the file, flipping through. "Bring the sister in. She has a child, so she has the most to lose." He closed his eyes, thinking. "Bring little Joseph in, too. Put her in interview room six and park him right outside on a chair. Make sure she sits where she can see him." He smiled thinly. It would serve to get Danny's attention, as well. No more secrets.

Lucas's brows were bunched. "Not the brother? But he's the contact."

Alex said nothing. He handed the file back to Lucas.

"Not the brother?" Lucas asked again.

Alex had known he would, and with the hard edge to his voice indicating he knew Alex made him wait on purpose. It was a little game they liked to play. Well, Alex liked to play it, anyway.

"Okay. Not the brother," Lucas said. "You want me to bring the sister in now?"

Alex looked at the floor. He really needed to discuss how best to proceed with Thomas. Bring her in and keep her safe here while Alex worked on convincing her to join them? Or disappear her to Fort Nevada and worry about convincing her later?

"You know what? No," he said to Lucas, "we'll go get the sister tomorrow, after a morning strategy meeting. We'll pick her up at work. Get the boy from school. Make sure she sees we've brought him in, too. We can go together after we've hammered out our approach and questions first thing in the morning."

Lucas laughed. "You are a bastard, Alex. I like it. I'll have a team ready for when she cracks."

"Whoa. Hold on, cowboy." He shook his head, raising one finger up and shaking it back and forth. "Overconfidence is as bad as ineptitude."

"What the hell does that mean?" Lucas's smile vanished. The camaraderie went with it.

"It means slow down," Alex said.

"Slow down?" Lucas waved his arm at the window, seeming to indicate Lena, far off in the desert. "Think about what she can do. She's what the Council's been looking for. Besides, do you have any idea what a Neo-barb could do with that kind of power under his control?" Lucas was obsessed with the mostly nomadic people who lived independently of the Relo-Cities. The Council referred to them as new barbarians due to the quality of lives outside of civilization.

"She's not going to take up with a Neo-barb." Alex's voice held all the withering disdain he felt for the idea. "And even if you get a positive ID on her, you can't ride into Kewa country and snatch her. We already did this your way once, too fast, too soon, too hard. It's time for the Reyes way. Be patient. Be subtle. Let the woman come to you, Lucas. C'mon, man. You're making me think you haven't played the game before."

The muscle in Lucas's jaw twitched in fast-time. "I take it I'm no longer lead on this?"

"Oh, no, you're still the lead." The ink was dry on his reports. He gathered them up and neatly stacked them, setting them inside the top drawer of his desk. "But I'm still your senior. So come find me in the morning. We'll plan out a proper interrogation—together—and then you can go lead it." He stood, ignoring the ugly flush creeping across Lucas's cheeks, and leaned across to tamp out the candles with his fingers. "That's about it for tonight. Get some rest. It's been a helluva day."

Alex crossed to the hook on the wall where an old wire hanger held his black wool coat. He opened the door and held it for Lucas.

Lucas preceded him out but turned left instead of right, mumbling something about working on his interview questions for the morning. He continued down the hall to the big, open room where the junior agents shared desk space. Alex locked his office and pulled his coat on as he made his way through the hallways, down four flights of stairs, and through the locking security doors to the ground level exit at the rear of the building.

He stepped into the cold night, clamping his jaw to keep his teeth from chattering. He'd been born and spent the first five years of his life in the east coast's Zone One before being shipped across the country by electric car, steam-powered train, and then wagon train to the Ward School. In the decades of training there and after his assignment here, he'd never gotten used to the high desert temperature shifts. It had been a warm spring day, breezy but enjoyable. Now, even with his thin wool coat, his body hunched against the cold. His breath fanned out in front of him.

Alex shrugged deeper into his jacket, tugging it around

himself and fastening the buttons before shoving his hands into the pockets. He glanced up and down the road to be sure there weren't any horses or bicycles to be wary of, but no one else was out, so he bowed his head against the cold. He walked the two blocks home quickly. At his gate, he flipped the latch, letting himself into the small communal patio. He'd lived in the same lower level unit of a block of four for well over a decade.

All of the apartments faced out onto the little plaza. He could see the warm, hazy glow of a candle moving behind one of the windows of unit D. Either the Quiroz family meant to conserve as they headed into the end of the month, or they had used up their charge allotment for this pay period. Rough. No lights, no heat, no hot water, and no way to cook except in the communal horno here on the patio. He passed the huge, hive-shaped oven as he crossed the plaza, and the heat still radiating from its use at dinner warmed him.

He entered his dark apartment, not bothering to light a candle. He moved through to his bedroom by memory, crossing to the small closet to change into a warmer shirt. He shrugged back into his jacket then slid the small chest in the corner toward him.

As designed, it pulled the carpet back as it slipped out, revealing a trap door. An electric lock held it closed. He focused briefly, and the Dust stirred to life, cycling the lock open. He pulled up, spun around, and backed down the short ladder into the dark opening, leaning out to pull the chest and door back into place as he descended.

He followed the low, sloping tunnel that was his frequent route below the city walls. It emptied into a narrow branch of canyon outside. Once he reached the end of it, the top opened up again into a small vestibule barely wide enough to accommodate his shoulders, but six and a half feet in height. He gratefully stood and leaned to use the eyepiece of the tiny, real-time camera mounted just below eye-level, manually swiveling it to give him a view of the hatch and the surrounding canyon.

All clear. He took up the rare night vision goggles he'd brought from Fort Nevada and slipped them onto his head, then left the security of the tunnel. He moved quickly through the cover of canyons and arroyos that hid him all the way to the edge of old town, the largely crumbled ruins of what had been Los Alamos.

This close in to Azcon, the houses and businesses had been long-since stripped of any usable materials, right down to pulling the wiring from the walls. In the post-Industrial world, where the most basic products were again hand-made, everything was valuable. He entered a dilapidated former restaurant with one wall crumbled away and the roof partially collapsed after some long-ago fire. Tumbleweeds climbed the wall opposite the openings, trembling in the slight breeze.

In the back, he levered his body through an opening that had probably once been covered by a grate then walked easily through the sub-level drain to where it joined a larger pipe. He crossed to a sealed door. The faded scrapes and gouges that spoke of attempts to force it open always amused him. He worked through the security by memory—security box and code, hidden tube with a lens for his eye, and a quick green pulse of light. He keyed the code to reseal tube and box and waited.

He didn't doubt he'd be granted access. He was one of the few in Council Zone Three who even knew of the existence of the ancient train. Those who did know had graduated from the Ward School in the last twenty years. To a man, they gave their loyalty to Alex and Thomas, not the Council.

Locks at various levels cycled, and the metal hissed open, extending from the wall a few inches. In moments, he'd entered the controlled environment on the other side, nose twitching at the flat, stale smell of the air, and hauled the door closed again. As the edge of it engaged, it pulled itself back in and recycled through the locks, sealing him in.

He cycled on the lights and left the goggles for his return, then jogged down three levels of metal steps to reach the locomotive of the old mag-lev train. It had long since been disengaged from the passenger cars. Whatever the cars had been used for by the old military before the collapse, the need to transport so many people through the secret tunnels had died with them.

He stepped into the cab and crossed to the controls. After a brief pause to power up and run a check, he pulled it away from the platform. It moved slowly at first then built speed through the deep tunnel. A trip that might take him weeks by horseback had been cut to half an hour.

# FOUR

A lex stepped off the mag-train in a station very different from the abandoned, hidden base he'd left behind. Likely nowhere near what it must have been during its heyday of military industrialization, Fort Nevada was nonetheless busy. The lights shone permanently, and the air cycled continuously, as all of the students at Fort Nevada took a turn in the power stations.

Alex strode across the metal platform and then down the short staircase. He exchanged a brief greeting with a young agent whose hands were deep inside a metal-plated control panel. Down here at the train level, a handful of Ward School graduated agents worked maintenance and inspected the lines and wires.

Both students and agents were required to have the knowledge and ability to maintain the infrastructure of civilization. They expected the young, highly powered Wards that came through be infused with a sense of responsibility not only to what was left of society, but also to themselves. Sparks should no longer be tools in the hands of others, and part of claiming the role they deserved meant ensuring Sparks weren't rendered obsolete.

As Alex made his way toward the elevators, the duty officer appeared at his shoulder.

"Good evening, sir."

The duty officer was a serious-faced young man whom Alex didn't recognize. Once upon a time, Alex knew them all. Now he spent the majority of each year in Azcon.

"Good evening." Tired and hungry, he kept moving.

The officer stayed apace next to him.

"I have a report for Councilor Five. I'll be in the mess until he's available."

The officer nodded his understanding and peeled off, heading for his desk. He'd send a messenger up to Thomas's offices. When Thomas wanted him, they'd send someone down to the mess to bring him up.

This was standard procedure on the nights when Alex came in unexpectedly via the train. The Council had long-since regretfully written off the tunnels and the trains, sealing off access points. Thomas had made reopening them for possible use against the Council a priority. It had taken decades to refurbish the mag-trains and the western tunnels, but it had been worth it. They still pushed east through tunnels they'd found and followed, exploring to see how far the old secret network had gone. The trains made everything easier, especially getting in to discuss critical new information.

Alex rode the elevator to the eighteenth floor and crossed the hall to the wide-open cafeteria. Out of consideration for those who worked the overnight shift, the cafeteria remained open twenty-four hours a day. At this hour, the hall remained uncrowded and hushed but brightly lit.

He picked up a tray and cruised through the empty line, choosing foods not available in Azcon. Every zone sent quarterly support to the Ward School, participating in the care and feeding of their future Council Agents as they trained. The Ward School always had goods you couldn't get in every zone. Alex added two rolls to his tray and debated taking another.

Bread was hard to come by in Azcon, as the Councilor chose to trade the Zone's valuable honey and pecans for other items. Wheat wasn't a priority for Councilor Three when his people could make do with mesquite flour. A terrible decision. The flatbreads made with the mesquite flour alternative never cooked right—the center stayed wet and mushy like pudding.

Alex sat, tore off a hunk of a wheat roll, and dipped it into the gravy. When he pulled off a bite with his teeth, he savored the chewy pull of the bread. A long sigh of pleasure slipped free.

A young man sitting a table away turned his attention from the maps and papers spread in front of him to Alex. He had dark, kinky hair cut close to his skull. His narrow dark eyes were crinkled at the edges in laughter while the rest of his long face spoke of bemused interest. He looked to be about twenty-four years old, so likely in or near his final year.

Alex raised his brows.

Caught, the young man dropped his head for a moment as he laughed wryly. "I apologize, sir." He gestured with his chin to Alex's half-empty plate. "I guess it's been awhile, sir?"

Alex glanced down at his plate. He'd been appreciating his meal at great speed. He shook his fork at the young man with mock severity. "Just wait until you've been out in the world enjoying regional delicacies. We'll see how much you look forward to reporting home so you can have some real food."

The young man barked a laugh. "Yes, sir. With all due respect to my instructors, I cannot wait, sir."

Alex smiled, remembering his own impatience. He nodded. "I know. I remember." He swallowed down another bite. "What's your name?"

He straightened in his seat when he answered. "Senior Ward Jackson Lee. First Class."

"Relax, son. And ease off the 'sirs'." He sopped up the last of the gravy with the last of the bread.

"Yes, sir."

He snorted. "Uh huh. I remember that, too." He pushed his plate away and sighed in pleasure again. "Senior, First Class, huh? You're almost done." Alex glanced at the maps and papers spread across the table. "Working on your out routes?"

In addition to the official graduation requirements set by the Council of Nine, he and Thomas imposed another final project. All Senior Wards had to create and defend three routes out of every Zone, including food and water resources, analysis of the local topography, and how local flora and fauna could be used as tools or weapons. If the panel of evaluating agents deemed more than two of the routes the Ward presented unviable, the Ward got scrubbed and repeated the year, regardless of his talent as a Spark. No graduation. No assignment as a Council Agent out in the world.

Jackson rubbed the top of his head with both hands as he looked down at the maps and nodded. "Yes, sir. I present tomorrow, sir."

"I don't need to tell you to take it seriously, but take it seriously. It's not just your ticket out of here, but it may save your ass someday." Reyes's own out route project had been unofficial, done to relieve the tedium of their last months at a Ward School still controlled by the Council of Nine. Now, the Council only thought they were in control of the critical school, tasked with training the strongest of the Sparks into the Council's elite Senior Agents. It was very much a mistaken belief.

Jackson's face lit up. "Yes, sir!" The prospect of seeing enough action that his ass might need saving clearly excited him.

Alex remembered that, too. He grinned, in spite of himself. It still was.

The muffled sound of boots on flooring approached from behind him. He turned. A lower ranked Fort Nevada security officer greeted him with a crisp nod and started pulling to attention.

Alex waved him down. "Is he ready for me?"

"Yes, Councilor Five is ready to see you now, Agent Reyes. If you'll follow me?"

Alex nodded. He winked at Jackson Lee as he rounded the table to follow the man out. "Good luck, Senior Ward Lee. Make sure you cover your ass from every possible angle, and you'll be fine."

He dumped his plate and utensils in the appropriate alcove and followed the security officer out. Instead of continuing straight onto the elevator as they left the cafeteria, the officer turned right and led him into the warren of hallways on the eighteenth level.

Before they got there, he figured out they were heading to the gym, a path he remembered well from his years at the Ward School. Most of the time he'd spent there had been in the company of the man waiting for him. Their brilliant leader had once been an eighty pound weakling who came to the school late, at age thirteen instead of five. He had been the strongest Spark at the school, for sure, but as physically unimpressive as a young man could be. Alex, whose favorite part of every year had always been the six months spent boxing, was already bigger, stronger, and faster than the other boys of their class. He had seen Thomas's potential. He'd defended him. Then he'd taken him under his wing and trained him.

The wiry, leanly muscled man currently hitting his gloved hands in rapid succession against one of the sand-filled canvas bags in the corner had clearly taken that training to heart. Alex strolled across the gym, his gaze darting over the Councilor to check his form, but he had nothing to critique. His friend was a weakling no more. He wasn't an underdog anymore, either.

Somewhere along the line, their relationship had shifted. As they'd become friends, they'd become equals, then partners, with Thomas running their nascent empire and Alex handling the expansion of it in the field. Their roles fit their gifts. It was the best way to achieve the goals they'd hammered out together as young men.

The Councilor's familiar pale eyes were small over a hawkish nose, and the old scar where he'd cut away the slaver's brand was a flat, shiny patch under his right eye. His piercing gaze flicked out. "Alex." It was all the greeting he'd get.

"Thom." Amused, Alex mimicked his friend and partner.

Thomas's lips turned up on one side. "So?" He grunted, fists still pounding the bag.

"Sooooo…" Alex dragged out the word. "Remember your theory about how the strongest Sparks, if left to their own devices and totally untrained, will come up with new ways to do things? Will even make themselves stronger? Kind of like…oh yeah, kind of like *you*?"

"I do." The pace of his hits slowed as he listened, but not the force. "You found one?"

"Oh, yeah."

Thomas's quirked lips grew into a smile. "How strong is he?"

Alex waited a beat, drawing out the moment. He'd only get to do this once. "*She* is the brightest thing I've ever seen. Her bloom was so bright it hurt to look at it, and she was still fully functional."

His friend stilled, one hand poised for a blow that didn't fall. "*She?*"

Alex could almost hear the click as the final piece of Thomas's grand plan fell neatly into place, making the largest, most theoretical of his ideas a reality.

His arms fell to his sides. He turned to Alex. "Tell me."

"Do you remember Three's Senior Councilor Aide, name of Gracey?" Alex asked. "Caught being curious about things he had no need to know? She's his daughter."

Thomas frowned his disagreement with a slight shake of his head. Unlike Alex, who had to use mnemonic devices to keep track of information, Thomas could flip through memories like file folders. "Gracey had a daughter and a son. The daughter's just a mid-level. Like all girls." His voice was disappointed.

Natural women and men had a roughly twenty-five percent chance of parenting a powered child. Add in a powered father, and the rate rose to fifty-fifty, but the children were always mid-level strength or lower. Powered women always produced Spark children. However, mid-level powered woman had an almost thirty percent chance of producing the coveted highly powered Spark, although those children were always male; with a highly-powered father, the rate rose to almost fifty percent.

The official story said every female born with power was naturally limited to mid-level or lower. Thus far, the records supported the story. At some point, it was widely believed, a hiccup in nature would produce highly powered girls. Since female Sparks bred true, they would produce only high-powered children. If one of these theoretical females produced children with a high-powered male, the possibilities for their children, and for the future of Sparks, were limitless.

There were communities—Neo-barb run—that patched together hydroelectric power or made do with windmills built from scavenged materials. But the Council had invested in humans they could control since the beginning. Their obsession with finding any such girls had been growing over the last half-century, a response to fear of hypothetical children strong enough to resist the growing restraints on Sparks. If they lost control, they lost power—literally and figuratively.

Thomas, of course, was obsessed for the same reason. The girls were the key to the long-range goals of Fort Nevada's move toward revolution. He saw the children born of such high-powered women as the future of free Sparks.

He believed the Council was spiriting away girls as they were found to be highly powered, before even their parents were fully aware of the magnitude of their difference. They hadn't been able to discover to where or by whom yet—the occurrences were too unpredictable. Now they'd found one that had escaped that fate.

"He had another daughter. He faked her death. He hid her away, which may explain his varied interests." Alex took a breath. "After his death, as soon as she was old enough, she left the city. She's been living on the edge of tribal lands and working as a black market Spark. That's how we found her. We heard rumors and put ourselves on her schedule so we could bring her in." His voice turned mocking. "Can't have any Sparks not pulling their weight for the good of the Council, now can we?" He shook his head. "Imagine my surprise when we pulled up and she had a corona around her like the sun at full eclipse. Like I said, it hurt to look at her.

"It was the most beautiful thing I've ever seen," he said. Emotion tightened his throat, and he swallowed to clear it. It had been beautiful, but still. Clearly, Thomas's obsession had wormed into his psyche and latched onto Lena. He crossed his arms and continued. "And it was only the beginning."

Thomas was still now, utterly focused on his friend. Alex recognized the excitement bubbling beneath the surface. But that surface? Calm.

"One of the disappeared girls," Thomas said. "How old?"

"Twenty-four. Young enough, and old enough. Tiny thing. Big green eyes. Coated in freckles. Not pretty, exactly, not that it matters, but stunning in her own way." He frowned. What did that have to do with anything? He barked a laugh as he focused on what mattered—the personality they'd have to work around to get her to join them. Just because he admired her ballsiness didn't mean he couldn't recognize that her strength would make things harder. "She's a tough little pain in the ass."

Thomas took a deep breath. "Please tell me you've brought her here?"

He shook his head. "She got away—"

"Dammit, Alex! This is important!" His gloved hands shot up to frame his head in anger and disbelief.

"I damn well know how important it is! She took us out. Took. Us. Out." Alex made sure he had Thomas's attention. "She can do shit nobody else can do. Not me. Not you." He took a deep breath and released it in a noisy gust of frustration. "She had some kind of early warning system. Probably Dust. One minute, we were in the middle of a conversation, our guys scheduled to start moving in, and the next, she *knew*. Who we were, why we were there." He shook his head.

What came next had been terrifying. Once he'd recovered, he'd felt such a euphoric rush at having found her that he'd had to tamp it down and twist it into rage. "I didn't even have enough time to react. She just—our lungs stopped working. Our muscles contracted. It was agony. And she had enough control to put us on a fucking timer."

They had hoped to find a Spark evolved to a dangerous, exquisite extreme. They'd found her, and that presented a danger all its own.

Alex ran his hands through his hair. "She took us out long enough to get out through her escape tunnel. Dust-made. Dust-protected. I found the exit in the side of an arroyo before we cleared out. The damn thing was a good three hundred feet long." He shook his head again. "She made it to the tribe. I couldn't do anything at that point."

"You know where she is?"

Alex nodded.

"Then we'll go get her. Tonight."

Alex closed his eyes for a moment. *Shit*. He'd figured

Thomas's reaction would be strong. But this was on the extreme end.

"No, Thom."

"Yes! She cannot get away. She belongs with us."

"We're not ready to go to war. And that's what it would be. We have to do this the way we do things. We have to be smart." Alex stared down into Thomas's pale eyes, holding onto his calm. One of them had to.

Thomas took two quick steps to stand inches from Alex. "We cannot allow her to disappear. She is—she's our Eve."

"I know. And I'm working on it." Alex grimaced. "My partner knows he's onto something big. And as soon as the Council gets wind of this girl, they will scramble everything to ensure she is taken into custody."

"Then you get to her first, Alex. Because if they get to her first and they can't figure out how to harness her, they will kill her. And either way, they win. You get to her first. You bring her home to us. I don't care what you have to do."

Alex took a long breath. "Decades of work," he reminded his friend. "Decades. Of *my* work. And we are so close. Zone Three is primed. I'm not willing to undo that for a girl you didn't know existed five minutes ago."

He wasn't. Was he?

"I knew she should exist. And now that I know she's real, we will do whatever we have to do to bring her home."

Arguing would be pointless. Thomas had anticipated this moment for too long. Alex nodded, his mind working angles.

Like this reaction wasn't exactly what you wanted: an excuse to do whatever it takes to bring in the perfect Spark. The perfect weapon.

"We can have both. I can make it happen."

"Then do it." Thomas stepped away, raised his arms to resume his workout. "But remember, she's our priority now. Once we have her, we have the future."

# FIVE

Lena sat cross-legged on the hard-packed earth floor of the medicine woman's home. Soft, bright wool pooled before her knees as she worked the yarn and knitting needles above her lap. For the first hours after the agents had driven her away, she'd paced restlessly between the small bluff rising above the arroyos and Santo Domingo to the east, watching agents move in and out of her home.

Finally Gloria, the Kewa woman closest to Lena, had tired of Lena's temper and sharply told Lena to wait at Gloria's adobe house. As the afternoon melted into evening, a trio of young women appeared at Gloria's door. They had gone to Lena's home to retrieve clothing for her, as well as her knitting and needles.

Her mind worked as her fingers threw the yarn and moved the needles at a furious pace, everything soothing and meditative about the activity gone. She had turned her focus down to her hands, but instead of yarn and needles she saw Reyes and Lucas standing in her doorway and agents darting in and out like wasps. Could she reclaim her home?

It's done. It's done. No going back.

The rage built. It beat in tandem with the violence of her feedback headache. She needed to ground, but she couldn't trust the agents were truly gone. Instead, she knitted.

What about Danny? If they'd made the appointment through him, would they arrest him now? Had another Gracey man been put in danger because of her? The memory of the night the men had come to tell her mother that her father's body had been found, and the devastated, blaming eyes of her sister, rose up like dark water. She fled from it, as she always did, blinking away from her thoughts before the memory could suck her back down into the drowning depths of grief.

Her head jerked up. The light inside the little house had dimmed with evening, and Gloria entered through the front, a basket of eggs in one hand and an earthen jug in the other. She caught Lena's attention.

"Light the lamp," she said. "My hands are full of your dinner. Then we'll talk."

At home, Lena would simply spark it, but she couldn't spark anything until she'd grounded. She rose to use tongs to pull an ember from the little round-bellied stove and lit the wick of the fat lamp on the table in the middle of the room. When she was done, she returned the ember to the stove.

"Put water on to boil. And heat the comal," Gloria told her, referring to the large flat frying pan. She dipped out blue cornmeal and mesquite flour and mixed it in a chipped bowl. While she dropped spoonfuls of batter onto the hot comal and used her strong fingers to break apart pinon nuts and scatter them over the cakes, Lena set the table.

In moments, Gloria had flipped the pancakes onto the waiting plates and they were sitting together, a covered bowl of honey on the table between them. The crunch of the bits of toasted pine nuts and the distinctive tangy sweet flavor of the mesquite flour improved Lena's mood.

Of course, her bliss might be related to her terrible sweet tooth. She pinched the last bite of the delicious cakes between her fingers, swirled it in honey, and shoved it into her mouth. She licked her fingers.

Plenty of mesquite flour and honey in storage up at the house. I should barter for more baking powder and cornmeal.

The realization that she didn't have plenty of anything anymore hit like a slap in the face. How could she plan her cooking? It wasn't even safe to return home. The delicious dinner settled like a hard ball in her stomach.

Gloria spoke to her in English now, the words coming in the odd, jerking cadence of a native speaker of Keresan. "It is hard to think of making a choice now, but you have to decide whether you are staying or going."

Lena swallowed. "Am I allowed to stay here?"

Gloria made a small shrug. "It's not for me to decide. Before you ask, you should think about what you ask of us."

Lena stared at her. "I'm a hard worker. I would never be a burden, and I can help—"

Gloria shook her head. "It isn't food and shelter that will cost us. It will be defending our friend from those who return for her."

Lena's shoulders slumped again, and her gaze returned to her empty plate with the bits of cake and nuts sticking in honey.

"They will return for you, Lena. You shine as bright as the Sun, and they want your light. They would do anything to possess it. They will come."

Lena jumped at the faint knock at Gloria's door. At a Keresan word from Gloria, a boy of about twelve entered from the deep of night. Lena recognized the Keresan words for *one man*, "ishk hachtzeh." Reyes? Back again already? Was she already bringing unwanted guests to the Kewa? Gloria and the boy spoke for a moment before she turned to Lena.

"There is a man who says he is a friend come to warn you of danger. He says it's important that he speak with you."

Lena waited. One didn't just get up and go when Gloria was speaking. Gloria held her gaze for a moment. When the woman spoke again, she spoke quietly, like always.

"You have to make a decision soon."

"I know," she said. "And I know I should go away somewhere. But this is my home. It's all I know."

"Fear of the unknown is a reason to go, not stay." Gloria's voice had taken on a chiding tone. "If you stay, it should be because you love a place, not because you're afraid to move on." She slid her hand along the tabletop. "If you're going to stay because you're afraid, then you might as well go live with them in their city. Everyone there stays because they are afraid."

"I won't go back to the city. Life isn't worth living under

their rules. I'd rather die."

"So. You would die for freedom. What would you live for?"

Lena stared at Gloria. She could feel her brow furrowing. "I don't—for the same thing?"

"No. You said you would die to be free. If you are given a choice, if you must choose between freedom in death and the life they offer, what would make you choose to live? Figure that out, and you will know what is really at stake. You will know why you must return."

Lena's brows rose almost to her hairline. She wouldn't return to the city. She opened her mouth to say so, but it was too late. Gloria pursed her lips in the direction of the door.

She rose to her feet as Gloria nodded at the boy. Lena followed him out, giving herself a moment to allow her eyes to adjust to the dark. The boy waited for her in the middle of the narrow road. When she moved forward, he trotted off into the night. She quickened her steps to keep up, arms going around her own body to ward against the cold. When they turned onto the Pueblo's main road, she could see the twin beams of a car's lights, the silhouettes of armed Kewa warriors to either side. She shook her head at the waste of energy.

It wasn't the Volt. Not Reyes. She hissed silently at the quick flit of disappointment through her belly before the man behind the wheel leaned out.

"Ace!" She sped up, jogging the final distance to the car. He unfolded himself from the front seat, relief spreading across his face with his smile.

"Lena!" He bent down to pull her up into his arms and shake her like a rag doll. "Damn, girlie, you're going to be the death of me."

She laughed as she pulled away. The laughter faded at the worry on his face. "What are you doing all the way out here? And at this hour? Do you want agents knocking on your door?"

He cocked a brow at her and rubbed a hand across his bald head. "I've already got agents dropping my name. Yours, too."

Her eyes closed. She shook her head. "Ace, I'm sorry. I never meant to bring trouble on anyone—"

"You didn't bring any trouble on me. And even if you had—" he flicked the tip of her nose and then pulled her back in for another hug "—you know you're worth every minute."

She wrapped her arms tight around his waist and leaned her head into his lower chest. She regretted, not for the first time, that she and Ace could never be together. She wasn't the correct gender. Other than her father's, his were the only arms she'd ever felt safe in. Now the Council had found Ace, too.

"What happened? They didn't bother you at work, did they?" She tipped her head back to look up at him. He worked for Wallace & Aceves Imports, also known as the Dragonfly House, one of the most powerful trade groups. They had their fingers in all nine Council Zones. They were powerful. They were also paranoid.

"No." He shook his head and wrinkled his forehead. "He found me at the Piece of Asp."

"He?" She knew who before Ace even answered.

"Uh huh. Beautiful, dangerous man. Likes expensive tequila. And pain-in-the-ass redheads. You know him?"

"Reyes." Lena rolled her eyes. "He does not like me, I promise. He came out here to arrest me."

Ace reached out to gently grasp her chin and pull her face up. He examined her with a familiar, searching look. "Oh, hell no. Lena. No. Not that man."

She pulled her chin away and scoffed at him. "What? Whatever you think you're seeing…no. I don't want him." She crossed her arms over her chest and hugged herself against the dropping temperature. "He's an *agent*. He works for the *Council*."

"Screw being an agent. And screw the Council, too. The man is dangerous. You think you're tough, playing with little boys. This is not the kind of man who plays games. He will eat your soul and make you like it."

"Well, if I'll like it, then what's the problem?" She tossed the words back lightly.

"Lena."

"He's an asshole. Whatever you think you're seeing, you're not. I promise. And by the way, I *am* tough. I kicked his dangerous ass today, thank you very much! So don't be underestimating me." She scowled up at him. "And don't go thinking he's interested in anything but my kilowatt per hour output. The only thing I am to Reyes is a check on his monthly quota."

"Yeah? Then why did he tell me to warn you that they're not interested in hooking you up to a power plant? That you need to come in to him so he can get you someplace safe and keep you away from the Council?"

"I—what?" She stared at him.

"Yeah. He said you had their attention now. They're going to ship you away and do Dust knows what to you. Don't look at me like that!"

"Ace, he was playing you. It's what they do. He's just better at it than the rest of them."

He leaned down and gripped her slight shoulders. "He wasn't playing. He was pissed. And worried. He said he wasn't sure he could get you someplace safe now, and the sooner you get back, the safer you'll be." He released her shoulders, but he kept his hands on her arms. "He knows you're different. They do, too. The secret's out. Agent or not, this guy wants to take you someplace safe. Maybe you can have a real life, one where you're not hiding who you are. It's hard, but it's worth it."

She stared up at him, fear beating inside her chest. No one was allowed to know what she could do. That was the rule. It had been the rule for as long as she could remember. "You don't understand."

"I don't understand? You're funny, little girl. I am the one person in this world who definitely understands." He gestured at the car next to them. "I dropped everything and came out here to get you because I understand." He smiled at her. "Jimmy's pissed, too. He thinks I left to go meet up with your agent somewhere."

A quick bark of laughter erupted from her. "What? He's not even your type!"

Ace raised his brow again. "That man is everybody's type."

"Shut up." She rubbed her arms and tilted her head back to stare up at the stars. Their brilliance took her breath away but gave her nothing in return. She had to find her own answers. "I don't buy it, Ace."

"You don't think he's everybody's type? You going blind out here with the sun in your eyes?"

"No, and you know what I mean. I don't buy this concern. There's some magical safe place? I don't buy it." She tucked her hair back behind her ears, smoothing it down as she bit her lip. "I don't buy it," she repeated.

"Are you trying to convince me or you? Come back with me. I didn't drive all the way out here for nothing. Guy like him gets worried, you pay attention."

"I just—you didn't see him when he came in today. He was totally convincing as a bored rich boy. And then as the good-citizen agent trying to talk me down. I don't buy that he's scared of the Council or something. I think it's a trap." It didn't matter how beautiful the man was. She'd seen him be two different people already. How could she trust this new double agent role he'd sold to Ace?

Lies. He told them—became them—very well. He's an agent, *for Dust's sake.*

She gave voice to the fear simmering inside since she realized she'd somehow brought attention to Ace. "I go back with you, and then they take us both, me for the power plants and you to the work farms for helping me. I can't be the reason you—" She swallowed the heat back and blinked away welling tears.

"I don't think it's a trap." He lifted his hand to gently brush away from her face the hair the wind fluttered. "It's hard to play a player. I looked into his eyes. He's spooked for you. That's not a lie. It was real."

She shook her head. "I don't believe it. I love that you came out here to get me. But I can't come back with you. I won't put you at risk."

"You have to trust somebody sometime, girlie."

"Maybe. But not Reyes."

They stood in silence then. He pulled her back for a long hug, and she leaned in, loving his warmth and the spicy male scent clinging to him. They'd been friends since before her parents had made her disappear, each hiding a secret from the world. Ace had come to terms with who he was long ago, and screw anyone who had an issue with him. But he still always made time for Lena and her struggle to exist. Her brother helped her out of a sense of duty. Danny loved her, but putting himself on the line? That he did for the memory of their father. Ace had no reason to drive out to the middle of nowhere to get her except that Ace had chosen her. And she'd be damned if she put him in danger, too.

Except Reyes had shown up at their favorite club to find him. They'd somehow made the connection. Ace was already in danger.

How long until he isn't the only one?

She pulled away, staring up at him, stricken. "They found you already."

Ace shook his head. "I can handle me."

Her breath creaked out of her throat. "How long until they find my family? I thought if I ran away, everyone would be safe. But if they found you, they already know who I am. No one is safe." Her hands tightened into fists. "They'll go after my mother!"

It was her father all over again. He had tried to protect her, keep her hidden. After she'd messed up the first week of school, they'd never sent her back. They'd told everyone she had a terrible fever. A week later, she had officially died. It wasn't a difficult lie. Disease was a constant danger; even hardy Spark children sometimes died. Lena had ceased to exist. Her father used his position to make it happen.

When the Councilor had discovered her father had secrets, had been hiding things, they'd taken him. Whatever they suspected he was doing, they'd never been able to discover what he'd really been up to. He took her existence with him to the grave.

The night they came to tell her mother, Lena had been helping Danny work on a circuit breaker for school. With the knock at the door, she'd hopped up and hustled to her hiding hole behind a loose board in the closet. She'd risked slipping back out into the closet and peeking through the crack, though, when she'd heard her mother begin to wail. Lena stood in the dark, alone, and watched as her family grieved. Danny sat in shock, one hand poised over the electric panel, head bowed. Teresa went to their mother and wrapped her arms around her. Over their mother's shoulder, she'd stared with venomous hate at the closet where Lena hid. Teresa blamed her and had never made a secret of it. Lena had cost them their father.

Would she cost them their lives, now, too?

Ace shook his head. "I'll protect Mercedes. I work for Dragonfly House. You go find somewhere safe to live, and I'll get her to another zone—"

"But Teresa would never leave. My mother couldn't leave Joseph behind." After all of the loss in their lives, the birth of Lena's nephew had brought joy back to her mother's life. She shook her head. "I have to go back. I have to convince them. I can't lose my mom."

"Are you going to talk to Reyes, then? See if he can protect you all?"

Back to Reyes again.

She grimaced. "I don't know. But I have to go somewhere. And I have to protect my family. I'm going to have to go back and figure it out."

She looked down at her hands, fisted on the sides of his shirt, and then back up at him. "Except…it's kind of a long walk. Can I have a ride?"

Ace nodded, face grave. "Yes. But you're a wanted woman. You don't mind riding in the trunk, do you?"

She blinked.

A broad smile spread across Ace's face.

Lena rolled her eyes. "This is serious, Ace. You're such a jerk."

He chuckled.

"Seriously."

"Mm-hmm."

—✳—

Before they could leave, Lena had to ground. Whether agents still lurked out there or not, putting it off would be dangerous. She couldn't go into the city glowing this bright. She tried to get Ace to stay behind, just in case, but he would have none of it. He'd go with her into the desert, or she'd take her chances going back without grounding.

The desert undulated before her, lit by bright starlight and the half-moon above. Rocky outcroppings and twisted juniper trees scattered across the low hills threw pale shadows across the sand. She avoided them and her home, leading Ace toward the wide strip of broken asphalt that had been the big road to Albuquerque. The road was cracked and lifted in chunks, melted black ribbons crumbling. The road led nowhere now. The people who had been the heart of Albuquerque were long gone, and past it was Native Nations desert territory and the Hell City that had been El Paso.

She preferred to ground near the road to nowhere. It was already broken and glassy in places, so she wouldn't disturb the desert. But she couldn't risk hiking four miles from the Pueblo tonight. The pride of lions roaming the Zone Three desert hunted at night. So did wolves. In her current condition, she couldn't defend herself and Ace, and she had no desire to find more trouble.

You've already got enough trouble, Lena.

Her lips quirked, although it was pain not mirth behind the smile. She had cataloged the four-legged threats to their safety when the real danger to her life came in the two-legged variety.

She reached a long rise jutting out over a shallow indentation in the land, not quite an arroyo. It was clear of brush and junipers. It would do. She hopped down from the rise and quickly removed her clothes. Her hands, shaking now from cold, flipped and creased the fabric in sharp motions before handing it off to Ace and reminding him to stand back. He'd seen her ground before. He planted a quick kiss on the top of her head and moved well away. He couldn't help her with this anyway.

Naked and shivering, she returned to the middle of the shallow bowl. She rubbed her hands together and took a deep breath. She paced for a moment, pushed her hair back behind her ears, and waited for the anticipatory nausea to subside.

With a cry that was half sob and half angry shout, she planted her feet and wrapped her arms around herself. Her head fell back, and her eyelids closed as she sent her mind down into the ground below her, burrowing deep into the cool dark of the earth. Even as she pushed down she could feel the Dust swarming up, coating her invisibly, to protect her from the worst of the discharge to come. She gritted her teeth and opened herself to the earth.

She forced the Dust immersed in her cells to unfold in a ripple of will and energy. They spiraled open like flowers, revealing the pulses of stored energy at their core. She harvested the charges, and each pulse joined together and flowed down her body in spurts, pulled by the charge-craving earth.

As they moved, they drew the earth's energy up toward themselves. It seeped into the bottoms of her soles and pooled before creeping up. The flow down from Lena slowed and steadied, grew together, and filled her until she could taste the metallic tang, and the rich electricity filled her nostrils.

The initial crack of the electric channel forming as the two forces met within her deafened her to those that followed. The sound waves came so fast that they were indistinguishable from each other. She felt each one. The sear of the white hot energy was muted by the Dust coating her skin, but only enough for her to survive it. The terror of the heat grew. It filled her mind as it licked at her body, outside on her skin and inside at her muscle and bone. Her blood burned. She screamed; the sound became lost in the crash of discharging electricity. Heat filled her mouth, white static arcing between her teeth and then out, up from the ground through her to sheet across the sky.

As suddenly as the channel had formed, it released. The last of the feedback energy curled away as the lightning dissipated. Her collapsing body threw no shadow in the absolute dark following the loss of brilliant white, but as she broke the rippled glass that had been desert sand, the dull crack echoed.

A ghost of sound whispered through her lips. She curled onto her side until bile rose from her stomach and made her roll forward and lift herself to hands and knees. Her throat and sinuses burned, waking her from her grounding-induced stupor. She eased back onto her heels. Ace's hands were there then. He was with her, easing her hair away from her face, checking to be sure the desert glass hadn't cut her after she fell.

She needed time to recover, but the final bolt shooting up and sheeting across the sky might well attract those two-legged predators. Instinct would have animals headed in the opposite direction. Slavers were the danger after grounding. Those willing to trade in humans found a booming market for Sparks. Slavers didn't often come this close to Native Nations territory, but it was good practice to not make oneself obvious. She usually grounded during the day when figuring out more than the general direction of a bolt was made more difficult. The hour after grounding was not the ideal time to try to fight away some bastard intent on dragging her off to sell to the highest bidder.

Or to best an agent intent on dragging her back to the Council.

Four shaking hands pushed at the hair hanging over her forehead and cheeks as she and Ace both attempted to help her see. Every breath rasped in her throat and her teeth ached. Ace helped her get back into her clothes. She wouldn't win any awards for presentation, but she was clothed and shod.

The stars lit their way back. She blinked up at them. She loved the light they provided in the open desert. Starlight was never as bright in Azcon. Perhaps it was a factor of the taller buildings or the grounding platform for the city Sparks that rose above them, where lightning lit the sky every night, the jagged discharges visible from miles away from the city. Maybe the darkness of roads and buildings sucked the light from the sky. Here in the desert the sand reflected the light back to the stars like a lover returning a smile. The vastness between them should have felt lonely. Instead, it was healing.

They made it back to Gloria's to gather her clothes and knitting, the only things left of the world she'd built that she could carry. Gloria wished her well, and Lena and Ace trudged back to his car. Lena looked back over her shoulder, her head turning with every step, as if to sear the memory of the village and the Kewa into her memory through sheer force of will.

SIX

The frigid mountain air Alex sucked in as he jogged to Council headquarters cold-seared his lungs. He ran through darkness. He'd gotten back from Fort Nevada late—or perhaps it would be more accurate to say early. After he'd hiked back in through arroyos and tunnels, he'd fallen into the shower. Under the spray of the water, his mind woke and started working through the puzzle of Lena Gracey.

Finding her was a coup. Where there was one, they had to anticipate the possibility of others. Before he'd returned to Azcon, he'd left messages on three desks at Fort Nevada, to be seen whenever the others came in to make reports.

Believing Lena was not unique did not lessen her worth in Alex's eyes. She wasn't some abstract concept of the Spark's Eve like she was to Thomas. She was a real woman, troublesome and smart and intriguing. He felt a little smug that he'd been the one to discover her. Unlike Thomas, he did question their ability to control and bend her to their will. He'd dealt with the maddening little thing. And the damnedest thing about it was he couldn't wait to have the chance to do so again.

He tried to imagine what it must have been like for five-year-old Lena to suddenly be hidden from the world. He didn't know the specifics, but she had to have lost contact with everything and everyone she knew except for her family. And as her taunt in the desert had reminded him, he understood that trauma all too well. He'd lost his family. She'd lost the world. Flip sides of the same scarring loss. He knew what made her so strong. He recognized it because it lived in him.

It had hardened him, that rage and grief, and his training had honed it into a weapon. He had survived the process, turned it against the people who had made him, due to the influence of Sam, one of his early instructors. Sam had seen something in him and had worked hard to bring back the humanity in little Alejandro. He hoped Lena had her own Sam. Was it Ace?

By the time he'd finished his shower, he'd decided to head back out and have a non-threatening conversation with her, to be honest and explain everything at stake. Surely, she had seen something of herself in him, too? It might explain why she'd stopped to speak with him outside Santo Domingo instead of merely running to safety.

He dressed, eager to start the day, regardless of the hour. He'd wait for Lucas to come in, coach him through a strategy session, have him collect Lena's sister, and then head out while Lucas was distracted by his "interrogation." He could be down to Santo Domingo, convincing her to cast her lot in with the men of Fort Nevada, by noon. If he could convince her, Lucas would be chasing a ghost.

A very well-protected ghost.

Alex jogged to work and took the stairs to his floor two at a time. He pulled open the door, sending it swinging behind him to bounce off the wall, then continued down the hall to the wide-open office space and crossed to Lucas's desk, where he scrawled a note: "SEE ME. -Alex." He left it on Lucas's desk and went to unlock his office.

After lighting the candles on his desk, he pulled out the reports from last night. They were in need of changes now that he'd spoken to Thomas and knew what their goal would be. By the time he finished rewriting them, the candles near his head sputtered and popped. They were nearly burnt down. Sunlight had been flooding in through his window for the last few hours. He tamped the candles with his fingers and stretched.

Where the Dust was Lucas?

He rose and left the office, intending to march down to

Lucas's desk again. Before he got to the end of the hall, he heard his name behind him. Fernie Salas waved a wax-sealed folded paper at him as he came down the hall.

"Downstairs asked me to let you know—messenger dropped this for you. It's urgent," Salas said.

"Oh, yeah?" Alex stopped. "Urgent, huh? I've been so wrapped in urgent reports I don't even know what day it is."

"Tell me about it." Salas grimaced in commiseration as he passed Alex and handed off the note.

"Thanks, Salas."

The man raised a hand above his shoulder, waving back to acknowledge the thanks without turning. Alex changed directions, returning to his office. He closed the door behind him and examined the wax seal. A dragonfly. Dragonfly House, then, which meant Ace. He broke the seal and unfolded the paper.

> IN THE CITY WORKING ON TRUST. IF YOU
> DON'T HAVE YOUR ANSWER BY THIS
> AFTERNOON, MEET ME AT THE BAR AT THREE.
> NO PLAYING.

Alex felt a grin spread across his face. She had come to the city, and Ace would get her to contact him.

Three o'clock at the Piece of Asp, if he hadn't heard from her before then. It gave him enough time to wrap things up and send his partner on a goose hunt.

No playing. No doubt Ace meant it as a threat. A wheeze of a laugh escaped Alex. "Yeah. We don't have to do the whole threatening thing, Ace. We want the same thing for Lena. I promise."

He crossed to his desk, relit the candle, and burned the note. He checked to be sure the wax seal had melted away before discarding the ashes. Assuming she didn't decide for herself before then, Alex would be there at three, and Ace would take him to Lena. A man like Ace was as good as his word. Occasionally, that presented problems. Not this time. Not yet.

—✺—

Lucas wasn't at his desk, and Alex's note sat untouched. He crumpled it into a tight ball and glanced around the large room. Junior agents hunched over desks, dipping their pens in ink and then laboriously scratching out their reports. A laugh bellowed from a group of agents standing together in the far corner under a wide window.

They saw him coming. They also saw the closed, unhappy look on his face. The loud laughter died off, and several of the men who had experienced Alex's wrath in the past turned away and scooted back to their desks, busy again. Alex tossed his head at Hilliard, one of the more senior of the men.

"Have you seen Lucas this morning?"

Hilliard's face flashed surprise for a moment. "I haven't, no. But…"

"But what?"

"He logged out early this morning. Noticed when I signed out mine." Hilliard pulled a set of car keys from his pocket and gestured to the closed door across from them. The keys to the official vehicles were kept in a storage box mounted on the wall of the equipment room. Junior agents were required to log their usage of the vehicles.

Alex glanced over and then looked back. "Thanks, Hilliard. I appreciate it." He strode away.

Lucas had checked out a vehicle? Had he decided to pick up Lena's sister and nephew before meeting with Alex this morning? It would be just like Lucas. Not only was it insubordinate, but Lucas appreciated any opportunity for bullying. The man represented everything Alex knew was wrong with the Council agent system.

He gritted his teeth. If Lucas managed to stumble upon Lena and drag her into custody, making his real mission that much more difficult, what was left of the little jerk's life would be short and intensely painful.

He walked into the equipment room. It appeared to be long and narrow, as walls closed it off on either side of a long desk.

They shielded the wide, shelved space behind the agent manning the desk. Alex greeted him and slid the thick paper logbook down the desk to himself.

"Checking on my junior," he told the agent. He scanned back up the entries for the morning until he found Lucas's scrawled name. He traced across. Six a.m. Lucas had left the building while Alex had still been deep into his paperwork. That made no sense. It didn't take that long to pick up a set of potential witnesses and bring them in. Where had he been since then?

His eye caught on a scrawled word down the line. Lucas had checked out the Tesla, the long-range vehicle reserved for the Councilor. When not scheduled for use, it could be checked out by senior agents. Breath slid from between his tight lips in a thin stream of whispered sound. Wherever Lucas was, and whatever he was doing, he'd given Alex the means to hang him high. He returned his scrutiny to the agent before him.

"You signed out the Tesla to him?"

The man looked down to Reyes's pointing finger on the log. It was all show. He'd remember signing out Councilor Three's vehicle. "Uh, yeah. He had the req form signed and sealed by his senior."

"Is that right?"

The man nodded, but the expression on his face turned from efficient detachment to dread.

"May I see that req form?"

The metal drawer of the desk rasped open, and the agent reached into a bin of papers inside. He leafed through them quickly before pulling one out. He handed it to Alex without a word.

Alex stared at the signature blocks. The little rat had forged his signature—and done a piss poor job of it, too. His seal imprinted the glob of wax, and the mark was authentic. He kept the seal in a locked drawer in his locked office. When had Lucas taken it? Not that morning. Alex had been in his office. But Alex had used it himself the night before. Lucas must have broken into his office overnight.

Alex took a deep calming breath. He tracked up the paper to

the Need/Destination section of the requisition form.

The words were scrawled in clotted ink.

APPREHENSION OF ILLEGAL & POSSIBLY OVERPOWERED SPARK POSING DANGER TO THE COMMUNITY & COUNCIL OF 9. AGENT ACTING ON TIME-SENSITIVE INFO REGARDING LOCATION OF FAMILY MEMBERS IN ORDER TO FORCE COOPERATION OF TARGET.

Alex gave his attention back to the agent before him at the desk. The man leaned away from him.

"There's only one problem. *I'm* his senior. And I didn't sign this."

"But your seal?"

He didn't even blink. "Yes. My seal. So we have a junior agent who broke into my office and desk, stole my seal, and drove away in the Councilor's long-range capable vehicle. Sounds like an idiot going rogue." He placed the form on the desk and used one finger to slide it back across to the agent. "Don't worry. I'll retrieve him." He tilted his head toward the rack of keys. "Any of the Volts will do."

The man turned and snatched up a set of keys from a hook.

"You should probably get started on the incident report right away." He pocketed the keys. "I'll sign off when I get back." It would look better if the report had been timed and signed by the man before Alex got back. Since it involved the Councilor's vehicle and the man would be eager to distance himself from the mistake, he'd likely go up his own chain of command as soon as he could.

"Yes, sir." Before Alex left the room, the agent gathered sheets of forms from a drawer on the other side of the desk. *How cooperative.* For every agent who knew Lucas had gone rogue, it would be that much easier to return with Lucas's corpse.

As he passed through the bullpen, he snagged Fernie Salas's junior agent, clapping him on the shoulder as Alex passed behind his chair. "Mark, grab Salas and come to my office. I need you to process it for a break-in."

The man's eyes widened. He nodded and rose. Alex returned to his office. He stood at the door, examining the lock of the knob for tampering. Inside his office, he did the same at his desk. The evidence at the desk was clear, a scratch veering away from the drawer lock where Lucas's hand had slipped. Nothing too obvious, though. Lucas had done his thieving well.

He turned at the sound of shoes scuffing the floor behind him. Salas was framed in the entry, Mark hovering behind him.

"Someone broke into your office?" Salas asked. At Alex's nod, he shook his head. "You're on the main corridor. Do you know when? How'd it go down without someone noticing?"

"Early this morning or last night. And no one noticed because they assumed he had a right to be in here, I'm guessing. You'll have to see if anyone saw him."

"Right to be in here?"

Alex nodded. "It was Lucas. He came in to get my seal so he could forge my signature on a req form. He wanted the Tesla."

Both men stilled. Salas recovered first. Mark looked as though he'd like to ask if Alex were sure, but not Salas. Alex wouldn't have said anything unless he was certain.

"If you don't mind processing the door...my drawer.... Nothing else appears to be missing, but it'd be helpful if we could see if anyone saw him." He shrugged into his jacket. "I'm going to go find him."

Salas glanced around. "Mark can handle this by himself. You want back up?"

Alex's eyes crinkled, and he snorted. "For Lucas? C'mon." He focused on presenting a confident and trusting face, not a cocky one. It would be more believable that he'd had to take Lucas out after the younger man gave him no choice if he didn't give the appearance that he was out for the man's blood. "He's my partner. He's not gonna give me any trouble. I'll bring him back. We'll figure out what the Dust is going on in his head." He shook his own head.

He allowed his attention to return to Mark as if a thought had just occurred to him. "Hey, you two have your heads together in the bullpen a lot. He didn't say anything to you? I know I can be a hardass, but this? This is crazy." He shook his head in wonder and lowered his voice. "He took the Councilor's fucking Tesla. Requisition already has a report going up the damn chain. Got any idea what's going on with him?"

Alex wanted to be sure the problem was limited to Lucas. If he had a larger problem, it would be better to root it out now. It sucked to be detached about the loss of life, but he had too much riding on his success to be sentimental. There was too much riding on Lena, too. Separate issues, but both had huge repercussions. If he failed, the loss of life that could follow would be devastating—to Sparks first and then to humanity. No more limping away from the brink of collapse; they would all be sucked right down, courtesy of the Council of Nine.

If it was in his power to end the cycle of clinging to the old ways, old technology, and old corruption, he'd make it happen no matter what it took. The oligarchy masquerading as a confederacy needed to end. With Lena, they could stop it. The power they could gain from her to change the order of everything promised to shatter the Council.

He scanned Mark's face, but the younger agent's only agenda was distancing himself from Lucas's fall.

Mark shook his head. "No. He was working hard on something. But he always did." Mark gestured to the doorknob, a symbol of the transgression. "But this—no. I got nothing to explain this."

Alex sighed and shook his head in regret. "Damn," he murmured to himself, loudly enough for them both to hear. "The kid had potential." He stared out the window in disgust for a beat and then turned to them. "You got this?" he asked Salas. At his nod, Alex told them, "I'm gonna head out, then. See if I can salvage this." A little bit of honesty always made the lie sweeter to the ears.

He left them in his office, working out the details of Lucas's mistake. He wore the mask of concerned partner as he made his way through the building, but his teeth were grinding. He'd been so close to being done. Councilor Three departed for the annual

Council Meet in three short months. The Councilor would travel cross country with his lackeys, security, and Zone trading partners to meet the other eight Councilors. They'd set mutual policy and deal with any disputes. Alex had positioned himself as the only choice as the Zone's agent liaison to the delegation, a position affording him the luxury of bringing in his own small support team. He'd quietly done favors for and tolerated time spent with men he would have preferred to arrest or bury. He included Councilor Three on that list. Even the suggestion of a scandal could scuttle all of Alex's work.

Alex's mind worked the problem. If he could bury what Lucas had done by planting key pieces of incriminating evidence that suggested Lucas was part of a splinter group, he could pull it off. Not only would he discredit even the memory of the steaming pile of Sparklet crap, but he'd also cement his own position.

As his mind ticked through and created a list of upcoming activity, he almost missed the conversation ahead of him down the short hall.

"I'm sorry, Miss. Agent Reyes may not even be in the building." Margie, the Council receptionist, used her best ice queen voice. "I can schedule an appointment for later in the week—"

"I need to see Agent Reyes now." Lena said, quiet and determined, but with a little edge of fury.

In spite of the anger in her voice, he grinned at the sound of it. She'd made her choice. She had come to him. If he could get her out of the building before Lucas returned, she'd be safe.

"You need to go get him." Lena had replaced quiet and determined with scorn.

He winced. Margie wouldn't like that at all. He moved to step forward as Margie responded, her voice having sunk to frostbite level chill.

"I don't know where he is, Miss."

"I do." Lucas spoke from the hall that emptied into the lobby from the rear of the building. He meandered out to Lena and Margie, hands in his pockets. "Agent Reyes is sitting in his office," Lucas lied. "Waiting for me to let him know how best to hunt you down. Do you know how it is I'm supposed to find out?"

The heat and loathing in Lena's voice increased. "I imagine you'll use my family," she said. "But it's not necessary. I'm here to turn myself in. You can leave them alone."

"Oh, I don't know that I can convince Agent Reyes to do that. We've already picked up your sister. And your little nephew Joseph, too. I spent the morning catching up with them." In the beat of silence, Alex imagined Lucas was smiling. "And there's no telling what a man like Agent Reyes will do. Or which room he'll start with."

"You're pretty brave," she snapped, "to say that to my face after what I did to you yesterday. If I've got nothing to lose, what's to keep me from hurting you again?"

"Because, Lena Gracey, I will make sure your family suffers for every moment you resist us."

His voice was pleasant, but Alex's ire at his younger partner multiplied.

"I'm not resisting you." Her voice throbbed, thick and pulsing with hate, proof of her struggle not to strike at Lucas. "Let Teresa and Joseph go."

It was time to intervene. Unfortunately, it wouldn't end well. He couldn't see any easy way out. His mind scrabbled at scenarios, flipping through and discarding almost as rapidly as he could form the thoughts. He stepped out, a smile on his face. Lucas and Lena both caught the movement and turned. Neither of them seemed happy to see him.

He sauntered down the short hall toward them. Venomous intent glared through her eyes. He could feel his body begin to respond, his throat constricting around the urge to cough. But he'd spent a good portion of the ride to and from Fort Nevada deconstructing what she'd done to him. He couldn't reproduce it. He could damn well resist it. When he reached them, he cocked his head to the side and smiled at her.

"Did you really think that little trick would work on me again?" He raised his hand and shook his index finger in the air, making a tsking noise. "Fool me once...."

Her face reddened with rage, but she behaved. She was

probably plotting her next move. He imagined it would be painful. She'd make a hell of a weapon.

She's already one hell of a woman.

Thanks to Lucas, he'd lost any influence he might have gained from Ace's trip out to reassure her of his intentions. She had worked up the courage to come directly to him, made the choice to do what would be best for her family. Now, whatever kernel of trust had started to grow, Lucas had destroyed. Regret for that loss weighted Alex's belly.

He swung to face to Lucas. When he spoke, he had lowered his voice to a near whisper. "And speaking of fools," he said. "What in Dust do you think you're doing?"

Lucas had the gall to sneer at him. He wasn't even bothering to hide his dislike for his superior. He thought he'd completed a coup.

Speaking of fools, indeed.

"I just lured in a dangerous, illegal Spark. By myself," Lucas declared, allowing his voice to carry. "And I did it in spite of the interference and delay tactics of my supposedly superior officer, who is clearly too much of a coward to do his job."

From the corner of his eye, Alex caught her reaction. He paused a moment to allow the realization of what Lucas had said to sink in. *See?* He told her in his mind, *not involved.* Not this time. She turned the force of her blue-green, venomous eyes, and her fury, from Alex to Lucas.

He gave his attention back to his puffed up junior partner. "Actually," Alex said evenly, allowing his own voice to carry without it being obvious, "what you did was break into my office, forge my signature, and illegally use my seal to gain access to the Councilor's vehicle, and then taunt a dangerous, illegal Spark in a lobby full of unprotected citizens of Azcon, and in the building where our Councilor works."

Would that be enough for her to figure out he wasn't responsible for any of this? That he hadn't betrayed her? It should be. She was a clever woman. Whether or not she would realize he didn't have a choice about what came next was the question. That, and whether she'd forgive him.

Citizens who had been waiting for appointments with various Council officials began to move away from them. With the movement came whispers and fear. Alex caught a brief flash of fabric and skin to his right. An agent who'd been coming around the corner from the other side of the building sank into a crouch and moved into position behind the low wall separating the back of the building from the lobby area.

"But you're right," he told Lucas, "you did do *that* alone, in spite of the direct orders of your senior agent." He needed her to strike out at Lucas. Surely knowing what the ass had done would incite her. *Any time now, Lena.* "Orders that were born of caution and experience, Junior Agent Lucas, and extrapolating what one Spark like this woman might be capable of doing if she's brought into a room full of people while she's still conscious."

Hello, Lena? Any time.

Lucas looked uneasy. The agent crouched just to Alex's right, out of sight of both Lucas and Lena, was also distinctly uneasy. He removed a Taser from his belt. The weapons were even more effective at controlling Sparks than the regular population.

Alex hammered his point home to Lucas, raising his voice as if genuinely worried. He had the attention of the captured audience of agents and citizens. He hoped it would be the final push for her. "Have you forgotten what the woman did to *us* yesterday? Two experienced agents? You're a fool, Lucas!" He turned to Lena then, raising one hand in a calming gesture.

Her lips were turned upward in a mean smile directed at Lucas. "Maybe he's not a fool, Agent Reyes. Maybe he's just a slow learner?"

Finally!

Lucas paled. He fought her for a moment, lips pressed together. They parted to allow a sound that was half-gasp and half-cough to wheeze out. Beside Alex, the agent swung his hand out, preparing the Taser. With her attention focused on Lucas, Alex shot a hand out to intercept the weapon and took it, holding it down behind his thigh.

Lena's chest rose and fell, her face mottled red beneath dark freckles. "All I wanted was to be left *alone!*"

Lucas stood, knees locked, fighting for consciousness.

Her glower dipped down to his knees. They buckled, and Lucas collapsed to the floor at her feet. The mean smile crept back.

Alex took a deep breath. "Damn, Lena. You are truly amazing." The words were soft, but not so soft that she wouldn't hear them. He shook his head. "I am so sorry."

Her brows knit together. She slid one foot back in a cautious step away from him. "What are you sorry for?"

"The headache." He flipped his hand out and up, pulling the trigger. The darts shot out and impaled her with small barbs to deliver their voltage and shatter her concentration. She went down. Her head cracked on the floor, and she remained down, small and crumpled.

Bitterness flooded Alex's mouth and coated his tongue. He sighed and shook his head.

She's definitely going to hold this against me.

SEVEN

L ena came back to a world of crackling white energy. White light glowed from under her cracked eyelids. White noise hummed in her ears. The white buzzed beneath her skin. It crawled and bit in stinging waves over her head and down her body.

She opened her eyes. Light blazed in. She squinted and tried to turn away from the twin lamps hanging above her head, shadowy metal arms bent behind them. A strap ran across her brows, pinning her head to a hard mattress. She jerked her arms up to reach for it, then her breath caught in her chest like a fluttering bird of panic. Restraints yanked her wrists back. She tightened her fists and lifted, pulling up more and more violently. When that failed to free her, she bucked her body up. Restraints bound her at chest, hips, and ankles. Air chilled her skin. They'd taken her clothes?

Her breath sawed in and out. She blinked tears back and rolled her eyeballs, straining to see past the light. It was no good. At the edge of her field of vision, wires curled away from her temples and down.

Were the wires the source of the constant biting sting at her temples?

Lena lay still. She had to stay calm, to focus, and to think, so when an opportunity presented itself she could take it. But she couldn't stay focused. Each time she almost had her breath under control, the controlling thought would slip away, lost in the white noise coating the inside of her head or in the stinging that caused her flesh to crawl. She'd have to start again.

After the fifth or tenth or twentieth attempt, her tenuous hold on control snapped. Her breath gasped out again, wet and raw with tears. This was it. Everything her father had warned her about. She'd failed. She'd taken a chance, grabbed at an opportunity to keep her mother safe, and had walked right into the trap. The Council had her now, and the Council did terrible things to powerful girls.

Please no please no please no.

Her father's serious, freckled face flashed before her. He smelled like heated metal. Fear. His hands held her shoulders as he reminded her again. But when he opened his mouth, she heard no words, only the buzz of static.

Stop stop stop stop stop.

Her mother came to her, pushed her father gently away and stroked Lena's hair away from her face. Her mother had been the patient one, the one who'd reassured her when her father's insistence made her cry. She had a gentle touch, like her smell— rain in the desert, sky and earth, clean water. Mama had been as soothing as cool water before Lena's father died. Before Mama began to blame Lena.

Mama I want to go back. I want to go home. I want to go back. I want to go home. I want to go home.

A moan filled the air. She listened, rigid and still, straining to hear beyond the soft static. Had it been her own voice crying the words aloud? In the wash of shame and fear following the realization, there came another sound from outside her own body. Voices.

Lena closed her eyes to the bright light and her mind to the static. She breathed deep once, twice, calming the hysteria-tinged hiccupping breaths. She listened. Yes. Voices. The low rumble of men talking outside the room. Not talking. Arguing.

Reyes.

A stab of hatred arrowed through her, so pure and strong that it almost felt good. Trust him, he'd said. He'd get her to safety, he'd said. Lies. She'd believed them, too, just before he betrayed her. She'd wanted to believe them. She'd looked for a reason to. And now she was strapped naked to a table in Council custody.

The voices ebbed in volume. She strained to hear them, to pick out intelligible words from the stream of low sound, but she failed. After a moment, a lock turned over behind her and to the right. Footsteps shuffled on the floor as several people entered the room. The door closed again.

Lena waited. She held her breath, paralyzed, only her hammering heart reminding her that she lived. For a moment no one moved. They stood outside her limited field of vision. One, then another, walked crisply across the floor. Blinded by the lights shining upon her face, she still couldn't see them. Dark shadows examined her.

Slow steps came from her right. An arm reached across and snapped off each lamp in turn. She blinked in the sudden absence of light. By the time her eyes adjusted, Lucas had pushed each lamp back and up, away from her face, and then retreated to the side near her knees.

Another man joined him, moving in from the corner to flank her on the other side of the bed. He was older, his hair mostly grey except for an odd pocket of black along the hairline above his left eye, his face crisscrossed with seamed frown lines. He wore matching pants and shirt, an electric blue flecked with green, and both were prohibitively expensive silk relic-wear. He looked at her as if she were a specimen, a mixture of revulsion and dark fascination on his face. She recognized him.

"You've got your second chance, Agent Brayer, so then tell me," the Councilor of Zone Three said, gesturing to indicate Lena, "how all of this works? You're sure she's incapacitated?" His voice had the resonating quality of someone who spoke and expected to be heard.

Agent Brayer? Second chance? Am I the second chance?

Lucas smiled and nodded, opening his mouth as if to answer, but another man stepped forward. He was middle-aged, older than Reyes and Lucas, but not as old as Councilor Three. Tall and broad, his bullish shoulders sloped into a thickly muscled neck.

When he reached the end of the bed, he looked at the doorway. His gentle, soft voice surprised her. "Alex? If you'd care to leave the guards and join us?"

Five slow footsteps later, Reyes appeared at her shoulder. "Lena." The greeting came low and even. His eyes were hooded, eyelids sheltering his expression from the men.

From her angle below him she could see directly into their dark depths to the emotion he seemed to struggle to bury. Disgust? Anger? Regret? Each time she tried to put a name to it, the word skittered away in her mind, driven out by the buzzing that filled her thoughts. She grunted her frustration, the sound barely registering as a huff of air. She swiveled her view from Reyes to focus on the ox at the foot of the bed, already talking.

"Councilor, if you'll notice the electrode pads at temple, chest, pelvis, and ankles? We have a constant feed of electric current flowing into the subject—"

"Lena," Reyes interjected. "Her name is Lena."

The big man's brows lifted. "Alex. I had no idea you were a sentimentalist." The corners of his mouth twitched.

Reyes met his stare without flinching. "I'm not, Director Hernandez. But if I'm going to do something for the good of the people, then I will do it without shying away from full knowledge of exactly what it is I am doing and to whom. I take that burden because it is part of the job I believe in. I don't look away. I don't close my eyes. And I don't try to make the weight of it less by dehumanizing the people who suffer for it."

She glowered at him. Was that all it took for him to excuse his dishonesty?

The thought slid away from her.

What about trust? Broken trust?

"Alejandro." The Councilor's voice expressed his oily admiration, even if his words were a rebuke. "Please allow Director Hernandez to continue. I'd rather watch you gentlemen work tonight—" His speculative leer fell upon Lena.

She shivered and shrank back, aware enough to be afraid of the avarice in his gaze. He wanted to see her hurt.

"—but my presence is required elsewhere. This is all the

demonstration I will get."

Reyes extended his head in a nod. "My apologies, Councilor Three. Of course, you're right." He waited a beat before speaking again.

She tried to bring her focus back around to his words. But the static in her head crested. She lost his words in the wave of the damn buzzing. She widened her eyes, as if it would help her to understand if she could see them all better, and turned them to look from man to man.

The Councilor preened. The ox was amused. The rims of Lucas's ears reddened, and his lips compressed into a white line. Reyes was neutral. Always neutral.

Was that part of the burden? The thought snaked away. She clung to it, and the flesh under her skin began stinging again, ant bites spreading. It hurt worse when she tried to cling to understanding. If she let go, hazed out her focus, the burn subsided. By the time she brought herself back to awareness, the ox's voice filled the room again.

"...began experimenting with different levels of current after a riot at Madisonville."

She recognized the name of the Council prison reserved for criminal Sparks. It was in Zone Two. No. Zone Four? Yes, it was in Four.

"It was an accident." The man smiled. "But when even the strongest of our Spark offenders were incapacitated, we realized what we should have known after experiencing the grounding hangover." The man was pleased, rocking back and forth on his toes. "That happy discovery led to different modes of application. All of the Madisonville prisoners are fitted with electric collars like the shipment we've been promised."

His voice became a buzz again, blending with the buzz in her head.

"...can see it disrupts the critical processes we Sparks use to maintain Dust activity. No focus. No Sparking. It will also reduce her resistance to suggestion. We'd like to find out exactly what she can do, but without the demonstration Agent Brayer got." He clapped Lucas on the shoulder and laughed.

The Councilor's leer raked over her again as he spoke. "...like to make sure the current fluctuation will be effective before I go. I'll be very disappointed if this one—" He broke off and turned a more respectful look to Reyes. "If *Lena* is as big a disappointment as the last one because I could use the prestige of—."

The last one? She pulled in her focus sharp and tight, gritting her teeth against the pain. There had been another?

Reyes's head snapped up though he shifted the movement into a casual back and forth stretch of his neck. The ox immediately spoke over the Councilor, offering reassurances and making a display of sliding up a handle from the end of the bed to prepare the demonstration.

The last one? The last one like me? Or the last little girl? Her father hadn't been wrong.

Wait. Her mind tracked back. *Demonstration?*

Current poured into her like acid, ate down into her flesh from the electrode pads, and then spread. Her body arched, straining against the restraints holding her flat. It had the battery acid, electric burn, white heat of a grounding with none of the protections offered by the Dust. The raw current seared down and out, arcing through every part of her skin in contact with the table beneath her.

Then it was gone. Her teeth unclenched, and she found her voice, a hiccupping negative moan so raw it echoed back down at her from the ceiling. Her arms and legs and neck trembled with the memory of the spasms. She tried to catch her breath. She failed.

It took time for her to regain awareness and the moan to fade to ragged sobs. The men stood around her bed in silence. She opened her eyes, feeling the heat of tears tracking back into her hair.

Reyes stood over her, his face a mask of detachment but for one tiny muscle that jumped at the back of his jaw.

None of the other men, however, were remotely detached. The ox man, Hernandez, wore an expression of anticipation, expecting that whatever he wanted from her, he would have. The men to either side of him wore nearly identical expressions of pleasure. Lucas's face was a study in vengeful satisfaction, and the Councilor....

Lena squeezed her eyelids tight. Bright, raw lust lit the Councilor's face, and his chest heaved. Had he been this excited when his men murdered her father?

Her hands clenched and unclenched. Her father had tried to protect her. He'd raised her in hiding, taught her to live a lie to keep her out of the clutches of the Council. But even the loss of her childhood hadn't been enough. He had been as unable to keep her safe as he had been to keep himself alive. He hadn't been powerful.

But she was. She was so powerful, so different, that her father had been willing to die to keep her hidden. He had paid the price in pain. So could she. Her breathing calmed. Her hands relaxed. The tears still flowed, but they were for her father. She could do this.

She opened her eyes.

As if he'd been waiting, Reyes finally spoke, his voice hushed. "Councilor Three, I would like to reiterate my protest for the record. This is unnecessary. If you would allow me to use my methods, I could discover what you need to know without damage to her trust."

"Oh, please, stop with the trust." Lucas had clearly had enough. "Like it's going to matter where she'll be?"

"Sir, we don't have to lose her to use her." Reyes's face was bleak, as if it pained him to say the words.

That, or even he didn't believe his words would move the Councilor. Why did he bother? He had her in custody. He'd achieved what he'd set out to do. So let them have her, and enough with the charade of charm and caring.

The Councilor turned to Lucas then, the heat in his expression tamped down. "What would you do, young Agent Brayer? You are the one who lured her to us, after all."

"He's the one who endangered everyone in the building, you mean!"

The Councilor managed to raise his voice over Reyes without

increasing his volume. "Yes, Alejandro, I know. And your quick thinking saved us from his irresponsible actions. But were you never a junior agent with more enthusiasm than sense?"

"No, sir." Reyes's denial came quickly, flat and final.

"I value enthusiasm, Agent Reyes. I've already said I think an enthusiastic agent should be allowed a moment of redemption." He turned back to Lucas. "Tell me, Agent Brayer, would you like a further opportunity to salvage this situation?"

Reyes was still. Disbelief flared in his eyes.

"I would, very much, sir."

The Councilor nodded firmly. "You'll have it, then. Do what you must to get what we want. You have full authority."

Hernandez nodded his agreement. The Councilor clapped his hands once. Reyes made a suspicious survey of the other three men, lightning fast, before dropping his gaze back to her. He seemed confused and angry. Had he fallen from favor? Good.

The Councilor's gaze raked over Lena once more before he left them, his satisfaction evident in the angle of his chin and the gleam in his eye.

Reyes managed to catch her eye. He held her, staring down as if trying to impart something to her without words. She wasn't interested. She returned his gaze, feeding him all of the rage and betrayal that she felt in one hateful look. His lips parted. He took a step back, then turned and walked away to a corner of the room, outside her field of vision.

Lucas, smug, tracked him. "What are you doing?"

Reyes's low voice rasped out. "You want to salvage. So salvage. Don't worry about me."

"You're not leaving?"

His brief laugh slashed across the room at the younger man. "No. I'm not leaving, Lucas. I'm witnessing. And I'm waiting for the inevitable fuck-up."

If not for the current creating burning static through her body and her mind, Lena might have laughed.

Lucas curled his lip. He turned his back to Reyes and breathed in through his nostrils. After a moment, he reached into his pocket and removed a small folded packet of papers. After tearing off a square, he carefully refolded and pocketed the packet. He crossed to one of the agents guarding the door and passed him the slip of paper. "Go to this address. Ask the woman there to accompany you back."

Reyes snapped, "Whoa, whoa, whoa. I thought you were going to salvage the situation, not compound it."

Hernandez spoke up, too. "Agent Brayer? What are you doing? We have everything we need here."

Lucas turned his head back and spoke to the Councilor's Director of Security coolly. "The Councilor gave me his authority. I'll be doing it my way. Do you understand?"

Hernandez blinked his displeasure, but shrugged and crossed his arms. He said nothing. Lena held tight to the threads of her concentration. Why was Lucas allowed to speak to a superior like that? Why had he been given another chance? She didn't think Reyes knew, either.

After the agent who'd been sent to retrieve the mystery woman had gone, Lena tried to work through the puzzle of who could be coming to assist Lucas, but her mind began to fuzz out again.

Lucas put his hands into his pockets and wandered back to his place beside Lena. He looked down at her with a broad smile. "Look at her," he said to Hernandez. "She's already recovered. They have incredible recovery from pain, even more than the average Spark. It would be amazing if they weren't such monstrosities." He shook his head and glanced over at the larger man. "Your current may be keeping her from zapping us. But it won't work again to hurt her. She'll adapt. She's trying to figure out how right now, if she hasn't already. She'll make herself immune to the pain."

Hernandez's eyes narrowed. His hand moved on the slender handle before him.

Current sliced through her again. She was ready. She couldn't focus enough to talk to their Dust, no. But she could get her own to act, even if only sluggishly through the interference in her head. She'd already moved thin insulating layers of Dust between her skin and the eight pads. Electricity still arced through her, heated pain pouring through her flesh and blood and bones and then out into the surface behind her. She could bear it. It wasn't even a grounding.

The current abruptly stopped. Hernandez ground his teeth together loudly in the silence that followed.

"And how is it," Reyes's voice grated from the corner, "that you know so much about this, *Junior* Agent Brayer?"

A gloating smile ghosted across the younger agent's face. "Because there's a lot you don't know, Reyes. Now you're the junior, and I'm the master. You see that much, right?" Lucas said. He walked toward her head, searching her face as she gasped in recovery. "She adapted, just like I said. But there's pain. And then there's pain. It's time to do things the Brayer way." He grinned suddenly, the tight skin of his face pulling down with his leer. He purred the next words like a promise. "Because there are some things for which there's no immunity."

EIGHT

What was Lucas waiting for?

He perched next to Lena on the bed, one leg dangling, in obscene parody of a concerned friend visiting a patient. He didn't ask her any questions. He didn't speak at all. He waited.

Hernandez leaned against the wall to her left, hands clasped across his broad front. She assumed Reyes still stood in the corner.

She tried to figure out what Lucas had meant with his pain comment and who he'd called in as back-up. Someone better at causing her pain? What kind of pain? Her current-addled brain couldn't hold onto the start of a circular thought long enough for her to come back around and begin to analyze it. She had to let it go.

Pain is pain is pain, and I have the advantage. She had managed to regain even more control over her own Dust, both that which lived inside of her and that living on her skin. Lucas could do little to hurt her now. She only wished she could hurt him.

She couldn't send commands out beyond her body. She'd tried. Oh, how she'd tried, staring at Lucas sitting smugly beside her, to force her thoughts and will to pulse out at him in the gaps of focus between waves of static. It simply hadn't been enough. It hadn't been enough to work on the generator or Hernandez the Ox's charge-producing machine, either.

If she could gather enough Dust both above and beneath her skin at each electrode point and ask the Dust to send out a quick pulse of energy at each point, she might be able to short them out. The trick would be to do it not once, but eight times. Once she'd done that and regained the ability to focus....

She turned her eyes to look at Lucas. He stared at the wall behind her, face relaxed, hands loose in his lap as he meditated. Focused on how best to hurt her? Why?

She pursed her lips to ask him. The static made her lips buzz, and the word came out heavy with a buzzing *wwhhhh* that overpowered the long "I" sound of the end.

Nonetheless, Lucas's gaze moved from the wall to focus down on her face. A restless shuffling from the corner of the room was the only sound in the long pause as he examined her.

"Why?" Lucas repeated her question in a voice so soft she had to strain to hear.

It would be impossible for the others to hear his soft words.

He made a small sound of amusement, but his lips were twisted. "Good question. I've asked it myself. Every time I ground, I ask why. Every time I think about how I am the only one in my family to be cursed with the Spark, I ask why. Every time I think about being less human than my brothers, I ask why. I grew up asking why—why did I have to be the spawn of the men who caused our destruction, a living reminder of those who ruined us all?"

The first Sparks? The soldiers? She blinked, trying to find her way through the static. The people had been dying. The Sparks brought them out of the dark. Hadn't they? She tried to follow through, but could only remember that Lucas blamed Sparks. But he was an agent?

Lena swallowed. A feral light bloomed across his face. No, more than feral. Rabid. She tried again to make sense of his words, but her mind turned and fuzzed out. It made no sense. If Lucas hated being a Spark, why become an agent?

Lucas pitched his voice for her ears only. "I learned long ago that asking why is pointless. We must follow where the Council leads and do what the Council compels without question and without complaint. That's how we earn the right to l—" He stopped to swallow spasmodically. He looked at her, expression icy. "We earn the right to live and contribute as citizens." His lip curled in disgust. "Even you. I begged him to let me kill the aberrations. The world would be a safer place with none of you bitches in it. It would be cleaner. Would you like to know what he told me?"

She stared back at him, silent, stunned as much by the rictus of hatred that contorted his face as the electricity that buzzed through her. *He? He, who?*

"He told me that even things like you have a purpose. For now, you can be used for testing, for twisting, for helping us learn to protect human citizens against your kind. And someday, soon, you get to be the catalyst that ignites the world and cleanses it of the powered filth who would make us servants." His eyes widened, and his fingers, hidden in his lap from the other men, made an exploding motion.

He's crazy. She licked her lips, but it did nothing to relieve the taste of ashes in her mouth. "How can you...?" The question drifted away. She managed to pull it back in. "You're like me?"

Lucas leaned in. His voice rose as he spat each word at her. "I am nothing like you."

She held his crazed stare, refusing to back down. She would not give him the satisfaction. If she could help it, she wouldn't give any of them any satisfaction at all.

Lucas's hand curled into a fist in his lap. She could see the hint of the movement.

The door opened. Lucas looked up, his hand uncurling, and smiled. "Thank you, Agent." Delight colored his voice. His gaze shifted and moved up and down, taking the measure of someone hesitating in the entry. "Welcome."

Did he intend for his voice to be a sinister purr?

"Please." Lucas gestured to the area beside him as he stood. "Come in."

Three hesitant steps lightly tapped the floor as the person came closer. They stopped on the sound of a quickly indrawn breath. Lena's heart twisted when the woman spoke.

"Magdalena?" Her mother's voice, filled with despair.

He'd brought her mother to help them break her. Her mind

refused to acknowledge how.

"Come." Lucas gestured her over with a beckoning motion from his fingers. "You can come closer."

Those light tapping footsteps brought her mother near.

Lena turned away from Lucas's gloating face and stared up at the ceiling. If she didn't look, if she didn't see her mother standing at her bedside, then maybe Mama wouldn't be there.

She swallowed. *There is pain, and then there is pain.* He'd promised her pain from which she wasn't immune. She had to look.

Her mother's face was drawn, her smaller bloom a bright halo around her, as if she hadn't grounded in far too long. Her skin seemed yellow and thin. Most Sparks wouldn't ground if they were sick or over-tired. It was too hard on their bodies. It made the Spark hangover much worse, even dangerous. Most also wouldn't charge when they were ill, making sure not to build up a dangerous amount of feedback energy.

Lena had never known her mother to go more than a week— her job at the Council plant required regular discharges. She had never seen her mother glow this bright before. Had she been sick? And still working every day?

She felt a pulse of guilt at how long it had been since she'd made her way into Relo-Azcon to see her mother. She always told herself she stayed away due to the danger to them. She just couldn't stand the guilt. She'd broken her family. Everything that had happened was Lena's fault.

As was this.

"I'm sorry, Mama." Her voice shook.

Her mother reached out a hand. As soon as her fingers touched Lena, a spark leaped between them, and her mother yanked her hand back with a cry. When she spoke, her voice still shook. "No, Magdalena. I'm sorry." Her throat moved spasmodically as she swallowed back tears. "We always knew it would end like this. The three of us tried to protect you." Her mother shook her head. "From the moment we realized what you were, we tried to spare you this."

Three of them? Spare me this? Her heart stuttered.

"Mama…?"

Her mother continued. "We hoped when they came for us, it would be after you had made your own way. We wanted you to be safe, Magdalena. I thought you were safe now. We always wanted you to be safe."

Her mother's shoulders hunched as if she were resigned to fate. It didn't matter what she expected. Lena wouldn't allow them to hurt her. She'd give them what they wanted and end this now.

She moved her focus to Lucas. His face was bright again. He'd moved closer to her mother, standing beside her elbow. His nostrils flared as if he inhaled the scent of her mother's fear. Reason wouldn't reach him.

She raised her voice so she could be heard in the corner of the room. "Reyes?" He had lied to her. He had broken her trust every step of the way. But he wasn't a sadist. "Reyes, I will tell you whatever you want, just get this freak away from my mother."

Her mother didn't stir, her face rapt as she surveyed her daughter's face with love and tears and regret written on it. Except for the long sound of a breath drawn in and exhaled heavily, neither did Reyes.

"Reyes!"

His husky voice came from the corner. "Lena, Councilor Three allowed this. I can't stop it. But I promise I won't let it go further than it needs to."

She stared up. Her heart thumped hard. He had to stop it now. They didn't have to do this. "You promise?" Her disgust echoed off the ceiling above her. She vibrated on the bed with rage. "We know how much your promises are worth, don't we?" She spat the words then turned back to Lucas. "What do you want me to tell you?"

He cocked his head, and his mouth twisted at the corner. "Tell me?" His voice still had the purring, pleased burr beneath it.

She gritted her teeth. "What do you want to know?"

"Oh." He frowned as if puzzled. "I thought it was obvious." He leaned in, careful not to touch her. "I want to know your limits." His nostrils flared again. He pulled back, sinuous as a cobra. Then he struck.

His right hand shot down across her, ripping off the electrodes at her temples. His left hand gripped her mother's hair. He pulled her head back and stuck the electrodes to the skin of her temples.

Her mother didn't even try to fight him. She stood almost serenely beside Lena.

"Mama, please. Do something. Fight back." The buzz in her head quieted with the electrodes gone from her temples, but the current still burned into her from the others.

Lucas grinned. "Fight back? Against the three men in the room? How should she do that?" He flexed his hand in her mother's hair, moving her head with the tightening of his fingers. "She's not like you. She's not strong, is she?"

"Strong enough to keep me hidden from you assholes." She swallowed. She looked back up at the ceiling above her. Perhaps if he couldn't see her into her eyes, he couldn't see her fear. He couldn't enjoy it.

He laughed softly. "It's up to you, Lena. If you want to help her, you're going to have to show us what you can do."

A soft curse came from the corner. "You're a fool, Lucas," Reyes said. "What do you think is going to happen if you piss her off enough to break free? What if your little set-up there can't hold her?"

Lucas rolled his eyes at the interference. He didn't bother to turn to Reyes. "It'll hold. It always holds. And we always get what we need out of them."

"We? Them?" Reyes demanded. "What the Dust are you talking about?"

The Ox straightened his shoulders. "Enough, Alex. You're not cleared for that. Not yet."

"I'm not, but this asshole is? Bullshit! He's my *junior,* and he should be in an interrogation room himself," Reyes flared. "I bring her down for this idiot and save everyone's ass, and yet I'm the one standing here without clearance to know what's really going on? Everything I've done for Councilor Three? Are you shitting me?"

"This clearance doesn't come from the Councilor." Hernandez stopped and shook his head. "Enough." His soft voice held a thread of menace. "Get on with it."

Lucas's face reflected his calm anticipation. "Lena, I'm going to hurt your mother now. You should pay attention." He reached his free hand out and unstrapped her head, working the buckle with a sawing motion that pressed the metal and leather into her skin. He flipped the straps apart, and the metal buckle swung out and rang against the edge of the bed. "There you go. You'll be able to see everything now. That's much better."

She refused to give him the satisfaction of lifting her head. She urged the Dust along her body. It didn't swarm to do her bidding like it usually did, but it wasn't the sluggish mirror of moments ago, either.

Lucas nodded to Hernandez, released her mother's hair, and stepped back from them both. Her mother lunged forward to put one hand on Lena's chest, over her heart. Her other hand gripped Lena's hand right below the strap holding her to the bed. Lena had enough time to note both of her mother's hands were shaking, little tremors from deep within before the current running through her roared from a trickle to a torrent. Her mother's hands tightened, spasming, as the loop of energy between them began. The electricity burned across her nerves and into her mother through their skin contact. It burned through her mother and into Lena.

Lena's head twisted against the bed as her neck arched. She set her teeth, and her body tightened, straining against the restraints. But the Dust had collected at the electrode points. It offered some meager protection, even without her focus.

Her mother had no protection.

It stopped. The pressure of her mother's hands disappeared. She slid bonelessly away. A grunt of air escaped as she hit the floor, followed by the hard thunk of her skull on the tile. Lena gasped in a breath, then another. She tried to call out to her mother. A croaking sound came from her throat. She pulled a breath in through her nose and swallowed to try again.

"Mama." She raised her head. To her right, unmoving on the

floor, her mother's back and side curved. The edge of the bed hid her head. "Mama!" Her mother's bloom pulsated, the painfully bright then dim flicker of a light about to go out.

Lucas stood a foot away. He didn't move. He watched Lena, a curious satisfaction written upon his face.

"Please!" Lena didn't know to whom she directed the imploring word. None of the men would do a thing. "Please, please, please...."

Reyes darted around Lucas to crouch beside her mother. He turned her body over, half into his lap, cradling her neck and the back of her head in one hand as he checked for a pulse. Lena stilled, her neck straining, stretched against the limits of the straps around her chest. Her breath came in harsh sobs. She stared at the slowing flick-flick-flick of her mother's bloom.

"Put her down, Reyes." Lucas's command came, sharp and cold. "The protocol is three shocks in rapid succession. They're about to get another."

"No, they damn well are not."

Reyes leaned over her mother, his fingers still at her throat. She stared at him.

"Do something." The words from Lena's throat were a thin thread of sound.

Reyes's shoulders moved helplessly. His eyes tracked the pulse of the flickering light. He looked over his shoulder to Hernandez, ignoring Lucas. "Get a medic."

Hernandez sighed, and Reyes half-rose.

"She's not a criminal, she's a citizen of this city. Get a fucking medic!"

Her mother's dark eyes were wide and staring, only slight movement in them. Was she trying to turn them to Lena?

"I'm here, Mama." She strained against the straps. They bit into her skin and her rigid muscles. "Please don't go. I'm right here."

Her mother's lips moved. A breath of sound escaped. The pause between glimmers grew long now.

"Please fight. Mama, just fight." Her words turned to a hoarse moan. "I can't lose you, too. Fight, Mama. I'm here. I'll be a good girl. I'll do what they want." She turned to Lucas, to Hernandez, desperate, gasping. "I will do whatever you want. Please go get a doctor. Please don't let her die." She strained against the straps. "Please. Please, please." Her eyes fell back to Reyes. His head bowed in regret. He lowered her mother to the floor.

Lena stared at him. "No! She's not gone. I can help her, Reyes. Get me off of here. Reyes!"

Her mother's bloom didn't pulse back. Lena could help her if she could get off the damn bed. Her mother blurred as tears rose.

She opened her mouth to scream, but the sound building within her chest caught in her throat. Her muscles slackened. Her watery view of her mother, of Reyes placing her upon the floor and closing her eyes, faded away as her body sank back. Her mouth hung open, the scream still caught, beating at her vocal cords, waiting for an exit.

She sagged onto the bed. A memory flashed into her mind: crying as her mother brushed her snarled hair. The brush caught; Lena's breath stuttered with it. Her mother's hands stilled as she held the snarl in her fingers and gently untangled it, urging Lena to recite the Spark's Rede, the code that all of the Spark children learned in their earliest years. She began, voice quavering, high and pained, "I will do no harm with my power. I will follow the will and the good of those without. This gift is my virtue; My Councilor is my guide." By the time she'd finished, the knot, and with it the pain, were gone. Her mother had told Lena many times the act of focusing on the words could keep pain at bay.

Her lips moved. The Rede came back to her, as if she were young again. The pain didn't recede.

Lucas's voice intruded, disgusted. Put upon. "I should have sent for the sister."

The Rede stuttered in her mind. *I will do no harm....* But they could? They could do whatever they wanted to the people she loved? No more. *I will do harm. I will be free.*

She focused the grief inside, rage making her immune to the effects of the current. Dust swarmed to answer her. The scream howled free. With it, white light arced across the room, seeking the men. Her electric-coated shriek of rage and grief released something within her. She convulsed, her body arching up in a corona of white light that flashed up and across with a concussive boom of sound that drowned her out. It sucked away her breath, and her voice died, the electricity following it back, crackling away into nothing.

When her eyes fluttered open, the windowless room was dark. The brilliant after-flare of the branching white heat etched her vision, glowing in the black. From somewhere nearby, a metal fixture squeaked as it swung. Voices shouted from outside. Someone banged at the door.

No sounds came from inside. She pulled her body up to the right, trying to roll to the limits of the straps, but they didn't hold. As her body pressed against them, the leather cracked and fell away from the buckles with dry pops and faint metallic tinging. Waiting for the pull of the taut, thick restraints, she rolled up and almost off the bed. She caught herself with one shaky hand.

She leaned her face over the edge, vainly searching past the vivid memory of light into the darkness below. Her mother was down there. She'd freed herself to go to her mother.

"Mama?" It hurt to make even the faint, hoarse sound she managed.

No response.

She pushed with her hand and eased up to sit, pulling her legs free of the cracked restraints to swing over the edge of the bed. She turned in the darkness. Something brushed her head, and she jumped back from the sound of swinging metal. Pushing her hand out in front of her in the dark, she reached up, searching. Her fingers made contact with one of the metal lights that had been trained upon her when she woke. It hung down over her now, loose and broken.

What had she done?

She eased her way back to the edge of the bed and slid her legs down. "Mama?"

Her feet found the floor, a coating of dust and small hard pieces of rock spread over it. Lena slid to her knees and reached her hands out, searching. She made contact with cloth, and then with the firm resistance of flesh beneath it. She ran her hand lightly up, crawling along. She'd found her mother, yes, but she was wrapped in Reyes's arms. His body curled around on top of her as if he'd tried to protect her from the electrical arc before the blast.

She pushed at him. She had to pull her mother away. She could restart her heart. Reyes was heavier than he looked and solid. She pushed harder, the motions becoming short and hard with desperation. *Get off. Get off. Get off.*

"Get off!"

He coughed. He coughed again then rolled away from Lena's pounding palms. Barely a second later, his hand shot up through the black and caught her hand. "Stop." The command was low, his voice even more hoarse than usual. He made a soft, guttural sound as if trying to clear his throat with the least amount of noise. He coughed again. "Listen."

In spite of her panicked need to reach her mother beneath him, she stilled. What was she listening for? The shouting in the hall? Someone called for a saw, a gun, anything. The door must be well and truly warped into the frame. They should have been able to access the room already. What else should she hear?

"Reyes, please…my mother." She pushed at his shoulder.

He didn't move.

"If I'm awake, they might wake, too. We need to get you out."

Get her out? But he'd brought her in?

She shook her head in confusion before she remembered he couldn't see her in the dark. "No. You were on the floor. They were standing where the blast—"

His hand moved up her arm to her neck and slid around the back of her head. He pulled her forward with gentle pressure, moving her head toward him. "I can't hear you. My ears. But don't speak louder, speak closer."

Her lips touched the side of his head. She felt his ear, wet with fluid. Blood? The concussive noise had burst at least one of his eardrums.

She tried again. "You were on the floor. They were beside me and took a direct hit. They're not waking up now. Maybe not ever." She wasn't sorry. She regretted that Lucas wouldn't have suffered. "Reyes. My mother. I can restart her heart. You have to move." She pushed again. "Move."

"No. You can't." He shifted away, his hand out, keeping contact, bringing her head with him. "It wasn't her heart, Lena. It was her head. I saw her face. Her brain bled."

She made a small noise of negation. He had to be wrong. She could do it. Now that he'd moved, she would. She reached out for her mother, felt the soft, cool skin of her mother's face under her hands.

"Lena." Reyes's voice denied her hope. "Even if you start her heart, her brain is gone. You can't fix this."

"I can!"

"You can't. And if you don't get out of here right now, they're going to kill you, too."

She sat. Her hands fluttered over her mother's face, fingertips feeling the familiar shape of eyes, prominent cheekbones, delicate nose and jaw. She had always been jealous that Teresa got to look like their beautiful mother.

"I can. I have to. You don't understand." She shook her head back and forth, her hair brushing the side of his face. "I have to. She's all I have."

"No, Lena." He gathered her up then pulled her across him and away from her mother. "You have your sister. Your brother. You have people you've never even met." He set her on his other side.

He released her, and she sat, sobbing quietly. The banging on the door directly behind her had shifted, become methodical as they smashed something heavy against it.

Debris rustled as Reyes crawled away in the darkness. He pushed something large and heavy away, the grit on the floor scratching beneath it. One of the other men? Reyes grunted. After a pair of thumps, small rocks pattered across the floor. He made a hiss of satisfaction. A moment later, he returned, scrabbling in the dark as he crawled back across the floor. He sounded like he was right on top of her mother.

"I'm here," she said sharply, forgetting for a moment that he probably couldn't hear her. She should swing her arm out to catch him and lead him back. She didn't. It didn't matter what he was doing. Her mother was gone.

He came back to her. His reaching hand found her bare stomach. His fingers slid up to her face. She shivered, and then shrank away in shame. Reyes dropped something over her head, pulled it down to her shoulders. Fabric. Clothing?

"What are you doing?" And why? The bastard had done this to her. She shook her head. Nothing made sense.

"You're naked. You can't get away like this." He took up each of her numb arms and slid fabric onto them then pulled it down over her torso, letting the leftover cloth pool around her hips on the floor. It smelled of sweat and fear and a familiar soft musk. Before she could identify it, he slid his hands back up to her head and pulled her close. The warmth of his breath tickled her ear.

"That thing you did?" His voice was a bare whisper of sound in her ear. "It weakened the ceiling and the walls. The exterior wall is cinder block. It's ready to go. Do it one more time, and the wall will fall. Behind it is—"

"Do it again? I can't do it again. I don't know what I did the first time."

"Be quiet. Listen. You will do it again. Behind the wall is a side street that leads to the rear of the building. Stay away from there. Follow the side street up behind the next building over. Block and a half up, turn right. Across the street is Citizen's Park. Get across it. Keep moving. It empties into Market Square. Do not stop. Get to Ace. Tell him to hide you until I come. I will come." He pulled away as a particularly violent thump against the door caused debris to rain down. He pulled her up then, dragging her by the hand across the room. "Do you understand?"

"I understand. I understand. But I can't. Reyes, I don't know what I did—"

He stopped. He must have found the wall again. He yanked her around him, pushed her in front of himself, and pulled her arms up to stretch out and make contact with the wall. He spread her palms flat against the wall, his own hands pressed against the tops of hers, holding her down.

The pressure of his hands above hers hurt. Her fingers ground into the wall. The pain caught her attention, lit a fluttering something inside of her. It was too close to that feeling of being restrained, the helplessness and rage she'd just escaped. She tried to pull away. He held her fast, pressing his hands and his body hard against hers. She scooted forward to escape him, but he followed her until her arms bent and her body pressed against the wall. He held her there.

Her breath came in small, panicked puffs. Why had she trusted him? Why had she listened?

He spoke then, his lips pressed against her skin. His hot breath puffed her hair away from her ear, his quiet, hoarse voice laced with menace. Her heart stuttered.

"Councilor Three killed your mother, Lena."

She stopped struggling. Cold wrapped around her. The heat of rage chased it away.

"We hauled her in, sick and weak. Put electrodes on her head and charged her until her body couldn't handle it, and she bled out."

He crushed her in tighter. The dusty grit coating the wall bit into her forehead and chin. The pebbled surface beneath the paint pressed her breasts and belly and thighs. Her breath sawed in and out of her raw throat. She tried to fight, pushing back against him. Dust swirled across her skin in agitated reflection of her anger and confusion.

"Lucas liked it," Reyes growled into her ear. "He liked seeing you naked and helpless on that table. He liked watching you jump and fight when they shocked you. And he really liked hurting your mother. Councilor Three let him do it. He gave Lucas permission to charge you both until your mother's brain exploded."

She shoved away from the wall, managed to gain several inches. He slammed her back. Her forehead cracked against the cinder block. A scream of rage erupted from her. Bright clawing branches of electricity spread across the wall before her then sheeted back behind her, flinging Reyes away from her a moment before the enormous boom of sound and light and pressure erupted from her chest.

The wall disintegrated, and she fell forward through it, stumbling across the broken blocks and skidding across the debris-coated street outside. She hunched over painful hands and knees that had taken the brunt of her fall and curled away from the noise of her discharge. Unlike before, when the boom had been loud and then gone, this one went on rumbling loud in her ears.

But it wasn't the echo of her thunderstrike. The building collapsed behind her. She turned her head to look back. The wall slid down into the street. The ceiling had collapsed. Rubble filled the opening.

Her mother was buried within.

Lena's heart squeezed. She swallowed the pain back down. At least she'd also buried the bastards who'd killed her mother.

And Reyes?

She turned onto her butt and pushed away from the rubble that slid through the opening. His remembered voice growled, vicious and low in her ear. *Councilor Three killed your mother.* But Reyes worked for the Council. He worked for Councilor Three. He was one of them, wasn't he? Why had he helped her escape?

Councilor Three killed your mother. He *was* one of them.

Lena lifted herself up from the ground, knees and hands bloody. A fine dust covered her. She shook her head, trying to shake the worst of it off her skin and hair.

Councilor Three killed your mother.

She turned and limped down the street as quickly as her knees would allow, angling up behind the building next door, moving away from the shouts and activity behind her.

Councilor Three killed your mother.

NINE

Grit filled Alex's nose and coated the inside of his mouth. Hands gripped him, holding him in place as he tried to roll away. They snapped a neck brace around him and then counted off. He didn't need a damn brace. He tried to tell them, but remnants of the ceiling gummed in his mouth and made him choke again when he inhaled. On the count of three, the techs rolled him to slide a backboard behind him. His bellow of pain became snorts and hacks that cleared the worst of the debris and allowed him to breathe easier. At least he wasn't choking anymore, as he had been in the time it had taken them to get in the door.

Each breath burned agony in his chest, but it was infinitely preferable to choking. Every move lit a fire in his ribs. When he'd been thrown back like a rag doll in the last moments before Lena had exploded the wall, his left side had slammed into the end of the bed before he'd fallen. The toss across the room had protected him when the ceiling came down like a hinge, but his ribs were in misery.

And her explosion? He couldn't wait to learn that trick—once he had gotten her back to safety. He groaned. Someone above him shouted some drivel about being okay. *Yeah. Whatever.*

They lifted him and carried him down the long hall to the old wing before handing him off to some waiting medics. He managed to crack his eyelids open. Grit fell past them and burned like cinders. He squeezed them shut and grunted in displeasure.

Someone swiped his face with a cool, wet rag, carefully easing it along both eyes and then down and around his nose.

He tried again, fluttering his lashes and then lifting them. A nurse with a grim face but a gentle touch cleared the worst of the dust and debris from his face and ears. Someone else examined his chest and legs.

"What happened?" Alex frowned at them. He hadn't lost consciousness after the second blast. But he hoped to pass for woozy and newly conscious. "Where are the others?"

The nurses exchanged a look over him. He could hear someone shouting in the hall outside. Though his damaged right ear muted sound, he thought it might be Lew Merritt, Councilor Three's Junior Security Director, who served directly under Hernandez.

One of the nurses said something about being right back and stepped away. She called down the hall, informing someone of his status. A moment after she returned, running her hands over each arm in turn, he could hear Merritt's heavy footsteps.

"I said, what happened?" Alex repeated, raising his voice for effect.

Merritt's clipped voice sounded from somewhere behind and above his head. "We're hoping you can tell us."

Alex made a move as if to turn and see Merritt. The nurse hissed at him and held him still. Merritt came closer, standing behind the nurse. He was a big man, both tall and wide. Even his features were big—lantern jaw and long, wide boxer's nose over a bristling blonde mustache.

Alex furrowed his brow. He needed to know who survived before he made a move. "Where are Hernandez and Lucas?"

"They're working on prying Lucas out. He's alive, but barely." Merritt paused, the muscles around his brows tightening. "Hernandez was killed, along with one of the women. The suspect's mother, I'm told. What happened?"

"We were interrogating the Gracey woman. Hernandez was charging, with Lucas questioning. I was observing." Alex made a show of thinking.

With Hernandez dead and Lucas down for the count, things

were easier. However, he had no doubt there was more going on within the Council than Alex or his people knew about. Without knowing the parties involved or being able to guess the end-goal, he'd have to tread carefully. Carefully but quickly. His mind flashed to the lost, broken quality to Lena's voice in that dark room. His stomach turned over. He had to find her.

"We brought in her mother," he continued for Merritt. "Gracey flipped out. It seemed—like she maybe grounded through the table or something?" If grounding included a concussive thunderclap that destroyed walls and ceilings, sure. He slowly nodded his head, filling his voice with disbelief. "She used her ground as a weapon?"

Merritt grunted. "I'm surprised no one's thought of it before, actually. You'd have to be pretty desperate. What did you get out of her?"

Alex growled his frustration. "Not a damn thing yet. Where is she? Let me have her for a few minutes, and I'll get it out of her."

Merritt shook his head. "She's gone."

"What? How?" He kept his stare locked on Merritt's.

The man shook his head again. "She blew up the damn place. Room upstairs came down on it. Exterior wall is blown to Dust. Looks like she climbed right out. She should have been restrained."

"She was," he answered. He shook his arm in a small movement meant to show his displeasure at being strapped to the board. "Let me up. This is my case. I can find her."

The nurse above him shook her head. "You're not going anywhere until we can get a doctor down here to make sure you haven't broken anything."

"Then get me a damn doctor," he snapped.

"I can't," she snapped back.

"She can't," Merritt said simultaneously. "Gracey blew the whole building. Every area behind a security door is locked down. We're trying to figure out the extent of the damage. We can't get anything back up yet. Right now, the Council building is dead, and almost all of our people are trapped."

Alex stared at him, his mouth hanging open. The entire

building?

She was a hell of a woman. He wanted that trick. He had to get her to teach him all of the fun things she could do.

He recovered a moment later. "Unstrap me," he commanded the nurse above him. "I'm fine."

She pushed on his left side. Alex roared, tears springing to his eyes. When she released, the sound faded to an angry hiss.

"Fine, huh? And what about your ear?"

He glowered at her. "I'm a Spark. My ear's already healing. My ribs will be fine in a week. My back's fine. My legs and arms are fine. Wrap my chest. Give me something for the pain. It's not the first time I've had broken ribs."

Merritt looked at him appraisingly.

"Wrap me up and let me go. This is my case. She may be long gone, but if anyone can find her, I can."

Merritt nodded at the nurse. She sighed and shook her head, but she unstrapped Alex from the back board. He braced himself before pushing up, gritting his teeth against the pain. He kept his breathing as shallow as possible while she wrapped his ribcage with tight bandages.

"Who's out there, and where are they?" Alex asked Merritt.

"We've got four teams out at a ten-block radius, sweeping in. She can't have gotten that far."

"Four teams?"

"Everyone else is on recovery or locked down. Even our strongest Sparks can't get those shorted doors to respond. We can hear them working on them from the other side, too, but they're not coming open."

Alex shook his head. "Shut down the city gates."

"She's not getting past—"

"She'll get past. She might already have. She's got resources. She's slipped us twice now. Twice. Shut down the city gates. Nobody in or out. Give me forty-eight hours." Alex needed that time. He needed them focused on the commotion that shutting down the gates would cause, allowing him to get her out via the tunnels.

"I can't shut down the gates for two days. There's no way.

We have people out there—"

"She killed the Councilor's Director of Security."

"I worked with the man every day. I damn well know what the situation is."

"Twenty-four hours." Alex stared at Merritt. He had to get something from the man.

Merritt chewed his mustache. "Twenty-four. Who do you want with you?"

"My junior."

"He's down. Maybe permanently."

Alex shook his head. "I don't want anybody. My case."

"That's not happening. You're not in any shape to be out there alone. If you can't think of anyone you want then I'll—"

"Fernie Salas, if he's not locked upstairs." He straightened and rocked gingerly. The pain stabbed through him.

The nurse gave him a look.

He had to be sure he could move.

Merritt nodded. "Fine. You should know before you head out—Councilor wants her alive." Merritt raised a brow and made a small shrugging movement with his broad shoulders.

—⁓—

Alex turned the corner behind the reception area and stepped around the crew of Spark agents and building techs clustered around the electrically sealed access to the upper levels. A heavy rock propped open the rear door, and a pair of agents stood to either side of it. The lock plate was blackened and melted, so they had managed to get some opened, even if by force. Was the Councilor stuck upstairs in his offices? The thought of the man having a panic attack over being confined to his office made Alex's lips twist briefly into a smile. Then he sobered.

The Councilor was far more likely to be having an apoplectic fit of fury, which would not bode well for Lena. Especially with the speed at which they were getting everything open. The more agents flooding Azcon looking for her, the harder it would be for him to smuggle her to safety.

Alex didn't pause when he hit the parking lot. Salas and the

Security boys Merritt had insisted on including in the search trailed behind him. "Understand the assignment and the goal?" He tossed the words back over his shoulder.

At the affirmative sounds from behind him, he crossed to the little Volt. He tried to swing into it as he normally would. Agony hitched in his chest and caused him to stop. He pressed his curled arm tight against his ribs. Once he'd caught his breath, he eased his way into the car and gingerly swung his legs into the foot well.

He'd sent Salas to her mother's house, and the Security team had instructions to go to Danny's house. Alex had chosen to check on her sister. He hoped Lena had listened to him and gone straight to Ace, but if she hadn't, he was betting she'd go to her sister. It made sense that she would go there to check on them after Lucas had pulled them in for questioning.

First, he'd stop at the Piece of Asp to be sure Ace wasn't there waiting. It was almost three. The bar sat on West Alameda, which fed into the Northwest grid, where Lena's sister lived. While he was on his way to her sister's, he'd double check that Lena had gone straight to Ace. Assuming she'd followed Alex's instructions, she would have made it to Ace's before he'd left for his appointment with Alex.

He cursed at himself. He was making a whole lot of assumptions lately. Lena was screwing with his head and his standard procedures. He needed to get her to Fort Nevada and get himself back on track so he could repair the wide wake of damage she'd unwittingly done to all of his plans.

And to your focus, asshole. You've spent too much time distracted by big green eyes and freckles. What do they have to do with what she can do with the Dust? Get the girl safe. Dump her at the fort. Get your head back in your fucking sweet spot before you get yourself killed.

He forced himself to take deeper breaths as he shifted into drive and pulled out of the lot. He had to breathe, even if it hurt. He needed his mind clear. He worked on his focus as he drove to the bar. When he parked, his ribs still hurt like hell, but no more sudden moves, and he'd be fine.

He pushed into the bar. Light from the sunny day outside fell into the room, illuminating Ace. He sat at the bar, spinning a glass of water between his palms over and over. Alex stopped, and Ace raised his glass a couple of inches in greeting before gulping the water down.

"Hey," Ace said to Alex as he crossed to him, "You ready?"

He shook his head, already furious. "Were you at home before you came here?"

Ace frowned. "Yeah. Why?"

"And Lena wasn't there?"

"No, she left a note. Said she was going to talk to her family, and she'd be back. She'll be back."

He looked at the floor, cursing. When he looked back up at Ace, he didn't bother to hide his anger. "Stupid girl. I don't have time for this."

Ace pulled his head back, brows furrowed.

"Go home and wait for her, Ace. I told her to go there. But she didn't do as she was told."

"What are you talking about?"

"She came in. Came to find me. But my partner got to her. I tried to buy some time, but then he brought her mother in." Alex stopped. He shook his head. "They killed her mother. It was an accident. Sort of. And Lena—"

"Council agents killed her mother?" Disbelief warred with outrage on Ace's face. "In front of Lena?"

He nodded.

"In front of her?"

"I said that, yes."

Ace's eyes narrowed. He leaned in toward Alex and whispered tightly, "Don't you get short with me, Agent. You say you'll protect her, then the next time I see you, you tell me Mercedes is dead? That they killed her in front of Lena? While you were buying time?" Ace leaned back. His face twisted, as if he had tasted something foul and was ready to spit it out.

"I got her out." Alex said flatly. "I told her to come to you and wait, that I would get her out of the city. And I can. But she didn't go to you, so now I have to find her. I'm running out of time." He turned and reached for the door, bracing himself to pull it open.

Ace grabbed his shoulder and spun him back around. "Then you should have done a better job of getting her out. What the hell were you doing?"

Alex's breath caught in his throat. The pressure built, waiting to be expelled, but the agony that had flared in his side would explode. He allowed the breath, and the pain with it, to hiss out between his lips. "I was busy trying to get the rubble of the side of the Council building off of me. It took a while."

Ace searched his face.

The man had been thrown, even harder than Alex expected. He hadn't anticipated that Ace might have been close to her mother.

Alex shook his head. "This is bad. And I don't have time to explain it all now. Later, after I've found her, okay? Right now, I need you to go home and wait. If she shows up, keep her there. I'll check back." He held his finger up to Ace's face for emphasis. "Do not let her leave. This city is not safe for her now. If they take her again—assuming they don't shoot her out of hand for the death of the Director of Councilor Security—there will not be a damn thing I can do."

Ace pulled back when he mentioned Hernandez's death. "She killed him?"

"Him. Maybe my partner. Almost me." His hand twitched, but he managed to keep it from reaching up to support his ribcage.

"Good for her." Ace pushed past him and out the door.

Alex barely managed to avoid being knocked into by the larger man. The sudden jerk away sent a searing wave of pain through him. He ignored it, his breath gasping out as he followed. "Ace—"

Ace spun back, rage flowing freely across his face. "I'm going, Agent. You said you could keep her safe. So go find her. Or all bets are off." He turned and strode away, his heels beating against the ground. "And if she shows, I'm making you no promises. Not anymore."

"I am the only one—"

Ace didn't slow, just waved him off and turned the corner,

his long stride carrying him away.

Alex shook his head. The day had gone to hell. It was time to do what he did best and turn it around. Of course, it would be helpful if he had all of the information he needed.

At the top of his to-do list, right behind getting Lena out of Azcon and covering his own ass, was figuring out what Lucas, Hernandez, and the Councilor were a part of that he hadn't even known about. The fact that he wasn't aware of any other factions operating within the Council or on behalf of any individual Councilors left him cold. They had plenty of reports about the Tribulationist influence on Councilors Four and Two, and on Two's panic as the Native Nations carved away her arable land. But an unknown internal faction operating at this critical point? Not good.

It wasn't far to her sister's grid with the tiny new homes that were meant to emulate the old neighborhoods of Santa Fe and Los Alamos. He parked and approached Teresa's earth-toned adobe home on foot. Just inside the gate to the little private plaza, a large earthen bowl of pecans still in their brown and black striped shells overflowed onto the terracotta tiles. Alex cocked a brow at the extravagance.

The nut somehow affected the brains of Sparks, giving them a boost in strength and longevity between grounds. The valuable commodity grew almost exclusively in Zone Three. Their trade value dictated most of the crop be earmarked for shipment out of the zone. The overflowing bowl on Teresa's porch was meant to say a great deal about her, though she made sure they were out of reach of anyone at the locked gate. He sourly shook his head.

He pulled the rope to the side of the gate, and the bell clanged. Through the front window, he could see two shadows, one large and one small, moving in a back room. Not Lena small, though. Child small. As the notes of the bell sounded, the shadows melted to the walls. He shook his head and pulled the bell again.

After the bell sounded a third time, he raised his voice so Teresa could hear him from inside. "Teresa Gracey Luevano? Council Defense Agency. Open the door." He pulled the rope another time for good measure. He wasn't going away. He repeated himself, louder, deliberately throwing his voice so her neighbors could hear him as well.

The larger shadow peeled itself away from the wall and hurried up the hall. Locks flipped, and an attractive young woman in her late twenties came out and hurried across the courtyard.

Teresa looked like Mercedes, all large dark eyes and thick black hair worn loose and long. Their mother had been tired and likely sick, but he had still recognized the faded beauty of the woman beneath the sallow skin and timid demeanor. Teresa had her mother's beauty. But Teresa did not have her mother's manner.

She stopped and stood back from the gate, her arms crossed tight across her chest. "Show me your badge."

Alex had anticipated her demand and already had his wallet out. He slapped it open with an irritated flick of his wrist. She leaned closer to see it better, as if anyone else had the capability to make a mock-up of the rare metal blend with a stamped engraving of his face.

"Teresa Gracey Luevano?" He made sure his voice still carried and nodded at the gate between them.

"Do you mind?" She darted forward to unlock the gate, looking quickly up and down the street behind him. She closed the gate then turned away from him to hurry back into the house.

He followed her.

Once he'd crossed the threshold into the cool house, she swung the door closed behind him and whirled to face him. "What do you people want? I already told the other agent that I have nothing to do with my sister!"

He held up his hand. "When was this?"

Her nostrils flared with her emotion. "This morning. Early." She spat the words at him. "When agents came to my home and took me away like a criminal. When they pulled my son from his bed and carried him away." Teresa gestured down the hallway. The smaller shadow, no doubt, was her son making himself scarce.

If Lucas had picked them up, Alex couldn't blame her for

being angry. But she wasn't just angry. There was fear. Fear and—? Her hands trembled. The pulse in her neck was racing. Her eyes were red and her lashes wet.

Fear and grief. She knew her mother was dead. And only one person could have told her.

"I'm sorry for your loss," Alex said.

She swallowed hard, shaking her head, as if to deny it.

"Lena? Lena!" He called out to her, his voice a bellow of frustration. Why could she not have gone to Ace's place like he'd told her? Why did she have to push every step of the way? He pressed his hand up against his ribcage and stalked down the hall.

"She's not here," Teresa called after him.

Her footsteps slapped the floor behind him as he called out again.

She raised her voice over his. "She's not here! I threw the little bitch out of my house!"

Alex turned. "What did you say?"

Teresa folded her arms across her chest again. Her jaw set, and her lips turned down with hate. "I threw her out. She's not here anymore, and she won't be back, so you can go, too."

"You threw her out?"

"Yes."

"Your own sister?"

"Half-sister!"

There was nothing in the file to reflect that, so he merely filed the lie away. "And where was she going?"

"To one of the stupid boys she sleeps with? To her awful friend? To my idiot brother? I didn't ask. If they're smart, they'll throw her out, too." Teresa tossed her long hair back behind a shoulder. "Maybe she ran to the park or the market to creep around pretending to be a normal person like she used to do. How should I know? And why should I care? She got my mother killed!"

He felt his disgust mirrored on his face. He continued to the back of the house, a long open space with a kitchen at one end and a living area at the other. Teresa stalked after him, ordering him to leave her boy alone and spewing half-formed threats. The room was empty but for furniture and the small boy squeezed between the wall and the back of a wooden chair. Alex crossed to the boy.

"Joseph." He squatted, back straight to ease his ribs, as he regarded the scared child half hidden behind the slats of the chair. Wide, dark eyes stared back at him. "Was your aunt here?"

The boy peeked at his mother.

Alex had to have his attention. "Joseph!"

The boy jumped.

"Do you know who I am?" Alex asked.

"A bully!" Teresa spat at his back.

Alex ignored her. He focused on the boy, hating that he needed to question him. The pit he'd waded into kept getting deeper and deeper. "Joseph, do you know who I am?"

Joseph nodded. "Council agent." His voice was so faint as to be barely heard, especially with one eardrum still healing.

"That's right. And if you lie to me—no matter who tells you it's okay—it is very wrong. Do you understand?"

Joseph nodded again.

"Okay. Now, was your aunt here, Joseph?"

"Yes." Joseph kept his gaze fastened upon Alex's.

"And is she still here?"

Joseph shook his head. "She had a fight with Mama." Tears welled. "She said my 'buela was gone. She said the Council killed her." He sneaked a glance at his mother and then back again. "But Mama said no. That Tia Lena killed her?"

"Actually, she tried to protect your abuela. Okay? It was a terrible accident, but she did try."

Joseph nodded. His small hands, still baby fat, curled around the back bars of the chair he hid behind.

"She tried, Joseph."

Alex rose. He made a quick circuit through the two tiny bedrooms and the bathroom joining them. No Lena. Her sister really had thrown her to the wolves. Some family.

On his way back out to the main hall, he paused where Teresa stood, her chin high, nostrils flared, and eyes dark. The woman hadn't even bothered to comfort her own child.

"How long ago did she leave?"

Teresa shrugged. "I don't know. Thirty minutes? An hour? I couldn't tell you."

Alex didn't bother to answer her disrespect with words. He paced across the room, moved into her space, pushed forward even as she stumbled backward. Alarm replaced anger on her face. He didn't say a word. He didn't stop, either, until she had moved back and caught against the far wall. Movement flashed in the corner of his eye as Joseph ducked down further with a whimper. He hated Teresa for this. If she gave a single damn about her child's well-being, she would have cooperated. He'd have searched the house, been on his way to find Lena. But no, she had to try to prove how clever she was.

Except she wasn't clever, or strong, or tough. She was nothing like her sister. He had a new appreciation for why Lena had fled Azcon to make her home in an abandoned gas station in the middle of Kewa country.

"How long ago did she leave?" He breathed the question directly in her face as he stared down at her.

Teresa swallowed. "Twenty minutes. Maybe almost thirty? No more."

He waited, holding the invasion of her space, drawing it out.

"I swear," she blurted. "Twenty, twenty-five minutes. She ran out of here. And she really won't be back."

He understood. He was leaving, and he never wanted to return either.

He backed away. His heart wanted him to check on Joseph, but his head knew what he'd see: a terrified child, shrinking away from the Council agent, marked for life by the encounter. His lips twisted. Generally, he could assure himself that the things he had to do in order to change the world for the better didn't make him a bad person. Sometimes, like today, he couldn't avoid the truth. He was a very bad man. He did bad things. That he did them for a good reason didn't pardon him.

He left them. The gate swung open behind him. He hoped her neighbors scuttled over and stole all of her damn pretentious pecans.

—ᚼᚼ—

Alex rapped at Ace's apartment door, holding himself stiff. He'd experienced the pain of broken ribs before. He'd also been under the gun, literally and figuratively, trying to make things happen against the odds. The fact that Lena had him wound so tight was not good.

He raised his hand to knock again, his ire rising. Would they have the audacity to take off on him?

Ace opened the door. He stood framed in the narrow opening for a long, silent moment, his eyes hooded and smoldering with banked anger. Finally, he stepped back.

A long breath eased from Alex. She was here.

He only made it a few steps into the living area before he felt the shift in pressure behind him as Ace moved in fast. His ribs slowed his reaction. Before he'd even managed to make a quarter turn, he felt the hand drop to the back shoulder of his shirt, and Ace spun him around. Alex gasped, and then held his breath.

"Stop doing that," he managed to grit out. "My damn ribs are broken."

"Good. That's an excellent start. Because I tell you now, more than your ribs are going to be broken if you don't explain yourself in the next five minutes." Clearly, Ace had been catching up with Lena.

He took a shallow, tired breath. This would be pointless. Nothing he could say would appease the big man. "I did what I had to under the circumstances."

Ace scowled, shaking his head.

"And actually, I did exactly what I told you I would."

"You told me you'd protect her."

"I told you I would get her to safety. And I did. And if you'll notice, I'm still working on doing that." Alex pointed a finger in Ace's face. "I also told you I was running out of time and at some point my hands would be tied."

"Your hands would be tied? You shot her. *You shot her*. Then you handed her over to them." Ace's chest heaved. His lips thinned.

"I stunned her. And at that point, I had to. Lucas would have had her in custody in a matter of moments, and I had to be sure I would be included in her interrogation. It was the only way I could think to buy the time to figure out how to get her out of there." It sucked. It did. But it had been the first step to saving her. Did he even stand a chance at making Ace understand it?

"You stunned her? You betrayed her." Ace all but snarled rage and frustration at Alex.

Nope, not a chance. He sighed. "I never intended for her to stay in custody. It was just something that had to happen to buy time. There is more at stake than—"

"Like Mercedes's death?" Ace's voice rose now, enough that any neighbors at home might hear. Alex needed to end the conversation now. But Ace shouted, "You said you would keep her safe—"

"And you think I haven't?" Alex interrupted. "I've risked everything to help her. Who the hell are you to tell me you don't like the way I've done it? She would be dead right now if not for me. Dead or worse."

"Or worse?" Ace scoffed. "I've got news for you, man. There ain't anything worse than dead."

Alex snorted his disdain. He leaned in and lowered his voice. "I've got news for you, simpleton. There damn well is."

Ace's eyes narrowed to slits. "Get out. I'll keep her safe myself."

"You'll get her killed," he told him calmly. "And you'll die with her."

"Get out!"

"Stop it." Lena's voice, tired but strong, carried from the arched hall leading to the rear of the apartment.

Alex swept his gaze over her, checking her small body for injuries. She was whole, but she still wore her dead mother's dress. Somehow, it made her command more effective. He snapped his mouth shut and bit back the words he'd been about to growl at Ace.

Ace wouldn't give up. "I've had enough of his lies and doubletalk. I want him gone and—"

"I said stop!"

They stared at each other. She didn't move. She didn't so much as blink. Ace did, looking away.

"He helped me, Ace. Even when he was hurt, the first thing he did was help me." She was matter-of-fact, as if she'd been turning the thought over and over until it became clear. "You're focusing on the wrong part of the story, Ace. I get it. The whole time they tortured me, I blamed him, too. But as soon as he had the opportunity, he's the one who got me out." She shrugged. "And if I'd listened to him and come straight here instead of going to Teresa's...."

She shrugged again, but her focus scattered. It darted away from them, across the room, touching on a chair, a picture, the floor. She lifted her face back to them again with a sigh. The blue-green of her eyes was darker.

"Are you okay?" Alex asked her. He immediately winced. Stupid, stupid question.

Ace stared at him incredulously.

She laughed, the sound a little hollow. She reached both hands up to her face and pressed the heels of her palms against her brow. When she dropped them, she shrugged with her hands. "I am. I guess I really am. Wonder what that says about me." It was a statement, not a question, as if she'd already decided what it said about her. No doubt she'd had Teresa's help in coming to whatever conclusion she'd reached.

"It says you're a survivor." He looked from Lena to Ace. "So now we have to make sure you survive, no matter how motivated they are, and get you somewhere the Council can't reach."

"I'm pretty motivated myself," she said. "You say you have a place safe from the Council. Are you and your people working against them?"

"We are working *for* Sparks—"

"Yes, but are you working against the Council? I'll go with you if I can help destroy them."

Her soft voice filled with an intensity that took his breath away. The Council had carved a hole deep within Lena Gracey, and she wanted to fill it with vengeance.

Alex nodded at her. He could give her vengeance.

"Lena, no. He just wants to use what you can do."

"I want this. *I want this.* So let them use me. It turns out I'm a pretty good weapon."

She was an exceptional weapon.

"I can get you out," Alex swore, making the promise to all three of them. "I have a safe house. You get to it at dusk, when the streets are full of people heading home or to night shift. Wait for me there. I can get you out."

"Dusk is really soon," Lena said. Her hands picked at bits of the hospital room wall still embedded in the weave of her mother's dress.

Alex nodded. "Shower. Do you have any clothes here?" At her nod, he continued, "Good. Change. Then you and Ace can go for a walk. Take some food and water. I should be able to come for you tomorrow, but it may not be until late. Once Ace leaves, sit tight and wait."

"You expect me to just take her somewhere and *leave her?*"

"I expect you to do what needs to be done in order to assure her safety. You know, like *I've* been doing all along?" He was nonchalant, but the words were meant to dig.

Ace bristled.

"No, Ace, you aren't leaving me anywhere." Her voice had gained strength.

"That's exactly right."

The man had no idea how dangerous it was to give Alex that look.

"Stop smirking, Ace." Lena tossed out. "You aren't leaving me anywhere because you aren't going. You've risked enough. And I can take care of myself, as you well know."

Ace shook his head and opened his mouth. Alex turned away and tuned them out. He ignored the argument behind him and crossed to a desk. Deliberately slanting his letters far to the left and shifting his neat block lettering to a casual scrawl, he dipped a pen in ink and jotted down the address of the safe house. If she got picked up, this wouldn't come back to him. He couldn't save her ass again if he was in the cell next to hers.

He blew on the ink until it dried, then folded the paper and turned back to them. She stood serenely, as if waiting for him. Ace was still infuriated. Alex held the slip of paper aloft between his first two fingers, waving it back and forth between them as if unsure who would take it. After several seconds, he made as if he'd finally realized Ace would not be going along. He pulled a sad face at the man before crossing and giving the address to Lena.

Yeah, I'm an asshole. Oh, well.

"You should leave in about twenty minutes," he told her, all business. "You'll be traveling away from every area they have the manpower to watch so far. Blend in, and you should be good. Remember food and water. The address is between two storefronts, around back down the alley. Get in. Hunker down. Sit tight, 'cause the streets will be crawling with agents in a matter of hours. I'll be there as soon as it's safe to make a move."

She nodded. Her arms went around herself.

"I will be there," Alex continued. "This time...do us both a favor and actually wait for me."

She cracked a smile. That was good. If she realized how badly she'd misjudged him, maybe she'd stop.

TEN

L ena wove through a crowd of people. Some moved against her to get to their homes and others hurried with her to make it to work. She settled the knit bag holding flatbread, hard cheese, and water further up her shoulder for security and focused on blending in. At least she looked like she belonged. She'd quickly showered away the dust and grit coating her skin and hair and shed the dress—her mind veered from the memory and instead focused on the clothes she wore now.

Ace had found them on one of his trade excursions. She'd left them with him because she had little use for bright, lapis-colored, antique blouses and silky teal skirts in her everyday life in the desert. Now they helped her look like one of the brightly clad young women who worked the power plants but hoped to catch the eye of someone in the Council building. Well, except for the bloom so bright Lena imagined she could see it herself from the corners of her eyes.

Reyes had commented on it before he left, wishing that they had some way for her to ground. It wasn't like she could march into the grounding center. After what she'd done, the accumulated power zinging through her now would discharge spectacularly. She hoped anyone noticing the bloom would dismiss it as a young woman pushing her grounding way past the limits of what was smart.

So far, so good. Passersby were immersed in their own thoughts. The foot traffic was swift and free-flowing, citizens moving with heads down, hardly seeming happy in a city that billed itself as the comfortable, fair alternative to the unpowered wilderness.

A gust of southwestern spring wind roared through the street like a moving wall, pushing at the people. Dirt rose into the air in visible eddies. She automatically narrowed her eyes and turned her head away from the dust-filled wind that sent small, unsecured items rolling down the street with it. With her eyes squeezed into narrow slits and watering at the grit, she almost missed the faded lettering above the boarded up storefront. She darted into the small doorway. An equally faded notice informed her that Longoria General Goods had moved.

She steeled herself against the wind again as she stepped out of the slight protection the little alcove had provided. Only a few quick steps down from it, though, she could turn into the narrow alleyway between the two adobe buildings. When she reached the end of the building to her left, she turned behind it. The tiny little add-on building nestled in the far corner of the small lot. As promised, an electric lock secured it, tucked away to be as unobtrusive as possible.

Lena settled her hand against it, exhaling as she reached out to the Dust. The lock snicked open, and she slipped inside. She took the time to add her own special touch when she re-locked it. Now the Dust would send her a silent alarm if anyone attempted to open it.

She turned to the small, spare room. It covered only the essentials. A narrow cot ran along the wall across from the door. In the far corner across from the cot sat a lidded bucket. Being trapped in this tiny space with the smell of whatever waste she added to the bucket wasn't ideal, but at least someone had provided one. She'd wait as long as she could.

She took a long, uneven breath. She was proud of herself for managing it without tears. As a rule, she wasn't a crier. Being strong mattered, her parents had taught her. If the neighbors heard, they would question the sound of a dead child's grief. Tears were a mistake none of them could afford.

Instead of crying, she looked around again, making a memory

and knowing its import: this room was the first step on the road to revenge. She allowed herself a moment to savor the thought before setting it aside. She'd pick it up again later, when she could show the memory of her parents all that she'd done to make it right.

She crossed to a tiny table with a pair of three-legged wooden stools tucked under it and a book resting on its top. She set her bag of food and water down before picking up the book – *The Complete Poetry and Prose of William Blake*. It was very old, the cover dusty and worn, the edges of the pages yellowed. A small scrap of torn paper peeked out from the top. She carefully turned to it, hoping the thin pages wouldn't tear in her hands.

"Auguries of Innocence," she whispered to herself. She skimmed downward. Specific groups of lines were carefully underlined here and there, with tiny, neatly lettered comments written beside the poem. It appeared the words had been underlined at a different time than the comments, perhaps by a different hand?

> *A Truth that's told with bad intent,*
> *Beats all the Lies you can invent.*

The note beside the lines read, "Integrity versus Honesty?" She skimmed down the poem to the next set of underlined words.

> *To be in a Passion you Good may do,*
> *But no Good if a Passion is in you.*

She reread the line a couple of times. The carefully lettered note beside the lines read simply, "EXACTLY." Lena blinked. "Huh." She had to disagree. Maybe. If she felt a little more confident that she understood the words.

She raised her brows. Whose book was it? Did anyone other than Reyes use this safe house? Or were there others in Relo-Azcon who did similar work and might have need of a place to hide? She shrugged and hooked one of the stools out from under the table with her foot, dragging it back. She plopped down and bent over the ancient book.

It didn't take her long to decide she didn't agree with the mystery commentator's tiny notes, however thoughtful they might be. She had the urge to write a snarky reply. Good thing she had no pen and ink. On the upside, a one-sided debate while she read would give her something to occupy her attention while she waited.

By the next afternoon, however, not even puzzling over the ancient poetry kept her occupied. She paced the confines of the space, arms swinging loosely with nervous energy, as she had been for at least an hour. She heaved out a breath and fell onto the cot.

She'd tried to sleep the night before. Her efforts to beat the dust out of the pillow had resulted in a sneezing fit and streaming eyes and nose. Once she'd finally lain down, wiping at her nose every few minutes, she'd jerked awake every time she started to doze off.

While she was conscious, she could force her mind to focus on things other than the events in the Council building. The Kewa. Her home at the edge of their territory. The things she needed to get done to be ready for the harsh high desert summer. The puzzle of Reyes.

Every time she started to drift off, her mind flew back to that Council room with Lucas leering over her. She would force herself to wake, jerking up and away from both the cot and the pain. She'd finally fallen asleep out of sheer exhaustion. Hours later, she'd woken from a sobbing, cold-sweat nightmare. She couldn't remember the details. She didn't want to. Her hoarse cries had been for her mother. She didn't need to know more.

She popped up from the cot, arms still tight around herself. She paced, every step a slap of heels on floor, and swore savagely at herself. It was ridiculous. She hadn't seen her mother in months, and even longer before then. Neither of them had any real presence in the life of the other, and that was as they both preferred. Her mother hadn't been able to deal with the strength of Lena's "gifts," and Lena refused to hide.

After several tries, she swallowed down the lump in her

esophagus. She told herself her allergy attack caused her sore throat. It wasn't tight with tears.

The alert from the lock made her jump. She dropped her arms, looking wildly around, but with no bolt hole she had nowhere to run. Reyes swung open the door and entered. He barely spared her a glance before turning to re-secure the locks.

He turned and did a double take. His right hand came up as if to calm her.

Lena swiped at her nose. "I'm not crying," she lied. "I'm having a reaction to the dust in the pillow." She lifted her chin with stubborn pride, but she couldn't keep it from trembling.

Reyes's gaze swept over her as he evaluated whether or not he believed her. Finally, he nodded and crossed the room to stand in front of her. He chewed the inside of his lower lip as he regarded her. His eyes were deep and so dark his pupils disappeared. He opened his mouth to say something, closed it, then nodded and started again.

"You were right," he said, his voice soft, "back there outside Santo Domingo. They did snatch little Alejandro away from his mom and dad to make him a Ward. And it fucked with his head." He paused, swallowing, but not taking his steady gaze from hers.

"I was five years old when my parents handed me over to the Council. And the last words my father said to me before they put me on that steam train were, 'Be strong, little man.' I thought that meant I couldn't cry. Every night, all of the other boys cried. All the way to the Ward School, and after we were there, the sound of crying lulled us all to sleep. But not me. I was going to be strong. Except it didn't make me strong. It made me mean. It made me weak. It wasn't until someone showed me that crying could help me heal that I learned how to be strong. You have to mourn what's gone. You think if you nurse that wound, it will feed you. But if you let it heal, the scar will make you stronger than the wound ever could."

She shook her head back and forth, refusing. She held the grief back.

He lifted his hands to her shoulders. "Yes. It's okay to cry."

"It's not. It's not, because I don't deserve it," she whispered and dropped her face so she wouldn't have to look into his anymore.

"You don't deserve to heal?" The soft words were incredulous.

"No!" The trembling was spreading from her chin. The tears were going to come anyway. "Because it's my fault. They're dead because of who I am, decisions that I made—"

"No. They died because of the Council, for decisions that Three, and Lucas, and whoever else they're in bed with made. They died because they loved you, and they wanted you to live. You looked away at the end. You looked away. But I didn't. Your mother never faltered. She didn't falter, and she didn't let go of you. She didn't give you up, not even at the end. Do you think the woman who valued you more than life would say you don't deserve it?"

He kept talking, but she couldn't hear any of it. The tears had come, too loud and ugly for her to be aware of much more than being pulled close to his chest and the rumble of words inside of it. Finally, the rumble stopped, and he just held her.

A little while later, the tears stopped coming, too.

She stood still, even after the hiccuping breaths had eased, allowing herself to be held. It felt good. Not surprising. Under the scowls and barked orders, Reyes was a beautiful man. He was also solid and warm. She sniffled and rubbed her cheek against his chest, moving closer and sliding her arms around his waist. She drew in a deep, relaxing breath and enjoyed the familiar almost-tickle of the Dust moving within her. It pooled in her chest and belly, and all along her inner arms, as if drawn into the embrace as well. It swirled lower, too....

Under her ear, his heart skipped. So did the sound of his breathing.

Her eyes flew open. What was she doing?

Lena yanked her arms from Reyes and stepped away. She crossed her arms, and her mouth worked for a moment. "I—I'm sorry. I mean, thank you. I'm good now. So thank you." She didn't want to look up from the spot on his chest that was damp from her tears. She had to.

His lips twitched, but his eyes were still grave and concerned. "You sure?"

"Yep. All better."

"Lena—"

"Thank you, Reyes. Really, I'm good. Thank you. You went above and beyond. Thanks."

You can stop thanking him now. It was just a damn hug. It was. Why was her heart racing?

Reyes searched her face, as if looking for something. Whatever conclusion he reached, he nodded and crossed to the little table.

She moved in the opposite direction to perch on the edge of the cot.

Wincing and favoring his left side, Reyes pulled the straps of a bag he'd been wearing slung across his back over his head.

"Oh, yeah," she mumbled, mostly to herself. "Broken ribs."

He glanced over, shrugging his right shoulder in acknowledgment of his injury.

She'd forgotten to offer to help him back at Ace's. She hadn't offered when he got here, either. He had broken ribs because of her. He'd spent the last day and night in serious pain. And he was the one comforting her.

"Come here," she said hoarsely, beckoning him over.

Reyes made one startled sweep of her and the cot. His brows rose. "Enticing as you are, Lena," he drawled, "That's really not what you need right now. I'm going to have to pass."

Her mouth fell open. She snapped it shut. The heat of a redhead's flush flooded up her skin, from chest to face. "I'm not offering to screw you, Reyes. I'm going to fix your ribs. Or do you like being in pain and short of breath?"

"Fix my ribs?" He stopped working at the knot securing a rectangular flap over the bag's opening. She had his full attention now. "You can do that?"

She shrugged. Then, unable to help it, she smirked. "I'm multi-talented. I can smash a room over you and break your ribs. And then I can fix them."

His guffaw almost sounded like a cough of pain. He settled

the bag and crossed to her.

Lena gestured. "Take off your shirt."

He hissed out a breath as he pulled it over his head.

Her gaze rose with it, flowing over the skin revealed by the rising shirt, then made a slower return trip back down over his chest and abdomen. Yes, he was a finely built man. She couldn't resist needling him a little to remind him of how he'd come into her life and turned it upside down.

"I don't blame you for thinking I was propositioning you, considering you've talked to my sister. I know what she thinks of me. I am a little surprised you turned me down so fast." She tilted her head back so she could look him in the face as he pulled the shirt away. She cocked a brow, making her voice a pointed purr. "Especially since you did promise to be good to me when we met. Remember?"

Reyes rolled his eyes.

Lena laughed. Still chuckling, she inspected the offending ribs. Livid bruises spread across his side and curved around to his back. She made a spinning motion with her fingers.

He dutifully turned. "This isn't going to hurt, is it?"

She met his suspicious gaze, struggling to hold back another laugh. "No, Reyes. It isn't going to hurt."

"I'm fine with pain," he growled, "I just like a little warning."

She lifted her hands and placed them on his warm skin. She didn't have to be in physical contact in order to make the Dust heal another. It was all mental. But the contact made her feel more connected.

She traced the contours of his ribs around her hands. Where his skin curved over the muscle and bones of his chest and abdomen, his olive tone paled. She focused in, past his skin, her vision blurring as she called to the Dust living within him. They woke and swarmed to the site of Reyes's injured ribs. She told them how to pulse, and they sent currents of energy into his bones and the bruised flesh surrounding them to stimulate his cells. She could feel his skin warm under her hands and instructed a slight adjustment. She wasn't sure if it the warmth or the contact or maybe even the connection of moments ago spurred her, but the urge to turn the touch into a caress nearly overwhelmed her. Just a little more and then—

"Stop." Reyes's voice, tinged with alarm, intruded on her thoughts. "Lena! Stop!"

His rough hands pulled her own away from his skin. He held her arms between them and gave them a small shake to get her attention. His eyes were wide and alarmed. He searched her face.

She blinked. She gave a final instruction and sighed, pulling away from the Dust. "What?"

"You're glowing." He swallowed. He didn't release her arms, as if he thought he might have to hold her up.

"Yeah? Sparks do that. I'm overdue for grounding because of...because of what happened."

"No. Lena. You're...." His words trailed off. He shook his head. "It's not the Spark latent bloom. Only we can see that. This is different. You're actually...." He shook his head and released her to hold one hand up between them and the wall. The stark dark outline of his hand appeared on it, a shadow cast by her. "You're actually lighting the room. I've never seen anything like this. Are you okay?"

"I'm fine." Except she couldn't look away from the shadows she cast on the wall.

He dropped his arm to get her attention. "How's your head?"

From the way he looked at her, he clearly expected her to fall to the ground writhing in pain at any moment. She should be on the floor, incapacitated by pain and the need to ground, but she wasn't.

Instead of answering, she lifted her hand. She was glowing, the Dust beneath her skin incandescent. It wasn't subtle, either.

"My head is fine." There wasn't even a twinge of over-stimulation migraine. Nothing. She looked from her arm to his face.

Reyes stared at her, fascination and a kind of fear at war in him.

"What about you?" she asked him.

He frowned. "Me?"

"How are your ribs?"

"Oh!" He moved gingerly, then a little more vigorously. He raised his brows and tried an experimental twist to the side. He seemed to have close to full range of motion. "It's really good. So, you know, when you're giving lessons, that'll be a good one to know." He nodded before he added blandly, "Unless I'll start glowing."

She rolled her eyes and turned away from him, still admiring the light cast from her arm as she made her way back to the little table. She hooked a stool with her toes and dropped down. "Hmmm." She held her hand up again. "I guess this could make my escape a little difficult?"

Reyes pulled his shirt back on and walked over to join her, his movements smooth and cat-like again. "Nope. I've got you covered. Unless you're planning on escaping me?"

Lena raised her brows. "Do I need to?"

He laughed and started working the knot on the bag again as he shook his head. He didn't actually answer her, though, which made her nervous. The non-answer that was an answer, perhaps? What had the poem said? *"A Truth that's told with bad intent/Beats all the Lies you can invent"*? Her alarm grew into anxiety. She decided to push the issue.

"Reyes, do I need to?"

He looked up. The knot parted. He spread the cord apart without looking down. "No. You do not need to escape me. You don't need to fear me. And you don't need to be afraid of the people I represent, either. I am here to serve and protect," he smiled as the old words rolled off his tongue. The smile dropped, and he pointed to her with both index fingers. "You. Part of my job has always been to search for you."

"Search for me?" Her voice was sharp. "But Dad worked so hard to keep me hidden!" Her eyes narrowed. "Wait a minute. If you knew about me—"

"No, no, no. Nothing concrete." He shrugged and raised one hand to make a back and forth motion. "We knew about the possibility of you. Or we believed it, you could say. We actually expected you to be a child. That's what we expected to find. And if you happened, when you happened, we'd need to be ready to bring you in. Not to imprison you or use you or kill you, but to protect you from those who would do all of those things."

She digested that in silence.

He reached into the bag and pulled out flatbread, a small, paper-wrapped package of crumbly white cheese, several apples, and a skin of water. He pushed it all to the center of the table and indicated she should help herself.

She reached out hungrily, broke off a piece of the cheese, and dropped the crumbles into a torn piece of flatbread. She'd eaten the last of the food she'd brought early that morning.

"Protect me, huh?" she said after she'd swallowed her first two bites. "What if I don't want your protection?"

"Doesn't matter." Reyes produced a small folding knife and sliced an apple. He layered the thin wedges on the flatbread and then added cheese. "You need it."

She stared at the sandwich, mouth watering, even after he caught her. He grinned and offered it to her. When she unabashedly took it, he made another.

"I need it? Reyes, I don't need protection. All I need is for you to get me to the right place at the right time. Or have you forgotten that I pulled a building down on top of you?" The apple and cheese together was tangy, crunchy heaven.

"Yeah? Could you do it again if you needed to? On demand?"

She said nothing. She didn't have to. They both knew the first time had been a stress response of some kind. And the second had been a Reyes response. But he'd moved on to his next point anyway.

"And have you forgotten that I got the drop on you? If I can, so can they." He took a bite. "Might take a little longer..." He grimaced, perhaps at their chances, and chewed. "But they could. You're not omnipotent." He snorted. "Not yet."

She stopped chewing. An image flashed into her mind. A smell came with the memory. Perfume. Dust. *The dress*. She swallowed the dry wad of food in her mouth. "I know I'm not omnipotent. Believe me, I know. I never have been. If I was—" Grief closed her throat, and she choked on her words.

Reyes shook his head. When he spoke, his face and his voice were heavy with regret. "No, that was on us." He stopped for a moment, staring off as he gathered his thoughts. "She was sick. It was an accident. Not even Lucas, bastard that he is, intended to kill her. I promise. *I promise.* And I *never* would have stood back and watched if I had known she was that weak."

Tears gathered in Lena's eyes, but only for a moment. She drew in a shaky breath and straightened her spine. "I understand. I do. And I understand why you did what you did. Just—" She looked down at the floor. When she raised her face again, she could feel it was hot and flushed with hatred. "I'm going to make Lucas pay first."

Something flickered in his eyes. Regret? Maybe disgust, but not directed at her.

"I am coming back for him," she whispered.

Reyes shook his own head. "No coming back for Lucas." He took the fantasy away gently. "He won't be here. He's being shipped home to his grandfather."

She frowned and shook her head.

"When I left you at Ace's, one of the loose ends I wanted to tie up was Lucas. I went to check his condition—his head injury wasn't nearly as severe as they said. I'd decided, *again*, to kill him if the opportunity presented itself. But it didn't. He wasn't alone. Three was with him." Reyes used the familiar term for the Councilor. "Lucas was conscious, and they were talking." His eyes became hooded. He wasn't telling her something. He shook his head and gave a small shrug. "The reason Lucas got away with so much for so long is that his grandfather is Councilor Four. His forged identity papers showing he was born and raised in Zone Three were so damn good they didn't even change his surname. *Brayer.* Strings have been pulled from above."

"Is that the only reason?" She pushed for the something he wasn't telling her.

"You think there should be another?"

Another non-answer for an answer. She didn't push this time. She'd find out somehow. She'd use the answer to get to Lucas, and then she'd take care of him herself.

He must have seen something of what she planned on her face because his voice turned soft and persuasive. "C'mon, Lena. Don't pull away now. Let us help you."

"I don't want anyone's help. I never have. I don't need you." She glanced around the tiny safe house and grimaced. "Okay, so I need you to help me get out of the city."

He grinned knowingly.

She pushed on. "But afterward, all I want is an opportunity to be in a room with the people responsible for my parents. I can finish this. And then I'm disappearing again."

"Okay," Reyes conceded. "You can. But you're one person. Why not use what we have to offer? Education. Training. Resources. We're Sparks. All of us. We're like you, and we can help you. We can give you all of the knowledge you missed while you were hiding. You can be a part of us, an important part of us, long term."

"Uh-huh. And you'd do all of that out of the goodness of your little Spark hearts?" Her pointed question hung between them.

He seemed to be enjoying the beat of silence. His lips turned up in a slow, devastating smile. "If you decided to show your appreciation by helping us, we wouldn't turn you down. You could offer to teach us your wonderful tricks. But we're not going to force you to do anything you don't want to." He shrugged. "Look, I'll get you out of the city. At that point, you can decide for yourself. I'd like it if you stayed with us."

"Said the spider to the fly."

Reyes cocked a brow at her. "Hardly. I'm fairly certain I'm in far more danger the more time I spend with you than the other way around."

Hmmm. Is it wrong to like the sound of that?

She leaned on the stool, stretching her spine and pushing her clasped hands far out in front of her over the table. Her back eased with the stretch. She leaned forward again and sighed. The food was gone.

Reyes gathered up the detritus and swept the crumbs into his hand. He dumped it all into the cloth bag then lifted the bag across his back. "You ready to go?"

Lena blinked. "What...now?"

His eyes crinkled. "Are you waiting for a better time? I wanted to make sure you were fed before we headed out. You're fed. Are you ready? Do you need anything else? Do you want to use the bucket?"

She glanced at the bucket and then back at him, mouth opening to answer, but he laughed at her. She closed her mouth and shrugged.

Her boots were kicked half under the cot. She sat to pull them out. As she did, she noticed a corner of the book of poetry. It must have slid out of her hand at some point in the sleepless night. She pulled it out and held it up to him. "Is this yours?"

His eyebrows rose, and his face lit in recognition. "Yes! I wondered where I'd left it." He retrieved it, flipping through the pages in delight. "No idea how it got here." He sat back on the stool, his head nodding with familiar pleasure as he skimmed one of the early poems while she tugged on her boots. She tried to guess which it was.

"I kind of thought maybe it was left here to entertain anyone who might need the room. It came in handy."

His head lifted. "Not hardly. Do you know how much this thing is worth?"

At her shrug, he laughed. "A lot."

"Well, it helped anyway. I spent a lot of time on that poem you marked."

"The poem I—" Alex's brows dipped in puzzlement as he flipped it open to the page marked by the slip of paper.

His eyes moved as he skimmed it and noted the underlined lines. The lines hadn't been by his hand, then. He closed the book.

"Never mind. I know exactly how it got in here," he murmured to himself. "Would've been the last time I came through here. Can't believe I didn't notice, even if I was distracted." His face clouded over at some memory. Reyes shook his head, physically shaking it away.

He looked at her again. "Are you not a poetry fan, then?"

"No, I like poetry. Are you kidding? I was the weird, hidden child, remember? I read a lot. A lot." She nodded toward the book in his hands. "But I'd never heard of him. William Blake. His stuff was hard at first, but he's good." She'd keep the details of her snarky internal debate with Alex's margin notes to herself. "Is he your favorite?"

"He is good. But no, Stephen Crane is my favorite." A ghost of a smile came and went. "My father put a book of Crane's poems into my bag when I was sent to school. It had an inscription from his father to him. Then he'd inscribed it for me."

Lena shivered. He so casually referred to being shipped to the Ward School, the school for strongly gifted children. They were sent there to be trained and never returned home. Once they reached the age of majority, they were given an assignment in another zone, and that was that. Taken from home at five, they would never see their families again. After what he'd told her earlier, he clearly had lingering pain from the separation. How hard would it have been, if instead of hiding her, her parents had given her to the Council?

Reyes's eyes were distant. He came back to himself with a self-conscious grimace. "It took me a while to appreciate the book, of course. I was a pretty damn precocious child, but I wasn't reading Crane at five. Don't think I did more than read the inscription before I turned fifteen."

She nodded. "But I bet you had the inscription memorized by then."

His flicked a look at her then glanced away. He made a little shrugging, nodding motion, acknowledging the truth of her words but discounting their importance.

"Have you ever asked yourself why he wanted you to have the book? Other than, you know, his father had given it to him?"

Reyes barked a laugh. He pulled the bag back around and shook crumbs out of the bag and onto the table before stowing the Blake book inside. "I know exactly why he wanted me to have it. He'd marked certain poems, underlined passages, made notes to me, or maybe himself. It was all there, as if he were with me. The things he thought were important to know or to think about." He pushed the bag back around to his back and looked down at his hands. When he looked up again, he quietly recited a verse:

"In the desert
I saw a creature, naked, bestial,
Who, squatting upon the ground,
Held his heart in his hands,
And ate of it.

I said, "Is it good, friend?"
"It is bitter – bitter," he answered;
"But I like it
Because it is bitter,
And because it is my heart."

Lena sat, wordless, for a long moment after he'd fallen silent. Finally she ventured, "So, presumably he...*explained*...that grotesque poem to you in a helpful note?"

Reyes laughed, a burst of sound after the quiet of his voice reciting words written hundreds of years before. "Not that one," he told her with a grin. "But he did put a star next to it so I'd know to read it with extra attention. It was a very helpful star." He laughed again and then stood, telling her to rise with a cock of his head. "C'mon. Let's go."

She stood and turned to the door. Reyes went instead to the corner. He knelt in front of the bucket. *Was he...?* She averted her eyes.

His soft chuckle had her turning back again. "I'm not using it. I'm moving it. The passage to the store is through the basement, and it's under the bucket."

She tilted her head to look past his shoulder. Sure enough, he had popped a section of the floor up and slid it to the side.

"Well, I'll be damned," Lena murmured. "A bolt hole."

Reyes propped his wrists on his knees. His brows knit. She wasn't sure if his scorn was playful or real.

"Did you think there wasn't one?"

"Well, I didn't think to look under the piss bucket."

"Isn't that the idea?" His voice was droll. He gestured

gallantly. "After you."

She wiped damp hands down the sides of her skirt. Was she really going to do this? Blindly follow Reyes and hope he led her where she wanted to go?

She stepped around him to tread down the narrow stairs winding down into darkness.

Yes. She really was.

ELEVEN

Reyes disappeared over the lip of the surface above her as Lena climbed the rusty, pitted rungs of a ladder up the inside of a very old sewer access point. He'd already told her the tunnels from the safe house were the longest they had. Instead of having to make their way through the arroyos and canyons surrounding Relo-Azcon to their departure point, the tunnels would deposit them near their destination. It was still risky to be making the trip during the day, but according to Reyes, it was infrequently patrolled. Old Town had long been stripped of anything valuable and was not of interest to scavengers or the Council.

She tilted her head back, looking to see how much further just as he leaned over to offer her his arm. He hauled her up the last three rungs, her feet dangling in the air for a moment, before depositing her on the ground beside himself.

He had one finger pressed to his lips for quiet. He gestured with his head down the street and then held up two fingers. He pointed to a nearby opening. The doorframe had been pulled free and leaned down, almost touching a pile of broken cinder blocks piled haphazardly at the entrance. Desert sand had blown in to form a long, sloped drift on the far side. She quickly darted over and took a knee, leaning down behind the drift.

Reyes moved the sewer grate back into place. He joined her, glancing over his shoulder in the direction he had cautioned her about before tugging her sleeve and leading her the opposite way. He followed the contours of the buildings, hugging the walls when practical then darting out to move around the debris-based sand dunes when necessary.

He didn't take her far. Only four smallish buildings away, they crossed a wide open area of broken cement. They dodged inside the building, Reyes leading the way toward his goal. He dropped down into a drainage grate at the back of a long, narrow room. She joined him.

He led her through the dark sub-levels until they reached a large metal door. He popped open a security box, leaned in, and placed his eye on a small tube that extended from the wall. Reyes straightened after a pulse of green light, already palming the security box to reseal the little tube. She leaned in closer as the tube withdrew, trying to get a better view of the lock keyed to his eye.

Before the tube had even tucked back into its hidden hole, locks from within the metal door clicked and ground. It hissed and slid out from the wall. Reyes reached for it with a grin and hauled on the handle in front of her, completing the door's movement away from the opening. Her eyes widened. It was almost as wide as she was tall.

Where were they going?

Reyes entered through the wide opening, and she followed. Lights began to click on in the cavernous space. She continued across to the metal railing of the entry platform. She was dimly aware of Reyes closing them in and the sound of hissing air and cycling locks.

They were three levels up from the floor. Below, a train rested upon a track. She'd only seen trains from a distance, and they were the bulky steam engines the Council ran from zone to zone. They were nothing like this sleek machine. Its track headed into a darkened tunnel.

She turned to Reyes, eyes wide in spite of herself. He grinned like a little boy.

"Surprise." He tugged on her hand, pulling her toward the stairs. "C'mon. Let's get outta here." He trotted down the stairs.

Lena followed, her mouth agape. The implication of power and resources boggled her mind. Who were these people Reyes worked for? She didn't know what they wanted from her, but they had the resources to give her what she wanted.

She stopped in the entry to the train. Reyes crossed to the controls and powered it up. Her mind flashed to the scene in the Council room, when he had hidden out of sight in the corner. Even though she understood why he'd waited, and she knew that he'd worked hard to get her out since then, the memory was enough to leave her hovering outside.

Reyes glanced back over his shoulder. "C'mon." He jerked his head to urge her to step in. His smile froze when he saw her expression, though, and he turned to face her. "You know, we will protect you. I promise."

"You've made a lot of promises. You're asking for a lot of faith." She swallowed, but she stepped through. She didn't know who his people were, but if they could give her what she needed, then she was committed.

Reyes touched a button. The door hissed shut behind her as the train lifted. He turned back to the controls. They pulled away from the station, entering the dark tunnel. Regularly placed, long lights glowed high up in the tunnels. As they gained speed, the lights seemed to melt into each other until they were one long, continuous glow.

"How fast are we going?" Lena asked.

He grinned. "Fast."

She nodded. "Where are we going? Am I allowed to know now that we're on the way?"

He glanced at her sideways. "It was never a secret. Not really." At her snort, he protested, "It wasn't!" He shrugged. "We're going to a place we call Fort Nevada."

"Fort Nevada? I've never heard of it." She chewed her lower lip then asked the obvious question. "It's in old Nevada?"

At his nod of confirmation, she shook her head. "That's weeks away."

"About thirty minutes, actually."

She looked around the little train in appreciation.

Reyes chuckled. "Don't get any ideas. This train will only respond to those who have been keyed to it."

She raised a brow. "So I can't leave when I want?"

He kept his focus on the blackness of the tunnel before them. "You can leave. Once you're safe. I told you that."

She fell silent. Misgivings rose. Had she made the wrong choice? Trusted the wrong side? Reyes had saved her. He had helped her, all along the way. Was it all a sham? Maybe she'd been alone so long she didn't know how to read people anymore. Or was he really that good?

He glanced at her sideways, his eyes crinkled. "You still don't trust me?"

"I don't know you."

He barked a short laugh. "There are only two others alive who know the real me better than you, Lena. I'm not sure what more I can do to reassure you." A frown dipped his brows low and then disappeared.

What, because he'd told her about his childhood? And shared some poetry? What kind of life did he lead if that meant she knew him?

And who are you to question his life choices, Miss Desert Hermit?

She mulled it over, chewing her lip, fingers moving restlessly over the edge of the control panel in front of her. Reyes left her alone, immersed in his own thoughts. All too soon, the train slowed. The blur of lights began to thin and separate. A light grew ahead of them.

The tunnel opened into a huge space much like the one they had left behind. Multiple levels of metal-grated floors were connected by stairs. This area, however, was not empty. People moved around with purpose. Lena took them all in. Reyes had an army.

The train eased to a stop. Reyes's fingers tapped on the panel, and it powered down. The train sank beneath them, and a humming eased and then stopped. The door on the side of the cabin opened.

"You ready?" He waited for her, hip propped on the panel, the picture of relaxed ease though barely tamped energy rolled off of him.

She took a deep breath. She'd made this decision. She'd roll with whatever came of it, as she always did, and she'd take what she needed to make it all right. She shrugged one shoulder.

"Ready." Her answer earned her a smile.

He turned and gestured her out. She walked alongside him as he talked.

"It doesn't look like much down here. But I promise there's more to us than sewer tunnels and a gutted building." He waved at a young man who rose from a desk at the end of the platform. The young man nodded and saluted.

Saluted? *Military.*

Reyes responded and then placed his hand on the small of her back, guiding her down a short flight of stairs toward a set of double metal doors along the back wall. He went to the wall, palmed a small box with a button atop another. When he took his hand away, the top button had lit.

"Are you hungry?" he asked her. "Do you need a bathroom?"

"Yes, and *yes*," she answered.

The doors in front of them slid open to reveal a small room. He walked in. She hovered, hanging back as she looked for the exit.

He had turned and smiled, but his face showed the edge of nerves. "It's an elevator. It's like stairs. It's going to take us up." He pointed up.

"Oh." Lena walked inside the box. The doors closed behind her.

Reyes leaned around her and pushed a numbered button. Eighteen. He took a long, slow breath as the box shimmied slightly.

Her stomach dropped. Her hand flashed out to the wall.

He spoke, his words a little quick. "I hate the damn things, but it's perfectly safe." He nodded to reassure her, then continued, his voice distracting her from the strange sensation. "I'm going to take you to the dining hall. You can use the restroom, and we'll get you something more substantial to eat. Then I'll take you to your quarters, and we'll figure out—"

"My quarters? I have a room? Already?"

Reyes nodded. "It won't be much. After all, Fort Nevada is just a school."

"A school?" Her brows knit together. Her stomach lurched, and it wasn't because the elevator had stopped moving. "I thought this was like a military fort or something? That you were an army planning to take on the Council of Nine?"

The doors slid open, and he stepped out, his breath coming out in an audible sigh of relief. He turned back to her. "Well, yeah," he said, "that's the idea. But we're also the school."

The words barely penetrated. Behind him, painted on the wall, an eagle soared over words in some long-irrelevant language on a scrolled banner. Above the bird, large, black-framed lettering proclaimed, "The Ward School." At the bottom, below the scroll, the curving words, "Out of Darkness, Light" closed the crest.

The elevator tried to close, and Reyes's arm shot out to hold it back. "Lena?" He reached out to pull her toward him.

She shook him off. "The Ward School? You brought me to the Ward School?" Her voice was shrill in her ears. Her father had warned her about the Ward School. He had told her over and over that it was dangerous.

Reyes gave her a puzzled look. "Yes. I thought you understood. I told you we'd teach you the things you missed out on. Where else would I take you to learn?"

"Get me out of here." She couldn't catch her breath, even though her lungs rapidly pumped air in and out of her chest.

"What? Lena, what?" He stared at her. "What's the problem? If you're worried about safety, this is the one place you'll be safest, and I—"

"No! This is the one place, the single, solitary place my father told me I should never go. This is the place he hid me from."

A trio of young boys walked through the arch before them, arms laden with trays of sandwiches. The boys looked over at Reyes and Lena with interest, clearly wondering what her outburst had been about. He turned his head and gave them a blistering look. They picked up their pace and hurried down the hallway and around the corner.

Reyes turned back to her. He leaned in and lowered his voice to a persuasive murmur, lifting his hands to cup her shoulders as he had back in the safe house. "I don't know what that's about. I have no idea what your father thought he knew. But I can tell you that we will not harm you. It just won't happen."

"Then get me out of here. Now." She turned and waved her hand over the buttons on the wall. Nothing happened.

Reyes reached out and caught her hand. He turned her around. "I can't do that." From the tone of his voice, the slow, heavy regret already tingeing his words, this conversation wasn't going to end well.

"You won't."

"No. I won't. I can't and I won't. Not until you have all the information you need to make a rational decision." A muscle pulsed at the upper end of his jaw, just below his temple. "Tell me why you want to leave. Something besides, 'Daddy sacrificed my childhood for reasons he didn't share with me.' Something that makes sense."

"I don't know his reasons. He didn't share them with me. I was a child."

"That's right. You were a gifted child, and you belonged here." He was losing his temper.

"Well, my father thought otherwise strongly enough that he made sure I didn't come here."

"He did. But you're here now, and here is where you'll stay."

And there it was. She drew in a long breath. From his face, it was clear he hadn't wanted to deal with this. Not yet. The memory of his excited grin from the train was almost enough to quell her, almost enough to make her want to believe what he'd said about safety and belonging.

"So I'm a prisoner?"

Reyes closed his eyes, but not before an answering hard anger bloomed in them. When he opened them, it was gone, replaced by a formal neutrality. He'd slipped back into the mask. He dropped her hand, and his cool, clipped voice was all agent. "Not a prisoner, no. You are an indefinite guest."

He turned away and walked to the arched opening. "And as a guest, you should eat, make yourself comfortable, and then I'll show you to your quarters. We have a surprise for you. One I hope you'll appreciate for the effort it took to make happen." He raised his arm and gestured into the dining hall.

She stood for a moment. What could she do? Scream? Shout? Sit down and refuse to move? Knock them all out—the entire building—and race around trying to figure out how to get back? She couldn't even figure out how to make the elevator work, never mind that using that much Spark would kill her. She hadn't had a chance to ground since she'd brought down the side of the Council building. And get back? To Azcon, where they were hunting her? To the middle of nowhere, to hide again? What then?

No. She needed this. She needed their resources to get access to the Council. She'd gather her thoughts. Cooperate. And figure out what needed to happen to use them and then lose them. But she wouldn't pretend she wasn't furious at the deception. They'd know anyhow. She wasn't Reyes.

She did as he instructed. Used the institutional restroom he indicated then moved through the cafeteria line behind him, accepting the food he put before her. She kept her head down and refused to make eye contact with anyone, although she could hear the whispers and feel stares following her. The male energy, heavy and curious, pushed at her from every direction.

Lena followed him to a table on the far side of the cafeteria. She sat where he indicated and began eating. She tasted nothing except the bread. She savored every chewy, yeasty bite of the bread.

When she finished, she glanced up and wasn't surprised to see that Reyes had already finished and leaned back in his chair to watch her. Beneath the mask of calm, his glare roved over her face. She caught the stare with her own and held it defiantly.

His lips thinned, and he nodded, a curt movement indicating his impatience.

He stood, gathered their trays, and walked away. He set everything on an open ledge in the wall and walked to the archway to wait for her to join him. Then he moved off again.

She followed, glowering at the back of his head as they continued down the halls, sometimes skirting groups of boys. The boys always stared. She stared back, her animosity growing. They made several turns and wound their way deeper into the school.

He acted like this was all her fault. Had she asked them to come to her home and force her away? Had she asked to be lied to, tricked into going into the city? Had she asked to be tortured? Made to watch her mother be killed in front of her? A dry sob of rage and grief hiccupped in her throat before she forced it back down.

Reyes's head moved at the sound, almost a concerned response. He stopped before a door to palm the security box. He turned the handle and moved inside slightly, stepping to the side for her.

Reyes tilted his head, trying to catch her eye.

She entered, brushing past him to stand in the middle of the room, trying to pretend he wasn't behind her. She didn't see the spare furniture in the front, the table, pair of chairs, book shelves. She hugged herself. Items spread symmetrically on a low table near the bed tucked at the rear caught her attention. Small earthenware pots had been placed carefully in a line with tiny twig brushes fanned out before them. She stalked over. They were *her* earthenware pots, her powders and dyes. She turned to step up on the bed and walk over it to a low wooden chest on the other side. She flipped back the top. Her clothes. Her hand-knit curtains. She drew in a deep breath. *This* was his surprise?

Clearly it was meant to make her happy. Slip back in, beneath the watch of other Council agents, no doubt, and bring her some of the bits and pieces that made up her home. It was a sudden, glaring reminder of all she had lost—no, of all they had taken from her. What they had done, what *he* had done, was no less than tear her away from the life she had built for herself, and because of it, she'd lost more than just things. She'd lost her mother.

She turned toward him, head down, gaze lowered. She spoke, voice low and tight. "Is this supposed to appease me?"

He pushed away from the door and moved to the middle of the room. "Please you? Yeah, I guess. I wasn't really—"

"No! Not please me!" Her voice snapped out across at him like a whip. "Appease me. Is this supposed to *appease me?*"

Wisely, he chose not to answer this time.

"You brought my *stuff*. Great. Awesome. Thank you. Thank you so much for stealing back all this stuff. Never mind that I can never go back. Never mind the fact that you destroyed *my life*!"

"I destroyed your life? Because you lost access to a building?" A bare second later, he must have remembered she had lost much more. His mouth snapped shut.

"It wasn't a building! It was my home! She was my mother!" She stared at him.

He honestly believed he'd done a good thing for her. He expected her to be grateful. Happy, even. Her home was gone. She couldn't go back. Her mother was dead. This man had no capacity to understand either loss. How could he when he'd been made a Ward at five?

Just like that, her rage snuffed out. She deflated.

"Of course you don't understand what I've lost," she told him quietly, "because you've never had a home or a family. You've never built anything good. You've only been used to destroy. You're not a person. You're a tool."

And haven't you come here to be made into the same thing?

In spite of the mask, she could see the pain that flared in his eyes, quicksilver and then gone. *Good. I hope it hurts.*

Reyes opened his mouth to respond, but Lena held up her hand.

"Don't. Just leave me alone." She shook her head. "There's nothing you can do or say to please me or appease me. So, please…go."

He went.

A long time after he left, closing the door behind himself with quiet control, she sat on the edge of the bed and stared at nothing. She clasped her shaking hands together. When that didn't stop the violent trembling, she tucked them between her knees. She wished she could cry. But she had nothing left, not even tears.

TWELVE

A lex didn't wait for Thom's assistant to announce him.
"Is he alone?" He bit the words out as he strode through the outer area. At the startled assent, he snapped a nod back, and went in, closing out the office behind himself. He leaned his head against the door for a millisecond and then stalked over to stand in front of the desk, hands fisted in his pockets.

"That is not a happy face." Thomas's voice was guarded. He wouldn't want to be disappointed. Not about this. He tossed the thin sheet he'd been reading back down onto the surface of his desk. "What's happened?"

"Nothing." Alex answered. "She's here, safe, and installed in her quarters."

"Then why are you so pissed?"

His brows dipped into a brief frown. "I'm not."

Sure you're not.

Thomas made a small, doubting noise and cocked his head to the side as he waited.

Alex grimaced. "She can be difficult. You'll see." He let the promise hang between them. Her last salvo had been right on target, using what he'd shared with her. *So, you're the damn fool who let her get under your skin.*

"Soon, I hope. When do you think she'll be ready to be interviewed?"

He shook his head. "I wouldn't try interrogating her yet, Thom. She's not happy."

"I don't plan to *interrogate* her, Alex." Irritation tinged his voice.

"I know you don't. But that's not how she's going to see it right now." Alex ran his hands through his hair and turned to yank a chair forward. He sat back. "We knew she spent her childhood locked up because her father wanted to hide her from the bad people. We just didn't know it was us."

Thomas frowned at him. "Us? What did we ever do to the man?"

Alex nodded. "Good question. The answer? Nothing. Yet, we got here, and she saw the Ward School crest and froze. Demanded to leave. And when it didn't happen, she decided I am now her despised jailer." It bothered him a lot. It bothered him more than he'd ever admit to Thomas.

He'd gotten rid of the last woman who'd become this distracting. She'd been an agent. Only rarely did a mid-range manage to work their way out of mere Zone Security and into the Council Defense Agency and go toe-to-toe with the best of the Ward School. It was rarer still for a woman to do it. She had been exceptional. Alex had vetted and recruited her to join their movement himself. And as soon as he'd realized that she'd become more than a partner with benefits, he'd staged a crisis and had her reassigned to another zone. Erika had been the one who'd left that book of poetry in the safe house, the lines she'd underlined in the poem her way of telling him she wasn't fooled. Lena was very like Erika, but more. More strength. More independence. More power.

More trouble.

The sound of Thomas's fingers drumming a staccato beat on the surface of his desk brought Alex out of his head. After several long moments, Alex added, "This on top of the trauma of the last forty-eight hours does not bode well for her wanting to cooperate with me ever again."

Thomas's blue eyes sharpened. "Trauma?"

"Yeah. I was getting there." He sighed so deep his shoulders lifted. He spent the next twenty minutes outlining everything— Lucas's interference, Alex's own role in bringing Lena down in an attempt to control the situation, and how her inquisition had resulted in the death of her mother and the subsequent destruction of the side of the Council building in Azcon.

Thomas leaned forward and cupped his chin with the palms of both hands. "She did what?"

"She brought it down. Sent out some kind of energy shockwave that mangled the room and fried the circuits in the entire building, locks, lights, the works. Did it again a few minutes later after I woke up and got her pointed at the wall. I had her take out the wall to escape. Three's security director was killed in the collapse."

The other man grimaced, the expression pinching his already narrow face. "Good riddance."

Alex nodded his agreement. "I chased her down. We met up at her friend Ace's place. I sent her to a safe house to cool while I put out fires." He took a breath and pursed his lips, swerving his mind away from the safe house and the memory of how she'd moved the Dust within him when she touched him. Both times. *Focus.* "A few of those fires will require more long-term attention. Lucas is Four's grandson."

Thomas clearly hadn't known. He wasn't happy. "That explains a lot."

"It does," he agreed. "But it begs the question, why didn't we know about it already? We should have known. He came in as my partner. Was it deliberate or an unhappy coincidence? Who in Dust do we have up in Zone Four anyway?"

"No one, anymore," Thomas said. "There have been several incidents with the younger agents we've sent. Four is a cagey bastard, and he's always been paranoid with that damned Reintegration Program for Spark agents, but this is new. There's something else going on up there now."

"Damn straight there is. While they were interrogating her, Lucas let something slip about some 'they' who always got what they need out of people like Lena to test the limits of their abilities, and it was his turn."

"He could've been talking about accelerating the experiments on the prisoners up there." Thomas referred to the secret Council prison in Zone Four operating on the border of Council territory and the LDS Zone. They sent the strongest criminal Sparks there instead of to Madisonville. As far as the public knew, these most dangerous men were put to death. Thomas, as Councilor Five, received occasional briefs on the activities there that told him otherwise. The public didn't want men running around who could start fires and blackout fragile relo-city power systems, but the Council wasn't willing to give up the opportunity to figure out how and why Sparks worked.

"That's what I thought. The thing is…." Alex paused. "I had the feeling all of the advances they were talking about, all of the interrogations Lucas referenced that I wasn't supposed to hear about, they weren't on prisoners we know about. Thom, I think they've got the girls they've been taking up there."

They both had long since learned to pay attention to Alex's feelings on investigations.

Thomas's blue eyes narrowed now as he focused. "What gave you that impression?"

Alex cocked his head, thinking back. "Nothing concrete. Nothing overtly said."

"When you look at it sideways and take into account our lost agents up in Zone Four, it adds up," Thomas said. "Four is up to something."

"In response to us?"

"I wouldn't think so." His friend growled in frustration. "Our support shipments are still coming in, testing safe. And Four sent his Wards last summer, same as every year."

Alex could see Thomas's frustration at not having the answers. He felt the same. They had too much coming together now for it all to fall apart.

"I'll make certain we know more shortly. I've been considering sending an agent I think could slip under their radar. It's time to move on it." Thomas shook it off, shifting his shoulders. "We'll return to that later. Finish with the girl—"

"Lena."

"Yes, Lena. Anything else?"

Alex fell quiet. "There is, in fact." His hand reached across his chest to rub at his ribs where her small hands had spread warmth easing out through his body, healing. And doing other things. "My ribs were broken in the collapse. She fixed them. And—"

"She healed you?" Thomas tried hard not to sound incredulous. At Alex's slow nod, he said, "And there's an 'and'?"

He frowned, remembering, and continued the slow nod as Thomas's expression urged him to answer. "And it did something to her. She started...glowing."

"We all glow."

"No, Thom." Alex shook his head. "She was *glowing*. Casting shadows in the room because her skin or the Dust in her skin was a shining beacon of light, *glowing*." He swallowed and finished quietly. "It was the damnedest thing I've ever seen. She said it had never happened before. She didn't know what caused it." He shrugged. "It didn't hurt her that we know of, and it faded over the next two hours, while we were in the tunnels under the city. We got out. Came here. And now she's pissed. Welcome to Fort Nevada."

Thomas digested the information in silence, as he usually did. It unnerved most of the people who had occasion to report directly to Councilor Five. But Alex had gotten used to it long ago. He sat back and waited.

After several moments of silence, Thomas spoke, and as Alex had expected, he had moved on. "I have a plan B. I didn't know this would turn into such a production, but I figured you'd be due back in Azcon fairly quickly. So I've made other arrangements for her. Come with me." Thomas stood and came around the desk. "You can meet him."

"Him?"

Thomas nodded and strode from the room, his slight build somewhat incongruous when paired with his athletic grace. Alex followed him out of the administration wing and down two levels of stairs to the upper-level classroom wing. Thomas turned in to the Peer Assistance Center, where students who were struggling with their work could turn for help from carefully vetted Senior Wards.

The Senior Ward on duty jumped up when they entered.

Thomas pointed out a young man who looked familiar to Alex. The kid sat at a work station with his head bent down as he helped a boy of about twelve. "I require Senior Ward First Class Lee."

When Thomas said the name, Alex had it. Lee was the kid he'd talked to in the cafeteria two nights ago. He must've done well on his out routes. The kid likely didn't know yet, but Thomas would.

The Senior Ward nodded and hurried over to Lee and the boy. As soon as Lee looked up and saw them waiting, he nodded to the other Ward, rising and walking to them. Lee tugged on the bottom fold of his shirt to pull any wrinkles out. His face moved from nervous to become a study in cool indifference. The kid had potential.

"Councilor Five," Lee greeted Thomas with a salute then turned to Alex with the typical confusion from students when having to greet him, "And, uh, Sir? Reyes?" Alex had refused both a title in the Zone and a rank in the Ward School. Everyone who mattered knew his importance, both to the Zone, to Thomas, and to the overall plan to elevate the Sparks. He was perfectly content to allow anyone else to think he was a Senior Agent like any other. He had what he needed, and prestige wasn't part of it.

He chuckled. "I'm not a knight. Alex or Agent Reyes will do fine."

"Yes, sir." Lee answered gravely.

"Are you ready, Ward Lee?" Thomas was all business, his voice crisp and dry. "Your assignment has arrived. Time for you to meet her."

Lee's assignment? Alex raised his brows at Thomas. He understood now. Thom intended the kid to be a companion with hopes he could become a confidante. Alex appraised the young man. Young, good-looking as young men went, soft spoken and earnest. Perhaps Thomas even intended for more to develop. He wouldn't put it past his friend—he did consider her their "Eve," after all, and Alex could see the wide Spark aura around Lee hinting at his strength.

It'll never happen. He shook his head to himself as the three of them set off through the halls. The kid had potential and might be an excellent student and future agent, but he wasn't the same caliber as Lena. He made a mental note to talk to Thomas about the details of his Plan B. He told himself he didn't have any real opinion either way. He didn't have to have one. She would eat Lee alive.

If they wanted her, and any children she might have, to be stable, she needed a stronger and more experienced partner. It wasn't personal. It was just the smartest decision.

He took the lead as they neared her room. He keyed the lock just before he knocked, and waited several moments after it had popped open. She never called out, so he took a breath and slipped inside, waving his hand at the other two men to wait. Leaving the door ajar, he entered a few feet.

Lena sat on the edge of the bed facing him, watching warily.

Alex stopped and lifted his hands to his hips. "Any better?"

She sighed. "Not particularly, but I suppose I owe you an apology anyway."

"An apology?"

"For overreacting?"

He snorted. "That would be great. But I wasn't really expecting it from you." Alex winced internally. He'd tried for humor, and it had come out all wrong. She reacted about as expected.

He met a suddenly icy stare.

"About as much as I'd expect you to wait for me to actually let you in, I imagine." Her sarcastic voice was as hostile as her expression.

And here we go again.

"I did warn you that I was coming in. I did knock first."

"And what if I had been undressed?"

He sighed. "Then I would have seen you naked twice, I suppose."

She crossed her arms, eyes narrowed and fists clenched. "You know what? I take it back."

"You take what back?"

"My apology. I didn't overreact. You're just a jerk."

"You're taking back your theoretical apology?"

"Yes."

He nodded once. "Duly noted. But try to remember which jerk saved your life."

"After you placed it in danger in the first place." If she narrowed her eyes any more, they'd be closed. "Was there a purpose to this invasion?"

"There is, actually. I came to introduce you to my partner, and to your companion. Try to be nice to them."

Thomas pushed the door open fully and walked a foot into the room. His gaze moved back and forth between them. Two sets of eyes swiveled to him. Her anger still simmered.

"Come on in," Alex deadpanned. "The water's fine, really."

Thomas's lips twitched with amusement as he approached her and cautiously offered his hand. "Miss Gracey, I'm Thomas Washington, Councilor Five. I run the school. I've waited a long time to meet you."

As soon as the words 'Councilor Five' were out of his mouth, Lena jerked her hand back. She darted a look at Alex. "Councilor Five? But…. The Ward School is supposed to be independent of the Zones?"

She didn't like being at the Ward School. He imagined she liked it even less now that there was a Councilor involved.

Alex couldn't tell from his vantage point, but he imagined Thomas smiled at her. The look on her face was not reassurance. If anything, she'd just become even more suspicious.

"It is, yes." Thomas told her. "For the intents and purposes of the Council of Nine, the Ward School is independent of the Zones. But, as I'm sure you can guess by now, there's more going on here than just the school, and I am more than a Councilor. This is merely a convenient and temporary role used to conduct Zone Five's business while I take care of our other concerns."

Alex cleared his throat and ushered Lee in.

She inspected the young man from top to bottom. When she'd finished, she arched a brow at Alex. She was no fool.

Alex couldn't imagine Thomas would fail to notice the

pointed look Lena had given Alex. If he had, Thomas said nothing, merely urging Lee forward with a swinging hand.

"This is Senior Ward Jackson Lee, one of our top students." Thomas clapped Lee on the shoulder. "And he has volunteered to help you acquaint yourself with the facilities, get you to your appointments and lessons, and generally help us by seeing to your needs."

"My needs, huh?" She turned those blue-green eyes to Lee and swept them over him again.

He stood mute next to Thomas, overwhelmed by her energy, her bright bloom, and her attitude.

There's no way this is going to work.

She tossed her hair back, and it slipped free from her ears to fall around her freckled face again. "Hello, Ward Lee." She flashed a dazzling smile. "Or should I call you Warden Lee?"

Alex snorted softly. Yes, he could see this was going to go exactly as he expected. It was too bad his duties pulled him back to Azcon. The poor kid would need help. Ward Lee couldn't possibly be ready to handle Lena Gracey.

THIRTEEN

Lena tried hard not to like Jackson Lee. She'd made it clear in the beginning that she wouldn't be charmed by his easy company, no matter how lonely she became. Except at some point over the last month and a half, she had been charmed.

He walked back to her now from the cafeteria line, where he'd returned because she'd forgotten the maple syrup. She liked to dunk her toast, along with nearly everything else, in the sticky sweet. She'd discovered its rich taste, more complex than the honey those in Zone Three had access to, on her first breakfast at Fort Nevada. It wasn't all she'd discovered.

Jackson had a graceful lope that reminded her of Reyes's sinuous, confident movements. Unlike Reyes, he was neither jaded nor buried up to his neck in plots and counterplots. Reyes was a rugged mountain—beautiful to look at, but remote, exhausting, and dangerous. Jackson was a lush valley. His quiet offered comfort and recovery.

Then why can't you stop thinking about Reyes?

Jackson eased the little bowl of syrup onto the table as he rounded it to sit across from her, as he had every morning since Reyes had brought her to Fort Nevada. His narrow brown eyes, set high above prominent cheekbones on his long face, met hers, and he gave her a questioning smile.

"You didn't remember something else you forgot, did you?" Even his quiet, even voice spoke of his good nature. She had never liked her boys earnest before. Maybe the good food and easy days at Fort Nevada were making her soft.

"No, Jackson. Just eat your breakfast." She took a few bites of syrup-dunked toast before remembering and, exasperated with herself, mumbled around a mouthful of toast, "Thank you." A tiny piece of toast landed between them on the table. Lena's hand flashed out to swipe it away. *Ah, yes, Magdalena Gracey, such a damn lady,* she mocked herself.

As if he hadn't noticed, he raised his gaze to hers without glancing down at the telltale sticky smear. A genuine smile, broad and white with teeth, spread across his face. "You're welcome."

"What's on the agenda for today?" she asked, trying for crisp and detached to cover her mortification. Did he have to be so...gentlemanly? The word would have made her wrinkle her nose in distaste before she'd experienced Jackson Lee's daily attentiveness.

He swallowed the last bit of egg and took a moment to sip from his juice to clear his mouth. *That's what thoughtful people do, Lena,* she told herself, *so they don't spit food across the table when they talk.* He swallowed again.

"Well, you're scheduled to give me a private lesson this morning." He glanced up; her wide, wicked grin made him flush. "And, uh, afterward, um, you will go have a history lesson with Guardian Erwin. He's cleared his classes so he can clear up some of the history you're lacking."

She'd had periodic classes with the Guardians—the instructors responsible for educating the Wards—and the need for more wasn't a surprise. She had wide gaps in her knowledge. She had thought she knew the history of the Great Disaster, but recently a Guardian had referred to the Dust as "nanites," and when she'd responded with a blank stare, he'd sighed and told her she needed to spend time with Guardian Erwin. Apparently, today was the day.

"While you're having your lesson," he said, and then pointedly looked down at his plate, "Agent Reyes is coming in for a scheduled meeting. I get to go." Jackson tried to mumble the words because he knew the mention of Reyes might set her temper off. If only he could keep the excitement from his voice.

This hero worship of Reyes served as proof of Jackson's imperfection. She'd wondered if there might be more to it. Perhaps he was another beautiful, unattainable gay man like Ace, destined to be a wonderful, and very platonic, friend? But after several weeks of spending every waking moment together, that definitely wasn't the case. They'd progressed beyond sidelong glances and zing-tinged chemistry, thanks to her shameless aggression, and were moving nicely toward…more.

Jackson wasn't gay. He didn't want Reyes. But that didn't stop him from wanting to be Reyes. Her sigh fluttered the cloth crumpled beside her left hand.

He laughed to himself. His amused eyes, the corners turned up with dual laugh lines, met hers across the table again. "Why do you always do that?"

She arched a brow. "Because I don't like him. Because he tricked me into coming here. Oh, how about because he's evil?" None of that was true. He wasn't evil. He hadn't tricked her, not really. And as for not liking him….

It was one snotty hug, Lena. You're acting like a child. Get over it already. He has.

She just couldn't bring herself to let go of her indignation yet. He'd brought her here and dumped her without another thought. He'd been back. There had been meetings with Councilor Five, even check-ins with Jackson. Not one word to Lena, though. Not even to knock and barge in and say, "Hello, how are you coping?"

It had hurt, which was stupid because there had been *nothing* between them but a few days of intense drama and a bit of oversharing about mutual miserable childhoods. Then what she could only imagine was a deliberate slight had pissed her off. She decided to get over it as best she could—she'd enjoy the time she had here with the one person who did care whether or not she was coping. And she wouldn't think about Reyes constantly. She sure as hell wouldn't miss a man she barely knew.

So stop it already, little idiot.

Jackson shook his head, but his face stilled into seriousness. "Alejandro Reyes is a good man."

She snorted. "I think you're confusing being good at what he does with being good. And any man who does what he does, as well as he does, is by definition not a good man. Someday you'll be old enough to know that." That much *was* true. She hadn't reconciled what she knew and the stories she'd heard about his exploits with the poetry-quoting man who'd stuck his neck out for her over and over, even if he had hauled her to the last place on earth she'd have chosen.

"I'm older than you are."

"Chronologically, yes. Not in the ways of the world, Ward Lee." She folded the last quarter of bread around the end of a smooth-skinned sausage and submerged them in the syrup before leaning across the table so she could stuff the dripping mass into her mouth. She gave him a closed-mouth grin of contentment and hummed.

Maple syrup was the true blue secret to happiness. She didn't know why the Council of Nine didn't ship it off to every Zone in big vats. If they did, all discontent and crime would disappear with the regular ingestion of the sticky perfection. Look at her: she was a happier girl already. As soon as she cleared her mouth, she told him so.

He shook his head as if he could read her thoughts. He glanced up at her. "You're going to make yourself sick."

She smiled serenely, swirled her fork in the syrup and licked it from the tines. He did a double-take before he returned to his eggs, a slight flush creeping across the golden brown skin of his face. Hmmm. Thoughts of Reyes fled.

That's an interesting reaction, isn't it?

Jackson finished his eggs and then cleared his throat. "We should go get started, yes?"

She dropped the fork onto her plate and helped him clean up the detritus of their meal. "Yes," she laughed. "Absolutely."

She followed him to the out-of-the-way classroom they'd had her working in. They had started with teaching her centering and focus techniques. Washington wanted her to teach others to do what she could do. They hoped better control of her Spark would translate to being able to train others. So far, the attempt had been a resounding failure.

No one had been able to duplicate any of her offensive skills. She'd heard that Reyes, in a single evening lesson, had taught a group of Senior Wards how to protect themselves from intrusions into their personal Dust. And Jackson had shown remarkable aptitude manipulating the Dust to heal. The men could learn new skills, they just couldn't learn them from her. She suspected the failure had more to do with her lack of trust than with any lack of ability in herself or others.

Which was as good an explanation as any as to why she could teach Jackson. She'd never met anyone as steady and reliable. She felt safe with him. She laughed to herself as she crossed the room and hitched herself up onto a tall desk. He didn't always like how safe she felt with him.

He had paused by the door to fiddle with a rattling air vent. He hated distractions while he worked. While his back was still turned, Lena pulled out the small knife she'd palmed at breakfast. He needed an ego boost after failing abysmally at every attempt to use the Dust offensively. She could give him that. What he couldn't handle healing, she could take care of herself.

She drew the blade across the inside of her hand. The skin parted and blood pooled in her cupped palm. Jackson turned at the sound of her soft gasp.

She bit her lip. "New lesson."

He closed his eyes and let his head fall back. "I *hate it* when you do that."

"You can't practice healing if you don't have something to heal. You're an amazing healer, Jackson. You'll be better than me someday. You need the chance to practice."

"I don't. Not if it means you hurt yourself."

"Well, done is done," she said. "Are you going to come fix me or leave me to sit here and bleed?"

"I should let you bleed." He crossed to where she perched on the desk. He shook his head at her, a final admonishment before he took her hand in both of his. Even when angry, he had a gentle touch.

As he focused, her hand warmed. Her flesh knit back together. When he finished, he exhaled in relief and rubbed his thumb across her palm. He continued stroking even after he'd rubbed away the blood.

It felt good. It kept her focus solely on Jackson.

He sighed. "Please don't do that again."

She laughed. "You know if you couldn't heal it, *I* could. It's not a big deal."

"It is a big deal. It's a big deal to me. I don't like the idea of you being hurt. There's been enough pain in your life, dammit. You're overdue to feel good for a change."

She'd been waiting for the opening. She flashed him a grin. "What did you have in mind?"

He tried to lean back, but she shifted their grips and tugged on his hand to keep him close. She was small, but she was strong. And Jackson never put up much of a fight anyway.

He sighed. The sound fell somewhere between frustrated and longing. When he spoke, his voice was husky. "Lena. This isn't a good idea."

"You say that every time," she whispered. She slid one hand up his arm and pulled him closer.

He took a step, angled his body toward her, and leaned in. His free arm slipped around her back, sliding her down the desk until her body pressed into him. He leaned his head down, touching his forehead to hers. His breath warmed her lips. His whiskey gold eyes, inches away, stared into hers. "That's because every time it's a bad idea."

"And why is that?" She curled her hand around the top of his arm where the thick muscle rounded up into shoulder. His shoulders were her favorite feature.

He shook his head, a small movement, before he pressed his lips to hers. Like every time before, electricity arced between them, fed by their control of the Dust. With every small fluttery kiss across her lower lip, it was pressure and electricity and release. He exhaled hard against her skin, and she caught her own breath. Jackson's kisses were like nothing she'd ever experienced with the normal boys of Azcon. These kisses were filled with electric heat and longing as the Dust surged inside of her. She'd only felt that swirling, gathering pressure from the Dust with one person before....

She pushed away the intrusive thought. Rejecting the memory of Reyes, she leaned into Jackson's kiss.

He lifted his hand from her back to stroke her hair back from her face. His eyes were dizzy. "Ah, Dust, Lena, you have no idea how much I wish you could be mine."

She curved her lips up under his. "I can be."

He tightened his hand around the side of her head, gentle pressure, and his lips moved on hers. The soft kiss disappeared.

She'd waited for this hard, electric kiss, the one that took her breath away. Heat curled within her, pouring down from their joined mouths and pooling deep inside like the thick maple syrup she loved so much. She exhaled softly through her nose, and her breath fanned back to her from his cheek.

As if the movement of air across his skin was a signal, Jackson moved his lips on hers, parting them both. He darted his tongue out to taste her.

She moved with him, matching his slow pace. Their lips spread a little more as he turned into the kiss, one hand sliding across to the back of her neck, and the tips of their tongues touched.

Power zinged through her. She felt his body jolt as the wave rolled through him as well. Without thinking, almost without any awareness of it at all, she reached out to him the way she did when she healed. He became Dust swirling, blood surging, heartbeat increasing heat. She could feel his answer as he did the same. Dust moved low within her, curling and gathering in her belly and back.

He tugged his hand free from where she'd captured it and slid it around to her back, pulling her closer. He pressed his hand to her lower back, and her Dust darted to him in a cloud of energy, then flashed out, spreading rapidly through her to flare and pop everywhere they were in contact, at groin, and chest, and mouth. She shuddered again.

It was delicious. It was dangerous. She wanted this more than she'd wanted anything. But even as she leaned into the kiss, he pulled his mouth from hers, leaning back to put space between them.

"Lena," he said, his voice rough, "if we keep doing this, we won't stop."

Her head nodded, tiny movements signaling her agreement. "Okay," she said aloud, dazed. Her eyelids fluttered closed, and she leaned in again, wrapping her legs around him so he couldn't keep pulling away.

"We can't. Someone's going to walk in."

"So go close the door." She blinked at his expression. "What? Are you scared of being caught with me?"

He looked away and gave a pained laugh before nodding several times. "Absolutely."

She frowned. He was serious. "I'm trying to imagine sober, sensible Jackson Lee scared of anyone."

"Huh. Doesn't take much trying. I'm scared of you."

"I'm scary?"

"You are terrifying."

"Really?" She leaned in, grinning wide, determined to cajole him into going and closing the damn door. She nipped at his lip as she purred, "How so?"

"Hmmm," a familiar husky voice interjected from the other end of the room, "I don't think there's enough time left in the morning for Jackson to complete that list."

Jackson leaped back as if she'd scalded him. He didn't turn, and his hands had come up to frame his forehead.

She sat back. Reyes stood in the doorway, long and lean, with his hands in his pockets and his chin down.

She hadn't seen him in more than six weeks. She wasn't prepared for the jolt as her Dust recognized him. Already excited by what she'd been doing with Jackson, the Dust raged through her, battering her inside. She swallowed and sent angry demands that it stop.

I don't even like that man!

The Dust ignored the lie. Lena clenched her teeth and squeezed her legs together, tightening her back against the onslaught. She would *not* respond.

"Reyes." It was all the greeting he'd get. Her perfect maple syrup and make-out mood had soured. She could feel her face sliding into cold, unhappy lines. Damn her body anyway for responding to him more strongly than it had to Jackson. What the hell was that about?

"Well," he said, "if that isn't the damnedest transformation ever." His dark, displeased face turned to Jackson, who slowly moved to face the older agent. They remained on the younger man, steady and evaluating. "I thought Thomas spoke to you about this?"

"Spoke about what?" She looked from Reyes to Jackson.

"He did, sir. I apologize. Just—" Jackson shook his head. "I'll take care of it."

"Take care of what?"

Jackson looked away, shaking his head.

Reyes gave a strangled, disparaging laugh and shrugged. "Nothing, Lena." He cocked his finger at them. "C'mon. We're gonna be late. It's my day off, and I don't want to waste the whole day here." He turned and stalked down the hall, his back stiff.

Jackson started after Reyes then paused to wait for her. He still wouldn't meet her eyes. As soon as she hopped down from the desk, Jackson followed Reyes out. She trailed along behind him. What had just happened?

She wasn't in any hurry to catch up. She didn't know what was going on with Jackson, and she had no desire to engage Reyes any more than necessary. Lena had spent enough time examining her feelings to understand the source of her attraction, as well as her resentment. Reyes had been there. He had worked hard to keep her safe from the bad acts and intentions of the Council of Nine. When his plan had gone bad, he hadn't given up or walked away, he'd remained at her side, witnessing it all, and waiting for the opportunity to free her. He had kept his word to her. And after he had, he'd had no way to know he was taking her to the one place guaranteed to awaken all of her childhood fears. Intellectually, she understood.

But emotionally...every time she saw him, her teeth set and her shoulders tightened. She had trusted him. Doing so had cost her mother her life. As if that loss wasn't enough, Reyes had brought her to the school her father had told her wasn't safe, to the people he had insisted could never be trusted. Then he'd abandoned her. Mission accomplished. Outcome produced. He was done factoring that particular equation.

And that equation included her. Whatever connection she felt? Whatever lame response her Dust tortured her with? It was one-sided.

Jackson looked back over his shoulder. He flashed a sickly half-smile and indicated with a gesture that he was going to hurry up the long corridor to talk to Reyes. She waved her fingers at him, telling him to go.

The two men walked together ahead of her, Reyes dangerous and controlled and Jackson eagerly matching his pace. The men slowed, and Reyes turned to Jackson, finally engaged in whatever he was saying. She hung back.

She could see Reyes's nature now in the easy smile he flashed at Jackson. His dark eyes still calculated and ran through scenarios. Was his mind ever still? A memory rose, of Reyes reciting poetry as he remembered his father to her. She pushed it away.

Whatever he'd offered Jackson had lit up the younger man's face with relief. Her heart squeezed. Hope shone out of his smile like a beacon. Other than those wide, heavy shoulders, Jackson's smile was the best of many good features. It was broad and excited now as he nodded and shook Reyes's hand in agreement.

She returned her scrutiny to Reyes. He relinquished Jackson's hand and turned to flash her a satisfied smile before moving away down the hallway, his confident stride graceful and smooth.

Jackson stood in front of her, then, and she forced herself to look away from Reyes's back. "What was that all about? Did you make up?"

"Make up?" He gave her a puzzled look.

"Yeah. You said you were worried about someone catching us together. Obviously from your reaction, you were worried about what *Reyes* would think." She was pissed at Reyes. She shouldn't take it out on Jackson.

"I wasn't—Lena, I was worried, period."

She glared at him. "Why?"

"Why?" He stopped walking. "Really?"

"Yes, why really," Lena snapped. "You're twenty-four years old. What do you care if someone catches you kissing some girl?"

"I'm a Ward," he said, as if that explained everything. It didn't make it any clearer to her. "And you're not just 'some girl.' I've been trying not to jeopardize my graduation."

"Why would kissing me jeopardize your becoming an agent?"

He shook his head, closing his eyes. "Because of who you are. It just does."

Oh, so this is my *fault?* She couldn't help a sullen mutter. "It didn't look jeopardized to me."

"No. No, he understands. And he's not going to say anything to the Councilor." He looked away down the hall. "I hope you understand. I know you don't like him, but he's being very generous. He's even offered to mentor me when this assignment is over."

She couldn't keep the hurt from flaring. "This assignment? Is that what his comment back there was about?"

His face fell. "I—no. They don't want—I don't have permission to—"

"Permission?" Her voice wasn't sullen anymore, it was angry and loud. She didn't care. "You're waiting for permission to be intimate with your assignment?"

He shook his head, lips compressed and face unhappy. "I didn't mean you're an assignment. I meant—"

"I know what you meant." She lifted her chin. "Where's Erwin's office? I'd like to get this over with. And the sooner you drop me off," she added with brittle precision, "the sooner you can go report on the status of your assignment. Or maybe you were planning to ask for permission? If that's the case, don't bother."

He sighed, a whisper of sound that became her name.

Lena turned away, rapid footsteps carrying her to the elevators. She'd rather sit in an office with a Guardian than listen to whatever Jackson had to say.

—w—

Except for his luxurious lion's mane of golden brown hair threaded with washed out grey, Guardian Erwin was a middling man—middle-aged, mid-height, and of middling weight. Even his eyes were washed out, a watery hazel mix somewhere between brown and green. When Jackson ushered her in, Erwin distractedly told her to have a seat at a cluttered table shoved into the far corner of his office. In the same breath, he ordered Jackson out. Lena didn't turn back when he left.

With a long-suffering sigh, Erwin settled himself into the seat beside her. "How much did your—" his voice took on a note of distaste "—zone educators teach you about the history of the Great Disaster?"

She shook her head, willing herself to focus. She felt herself shrinking back into her chair and reversed course, straightening her spine. She refused to be cowed by any of them. "I didn't go to school."

Erwin blinked at her. "So...what do you know, if anything, about the beginning of the Second Dark Age, which many call the Great Disaster?"

She followed his lead, taking a long, calming breath to focus and remember what she'd been taught. "I know it was terrorists who released something over old Texas that was supposed to burn fuel and die, but something went wrong. The factories exploded, and the Dust went up into the sky and spread over the whole world. It burned all the fuel, everything, and when it went out, it took everything with it. Energy didn't work anymore. The first Sparks were special soldiers, and they tried to control the Dust, but they couldn't.

"People who lived in the huge cities suffered the most and the fastest. They couldn't get food. And the water stopped flowing. Most of them died." She swallowed. "And everything went dark for a long time. Almost fifty years later, Mark Peller went out and collected Sparks and formed the First Council."

Erwin held up a finger, indicating she should stop her recitation. He pulled a tube closer to himself and unrolled it, revealing a map. He moved the edge of it closer to her as he spoke. "That is a very basic, and incomplete, understanding of what happened—take that side there and pull it toward you—but at least it's not terribly tainted by Council propaganda." He gave a loud, indelicate sniff.

With the map spread before her, she could see the nine Zone divisions. Entire swaths of the green and brown of the land were covered with neatly inked, tiny black x's—most of the west coast of the country and a huge area sweeping up from the curving shoreline of the south. The ugly slashes crept away from the fat body of the inked areas in long, sinuous arms stretching across the country in every direction. Those tentacles represented the refinery-rich and pipelined Hell Cities and the lands surrounding them that had burned to slag. No one survived.

Erwin set a heavy ball of glass on one corner and a large and jagged black rock on the other. His hand ran across the map, gesturing like a magician about to make something appear from nothing. "This is the world as it was, two hundred and twelve years ago. Or at least our side of it." He pointed at the top and moved down. "Canada. The United States. Mexico. Central and South America further down." He stared down at the map and blinked several times. "The combined population of these three countries was 560 million people. Ten years after the attack, 300 million were gone. Ten years later, another fifty million. And on and on, the dying went. Starvation. Hard winters. Bad water. Illness. The influenza that struck the East Coast relocation centers devastated the population—and to this day, we on the Western fringes are stronger.

"By the time Peller and his cronies gathered together those few tens of thousands left alive in each of the relocation centers— if you can call what they were doing living—they were grateful for any chance. They would have agreed to anything. And the first Sparks did exactly that."

Erwin leaned back in his chair and the wood creaked and moaned, as if as disturbed at the loss of life as Erwin seemed to be. He shook his head. "That is what happened. But what *caused* all of this devastation?" He raised his brows at her.

Lena shook her head. She'd answered him already, hadn't she?

He smiled faintly. His chair creaked again as he shifted his weight. "The terrorists released nano-robots. Tiny, tiny metal machines too small for the human eye to see. In this case, programmed to destroy fossil fuels. They were specifically designed to work around safeguards, to be self-sufficient, self-replicating. Instead of a kill switch, they had an adaptation switch. The terrorists who made them did everything everyone in science had agreed to never, ever do. We have no idea why."

Her eyes narrowed. Tiny robots? Little machines?

"They might have only affected our fuels, if not for the government's response. You see, once they figured out what was happening, they decided to try to use their experimental nano-response team—"

"They had a team of tiny machines?"

"No, they had a team of soldiers, trained to reprogram the brains of the tiny machines."

"The Sparks."

"Exactly. They were chosen because of the strength of their brain waves, the ability to control things. And then the scientists manipulated their bodies to make it stronger. Their minds could contact and control nanobots. But by the time they were sent out, it was too late. When the explosions began—the refineries, the pipelines—the nanobots were sent into the atmosphere. It was already over. It took five days, roughly, for the nanobots to circle the Earth, a little longer for them to reach the Southern Hemisphere. Everywhere they settled, wherever they came into contact with pure fossil fuels, nightmarish fire. Even synthesized forms smoldered. And the nanites reproduced. It was over. They were everywhere. In the air, in the water, in us. Everywhere. The world was in flames."

"They were the Dust."

He sighed and ran his hand over his lips a few times. "They *are* the Dust."

"And the soldiers? What happened to the first Sparks?"

Erwin nodded. "They tried to stop it. They imposed their will over the adaptations. But it wasn't perfect. They couldn't stop only explosions, they had to stop all reactions above a certain threshold. When the bots finally responded, that's what they did. They stopped the combustion, and *every other large-scale reaction*. The nanobots muted every reaction wherever they were. Over the next year, the soldier Sparks were able to get the nanobots to adjust; they were able to get some energy back. External combustion mostly. They got us fire. But life as they knew it was done. The entire world paid the price for the anger of a handful of people."

"But, really, this is all guesses, right?" She held the map steady with her left hand, but she gestured her disbelief with her right. "I mean, we call it history, but there's no way we can really know any of this?"

"We do know, because we were told." His voice was steady.

"Told? By whom?"

"By those who were there."

Disbelief flared. "How is that possible?"

Erwin held up a finger for patience. "As you said, some fifty-five years after the world went dark, a government was formed. And its foundation was built upon the backs of those very soldiers. Peller had worked in the government as a young man, knew something of the program. He gathered together the soldiers he could find and convinced them to use their unique skills to work with the nanobots again. They handed out the first of the Spark-powered batteries. They handed out hope to the few masses remaining in exchange for the power to rule over them."

She shook her head. "How many soldiers were there? I may not know all of the details, but I can do math. How could there be so many of us now? Where did all of the Sparks come from?"

Erwin glanced down. He ran his teeth over his lower lip. "They came from the breeding programs, which of course necessitated the mandatory education programs that you know—"

Lena scoffed. "Breeding programs!" She let a burst of laughter erupt from her throat. "Those men had to be seventy-five, eighty years old!"

"Chronologically, yes." Erwin told her. "But the

manipulation of the scientists did something to them. Their lives are very much extended, as are the lives of their descendants." His stare bored into hers. "You must have noticed how quickly you heal from injury, how rarely you're sick? It depends upon the strength of the Spark, of course. The lives of weak Sparks run only slightly longer than an unpowered human, perhaps merely a few decades, although they are hardier. The strongest Sparks...." The man shrugged.

She leaned away from him, brow furrowed. *She* was one of the strongest Sparks. It wasn't ego. It was fact. What did this mean?

"The strongest...what?" She sat up straight again, back rigid, right hand clenched in her lap. "Guardian Erwin...how long—" She stopped and licked her lips. "How long did they live? The soldiers?"

"The oldest of them began dying sixty years ago."

She sat still, but her eyes wandered as she tried to run the calculations in her head. Almost two hundred years? When she spoke her voice shook. "Guardian. Will I...?" She huffed her dismay. "So, in addition to all the lovely things that make me special enough to kidnap and torture and lock away, I get to look forward to two hundred years of existence as what? Some desiccated old husk?"

Erwin laughed, his mouth wide. He did resemble a lion. "No, Lena. Your strength, your health, your vitality are all extended. You will not be what we consider old for a very long time."

She gave Erwin a long look. He had a very faint aura. "How old are you?"

"Well, for all I am a giant among the very few historians left in our world, I am not a powerful Spark. And I am eighty-two years old."

Lena gasped. She would have said he was not a day older than fifty, possibly younger.

He nodded, accepting her disbelief. "And this is why you find yourself the center of so much attention." His smile became rueful. "The strongest among us find your ability to keep pace attractive. If they were to be fortunate enough to win you, they wouldn't have to watch you wither. They won't outlive you."

"No," she ventured, her mouth twisting as she stared down at nothing, "they'll just have to put up with me."

Erwin laughed again.

She flashed him a sickly smile.

Erwin leaned back, the chair creaking long and low. His attention flicked over her shoulder. "There's more you need to know. More that explains—" he released his breath in a long sigh "—everything that has happened to you. When you're ready, ask. We know you're confused, but we are here to help you. And I think once you understand, some of your impatience and uncertainty will subside."

She looked up from the map. She blinked. Information swirled in her head. "Oh. Am I...? Are you dismissing me?"

Erwin raised his hand up in a grand gesture at the entry behind her.

Lena twisted in her seat. Reyes leaned against the jamb of the opened door, hands buried deep in his pockets. His face was as relaxed as his posture.

"Where's Jackson?" she asked automatically. She gritted her teeth at herself.

Something flitted over the calm mask, gone before she could name it. "He volunteered to go out on field exercises until tomorrow evening. He was worried he might lose his..." Reyes paused and smiled briefly. "Particular skills. Thomas agreed."

"Oh." She couldn't think of anything else to say. She couldn't think of anything at all, even though her mind raced.

He cocked his head slightly in the direction of the hall behind him. "C'mon. I actually have a surprise for you."

Lena looked back at Erwin. "Thank you. You've given me a lot to think about." She stood and shook the man's hand. A part of her watched with incredulous detachment.

She joined Reyes and walked with him back down the halls to the elevator, and then off the elevator to her room. She said nothing. She was aware of Reyes studying her. He even managed to look concerned.

When they reached her door, Reyes leaned to key the

lockbox. She grabbed his arm. He waited, staring back at her while her fingers held tight to his arm. She had to know....

"How old are you?" Her voice was low and hoarse and tense. She didn't know why it mattered, but it did. For all of his experience and authority, he seemed young and handsome and strong. He didn't look a day over thirty. And yet, all of the stories of his exploits she'd heard since she'd been here—if he was only thirty, how could he have packed so much into the five years since graduation? She answered herself now: he couldn't. "How old are you, Reyes?"

His head cocked to the side, and he searched her face. Bit by bit, he let the mask go. He let her see the pinched lines around his brown eyes, the lines of worry between his brows. He let her see his chin work as he chewed the inside of his lower lip. He took a deep breath and gave her the truth that she needed.

"I'm forty-eight years old, Lena." He nodded, acknowledging the shock that must be obvious on her face. "I'm forty-eight."

FOURTEEN

Alex held her shocked gaze. Her shock wouldn't merely be over his age, or the confirmation of what Erwin had told her, but must be born from the implications of what all of this meant for her. This wasn't simply news about her probable lifespan. It required a total reexamination of what she believed to be true, even of her own parents. Would she ever question if her mother had been older than Lena thought? She had been, by a couple of decades.

He waited for the explosion of denial, or more anger, even. He didn't expect the wobble as her knees let go. If she hadn't been holding onto his arm with her death grip, she might have gone down.

He wrapped his free arm around her, giving her support, and pulled her to him.

No, no. Danger.

He had no business holding her in his arms. For someone who gave such an overwhelming impression of fire and strength, she curved slight and soft against his chest and stomach. She even smelled good. The voice shouting in his head for his attention was absolutely correct: he didn't need the kind of trouble she could bring into his life, regardless of how much the rest of him was interested in exploring the idea. He'd spent the last month and a half avoiding her for precisely that reason.

Alex maneuvered her around and leaned her against the wall and put several inches of space between them. "Breathe," he told her, voice low. "Just breathe. And try not to think of it all right now."

She gasped out a laugh. "Don't think of it. Excellent suggestion. Tell me how."

He leaned away, and her hand tightened again on his arm. Okay, she needed the connection. Not a big deal. "I mean take it in pieces. Don't try to see all of it at once."

"Pieces, huh?"

He nodded. Her fingers were moving as she thought, back and forth as she gripped and released his arm through the sleeve of his shirt.

"I'm strong? I know I am, but…I'm really strong, right?"

He nodded.

"So that means…?" She must know what it meant, but she moved on, as if the concept was too big to apply to herself. "How is this possible? How does everyone not know?"

He shrugged. "The strongest, the longest-lived, they all become Wards, who all become agents. The mid-ranges, their life spans vary enough that it isn't that obvious to most people."

"But the Council knows?"

He nodded. Her nails were scraping through his thin shirt and against his skin. It was a thoughtless, automatic movement. It meant nothing to her, he was sure. But it felt like a caress on his skin. He swallowed. "The Council knows. And their policy until recently has been to ignore and exploit the differences."

"Until recently? How recently? What changed?"

The spasmodic movement of her fingers slowed as she calmed, allowing herself to be distracted away from shock and fear. The slowing movement should have been a relief. It wasn't. The intensity of his nerve response grew.

"Well. We don't know when it officially changed, or if it was even official at first. We started noticing it about twenty-five years ago."

"You were young then, right?"

Alex felt his eyes crinkling. "In the grand scheme of things, I'm still young." It was time to divorce himself from the sensations coursing up his arm. He took a deep breath.

"Oh. Right. I meant…you were a young agent then. I mean, you were new."

"Yes. And sometimes when you're new, you see more. Or maybe you accept less. Reassignments of older, powerful agents away from the top tiers of power. Whispers. Disappearances. A group of us were already watching, waiting. So when it started— we looked into it. And what we found made us decide to move, and move hard. We made a plan. We put it into motion." He shrugged.

She took a deep breath. Her fingers stilled. "Because if it comes down to them or us…."

"We choose us." He tilted his head, watching her face to make sure she fully understood. "*And* all of the people who depend upon us. We don't want more suffering. We're not about withholding power, but we won't be slaves to those who are weaker than we are. Do you understand?"

She stared sightlessly at his chest. She'd have to reorder everything in her head, line it up with her own experiences. It would make sense to her. Maybe she'd start trusting them.

Finally, she looked up at him and nodded. "So, all of this time, everything you've told me has been true?"

Alex nodded. "It has, yes."

"And everything you've done has all been for a reason? And that's what you've all been trying to teach me?"

He nodded. "Right."

She gusted out a breath. When she spoke, her voice was nearly back to normal. "So he was wrong? My Dad. You're not the bad guys."

"Right."

"And you're not actually a brutal, heartless bastard?"

He blinked. Her final question had been quieter, but her lips were curved. She was almost herself again.

He couldn't resist. One side of his mouth drew up in answer. "Well," he drawled, "I wouldn't go that far."

She laughed, the last of her tension releasing with the burst of sound. He laughed with her, his first genuine laugh in a long time. It felt good. He felt light.

She straightened, rubbing his arm almost affectionately before letting it go.

He stepped away, still grinning. "Ready for your surprise?"

"Ha. Are you?" At his questioning look she continued, "The last time you surprised me, I threw you out."

He laughed, again, at the memory. "So you did. It's a good thing I don't hold grudges. For long." He keyed the lockbox.

"In the grand scheme of things?" she asked archly.

He grinned at her as he pushed the door open. "That's what I like about you. You're a quick study."

She opened her mouth to reply, but her gaze shifted into the room. Her mouth fell open.

"Ace!" She ran inside.

Alex followed her. He closed them in as Ace swept her up into his arms with a laugh and swung her around.

"You're here!"

Was that laugh almost a giggle? Alex had never heard her sound young.

"What are you doing here? How did you get here?" Before Ace could answer, she whirled to Alex. "You brought him!"

He shrugged. "I figured you could use a friendly face."

Lena launched herself at him. Before he could even get his arms up, she had her own wrapped tight around his back.

She squeezed herself tight against him for a moment before leaning back and grinning up at him. "Thank you for this."

Alex worked hard to keep his smile in place as he extricated himself from her spontaneous hug before his Dust could start dancing inside for her again. "It wasn't a big deal. And he's kind of a pain in the ass, anyway. Two birds. One stone."

"It's a big deal to me," Ace said, his voice solemn.

She nodded at them both. "It's a big deal. It's—I needed this, especially today. Thank you."

He shrugged again. "Lena, you do need to know...you have to be discreet. Ace can't know where he is." He raised his brows at her. "It could potentially endanger too many people, including you."

"Wait. He doesn't know?" She looked between the two of

them.

Ace grimaced. "All I know is we walked for a long time. And then we rode." Her brows furrowed as he continued: "I came in with a sack over my head. Agent Reyes does paranoid very, very well."

She digested that for a moment. She turned back to Alex. Would the new understanding between them hold? Had he earned her trust back?

Alex held his breath. He hoped he hadn't made a mistake. Thomas had been adamantly opposed to the idea. He thought Lena needed a clean break with everything and everyone in her past. Alex had argued that she'd had a couple too many involuntary clean breaks in her life. Thomas should have understood. His childhood had been just as traumatic, but he'd put it behind him. Alex remembered what it felt like to be torn from people he loved, even forty-three years later. It wasn't something one should forget.

She was suddenly subdued. Did she suspect how hard he'd had to fight for this brief reunion? She searched his face. He didn't know what she found, but she nodded at him.

"I'll be discreet."

He returned her nod. "Good." He turned to Ace with a sardonic smile. "Looks like you get to go home, after all."

Ace squinted at him, and then he turned to Lena. "He's joking, right?"

She gave him a small smile. "Sure. Reyes is the comedian of the place."

"I'm a laugh-a-minute." He put his hands on his hips. "We know the rules, kids?"

She shook her head and rolled her eyes. "No going outside? No talking about where we are or anything related to where we are? And like that?"

"Exactly." He crossed to the door. "Unless Ace already ate it all while he was waiting for you to be done with your lesson, there's food in the basket by the table. Enjoy your lunch. I'll be back in an hour."

"Wait. You're leaving us?"

Ace crossed his arms and raised his brows. "You're going to trust us to be good? Funny, I kind of figured you'd be sitting here with us the whole time, holding our hands, and leading us in campfire songs." That earned a smile from Lena. "I wouldn't have guessed you were the trusting type, Alex."

The excitement and gratitude playing over Lena's face made it worth the hassle.

"I'm not. But everyone has to start sometime."

—⚹—

Alex left them and headed straight for his little-used office. After the frenzy of activity at the Council offices in Azcon following Lena's disappearance from the collapsed Council building six weeks before, he had earned an hour of quiet. He also had no desire to rehash this decision with Thomas. He had as much a right to make it as his partner did. That was a simple fact.

They had originally envisioned themselves running things together from this end. As soon as it was practical, Alex had taken a large step back. He'd reassured Thomas that he wasn't relinquishing his founding role, merely using his strengths in the best way he could to further their cause. He belonged out in the trenches. Thomas didn't always understand the decision.

Maybe Thomas needed help? He had to manage a zone, a school, and a quiet revolution's worth of reports on the Council's actions. Alex had only himself, the plan, and the people on the ground. It hardly seemed a fair division of labor. Perhaps it was time to find a replacement Alex, someone with the skills and the tenacity and the drive to bring their ideas to fruition on the outside.

Which brought him around to Jackson Lee.

Alex had a moment's warning when he heard the lock click over. Other than himself, only his partner had access to this office. He sighed.

Thomas leaned against the jamb. "Thought I might find you here. Left them alone, did you?"

Alex pursed his lips and nodded, unrepentant. He'd made his views clear. That Thomas had thought he'd talked him out of them was irrelevant.

Thomas came into the room and closed the door. He sat heavily on a chair placed at an angle to the desk. Alex leaned back in his own chair and hiked his feet up onto the desk, crossing them at the ankles. His friend was gathering his thoughts. He let him gather.

"My objections to this friend of hers, and to this visit, are not rooted in a desire to keep her isolated." Thomas raised his pale regard to Alex. "She is both young and volatile—"

Alex's mind flashed back to the scene he'd walked in on: Lena grinning up at Jackson, green eyes shining and full of mischief, legs wrapped around his waist. He forced the memory away. "Do you think I haven't taken that into consideration?"

"Let me finish, please." Thomas's stare bored into him. He waited until Alex had settled back in the chair, fingers laced across his stomach, staring up at the ceiling as he listened. "I manage things here. I read, I listen, I balance and weigh, and then I make decisions. You make them happen. You cannot be reckless, even if someone else must suffer a little. The price to everyone is simply too high. You go down, we all go down. You can't be replaced."

The silence stretched between them.

"Are you done?" Alex asked the ceiling. He took Thomas's silence as confirmation. He turned to look at his friend, shaking his head. "That's bullshit. What we've done in the last twenty years is bigger than both of us. We've talked about this, Thom. Neither of us is irreplaceable. Give Lee half a year, and he can handle most of what I do."

The kid had the skills. Short of Thomas and Alex, and now Lena, Jackson was the strongest Spark the Ward School had seen and a gifted young agent. He was also pretty compromised when it came to Lena. He said all the right things, but Alex would be shocked if he could extricate himself from their dalliance.

Like you'd be able to? He gritted his teeth at the taunting thought.

Perhaps it would be best for everyone to separate Lena and Jackson, train him, and let him take over Fort Nevada's interests in Zone Three. He'd already made the offer to Jackson earlier in the corridor. In a moment of frustration that admittedly had little to do with the kid, he'd asked the kid why he was so comfortable remaining behind and babysitting at the Fort. What had happened to the kid he'd met in the cafeteria, the one chomping at the bit for a chance to prove himself out in the world?

Lee's face had been a study in discomfort. He knew his responsibilities and his role, but she captivated him with her attention.

Alex had made him a promise. If Jackson could keep his distance and help Lena realize her importance to them all, then he would be assigned to Azcon to train with Alex. She would be free to focus on her lessons and her vengeance. Jackson would get the training and the experience he desperately wanted. Alex would get the skilled junior partner he had needed since Erika had been sent to Zone Six. A real partner, one whom he could train to take over the operations in Azcon in anticipation of the day Alex moved on to their next target Zone.

He could use a partner who was one of them. He was tired of looking over his shoulder. He had his people in the city, but they had other assignments and he expected them to keep their focus where it belonged. This thing with Merritt, the Junior Director of Council Security, served as a reminder that he needed someone to watch his back.

Alex and Merritt were both under the Councilor's consideration for the newly empty position of Director. Everyone in the inner sanctum knew Alex had a foot up simply because the Councilor had particular tastes and Alex was prettier. Merritt was looking for anything he could use against Alex.

He rolled his eyes at the thought and tipped his head to look at his friend again.

Thomas was still, except for one finger tapping on his thigh, likely as busy wrestling his thoughts as Alex had been. Finally, he leaned forward and told Alex matter-of-factly, "Well, he'd look better doing it."

Thomas loved to rib him about the youthful vanity he had indulged in so many years before, even more so since he had outgrown it. The memory made Alex wince.

He snorted. "Okay, see, now you're just being mean. Don't make me throw your ass in the sparring ring."

Thomas laughed. "Maybe that's what you need. It's been a while."

"It has. You done licking your wounds yet?"

"Ha!" Thomas narrowed his eyes. "Can you hear out of your left ear yet?"

Alex rubbed his ear in memory. That had been a shithead move. He told him so.

His friend shrugged and smiled. "It got you off me."

"It almost got you killed." Alex's vision didn't cloud with the red wash of fury often, but when it did, it could be hard to pull himself back into focus.

Thomas stood up. "I can take a drubbing, so long as you stay sharp."

Alex could see the genuine worry. He sighed. "Thom—"

"No. It's fine. I understand your motivation, and I even agree with it, to an extent. But she's a new cog in the machine. I want to be certain it will still run smoothly before letting her run."

"She's not the only new cog." He shook his head. "We need to get new people up there." Thomas would understand his reference. Something was going on in the Council of Nine. Even as a member of the Council, Thomas had no idea who or what moved in the background. Their missing agents in Zone Four spoke of a consolidation of power there reminiscent of their own start twenty years ago here in Zone Five. He needed to be there. He needed to get a sense of it for himself. "I don't like being blind. Not with Lucas back there. I can't be sure what he knows."

"I'm working on it." Thomas cleared his throat. "With Jackson gone tonight, she'll be on her own. Are you returning after taking the friend back to Azcon?"

"Not tonight, no. I need to go in and put in an appearance so my absence two days running won't be as notable." His lips twisted. If it hadn't become crucial to the plan, he'd pull out of consideration for the Director's position.

The mind-games and one-upmanship with Merritt, while

something he might have once had fun with, were another distraction in the post-Lucas era of looking for answers before he knew the questions. However, Merritt had made it obvious that if he got the position they both wanted, he'd make sure Alex wasn't assigned to the Council Meet delegation as Agent Liaison, which would scrap the original plan. It was Director of Councilor Security or nothing, and nothing wasn't an option. They couldn't wait.

"I'll be back tomorrow." Alex shrugged. "So have dinner with her. Answer her questions. Get to know her. *Her*, not your idea of her."

"Oh, I've abandoned my idea of her," Thomas said with a dry laugh. "And any notion of pursuing her myself. She's just not my type."

Alex raised his brow, a smile playing about his lips. As far as he knew, Thomas didn't have a type. Like Alex himself, he availed himself of female company when and where he needed without the complications of emotional attachments.

"Really? Untapped power beyond words isn't your type?"

Thomas cocked his head to the side. He pursed his lips. "I don't know. There's something off...."

"About Lena?" Alex winced internally at the sharp undertone in his own voice.

Before he could examine what made him feel so defensive, Thomas shook his head. "No, no. My expectation, I suppose. We waited so long to find a woman like her, and then—"

"If you tell me she's not as amazing as you thought one of them would be, I'll call you a liar." She was breathtakingly amazing. A huge pain-in-the-ass, yes, but she was also amazing. That was the problem.

"No. She is. Even damaged and prickly. She's just more than I expected. You don't know, because you're not here, but we can feel her. All the time. Her energy, her EM field, the amount of Dust she carries within her, whatever it is, it pulls all the time. She's almost too much." Thomas's eyes narrowed.

How like us fickle humans.

Alex's lips quirked up, and he told Thomas what had

occurred to him.

"Let me guess," his friend answered, a teasing note back in his voice. "There's a poem for that."

Alex laughed, not caring what his friend thought of his love of Stephen Crane. They were familiar enough with each other's foibles to be comfortable expressing them. "I was in the darkness," he began, quoting the poem.

"I could not see my words

Nor the wishes of my heart.

Then suddenly there was a great light—"

He stopped at the stanza break, grinning at Thomas for effect. "'Let me into the darkness again.' That's what we do, you know. We stumble around until we get what we want, and then once we see exactly what it was we really wanted we're terrified of it."

"Ah," Thomas said, "there he is, the warrior-poet I know and love. Take me to bed, Agent Reyes. Ravish me now."

"You wish."

"Ha. I know it breaks your heart, but you're not my type, either." Thomas laughed at him, shaking his head in wonder. "Seriously, why are you wasting your verse on me? That's good stuff, man. You should be reciting poetry to women, not keeping it bottled up. But you haven't. And you won't."

Alex was quiet. His face must have reflected the memory, because Thomas's brows shot up.

"You didn't? Really?"

"Shut up."

"To Lena? I get the lure of the power, but really? She's built like a boy."

"Shut *up*."

"She's just so…tiny. And freckled."

"I like her freckles." He gritted his teeth, pissed that his friend had needled him into the admission. He didn't have time for this. Any of it. "And not that I'm interested, but there's nothing tiny about her presence."

"Oh, no, she's intimidating as shit. When she figures that out, she'll be queen of the universe. I just don't get the whole inspiring poetry vibe off of her." Thom laughed again. "Congratulations,

Alex. You can still surprise me after all these years." He grinned in delight.

Alex pinched the bridge of his nose. "It's not like that. You had to be there. It was just…the moment."

"Aww. You had a moment? That's adorable."

"Get out. Get out now."

Thomas had gone from grinning to chortling laughter choking in his throat.

"Seriously." Alex was indignant. He'd never mocked Thomas's choices. Much. "Out!"

Thomas went. Alex could hear him still laughing as he closed the door behind himself.

FIFTEEN

After Ace left with Reyes, Lena curled up on the small couch. She didn't want to think about everything she'd learned. She didn't want to think about Jackson. She wanted to enjoy the residual happiness of Ace's visit. One moment she was smiling, the next she woke muzzy-headed with sleep and sitting up to an insistent knock. A second later, the lock turned with a click and the door opened.

Councilor Five leaned in, searching the small room. When he found her, he leaned back slightly, seeming relieved, and then embarrassed.

"I'm sorry. I didn't mean to invade your—" His hand indicated the space.

She shook her head. She blinked several times and yawned. "No. That's all right. I fell asleep."

He was uncomfortable, as he seemed every time he appeared. "I hoped Alex would have told you—"

"He did," she assured him. "I just fell asleep."

"Are you hungry? Or would you rather rest? I can have something sent to you."

"I am, actually." She slid forward and stuffed her feet into her low boots then ran her hands through her hair and shoved it back behind her ears. "I'm not fancy, but I am ready, Councilor Five." She stood.

"Councilor—?" He stepped back and shook his head. "No, call me Thomas, please." As he read her doubtful face, he insisted, "Thomas."

She followed Thomas through several corridors that finally emptied into a smaller elevator lobby. He pushed the button to call the elevator and then flashed her a smile. "We're not going to the cafeteria. I thought you'd appreciate some fresh air."

"Fresh air?" Her brows rose, as did her voice, with a surge of excitement. "We're going to the surface?" Since she'd arrived, she'd only been to the surface to use the protected grounding platform. They'd been very careful to limit her exposure to open areas where anyone watching the school might see her.

The elevator slid open, and Thomas rapped a button at the top of the board after they entered. She hoped along with the fresh air he planned to explain a few things to her. She had many questions, one of them how he and Reyes had come together to build their revolution in the first place. She wasn't sure she'd ever met two more dissimilar men. And yet, here they were, carving their alternative empire out of the Council of Nine without the Council even being aware of it.

The box slowed and stopped before they reached the floor Thomas had selected. The doors opened, and two men turned from their conversation to enter. The older talked with his hands, arms waving so violently that his thin blond hair fluttered around his face and ears. Both men paused when they saw her inside, brought up short in surprise. Two appreciative stares ran down the length of her and both lit with a speculative light.

Lena sighed and moved back against the wall behind her. She might get used to the idea that she was the only powered female in the school. She didn't think she'd get used to the looks. After her talk with Erwin, she understood their fascination better. She cast her gaze downward so as to not encourage either of the men.

"Guardian Wils. Agent Prentiss," Thomas greeted them, his voice dry. "Going up?"

"We are." The agent recovered first.

She still had the sense that Reyes would be unimpressed with his lack of self-control.

"We're joining Guardians Schroeder and Erwin for dinner on the Quad," the guardian told Thomas. Lena could feel his attention on her. "Perhaps the two of you could join us? I can't be the only one eager to meet our newest student."

Thomas cleared his throat. The sound was almost an apology. "Of course. Wils, Prentiss, this is Lena Gracey. Lena, one of our talented teachers and his prize student from several years ago."

She gave the men a weak smile before looking down again.

"She's shy," Wils purred. "How charming. Perhaps after dinner she'll be more comfortable with us."

She didn't think she had ever wanted to punch a man in the crotch as much as she did right then.

"I'm afraid we have to decline your invitation, Wils. We're having a working dinner." Thomas gave the Guardian another of his bland smiles.

"Oh, come on. The three of you can't keep her to yourselves indefinitely. It's not fair." The man was smart enough to keep his voice jovial, but it didn't matter.

Lena had looked up in surprise at his words and caught Thomas's reaction. The bland smile had shifted in some infinitesimal way to become dangerous. His eyes tightened barely perceptively, but she was glad the feral glint in the pale blue depths was not directed at her.

Had she believed he and Reyes had nothing in common?

The younger agent nodded. "But of course we understand the need for a working dinner. There are never enough hours in the day, are there?" He looked at her. "Perhaps another time?"

The elevator slowed, saving her from answering. Thomas ushered the men out ahead of them. They exited into another bare lobby with a set of heavy doors to one side. Thomas held out a hand at his side, pausing her progress. The two men preceded them, the Guardian's shoulders set and angry. As the door swung to close behind them, Prentiss looked back. He wasn't looking at her physically, but inspected her aura. The lascivious heat in his stare made it a violation.

Once she and Thomas were alone again, she let out the breath she wasn't aware she'd been holding. They spoke at the same time.

"Perhaps this wasn't such a good idea."

"What was that all about?"

She waited for him to answer her question.

He rubbed his nose. "Erwin explained the basics of our life spans?"

"Yeah, he did. And I understand, awesome, you guys live a long time and get lonely. But there *are* women here. I've seen them. Those two looked at me like they hadn't had a warm body in their beds in...ever. They're not the only ones. And really, I'm just not that beautiful."

"It's complicated," Thomas said. "It's not the life span alone. There are other biological adaptations at play. But to explain them.... I don't know how experienced you are in certain areas." He avoided her gaze. "I don't want to offend you."

Lena wanted to laugh. She would have if she wasn't so sick of being ogled by everything attached to a penis. Here in the Ward School, there were a lot of them. "Let's say I'm experienced enough. Please explain."

His face moved from side to side as he thought about how he wanted to phrase it. "So, look, your parents. She was a Spark and he wasn't. Did you never notice how powered men reacted to your mother, Lena? Or how they treated your father for having the audacity to be with her?"

She stared at the man for a moment. Male Sparks came on to her mother? What the Dust was he getting at? "I...no. I stayed inside. I never saw them interact with anyone."

He nodded in resignation. "Right." Thomas took a deep breath and shrugged. He looked at her now, his voice strong and direct. "And have you never been with a Spark yourself?"

"What does this have to do with anything?"

"Have you?"

"No, not—no." She crossed her arms and refused to think about Jackson. "I've avoided other Sparks like the plague. I couldn't risk being with someone who could recognize how strong I am."

"Okay." He nodded, licked his lips, and muttered to himself, "How did I get stuck with this conversation?"

She waited. Her brows were raised, and her amusement at his

discomfort twitched her lips upward.

He looked up at her, his own lips curved into a wry smile. "Don't laugh," he ordered her. "It's not funny. Look, it's like this. The Dust, the nanobots, they react to each other, a certain electric or magnetic pull. And they react also to those who can use them. We—" he gestured between the two of them "—and all of us, we have more Dust in, on, and around us than the unpowered. They prefer us. And the attraction grows with the Spark's power."

"Okay. Got it."

"And there are certain involuntary...discharges...that occur during times of heightened arousal."

"Right." She remembered how the Dust pooled within her in the safe house with Reyes. It had seemed drawn to where their bodies touched. Later, she'd definitely felt the involuntary discharges sparking and flaring when Jackson kissed her, and the frenetic reaction of the Dust when Reyes interrupted, as if it remembered him. That sensation got more intense?

"So, if you ever noticed or if anyone ever told you—"

"I got it," Lena said.

He moved his hands up in a gesture to appease her. "Okay. So, when you're with another Spark, it is more pleasurable. And the intensity of the experience grows with the power of the...participants. *Significantly*." The emphasis he put on the final word caused her brows to raise nearly to her hairline.

"So...what you're saying is, every single man I walk past in this place who gets a peek at my aura starts drooling and wondering if being with me would be a brains-on-the-wall final moment of glory?"

Was that why Jackson couldn't resist her advances? Not because he wanted her, but because of ...nanites? Had she been that wrong? Lena felt a wash of confusion as strong as nausea. No wonder he'd volunteered to go out on field maneuvers.

Thomas winced. "Yes..."

"Yes? But? Am I wrong?"

"Yes. You're not wrong. But look, it's more than the physical response. Although there's never been a woman like you, so that response isn't insignificant." His eyes were narrowed now, and he spoke rapidly and forcefully. Was this a favorite subject? "The things that you are capable of, the promise of what you can bring to us as a whole, and yes, perhaps, to one individual. If you choose well, your children will be powerful beyond—well, that's the draw. It's...you're the ideal. You're the great... tantalizing...possibility."

"I see." She did see. But she wasn't sure what to make of it. "So we're all slaves to the Dust we carry? Like, uber-Spark pheromones or something? Funny. Reyes doesn't seem all that affected."

He made a face. "Alex has more discipline than any ten men put together. He feels it. We all feel it. It's a matter of control."

She nodded. Control. That she understood.

"Thank you, Thomas, for being honest with me. It helps to know what's behind all of...." She waved her hand at the elevator, referring to what had just gone down with the guardian and the agent. It also explained Jackson's battle. She sighed. The confusion settled in her chest, heavy. Why couldn't someone have told her all of this *before* she'd fallen for one of them?

Oh. Really? Just one of them?

"You're welcome. Now...I promised you fresh air with your dinner." He clapped his hands together and opened the heavy door for her, evidently happy to have the conversation behind them.

After a short trip through more corridors, they passed through a locked security entry. Thomas keyed it and ushered her through ahead of him.

Sunlight flowed through the opening to spill at her feet. She scooted into a wide atrium. The main entry from the outside world opened across the room. Access to the rest of the area was blocked by a wide console running the width of the space that was manned by a pair of serious-faced young men. The back wall was glass, through which sunlight poured in. On the other side of the windows, a sheltered courtyard and garden stretched away from the rear of the building.

She tilted her head back to feel the sunlight on her face. You didn't realize how much you could miss that warmth until you spent a few weeks without it. She sighed happily and looked around again. They would be eating outside, he'd said. In the back garden?

One of the young agents guarding the entry left his post and approached. Thomas held up his hand, curtailing any salute. The guard opened the doors for the two of them. Lena stepped out into paradise, and everything else receded.

Benched tables were set at intervals around a wide stone patio. Most were occupied. Heads turned as they entered. She didn't care. Let them get an eyeful. She stared out at the grounds beyond the patio.

Paths led away from the patio to wind through tall, soft, pale grass waving in a summer breeze. Bushes and cacti were beginning to bloom. Mature mesquites, gnarled and bent, reached to the sky. Out at the end of the garden was a nothingness that spoke of a cliff edge. Beyond it, the desperate brown and red of the desert she loved stretched far below. Craggy, rocky desolation for miles, and then the jutting dark hulk of mountains rose in the distance. It was gorgeous.

She leaned her head back again. Eyes closed, she let the warm desert breeze brush over her skin. She could smell moisture, ozone, and dirt in the wind. She opened her eyes and looked out across the wide open land to the mountains. "Rain is coming."

Thomas tapped her arm and pointed past her. She looked at the sky beyond his fingers. Dark clouds smudged down to earth in a purple curtain. If anyone ever found a cure for drama of the heart, she'd bet it would include warm sunshine and the smell of rain in the desert.

She turned back to him with a wide smile. "I could smell it. I've missed that smell."

He nodded, serious-eyed and quiet. "It is intoxicating." He glanced around, as if aware of the curious, measuring looks from every table.

She was used to them.

He tilted his head to the side in a way that reminded her of Reyes. "Our food's here."

She looked where he indicated and noticed a young woman from the kitchens unloading covered plates and cups from a cart.

She crossed to the table behind him and sat, smiling at the girl. "What are we having?"

"Well, I hope you don't mind, but before he left, I asked Jackson what your favorite meal was. He said breakfast."

The young woman pulled back the cover from the plate before Lena.

It was pancakes, with thick-cut bacon and shiny rounds of sausage surrounding a small bowl. Lena dipped her finger and brought it to her mouth. "Maple syrup! And it's warm. They never put maple syrup out at dinner." Jackson might be gone on maneuvers, but he'd still managed to send her a gift. She flashed Thomas a wide, happy smile before turning to thank the girl who'd trundled it all up from the kitchen.

"Right." Thomas sat, glancing around at the rapt faces around them. "Well, clearly we'll have to rectify that."

SIXTEEN

When Reyes came for Lena in the morning, she was up and almost ready. Last night, Thomas had warned her that she'd have a full day of lessons, both as student and instructor. She'd already eaten her second round of breakfast in twelve hours. When Alex knocked and entered, she rose from her chair. He stood inside the door as she bent to tug on her boots.

"Did you enjoy dinner last night?" He kept his voice bland.

She straightened up. Yes, he was amused. He'd already been to see Thomas.

She marched up to him, planted her hands on her hips, and tilted her head back. "You could have told me, Reyes."

His lips twitched, and his eyes sparked with humor, but he mostly managed to keep from laughing. "First, enough with this 'Reyes' garbage. If you can call Jackson by his name, you can use mine. Second…" He paused, clearly trying a little harder not to laugh. "That is not the kind of thing you'd have wanted to hear from me of all people."

"Is that right?"

"Yes. It is right." He *was* laughing. "Pretty sure the last thing you want to hear from the guy who ruined your life is that you're irresistible."

"Irresistible." Lena crossed her arms over her chest and shook her head. "Ha. I remember you resisting just fine when you thought I was propositioning you back in the safe house. And you could have mentioned it then. Or when I started glowing and we were discussing my power."

The smile faded from his face. He cocked his head. "My ribs were broken. And I could not have mentioned it then. That glow was almost my undoing."

She pulled away a little at the intensity in his face. Her breath caught.

Then Reyes blinked, and it was gone. He tilted his head back and smiled again. "We never did find out what caused that, did we?" The question was light. "Remind me to ask Sam if he knows."

She reminded herself to breathe. "Sam?"

She was willing to be distracted. She had managed to convince herself that Reyes was nothing more than the weapon he'd made of himself. She was pretty sure it wasn't safe to do otherwise.

"Mm hm. That's who we're going to see. If you're ready?"

As Lena preceded him out the door, she could have sworn he made a small sound of frustration, or perhaps relief. When she turned back to him in the hallway, he was all business. He led her back the way she'd gone with Thomas the night before, making light conversation the whole way, telling her about the repairs to the damage she'd caused to the Council building and the ongoing search for her in and around Azcon.

They crossed into the atrium again, and the sunlight dazzled her. She looked longingly out at the garden, but Reyes...Alex...crossed the atrium lobby and through a locked entry point into a corridor behind it.

The corridor here was unlike any other in the fort. Thick, wall-to-wall carpeting stretched from one end of the floor to the other. The air felt cool and dry, unlike the humid underground air pumped through the main complex. The lights were recessed into the ceiling.

"What is this place?" She didn't know why she whispered, but it seemed appropriate in the hushed atmosphere of the hallway.

"Well, officially it doesn't exist anymore. If it is ever spoken of, it's remembered as Barracks Hall 13. The guys who lived here—" Alex made a little shrug and smiled "—they called it Sunny Acres."

She frowned. "Sunny Acres?"

Alex nodded. He gestured her forward with his head and padded down five paired doorways to one on the left. Once she joined him, he put his hand on the knob. He didn't turn it. He stared down at her for a moment as if trying to gain some measure of her. Finally, he gave her a bemused smile.

"You're about to meet Sam."

She nodded. "Yes. Sam. Who is…?"

"Sam's a friend of mine. He was one of my teachers. Later, he became…let's call him a mentor." He took a deep breath and laughed softly. Was he laughing at himself? "He was a light to a boy who didn't think light existed anymore. He was a light to a lot of boys."

She felt her brows rising. "Wait. You were a boy once? You had a *friend*?"

He rolled his eyes. "Cute. You'll see. Sam is going to blow your mind."

The room was hushed and comfortable like the hallway. Quiet, humming machines clustered around an empty bed. The wall closest to them was lined floor to ceiling with shelves bursting with books. The view directly across from them, however, captured her attention.

It was a garden. Or at least, it had been painted to look like one. A tree painted into the corner leaned out over the rest of the scene, sheltering it with thin, arching branches covered in pale green leaves. Grass moved out away from the wall, and hedges of flowers appeared to bloom as far as the eye could see. Birds seemed to hover, captured in mid-flight.

An ancient man hunched in a wheeled chair facing the wall. He stared out. His scalp shone through thin wisps of white hair, pale skin mottled with age spots like craters on the surface of the moon. His hunched back bent him forward, and his body bobbed with constant movement. Even his hands, misshapen fingers curled upon themselves, moved on the arms of the wheelchair, silent tap and then retreat. Tap. Retreat.

She felt her breath catching in her throat. She remembered Erwin's quiet voice the day before. *The oldest of them began dying sixty years ago.* The oldest of them began dying. What about the youngest?

Alex moved across to him. "Sam?"

In his quiet voice, she detected respect and affection.

"Who's there?" The old man's head came up and turned very slightly. His voice was strong, if a little breathy. "Is that you, Alex? Come around where I can see you."

He moved around the wheelchair to squat in front of it and smile up. "Hi, Sam."

"Hello, Alex. It's been awhile. I've missed you. Missed our talks."

Lena stepped forward and came around the wheelchair. She met his eyes, shiny and keen like a bird's. His body might be failing, but his mind remained bright and sharp. She sensed intelligence there, and humor, and a wonderful, comforting sense of humanity.

"Alex. You brought me a guest?"

He nodded. "This is Lena. Lena, this is Sam."

She leaned forward to touch the back of Sam's left hand where it tapped upon and retreated from the wheelchair arm closest to her. She held it for a moment. "Hello, Sam."

"You brought me a *pretty* guest!" His thin white brows rose in delight. He turned back to Alex, his lips twitching with amusement in a face crisscrossed with the seams of age and humor. Sam winked at the younger man. "You can go now. We'd like to be alone."

In spite of the tension and confusion curling inside her, or perhaps because of it, a laugh burst from her. Sam reached his shaking hand out for Lena's. Alex glanced at her for permission before he took her hand and placed it in Sam's. The old man's fingers closed around hers, and he closed his eyes. She could feel the Dust stirring within her, the almost-whisper at the back of her mind getting louder with his touch.

When Sam opened his eyes again, tears filled them. One rolled down his dry cheek. "Alex...," he breathed. "You've found a treasure."

Alex bounced in his squat. He swallowed and nodded his head. "I know." He glanced up at her and away. "But she's confused, Sam. She's been told a lot of lies. I don't think she knows what to believe. Or who. So I brought her to you."

"To me?"

He smiled. "You know the truth. You lived it. Tell her, like you told me."

The old man laughed, a dry, huffing sound that moved his entire body. "I had years with you. And you still didn't believe. Not all the way. Not until you saw with your own eyes."

"Yeah, well, that's the next step." Alex leaned in with an affectionate hand on Sam's thin arm. "Will you talk to her?"

"Sure I'll talk to her. What else do I have to do but stare at this wall?" He made his huffing laugh again.

Alex stood. "Do you need anything?"

"I wouldn't turn down some nice water. What about you, Lena? Can he get you anything?"

She shook her head. "I'm fine, thanks."

Alex crossed behind her, sliding one hand across her shoulders as he went. She shivered, and his attention dipped, noticing the involuntary response. He pulled his hand away and left.

Lena knelt down beside Sam. He regarded her, face serious. He still hadn't released her hand.

"Alex is a good man with a thankless job." His voice was firm. "But he does it so no one else has to. Remember that."

"I will."

He nodded. Once the bobbing motion started, it took him awhile to stop. "How much have they told you?" His voice had gone wispy and wan again.

She shrugged, at a loss as to where to start. "How it all happened. What the Dust really is. What we are. Where we came from." She hesitated. "A little bit about me."

"The basics." The grimace on his seamed face seemed an exaggerated expression of impatience. "So I'll start at the beginning of the end, then. My beginning. I was picked for the program when I was a kid, straight out of basic training. They were selecting for guys who had strong electromagnetic brain waves. Guys who could ace a biofeedback test. Once we were in, it wasn't just training, though. They manipulated our DNA." At her blank look, he explained, "They played with our genes, the stuff that makes us *us*. Made us stronger. Created a new dominant trait.

"I had celebrated my twenty-sixth birthday three days before we were called down. We were a secret unit, you know. An elite unit. They tried to play it cool, but after we ended the Pakistan Insurgency without a single casualty—dropped in the 'bots, keyed them to target human energy signatures, knocked 'em all out and sent in the ground crew to gather 'em up like apples off a tree. Well, we knew we were it then. The next generation." Sam smiled. It was wistful, and it faded quickly.

"We didn't go to the sites. Cloud servers don't have to move. We stayed here, actually. The scientists were the ones who went out to the sites with the bots. They were the ones who burned when it all went up a day later." He fell quiet for a moment. "We lost a lot of the country that day. We got it all under control as fast as we could. We found what we hoped was a solution, but we were operating under pressure." He smiled thinly. "It wasn't perfect, but the explosions stopped. The fires died back, from infernos to slag." His voice drifted off as he remembered.

Lena sat quietly, watching the pain move across his face.

"And then everything stopped. We didn't have any information, but we could figure it out. It was dark for a long time." She didn't think he meant only the lack of power and lights. "The first winter was brutal. No heat. No fire. Nothing. It was hard enough to make it where we were out west. I don't want to think about what it must have been like for people up north. But we did think about it, all of us who stayed to keep working. We knew people were dying out there. We wanted to get it all back. All we managed to get back was external combustion. Fire. Steam. And it took us most of a year. By then, we were falling apart."

He fell quiet again. It took a little longer for him to start again this time.

"I made my way to Canev Relocation Center. Tried to help, but I barely stayed alive. We had no hope. No reason to go on. By the time I noticed everyone else getting older and I wasn't, I just moved on."

Alex returned then, moving quietly into the room. He carried a chair in one hand and balanced a tray with a pitcher and cups with the other. He set the tray on the bed and poured Sam a glass of water. He brought it over, setting it in Sam's hand and wrapping his fingers around it. Then he set the chair beside Sam. "Sit," he told Lena as he sank onto the floor. He stretched his legs out and settled his hands across his lap.

She moved into the chair.

Sam sipped at his cup. He flashed a smile of gratitude at Alex and raised the glass to him. "It was a long time of just wandering then. I saw a lot of things. Some good. Most bad. One day, one of Peller's recruiters found me." Something in the way he said the word 'recruiters' told her Sam regretted that day. "I joined up. I was happy to. I wanted a chance to put right what had happened. I was ready. Ready. Some of the older guys, they weren't so sure. They told me Peller had been CIA. He'd been bounced from the program for some unethical behavior. They didn't know what. I didn't listen." He dragged in a long breath and let it out. "He knew what we could do. And he had big plans on how we'd help him fix it all." He nodded his head again. "And he did. He fixed it all." He raised his face to Lena. She could see it still angered him. "Except he didn't. We did it. He took the credit. We all felt so guilty about what had happened that we let him."

He fell silent. Alex watched him. She waited.

Eventually, Sam sipped then he took a ragged breath. "I don't want to talk about the breeding programs." His head dipped as he hid his face.

He's ashamed.

"It's okay," Alex told him, "You don't have to."

Sam nodded, head bobbing in decreasing arcs. "The program led to all of you, of course, and to this school. I retired here, to help teach the strongest of our descendants. So many children...."

His voice drifted off. His head lifted, and his gaze moved over her face and hair. "You could be one of mine, you know? With those freckles and eyes. You could be one of my...great grandchildren? Great-great?"

His forehead creased as he pondered the generations. He shrugged, and then his face split in a mischievous smile. He pointed to Alex with a shaking hand. "Not this one, though. He looks just like that bastard Castillo. Bred true, without a doubt. You never met a vainer, more egotistical sumbitch in your life." The huffing laugh had moved into a wheezing cackle.

Alex grinned. Apparently, he'd heard this before. Lena sent him a questioning look, but he merely rubbed his chin and winked at her. She turned back to Sam.

He settled back, moving his hips slightly to find a more comfortable position. "Peller always meant us to serve them. We were tools. *Peller's Pistons.*" His voice was strong again and angry. "From the beginning, it's what they intended. We started willingly, but when some of us tried to walk away—" He shook his head and lifted a hand, one finger raised. His lips tucked back into his mouth as he tried to compose himself enough to continue. "Then the prisons started. And now the collars. Did you tell her about the collars?"

Alex shook his head. "No. She'll see with her own eyes soon enough. But..." He hesitated before plunging on, "She's already been on one of the tables."

Sam went still. His watery eyes stared up at the younger man. His chin crumpled. "The tables? They had their hands on your pretty girl?" He shook his head.

He turned to Lena and the violence in his face shocked her.

Even after he began speaking again, his voice full of rage and grief, his head went on shaking minutely. "But look at you. Here. Strong. Strong, not like my Miranda." His voice broke, and he cleared his throat, a rheumy sound. "She was a strong girl, so feisty, but not strong like you are." His focus moved over her in the particular way Sparks had when they were looking at an aura and not a person.

"And she was too young. I had no business taking up with

her. I was almost a hundred and fifty years old by then. I knew what they were capable of." His voice moved higher, thinning with grief and tears.

Alex got to his feet and went to Sam, crouching before him and putting a hand on the man's slight shoulder. "Sam," he murmured, "it's okay. We can come back later."

Sam looked up at him, his face dark as he began losing himself to the memories. "They take what you love. They twist and break it. And then they throw it back to you and wait for you to break."

"I know, Sam. I'm sorry. I wish it was easier to focus on the good you had. I'm sorry our visit brought this back again."

The old man waved his hand and took several deep breaths, as if preparing to continue. But in a moment, his gaze unfocused, and he stared ahead. His eyes moved as if he watched something before him that they couldn't see. He closed them as he curled in toward his lap, crumpling in on himself, and he waved his hand at Alex again. This time the wave of dismissal was final.

Alex leaned his head in and whispered in Sam's ear. Sam shook his head. Alex sat back on his heels, sighed, and shook his head at Lena.

She rose and leaned in to press her hand to Sam's shoulder before crossing to wait in the hall.

Alex took the tray with the pitcher of water and set it on the chair she'd just vacated. He moved them within easy reach of Sam and then joined her. He turned back and gently closed the door behind them.

"Is he going to be okay?"

"Yeah." He took an uneven breath and ran his hands through his hair. "He's had a long time to live with what happened to Miranda. Of course, he only touched on the part I wanted you to hear. About what we're doing and why, so you can trust—"

"It's okay. I get it."

He turned to her, dark and inscrutable as he searched her face. "I spent a lot of time up here growing up. More than was officially sanctioned. I heard about Miranda a lot." He reached out and silently tapped his fingertips against Sam's door before withdrawing his hand. "C'mon. We have a lot to get done today before I have to be back in Azcon. Daylight's burning."

He moved past her, his feet making no sound on the carpeted floor.

SEVENTEEN

Alex led the way outside, but Lena hesitated behind him. He turned back. She squinted against the bright light, glancing side to side to check for others using the patio. He cursed silently. Thomas would have to call a meeting. She shouldn't be uncomfortable here where he'd promised her a safe place. The men of Fort Nevada would just have to have to learn to deal with her presence and with what it did to them. He had.

He walked backward and called out to her, "What's the hold up? C'mon. Thomas said you liked it out here. So move it." He turned back to head up one of the red gravel paths.

Her footsteps crunched down the path behind him.

He wound around on the path for two more turns and then arrived at his destination, one of his favorite spots in the garden. A gravel circle created a side area off of the path, somewhat hidden by a pair of desert willows flanking the opening. Benches faced each other from the edges of the gravel. He positioned himself in front of one bench and bounced slightly on the balls of his feet as he waited for her, psyching himself up for both the focus and the pain.

Lena entered the court and wandered toward the other bench, keeping her eye on him.

"I want you to try to hurt me," he told her. He tapped his chest. "Hit me."

She raised her hands up between them.

Did she think he wanted her to slap him? He rolled his eyes.

"No, Lena. Not with your hands." He smirked. "As if you could."

Her hands popped to her hips in attitude.

Yeah, she was tough. She'd lived in the desert on her own, chopped her own wood, trapped and hunted her food, defended herself and her home from animals and men. And he admired it. But being strong was entirely different from being able to fight. He hadn't meant to insinuate she was weak, but he guessed that's what she took from his comment.

She glowered at him.

He laughed. "You're adorable." If he had to make her angry to make this work, he was willing. Of course, since he wasn't exactly sure this would work, perhaps he should tone it down a little. "No, seriously. I dropped the defense I worked out. I've been practicing getting it up fast, in response to an attack, but I need to see if it works. So, hit me. With the Dust."

She arched a brow at him. "Why? I'm the only one who can attack like this, and unless you keep pissing me off, I'm not coming after you."

He made a face. "Actually, Thomas once managed something similar years ago. And I'm becoming more and more convinced you may not be the only one now, either. Or at least, not for much longer." He stood straight again and tapped his chest, grinning at her. "So, c'mon, you still mad at me? Even a little? Hit me."

He barely finished his sentence. His lungs and muscles shut down. His body stiffened, inside and out, as the muscles froze. She withheld the pain this time, but she waited impassively as he struggled. He pulled in his focus and visualized what he wanted.

My body. My response.

The squeezing in his lungs cleared, and his contracted muscles eased. He tilted his head back and drew in a deep breath. His hands unclenched. His head swung around on his neck. After a moment, he grinned at her, pleased with her raised brows and impressed expression. "Told you. Now do it again, but switch it up. Do something I wouldn't expect."

Lena nodded at him.

Alex doubled over at the sudden stabbing, twisting, acid burn of pain in the muscles and cells of his gut. He grabbed his belly, eyes wide. After a moment, he dropped to a crouch and groaned. How was he supposed to focus through this pain? He could hear himself panting, and he focused on that instead. He counted, visualized turning the Dust away from its attack, and used his sawing breaths as a countdown. Thirty seconds later, he raised his head, dazed but recovering. Did his face reflect how sick he felt?

"That wasn't nice," he said. "Another few seconds, and I would have shit myself." He couldn't believe he'd admitted that. He couldn't believe it had almost happened.

She tried not to laugh but failed. "Sorry," she told him, unrepentant.

It was his turn to glower at her.

"You told me to do it," she protested. "And besides, you did stop it. You're pretty good at this."

He gingerly stood, holding his stomach. "That was brutal." He tilted his head back and forth and swallowed. "Remember that one if you're ever in a tight spot."

"Absolutely." She paused. "Wanna go again?"

Obviously, she enjoyed this.

"Huh." He took a couple of steps to the side and back, trying to help the muscles in his lower belly relax. "Why don't I try to hit you? I've been working on it, too. I can actually make some sparks across a room now."

Lena shrugged. She was obviously of the opinion that sparks did not an attack make, and he'd been thoroughly unsuccessful at learning how to attack thus far. Everyone she'd tried to teach had been. They couldn't get it.

The failure frustrated him. They could heal. They could defend. They were getting better and better at doing regular things from a distance. Not a single one of them could learn her attacks.

Alex cleared his throat and prepared himself. He pushed the breath out of his lungs, reaching out with his mind to the Dust inside of her, on her skin, floating free in the air around her. He tried talking to the Dust within her, the way he'd recently learned to talk to his own.

It didn't respond.

Frustrated, he raised his inner voice.

Still nothing.

He took a long breath, closed his eyes, and tried again, calmer.

He couldn't sense even a hint of a response.

She cleared her throat, and the quiet noise echoed through their small clearing like a rock falling.

Alex opened his eyes.

"Not working?" Her soft question oozed disappointment. Clearly, she felt the failures, too.

He shook his head.

"Try again," she suggested.

He did.

Alex tried over and over, until his head throbbed. Finally, he sank down onto the bench behind him. He rested his aching head in his hands and breathed. When he looked up again, she had taken a seat across the little clearing from him. From her face, she had something on her mind.

"You have questions." He made a 'give it to me' gesture, flipping his fingers toward himself.

"I do have questions," she answered. "About Sam."

"Okay. Shoot."

"First...he said Peller was in the CIA. What's the CIA?"

"From what he's told us, it was a government organization of agents who watched and listened and kept order, but used questionable tactics."

"So, basically, exactly like all of you?"

Yeah, he walked right into that one.

He winced and tried to shake his head. The movement stalled, and he barked a laugh. "I suppose." He could hear how guarded his own response was. He had to work on that. Somehow, at some point, she'd have to learn to trust him.

"So our government was founded by a shady, deceitful agent. And the people who are trying to fix the system are...agents...who are basically the same thing?"

Fort Nevada was not filled with deceit. "No. No, we are not basically the same thing." Alex leaned back, his hand thumping on the bench beside him in frustration. He opened his mouth to speak, but she waved him off.

"It's okay. I'm not trying to antagonize you. I only wanted to know what he was referring to. So, my second question is a little more personal." She shifted on her bench and looked down at the ground. "The breeding program made all of us...all of the Sparks? So we're all descended from the same group of men?"

He nodded. "More or less. The ability is a native one. All humans could have it. But yes, the strongest of us are descended from the men the scientists...refined."

"How many were there?"

"Originally? Sixty-four. But only fifty-two of them participated." It wasn't a big number, which was why they had built in the safeguards.

"Fifty-two? That's not many."

"They keep records. They were very careful, especially in the beginning. It's one of the reasons why the Wards are sent out to new Zones when they become agents. And why they can't go back." The old pain twinged. With her, he didn't have to keep it from his voice. She understood.

"New blood."

He nodded.

"And it's the real reason all of you want me?"

He could see the fresh wound on her face.

"I can't speak for Jackson," he answered her. "But I'd be lying if I told you it wasn't a factor. Terrible as it was, the reason the breeding program was so effective is the Spark breeds true. Your Spark will, too. And as a weapon against the Council, a future filled with Sparks who can do what you do, maybe *more*? I'm sorry. That's more important to us than feelings."

"My Spark will *breed true*?" She shook her head. "You're all assuming I'll allow it to breed at all."

Alex felt his brows draw down. "Allow it? You can control your fertility—of course you can control that." As soon as he'd seen her expression, mocking him for thinking she wouldn't use her gifts to make her own life easier, he'd amended the question. "Here we all were, thinking the only issue would be who you chose. But it isn't just who, it's also when."

"No. It's *if.* I don't even know that I want children, and it's certainly not going to happen until I tell the Dust to allow it." She looked down at her hands.

Because she'd turned her face to the ground, he almost missed her next, soft question.

"Is that why Jackson kept backing off? Thomas decided Jackson was an inappropriate choice and he just...caved?" She nodded, a faraway look on her face, and it seemed to be an answer to her own question. "I thought he cared. I thought...."

She needed comforting. He didn't want to do it. What was the point of telling her a lie? Love gave the world a weapon it could turn on you. They'd both lived that.

But he found himself rising to his feet and crossing to her, anyway. He lowered himself to a crouch in front of her, taking both her small hands in one of his and using the first fingers of his other hand to tilt her chin up.

"If Jackson won't take a stand for you, then he's a fool," he said. He could tell her that much. It was the truth, even if the kid would have been bucking Alex's own orders. "A *fool.* And any man who is given the chance to win a piece of your heart and doesn't claim it...." He shook his head. "Worse than a fool."

"Is that right?" She searched his face, as if looking for the lie. Not finding it, she softly smiled.

The urge to lift his fingers a few inches to trace those lips surged through him. Instead, he stood up and backed away. He gestured for her to stand.

"C'mon. I have an idea. I want to try something."

She sighed.

"Seriously, I have a new idea. C'mon, get up."

Get up, Lena. I need the focus.

She rose and stood with her arms crossed, waiting.

He focused, grateful for the shift in mood. Instead of trying to affect the Dust inside the body, as she did in her attacks, he'd try for the Dust attracted to the outside of her. Perhaps the Dust living inside was simply too protective of their very strong host? He breathed out and reached with his mind.

Nothing happened, exactly like all the times before.

"Um." She wrinkled her brow. "Did you start yet?"

Alex groaned in frustration. He dropped his gaze to the ground at her feet, not wanting to see her expression after the latest failure. *Push, dammit!*

A flash of light and heat arced out in jagged white light from the ground. It threw Lena off her feet, over the bench and to the ground.

He stared, slack-jawed for a bare second. In two long steps he crossed the clearing and hopped onto the bench looking down at her.

She wheezed in an attempt to reclaim her breath.

He jumped down to her side, hands moving over her head and neck, and then down her sides, to be sure she was otherwise okay. She projected such a huge persona he was shocked at how fragile she felt under his hands.

She batted at him weakly.

Once he'd reassured himself she wasn't broken, he wrapped his hands around each of her thighs and pulled up her legs to inspect her feet.

The indignity of it helped her find her voice. "Get off of me!"

"Lay still! I could have hurt you!" He barked the words, guilt and dismay making his voice harsh.

"I'm fine."

She wasn't. Her voice came as a weak thread of air. She sounded breathless, small. She pushed his hands away, and then pushed at him as she sat up. He crouched at her side, refusing to give way. His heart still pounded.

With a faint grunt of disgust, she scooted herself back from him. She brushed the worst of the gravel and dirt from her hair with her fingertips. When she finally looked up at him, she seemed to freeze for a moment at whatever she saw in his face. "Reyes. Alex. I'm *fine*."

He propped one elbow on his knee in front of him and rubbed his mouth with the back of his hand. His eyes closed then opened on a gust of air. "Dust, Lena. I could have hurt you."

"Yeah." She agreed. "You could have." Her voice changed, and he could hear the sly grin under her words. "You really could have."

The mischief on her face was contagious.

"I did it."

"You did something." She wiggled a bit and then made a move to rise.

He jumped to his feet to help. His pull and her slight weight made her sail up into his side. He wrapped his arm around her to steady her.

She grinned up at him, mouth opened to make another wise-ass remark, no doubt.

He focused on her mouth just a beat too long.

She closed it, biting her lower lip. That wasn't a great help.

She stared back up at him, her eyes wide and her body very still. Before Alex had a chance to process the movement or talk himself down, his body shifted, turning to fully face her. He slid his other hand up to cup the back of her head, lifting her face as he lowered his.

Just a taste. One taste. I have to know.

The first contact of their lips was softer and more tentative than he intended, but the heat of it flashed down through his body. He pressed deeper, pulling her to him as he sampled. The heat responded, a spark spiraling up, rising through him and into her through the gentle contact of lips and tongue.

When it flashed back to him from her, the spark had grown. It slammed into him with the force and heat and intensity of a grounding, electricity arcing between them where they were in contact. It danced along his skin. Alex existed at that ecstatic line between pleasure and pain. His brain—always weighing, balancing, five steps ahead—simply stopped.

He was sensation. Electric heat chased electric heat, moving over them and flaring within them as their Dust wound together.

The sound of his breath stuttering out slammed him back to reality.

What the fuck are you doing?! His brain re-engaged.

He tore his mouth from hers, jumping guiltily away and lifting his hands up. The last flares of their shared power crackled against his lips. He could see the same blue-white flares popping across hers.

She didn't move. She was still, frozen, mouth still slightly open.

He was pretty sure he wore the same look, if thunderstruck stupefaction could be described as a "look."

He sucked in a breath, then cleared his throat. The noise seemed to snap her out of her trance.

You put her in a trance. He wasn't sure if his inner voice was outraged or smug.

Lena backed away, ducking her head and shoving her hair back behind her ears. It was her nervous tell. In a moment, her hair would slip back out, falling around her face again. He could feel his lips curl up in a smile.

No. Down, boy.

She laughed, a nervous sound. She turned away to move back around the bench, hands tucking her hair behind her ears again. She inspected the charred, scattered blast area where her feet had been, scuffing it with one boot.

"Damn, Alex." Her voice was husky. She cleared her throat, too. "At least I held back when I hit you." She rubbed her tail bone, underscoring that she meant his successful attack and not the insane heat of the moment before.

His brain sent her a silent, steady stream of gratitude for not making a thing out of the ill-conceived kiss.

You're a moron, Alejandro Reyes.

"You were not holding back." The memory of the pain in his belly warred with the more recent experience, but not for long. The warmth of their camaraderie, of her unrestrained laugh, of that impossible heat, felt too good. How the fuck did Jackson manage?

"I was mostly holding back." She finally looked up at him, expression mischievous instead of stupefied.

"I was...mostly pissed off."

"I see that." She scuffed at the blackened ground with one foot again and grinned at him. "You did it!"

"I did." He couldn't help the sly smile that spread over his face as he gloated. "And Thom is gonna be so pissed I did it first."

She cocked her head and narrowed her eyes. "We are talking about knocking me on my ass, right? And not...."

"No, no," Alex said. "Not talking about that. At all. Ever."

Lena laughed again. "Agreed."

Should he be insulted?

EIGHTEEN

Lena had laughed and agreed that they should never mention that kiss again. Why was it all she could think about? And why were all of the boys and men in the halls cutting her such a wide berth this morning? Usually they stared and whispered, the Wards sometimes pausing to watch as she moved past. This morning, they were avoiding her. Perhaps it had all been a dream or a joke. Not a single one of them was drawn to her, or her Dust.

Not freaking likely.

Reyes—Alex—had kissed her. The one man who had zero interest in anything other than her capacity to move their cause forward. The one man who had spent his life obsessed with and moving toward a single goal. His discipline was legendary. And somehow whatever Lena was had overcome his discipline and singular focus, and he'd kissed her.

No, he hadn't just kissed her. He'd melted her. The heat of it hadn't been an electric response, it had turned those little robots into molten metal burning through her flesh and veins and consuming everything she knew about feeling good. She'd been rooted to the spot. She'd been lost.

And then he'd jumped away, and his shock and dismay had been written on his face. So she'd pretended it didn't matter. She'd laughed. And when he'd said they should never mention it again, she'd agreed. Of course she had. How could she articulate how devastating that kiss had been, least of all to Alex?

And it wasn't just because it had been so far beyond delicious it made her chest ache, or that the devastation washed into guilt as she thought of Jackson—she hadn't been the aggressor, but she hadn't stopped Alex, either. Both the deliciousness and the guilt were part of it. But the devastation went deeper.

It meant she really was everything they said.

It meant she would never, ever know if anyone wanted her for her. How could she know if the feelings any Spark felt for her were true, or if they were merely a reflection of her power, her so-called gift? If Alex had been overcome, what chance did anyone else have?

Head down, she nearly walked into a young woman hurrying in the other direction. Lena lifted her head and opened her mouth to apologize. The young woman blanched, stuttered an apology, and stumbled in her haste to get away. Lena stared after her.

"I think you scared her."

She whipped her head around.

Jackson stood just ahead, body slightly turned as if he'd stopped when he'd seen her coming and hadn't decided yet which way he wanted to go.

"Which isn't surprising because your face is pretty terrifying this morning." He shifted his weight away from her.

"My face?"

He nodded. "Are you okay?"

She shrugged. No. But that wasn't going to stop her from doing what she'd come to do, which was learn how to make the Council pay. Instead of telling him that, she asked, "How were your overnight maneuvers?"

He took a deep breath, turning his attention to the people skirting them both in the hall. It seemed he had decided not to flee her and her terrifying face, and he eased closer.

"Good," he answered. "I had time to think."

Her stomach twisted. He was struggling to keep his agent mask of neutrality in place. Beneath the mask she could see flashes of guilt, even anger.

"Okay?"

He raised his head. "Look, you're upset about something. This can wait—"

"For me to start to feel better so you can upset me again? That hardly seems fair to anyone but you. If you have something to say, *Agent Lee*, then be a damn agent and say it."

"I asked to be reassigned. You don't need a companion anymore. You know your way around this place just fine. You're learning, adapting, doing everything you're supposed to be doing, and I'm...."

"And you're what?"

"I'm not. I don't want to deal with this anymore, Lena."

"Deal? With this...?"

"The temptation." Jackson swallowed.

She gave him the time to find the words he struggled with, though she wished he'd just get on with it.

"It isn't fair to ask me to resist doing what I want to do."

She smiled. She'd been wrong. The relief flowed like a wash of warm water, clearing away her doubts. "You do want to be with me."

He stared at her. His chest rose and fell as he took a deep breath, held it, and then let it go. "No. I don't. I want you, but I don't want to be *with* you. That's the point."

She froze inside. She could feel her head shaking back and forth, but her heart and lungs were frozen in her chest.

"I can't keep being dragged in by the lure of," he gestured up and down, indicating her. No. Indicating what she was. "I need to keep my eye on the prize. I'm sorry, but you're not it. Not for me."

That was it, wasn't it? The Dust, the power within her, was the lure. Not her. Not Lena. Not anything she herself had to offer. She looked past him and forced herself to focus on lifting her leaden legs, one after the other. She walked around him, down the hall.

"Lena."

She kept going.

"Lena." He moved around her and took her arm to stop her. "Look, the Councilor said he'd reassign me, but today I'm supposed to keep working with you."

"I have a lesson with Thomas," she ground out.

"It's been cancelled. Something came up, and he's dealing with it, whatever it is. He sent me to find you. We're supposed to—"

"I'll sit in his office. Alone."

"Lena." He sighed. "This is why I didn't want to do this. You're the one who said not to wait 'til later."

"I didn't want you to wait until later. And now I don't want to be around you. The two aren't mutually exclusive."

He grimaced and leaned in, his fingers tightening on her arm to keep her from moving past him. "I'm sorry." His voice was tight with emotion. "You don't know how sorry I am. I didn't want to hurt you. Can we just pretend, just for another day—"

She leaned in, too. "No. We can't. Now let go of my arm before I tell the Dust to melt your fucking hand off."

—⁂—

Lashing out at him with the threat had been childish. That didn't mean it wasn't satisfying to see Jackson's eyes widen as he realized she was serious and remembered she could do it. He let her go. She made her way to Thomas's office to wait for the Councilor to be done with whatever issue had come up. Messengers and agents buzzed in and out of his office for the better part of an hour. She tracked them while she waited. In. Out. In. Out. It kept her from having to think about anything that had happened in the last twelve hours.

She was about to give up and return to her room to sulk in privacy when the door opened again, and Thomas stood framed in it, ushering out the last three men who'd entered. He noticed her, and his brows rose.

As the men trooped out of his office, Thomas crossed to her. "Your determination to not do as you're told is a thing to behold."

"I am, in fact, an expert at not doing what I'm told," she answered, with a nod of her head.

"So I hear."

She returned his gaze, waiting. She wasn't sure to what he referred, of course, given her previous comment. She certainly wasn't going to try to guess what it was he'd been hearing and

from whom. She had no desire to tip him off to anything he didn't
know.

But he finally smiled, and the warmth made it all the way up
to his tired eyes. "Come on, then."

She rose and followed him back to his office. Instead of
walking around to the other side of his desk, he crossed to one of
the two chairs in front and collapsed into it. She took the other.

"I hope you weren't waiting because you actually expected a
lesson on control today?"

"I was waiting...." What had she been waiting for? Other
than to avoid everyone else in the school? "I don't know why I
was waiting, but I have zero interest in a lesson on control. So
you're safe."

Thomas nodded at the ceiling. He didn't say anything else.
He was either meditating or waiting for her to say something.

Finally, after what felt like an eternity, she ventured,
"Whatever it is that's going on, is it something I could help with?"

"Do you have any experience doing reconnaissance work?"

"Um. Nope. But I excel at making things go boom."

A smile flitted over his face. "A skill which we will no doubt
make use of." He groaned and pulled himself up, sitting forward
to clasp his hands between his knees. "We've gotten word that
there's going to be a big transfer—of what or whom we don't
know. Because of where it's coming from, we assume it's going
to be Sparks."

"Girls?"

He made a face. "Doubtful. It seemed more dangerous-
transfer big, not girls-who-don't-exist big. If I thought it was that,
I'd be playing it a hell of a lot closer to the vest. And doing more
than reconnaissance."

He'd go get them. Good.

"We know of one secret prison slash test facility, but not any
others. So...it might be a good time to keep an eye on them. We'll
be sending teams every few days."

"Can I go?"

"Didn't we just establish that you have no recon experience?"

"We did. But I have other skills. And you want me to be

involved, right? So involve me."

Thomas shook his head.

"It's just watching. It would be a learning experience. Please."

He looked at her, considering. When he spoke, his words were pointed. "I'd have to send you with Jackson."

She blinked, and her head shifted as if to shake it. She caught herself. "So?"

He tilted his head at her. "You know that I know everything, right? I see all, I hear all, in spite of what everyone else seems to think."

"Well, that's a little scary."

He grinned, baring his teeth.

She could pretend. And then he'd call her out on the lie. Difficult, omniscient man. "If I have to deal with Jackson, fine. I can deal with anything if it means I can be out doing something. Please. I need to help. I need to act. Alex told me I'd be helping."

"I'll think about it." Thomas wasn't promising anything. But that was enough for now.

NINETEEN

The ride to Fort Nevada gave Alex more than enough time to think about the potential folly of the trip and taking Lena north. He changed into his field uniform then sat back, blind to the reflected smear of light from the glassy walls of the tunnel. Since the beginning, when he'd convinced Thomas that fieldwork best employed his talents, Alex had been careful to balance his responsibilities at home with the maintenance of his cover in Azcon. This trip was not an effective balance.

His issue with the trip had nothing to do with securing the position that would make the rest of the operation fall into place. He'd been promoted over Merritt and had spent the last five weeks reveling in the intensity of his dual responsibilities— learning to control his Spark at Fort Nevada in the evenings and the workings of Councilor Three's Security at Azcon during the day.

It also didn't matter that Three believed the four days away were a pre-planned solo hunting trip, meant to keep Alex's skills sharp. A little praise of Three's intelligence and leadership of the Zone, coated with put-on sexual tension to flatter the omnivorous ass? It made Alex's skin crawl, but the Councilor rubberstamped whatever Alex wanted. Alex knew how to play the Councilor. It didn't make leaving Azcon right now any smarter.

It wasn't even the danger of taking Lena so far from Fort Nevada, and so close to potential peril at the prison. She needed to be a part of it all. It was time. This jaunt to run recon on the prison was both an established route and, since the transfer they'd expected hadn't happened, would likely be the most uneventful introduction to their activities they could manage. He agreed with Thomas: it made a good first mission for her.

No, his struggle had started the minute he'd written the message to Thom that he'd be going, too. He'd sent it off with their courier anyway.

When he'd challenged himself on the decision, his explanation was logical. There had simply been too many unknown variables to crop up in the past few months, and Alex wasn't willing to take any chances with Lena.

She needed to take a more active role, yes. It didn't mean they had to be reckless with her. She was too important to their future.

For every question or doubt he raised, he had a ready answer. But what about that constant itch to go back? His mind bobbed and weaved in an attempt to avoid the answer.

The train slowed, and the tunnel lights separated. He ran his hands through his hair in frustration. He still didn't have a solution.

After pulling the train in, he went straight to the ready room. The rest of them were already there. Lena sat at the end of the conference table, legs tucked up and crossed beneath her on the chair. She had on the same grey-green field uniform the rest of them wore, though hers was likely a Ward uniform—the only size that would fit her.

She leaned across the table to peer at the map Thomas and Jackson were reviewing. Her red hair fell around her face. The pressure that had been building inside of Alex began to ease, as it did every night when he showed up to work with her.

Was it the sight of her? Or a proximity response? He'd asked the same questions before.

With a deep breath, he buckled down and focused. Was it Lena? Or the Dust? She was young, damaged, and irritating. But she was also attractive, smart, and strong-willed, and her laugh echoed in his memory when he was far away in Azcon. It didn't really matter whether it was her or the Dust. He was compromised, period.

The final member of their little group sat at the other end of the table. The young Senior Ward might have been twenty years old. If all went well, he wouldn't be doing anything more than hauling the team they were replacing back to Fort Nevada and then returning to wait for Alex and his team to rejoin him after they were done on the surface in Zone Four. Alex approached him first.

The kid sat up straighter in his chair before deciding he should stand. He pushed back and tried to salute. "Senior Ward Third Class Xavier Herrons, sir."

"Third Class?" Alex's brows went up. He turned to look at Thomas, though his next words were directed at the youngster. "And yet you were assigned this duty? Your Guardians must think highly of you." He would have expected a Second Class, at a minimum.

"I hope so, sir. I work very hard."

"See that you do, Ward. I'd hate to see how far down their opinions would slide if you were to lose her."

The kid darted a startled look at Lena across the table and then back to Alex's impassive face again. Herrons swallowed convulsively.

"Alex." Thomas's voice was calm, but his face held both amusement and irritation. "Why don't you come review the route again?"

Alex guffawed. "Because I know the route like the back of my hand. Besides, he's the expert who's been in and out all month." He nodded at Jackson. "He'll be navigating."

Jackson's posture spoke of forced neutrality.

Alex snorted and turned instead to the four packs piled against the wall. He moved through them one by one, rechecking for contents, load and access. He finally stood, hands on hips, and turned back to the table.

Thomas and Jackson had turned their attention back to the map, but Lena wasn't watching them anymore. She watched Alex, arms crossed.

"Oh, hi, Lena." He gave her a warm smile, hoping for one in

return.

"Hello, Alex." She uncrossed her arms and reached up to tuck her hair behind her ears. "Can we get out of here now?"

He raised his brows. What had happened? She was already unhappy. And though they'd managed to build a friendly camaraderie during evening lessons, he knew there was a tension building in her lately that had nothing to do with him or their kiss. Why?

"Safety first," he told her lightly.

Were they putting her safety first? Because he'd had personal contact with her, simply knowing she was out there created a distraction, an irritating constant pull on his attention he couldn't shake. It posed a danger to him and to what they were trying to achieve.

But how much more of a danger was it to Lena?

If he was so affected that he hadn't been able to resist a taste of her lips, how were the others managing without his legendary self-control? He'd pulled himself out of it, and he made himself deal with it during their lessons, even if he hadn't been able to sleep a full night in the month since. Would the others be able to do the same?

She stared at the backpacks, tracing the lines of them, waiting. The eagerness to be on her way, to leave the Fort behind, was obvious. Clearly, they weren't managing well. What was she having to deal with that she hadn't been complaining about?

Thomas looked up. "All right. If we're good to go?" He looked askance at Alex, who nodded. "You all know what we're doing, and how we're doing it. You go up, relieve the team, observe from a distance, wait for your relief, and get out. Got it?"

As soon as the others nodded agreement, Lena abandoned her chair and hoisted her pack. The men hadn't cleared the table yet.

Alex worried for a moment the pack might pull her small frame over. He should have known better.

She settled the pack across her shoulders and looked back at the rest of them standing around the table. "What are you all waiting for?" She arched a brow. "Time's wasting."

And he wondered why he had an itch to get back?

—⚡—

Alex had to reach out and pull Lena back toward himself as she automatically headed for the train she'd arrived on months ago. He smiled and grabbed the back of her pack, steering her away from the front platform toward the back corridor.

"Hey!" she protested, craning her head to look up at him over her shoulder.

"It's this way," he told her, voice mild.

Her gaze swerved to Jackson behind him and the soft, suspect noises he made. Her face darkened. "It's not funny." The words she gritted were icy. She whipped her head forward again and marched ahead of them down the corridor.

He turned to the younger man and raised a brow in question.

Jackson shrugged. He focused straight ahead. "It's fine, sir." He cleared his throat. "No trouble."

Alex stopped. He grabbed the back of Jackson's pack as he had Lena's a moment before and dragged him to a stop. Herrons slowed, but Alex gestured him on with a nod.

Alex returned his attention to Jackson Lee. "There's personal business, and then there's business that could affect my operation. And the second is very much something I need to know. Tell me now." He gave no other option, and no wiggle room.

"There is nothing to know, sir." Jackson told him in his quiet, sensible voice. "No personal business." He paused. "I took care of it like you told me to."

"Did you now?" Alex could hear the skepticism in his own voice.

Jackson grimaced and said, "Yes, sir." He shook his head. "I told her I didn't want to be involved with her, sir, in no uncertain terms. I want to…." He looked down at the floor, miserable. "But I made sure she doesn't believe that anymore."

Good.

"I know who she is. Who she'll be. She's meant for something better. She's meant for *someone* better. Do you know what her children will be? What Councilor Five believes they'll be?"

Alex nodded.

Jackson continued, "She's not meant for me. So I told her.... She's very direct, sir. I was, too."

Jackson shook his head, focusing on Herrons and Lena turning off into the track bay ahead of them. Alex started walking slowly, and Jackson moved with him.

"And it didn't go over so well."

"It did not. I hurt her, sir." Shame and disgust colored his voice.

Alex nodded. He wasn't happy, was he? Lena had been hurt, after all. Why did he feel the need to swallow a grin? "Honestly, kid, I'm impressed as Dust that you were able to walk away."

Jackson grimaced, deeply unhappy. "I can't begin to tell you how hard it was, sir."

"You managed something most of the Guardians couldn't. You should be proud." He clapped the younger man on the shoulder. "Mastering yourself is critical, as you know."

They came to the corner, and Alex turned into the bay. "I appreciate your candor. Keep your focus where it belongs. The operation. Keeping her safe. Not worrying about how she does or does not feel."

Jackson nodded once, a sharp snap of his head. "Thank you, sir."

Alex grinned at Jackson's back. Perhaps he'd underestimated the kid? Where in the Dust had he found the strength to walk away from her?

Alex slung his pack into the far corner of the train. Lena seated herself in a forward left seat and stared out the curved window at the glassy black wall beyond it, ignoring all of them. He moved to the console, ran through the starting protocol, and eased them into motion. For Lena's benefit, he told them they were in for a slightly longer trip than from Azcon to Fort Nevada.

A moment later, she stood beside his seat. "How long will we be gone? Thomas said two days?" She looked at their reflections in the curved window instead of at him.

"That's right." They'd shortened the usual three-day rotation in deference to her training. "We'll leave Herrons behind and hike to our base camp location. Camp overnight, move into position before dawn, relieving the other team. Once we're in the hole, we don't leave it. We'll observe in shifts and head back the following morning after our relief arrives. We'll be back here late tomorrow night."

She took a deep breath. "Look, I know I'm not the best of company, but can we spend another night out? Like, head back to the base camp and wait until the next morning to hike back out?" She tried to make her voice brisk, but deep unhappiness threaded through her words. She refused to meet his eyes.

What the Dust had she not been telling him? It had to be more than just the thing with Jackson, didn't it?

He leaned back. Giving a little to keep her happy wouldn't cost him anything. Of course, she wouldn't expect him to make it easy. "Would you make an effort to be cooperative if we did?"

She finally met his gaze. "I'll be as cooperative as I know how to be." She rolled her eyes. "Which, I admit, isn't much."

Alex smiled at her. He waited until one side of her lips curved up in a returned half-smile. "You've got a deal."

She turned away then, exhaling a long sigh of relief, and returned to her seat by the far window. She still held herself apart, but her demeanor had changed. Her body wasn't tense and angry. More than anything, she seemed tired.

He knew from personal experience that they had all grossly underestimated the Dust Effect radiating off of a highly-powered female. They'd expected it, yes. Any of them who had ever spent time with a mid-range woman and felt the attraction and the buzz of well-being from her presence could have guessed there would be a stronger response to a woman who was a step up in power. None of them would have guessed it would be like this.

But what was the Dust feedback from all of them doing to her? They were affected by just one of her. How would it feel to have a hundred Lenas, all of them focusing their attention and expectations upon you?

His stomach sank. It would be overwhelming. Add on everything she'd been through before she'd even arrived, and the loss of the affections of the one person she'd spent every day with for months, and it was too much. He understood with sudden clarity: She might be pissed at Jackson, but all of it together was too much. She was doing the best she could with what she had, and if dipping past her reserves from time to time made her moody and difficult, perhaps they should all back off and let her breathe.

He intended to give her the time she needed in old Idaho. When he pulled into the station, he powered down and turned to Herrons while the others gathered their packs.

"Mountain Home is Zone Four, and it's too dangerous to risk the attention significant repairs might bring. The lights work, but the plumbing doesn't. If you have to relieve yourself while you wait, you'll have to go topside. I'd rather you did it after dark."

Herrons nodded his understanding.

"After you bring the relief team back here tomorrow, make camp here inside the train. We'll be back day after tomorrow, sometime in the afternoon."

"Day after tomorrow?" Jackson interrupted, surprised.

Alex nodded, his voice inviting no discussion, "Change of plans." He returned his attention to Herrons. "In the event something goes wrong, follow protocol. Do *not* attempt to begin a search or rescue on your own initiative. Is that understood?"

Herrons nodded once. "I understand, sir."

Alex nodded and trooped out, Jackson and Lena behind him. The station was bare-bones, on the off-chance someone native to the Zone wandered in. The detritus of its previous use over two hundred years ago hadn't been cleared, except to restore the stairs up to the exit. And that work was subtle.

When they came up to the exit from the station, he keyed open the lock box. Before the other two went through, he warned her. "This was a secure facility beneath a military base. When the power went, and the fuel-based generators didn't come online, the workers down here were trapped. Like I said, no restoration work has been done up here. It's too risky." He didn't expect her to be particularly squeamish, but better to be aware. "The bodies are still here. Keeps people out. Keeps those who might come in from going deeper. Just a heads up."

They moved through the corridors and up the staircases. It wasn't a big facility, nothing like Fort Nevada, so they made good time. Alex powered up each room as they entered and shut it down again behind them. It wasn't bad down here, on the third below-ground level. Except for the odd stray survivor who'd wandered off to die alone on the lower levels once they'd realized the inevitable, the lower levels were okay.

The top level was a mess. The entry and what looked to have been a meeting room were the worst. It was clear from the positions of the bodies that something had happened down here. People didn't die of starvation or suffocation crawling over each other in a vain attempt to escape. Someone, he'd thought from his very first trip through, had decided the air and the food would last a little longer if there were fewer sharing it. He had bleakly wondered if he might do the same. He'd long since learned not to second-guess himself.

They reached the entry. Alex powered up the lights and glanced over his shoulder at the sharply-indrawn breath behind him. Lena's face was pale but set. The body closest to the door through which they had entered was the most horrific.

He lay spread-eagle on his back, exactly as he had fallen. Skin, shiny and brown with age, had shrunken onto his bones. His mouth gaped in a centuries-long silent shriek while empty eye sockets stared up at the ceiling. Both hair and clothing were wispy and tattered. The brown-stained front of his shirt had several large, gaping rents in it, giving testimony to the wounds which had caused his fall. He was the worst. Once they got past him, the rest were too tangled to pick out the same level of detail.

Alex walked through the mass of desiccated, air-mummified bodies to the secured outside access point ahead, placing his feet carefully to show Lena where to step. He began the process of powering up the new security and keying it open as Lena and Jackson made their slow way down the path. The door cycled open, and Alex pushed at it, freeing them.

As they entered a final staircase up inside the long-abandoned and weathered building, Alex whispered an admonition to them. "No speaking at all from the moment we hit the surface. You keep your eyes on me and do exactly as I signal. Lena, we do not relax until we are within cover of the canyon two miles to the west." He gave Jackson a look meant to remind him they did not ever relax.

The building itself had mostly collapsed, leaving a skeleton of support beams and door frames. Only the rear wall and the stairwell remained intact. Alex slid from frame to frame, taking stock of the surrounding area.

They were doubly lucky. There was no one around—not many Scavengers would bother with an area as picked over as the former Air Force base, but Neo-barbs might move in anywhere they could find rudimentary shelter. Plus, dark clouds skimmed low. Not only would the temperatures remain cooler, but their shadows would be less defined. Anything making them less noticeable as they moved across the plains to the canyon was a good thing.

He gestured them forward, and first Lena then Jackson joined him. Alex headed out, and they followed, an irregular arrowhead darting from the scant cover of the building.

Tall grasses, overgrown bush, and the occasional scrub pine covered the plain. As they moved further away from the base, they passed through what might have been a farmed field many years before. The crop now grew wild, and Alex moved into high alert. Wild grain always caused worry. If food grew, any nearby people would be desperate to collect it.

They were almost to the canyon when dim shadows crawled up over the opposite lip of the canyon ahead, moving away from the river ahead of them and toward the first of the low, broad buttes rising out of the plain on that side. He dropped to the ground. Lena and Jackson did the same behind him.

It was a small party, but still bigger than Alex's three. They weren't in the well-made uniforms of Council security. Scavengers were vicious opportunists who'd be dressed in the mixed colors of whatever they'd managed to find, steal, or remove from the bodies of those not as strong. Even from this distance, he noted the telltale rough, earth-toned clothing marking them instead as Neo-barbs.

The group was well armed. Each of them carried a bow or

crossbow in addition to blades of various lengths strapped to their sides. He guessed they were a hunting party. So long as they continued in the opposite direction, he was content to let them go.

He waited until the Neo-barb party moved well away out of sight and hearing range. He back-tracked along their route to be sure there were no stragglers. The group had moved off toward the buttes ahead. He signaled Lena and Jackson to follow, and the three of them scuttled over the final stretch of open ground to the canyon.

The canyon narrowed as they passed, its steep sides choked with brush. The threatened rain stayed in the clouds as they cut south through the canyon to the Snake River. It was greener along the shoreline where the vegetation grew thick. The growth made for slower going, but it provided better cover. Alex hung back, watchful and wary, and let Jackson lead them up the river until late afternoon.

A piercing three-note whistle sounded from the underbrush ahead of them and off to the side. They stopped, and Jackson answered the whistle in kind. Alex joined them, waiting for the man on sentry duty to appear.

When he rose from the brush, he asked for the password.

"Bellwether."

The young man nodded. "Thank you, sir. Our camp is just ahead, in those pines." He pointed for them.

"Any activity?"

"No, sir. Nothing out of the ordinary."

Alex nodded. "Keep a close watch. We saw some neo-barb activity in the area when we were hiking in."

"I'll be staying behind and cycling back when you all go, so I'll watch your back."

"Shouldn't be a problem. They were headed toward the north side of the buttes, but it's good to know we've got you back here."

Alex lead the way up behind a rocky rise with scrub and pole pine clustered around its base on either side. He set his pack down and looked around. The base camp wasn't much, but it was protected from weather and view.

They were alone now. Only one man stayed behind to watch

from the rear. The other two were at the observation point, where they stayed for the duration of their shifts.

Lena slid her pack off and eased it down to her feet. She rolled her shoulders and then leaned down to take up her water and drink.

"Cold camp?" she asked him after she'd swallowed.

"Yeah," Alex said. "That's standard out here this close in."

Jackson bent to claim a small area. He set his pack down and then leaned back against it, propping his legs up with a sigh of contentment.

She did the same at the far edge, away from Jackson.

Alex still felt restless. He glanced around. "I'm going to make a quick circuit, make sure the campsite is as good as they think. Check in a little more thoroughly." He threw the younger man a sly look. "Don't do anything I wouldn't do."

Jackson blanched. Lena challenged Alex with a look, lifting a brow at him as if to remind him of the kiss they'd agreed not to mention again. He swallowed his mischievous chuckle and stepped back into the trees and brush.

TWENTY

They set out in the pre-dawn dark. Moonlight made artificial lighting unnecessary for this portion of the trek. The now cloudless sky cooperated, and the twilight glow lit the route before them. They hiked an hour up the river to the yawning mouth of the canyon that led to the prison. Their observation point was a third of the way into the canyon, up high on the steep canyon wall. They cut up and around now, to come at it from above.

Silence had been important earlier. At this point, it became critical. Alex was hyper-aware of every rock grinding under foot and every cricket that stopped singing as they passed.

As they perched above the opening to the canyon, Alex paused. He cocked his head, listening. He could hear the soft sound of the river being churned by a paddlewheel and voices floating across the water to bounce back from the sides of the buttes running along this section of river. A steamboat headed down toward them. He cursed silently.

They couldn't know if it would stop here, for the prison, or continue down the river. If it stopped, was it delivering supplies, or picking up cargo, likely of the human variety? Was this the long-overdue transfer they'd been watching for? The sounds were faint. Sound carried oddly over water, giving them no clear idea of how far out it was.

They entered the canyon, working over the sharply slanted wall, and then made their slow way down and across the right side of the butte that formed one of the inner walls of the canyon. The observation point hid the observers behind scrub and trees near the top of the butte, just to the side of an overhang.

The prison itself had been built along the curve of the butte, nestled at its base in the far opening of the canyon where two buttes rose up beside each other. The canyon ran between them from the river to the plain beyond. The plains spreading out from the prison on the other side were farmed, the labor to work the farms provided by collared Spark prisoners. The mouth of the canyon behind it had been reinforced and fortified against both water and intruders.

That was fine with him. They weren't trying to get in; they only wanted to watch the activity of the guards and prisoners. If Lena got an eyeful of the collared Sparks so she'd understand why he and Thomas had worked so hard to build a viable alternative to the Council, even better. Yes, these particular men were criminals. But it wasn't a leap in logic to guess how easy it would be for the Council to decide the easiest way to guarantee power would be to use the collars on all Sparks. It was barely a hop considering the recent delivery of a box of the damn things to each zone's Council agents, likely precipitated by the loss of Lena.

If Thom and Alex could move Zone to Zone, they would have accomplished a bloodless revolution, ending the abuse and harnessing of Sparks. Well, not exactly bloodless, he acknowledged, but they were doing all they could to avoid any large-scale fighting or casualties.

As the three of them approached the OP, two shadows rose from the ground. The men they were relieving lifted their gear silently and moved toward and then past them without a word, handing off a pad of paper to Alex as they passed. Jackson led Lena and Alex behind the brush-covered twining trunks of a pair of pines. A long, narrow ditch had been carved out of the canyon-side between the trees and a large rock jutting back up the side of the butte beside the overhang. The three of them settled in.

It would be a tight fit for three, but Lena was small and they'd make it work. Alex settled in next to her behind the juncture of the trees. Their bodies were hidden behind the earth.

He reached back for his binoculars, rare and prized, and held them to his eyes.

"Normal guard movement, focused in and not out," he breathed. "Nothing else stirring. We're good." He glanced back at Jackson, who nodded acknowledgment. Alex turned to the activity report he'd been handed as the other agents scooted away. It said much the same. He folded it up and tucked it away until he needed to scrawl his own update on it for the team who'd relieve them.

She pulled her legs up and tucked her arms in between them and her body. She appeared content to wait out the dawn, and with it, the promised camp activity, in silence.

Dawn came more quickly to the prison at the edge of the plain than it did to them. Their position on the near side of the butte guaranteed them several more hours in the shadows. As the first fingers of light crept over the buildings below, activity began to stir.

Alex peered through the binoculars, first at the river, where he noted the paddleboat still hadn't appeared, and then at the prison. "Shift's changing," he told them in an undertone, "won't be long now before the first crews are sent out."

He was right. Not even a full hour later, double doors opened up onto the yard and prisoners filed out. They formed into double rows. As the first of them headed out, turning to the left and heading out to the plains and the farms, more exited to shuffle into the center of the yard and form into lines.

Alex looked again, scanning over the men, trying to decide which provided the best angle.

"Let me look." Lena said, her voice less than a whisper, muted by concern of discovery and by the numbers of the men below.

He glanced at her, nodded, and passed the binoculars over, pantomiming what each of the knobs on top did to sharpen her view and vary the amount of light, although the amplification was almost unnecessary now in the strengthening light.

As she put them to her eyes, he leaned in and spoke into her ear. "The best, closest angle to get a look at the collars they use to keep them from Sparking is along the edge of the butte, right before they cross out of view behind it."

She nodded without commenting. She did focus down at the base of the butte as he suggested. He noted her heavy swallow and the thinning of her lips. She had not been collared in the room back at Azcon. Her experience had been traumatic but brief. They had to live with the current every hour of every day. After a moment, she slowly scanned to the side and up, returning her view to the prison. She was silent, but the anger radiated off of her in physical heat that Alex, sitting so close, could feel.

Lena stiffened. She sucked her breath in and her hands clutched around the glasses. She leaned in, as if getting those few inches closer to the scene far below would make what she watched clearer. Alex turned back to the prison. He didn't see anything amiss—or not any more amiss than so many men like them being tortured, criminals or not. A smaller group of eight, not the usual twelve, caught his attention. They were smaller than the others, as well, and more rag-tag. Had the Council brought in boys?

"There are girls down there." She kept her words low, but furious. She lowered the binoculars and passed them to him. Her face was pinched and mottled with rage. "In the yard. There are girls. Wearing those collars. I highly doubt they're criminals."

Alex looked at the rag-tag little group he'd marked as different. It had to be them. The view through the glasses arrowed him down the hillside as if he were standing right outside the yard.

The girls stood still, some of them shivering in waves in the peculiar way Lena had when she'd had the current flowing through her on the table. They weren't cold. They were fighting a constant flow of electricity.

One of them, the tallest, seemed Lena's age. Her long, dark blond hair hung lank around her shoulders. Her pale eyes burned with the same fury Lena's did. The bright uniform was too snug across her full chest and hips and too short at the wrists and ankles. The collar snugged against her neck had a small chain of lights flowing one to the next in a constant stream of light, like a macabre red slash across her throat. He shifted his view to look at the others.

The rest were girls: two teenagers, thin and awkward; a couple of pre-teens; and three smaller girls. The youngest was no more than five or six. Beyond a doubt, if she'd been a boy, she'd have been sent to the Ward School. They all would have. But they were girls. When their parents had taken them for testing, they'd have been powerful, unpredictable, and marked as capable of producing dangerous and uncontrollable children and sent here. How long had this been going on? How had Fort Nevada's spies missed this?

The littlest girl had enormous brown eyes, almond-shaped, with dark smudges of exhaustion and fear hollowed out beneath them. Her black hair was unkempt. Her collar, clearly improvised and too big for her thin neck, held her small chin up in an unnatural position. The lights running across her throat moved through their pattern slower than on the woman, but her body shivered constantly nonetheless. Alex swallowed bile.

"We're not leaving them here." Lena's voice brooked no arguments.

He lowered the binoculars and returned her gaze. Her face was serene and terrible.

"No," he agreed, "we're not." The words came before he'd even thought them through, but they were true. It didn't matter how much they complicated things. He rubbed the back of his hand across his mouth and passed the binoculars to Jackson. His soft exclamation told them when he'd found the girls.

Jackson leaned over, careful not to jar the lip of the hole they hid inside. He started to speak, hesitated as he looked at Lena, and then plunged ahead, voice no less emphatic for being barely audible. "Sir. We're supposed to—"

"I know what our objective was, Ward. It's changed."

"We were to keep her safe at all costs, sir. Has that changed?" Though his voice never rose above a whisper, Jackson challenged Alex.

Lena made a noise of disgust.

"No. You'll be leading Lena back to Herrons and then

returning here—"

"The hell he will!" Her exclamation was a strangled hiss.

"Lena, listen."

"No. You listen." She remembered to breathe the words in spite of her fury. "Those girls are me. If I hadn't blown up that building, I'd be down there with them. This is *my* fight. Tell me different!"

Alex sighed.

It was all the answer she needed. Determination set her face. "I'm not leaving them. I'm not going back. I can remove the collars. And I'm more dangerous than either of you." The last she whispered with absolute certainty.

He stared at her.

She stared back, refusing to give way.

Jackson sighed, leaning away again.

Alex finally turned back to study the rag-tag group who were heading out between the gates now with a guard on every side of them. There were four men to watch over eight girls, two more than went with each larger group of men. It seemed the Council was afraid of them.

Instead of following the dirt road winding away to the plains, the girls were led toward the reinforced canyon mouth. They followed the first guard up a rough path over the berm, and then continued down the other side into the canyon.

Lena reached out and gripped Alex's arm.

He nodded. This movement and the distant sound of the paddle-wheel moving down the river were likely no coincidence. These girls were the big transfer. They were being moved. Without a means to follow, he would get one shot at planning their rescue.

Jackson looked through the glasses. "Four sniper rifles, four side arms, four Tasers," he whispered. He turned back to them. "It doesn't matter how dangerous you are, a bullet in your head will kill you as fast as anyone else. The guards are Sparks, Lena, and they mean business."

"So did the team of men that moved in with Alex trying to grab me at home. So did Alex, for that matter."

He told Jackson to stand down with a gesture. She was right. Not invincible, but right.

She leaned in. Alex could read the eagerness and fury in the motion.

"Too close to the prison," Alex murmured. "We'll wait for them to get past us and then follow at a distance. When I have more of a plan, I'll let you know."

The group of girls and guards made their way along the narrow path at the bottom of the canyon. Their glazed eyes and the mechanical movements of the too-thin bodies coursing with the electricity keeping them docile infuriated him. He couldn't imagine what it was doing to Lena.

Lena remained focused on the girls, except to occasionally arrow her gaze to each of the guards, marking them. She was making plans of her own. He hoped Jackson would be ready to roll with whatever she improvised. He had little doubt that when he finally said, "Go," she would do whatever she deemed necessary to get those girls free.

Once the group made their way past, he leaned in. "When we finally act, we need to disarm first. We will have a much greater chance of making it back to the train if they don't fire a shot. No shots. No alarm. No pursuit. Got it?"

"I want to turn off the damn collars first."

He shook his head. "They rely on the collars. They're focused on them. The guards have to be dealt with first." He imagined the fists she clenched in frustration were a reluctant agreement. He leaned closer. "With four of them, paralysis is our best bet. Can you manage all of them at once? We'll finish them."

She nodded once, hard.

He leaned back and turned to Jackson.

The Ward gave him a silent thumbs-up, but his worried gaze fell on Lena.

The group moved into the far mouth of the canyon and off to the left in a diagonal line toward the river's edge, below the elevated path Alex had led them in on. He was willing to bet on his hunch now. The girls were being removed from the prison for parts unknown. He hated that he wouldn't be able to follow.

They'd be rescuing this group, but losing the opportunity to discover any others at the paddleboat's final destination.

Alex checked back along the path for any rear guards. Satisfied, he put the binoculars in their case and secured them in the pocket of his pack. He didn't want them damaged in what was to come. With no further movement along the pathway, he eased into a crouch and gestured for the others to follow him out of their hole.

They worked their way along the hillside and moved down to the path at the bottom of the canyon where they had more freedom to move. When they reached the mouth, Alex headed for the wall of the canyon. He eased out, checking along the river and down the shore.

The humming of the riverboat's engines drew closer, but it still wasn't visible around the curve of the river and the tall butte to the right. The guards had moved the girls further up to sit on the rocky shore, but not far enough to guarantee a gunshot wouldn't echo up the canyon to the prison. The guards, clearly bored, stood over the girls. They were waiting for the steam barge and its shore boats to collect their human cargo.

He was marking the position of each guard in relation to the girls when he felt more than heard a pressure shift behind him. He'd made it clear to Lena and Jackson they should hang back. He turned, brow furrowed.

Alex froze. A neo-barb crossbow hovered in front of his face, held in an unwavering grip that kept the head of the bolt pointed at his right eye socket. Alex tracked back along the crossbow pointed at his face to meet the implacable blue eyes of the long-haired blond man holding it. Alex was aware of the scene behind the man—Lena restrained by a neo-barb behind her with a hand across her mouth, Jackson with a pair of crossbows keeping him in place. Four more men ranged at varying distances around them, and a fifth crouched behind the brush at the opposite canyon wall, focused on the guards and the girls up the river shore.

The neo-barb hunting party had moved around the buttes and circled back while Alex had dismissed them.

He knew better than to focus all of his attention on the target.

It left you open to movement from the rear and sides. He'd made a rookie mistake that might get them all killed.

The man in front of Alex allowed his lips to curve up in a smile. He eased a foot back, cocking one finger along the side of the crossbow in a beckoning motion for Alex to walk with him back into the canyon.

Alex cursed himself for a fool.

TWENTY-ONE

L ena remained still and loose. She'd rather the man behind her, with his big hand wrapped tight across the lower half of her face, believe she posed no threat. She hoped Alex understood why she hadn't dropped them immediately. They were all too close to the group of guards. They couldn't afford sounds or movements that risked the girls. She would be taking those girls to safety today. She'd made a solemn vow on her parents' souls the moment before she'd told Alex the same.

The men holding them had the same general look and coloring. Their leader had lank, dirty blond hair hanging past his shoulders, pale eyes, and a nose that had been broken more than once. His clothes were a none-too-clean, hand-made combination of tanned skin and wool. He probably smelled as ripe as the one holding her.

Alex and the man backed away into the relative safety of the canyon. The two with bows on Jackson gestured for him to move, too, and all of the others but the man crouched against the far wall watching the guards and the girls moved back with them. She was ready when the one holding her unceremoniously wrapped his arm around her waist and lifted.

When the man with the bow trained on Alex deemed they'd gone far enough, he stopped. The others followed suit.

Lena stared at him, waiting. What did they want? Why were they interfering?

The man in charge allowed a ghost of a smile to cross over

his face again, before he asked in a voice so quiet it was less than a whisper, "Who are you, and what are you doing here?"

"I could ask you the same," Alex answered, his own words as soft.

"Except I've got the weapon." The man waited.

"We're from the South, near old Nevada," Alex finally gave him, "and we're here to rescue our girls."

The man's square jaw jutted out and his eyes narrowed. "Your girls?"

Alex shrugged. "Not all of them. But it's not like we'd take ours home and leave the rest to suffer with these Council bastards." His low voice throbbed with honest emotion. "So if you're going to shoot us, shoot us. If not, back the fuck off so we can finish this and get home."

"Old Nevada, huh? Wanna be more specific?"

"We call it Fort Nevada. Southern end of Zone Five, far away from everything."

"Fort, huh? Military group?"

Alex nodded, the movement slow and deliberate.

"You think you're strong enough to take on the Council?"

He shrugged. "We already have. They just don't know it yet." It was the truth.

The man searched Alex's face with a long look. "I thought you were Council yourself, or maybe LDS. Too well-provisioned to be one of us." The man pointedly looked at their gear. He stepped back and the bow went down, although he still didn't remove his fingers from the trigger. "I guess Fate's working in both our favors today. One of those girls, the tall one, she's ours. And we mean to get her back."

The two men stood, silent, weighing each other.

"I'm Roddric," the Neo-barb offered.

"Alex." He nodded at each of them in turn. "Jackson. Lena."

Roddric turned to the others, and with a lift of his chin, told them to back off.

She stepped away as soon as the Neo-barb's arms unfolded, side-stepping closer to Alex.

Roddric kept his focus on Alex. "Plan?"

Alex hesitated. Roddric's fingers tightened on the crossbow. Alex raised a hand. "Trust comes hard."

"It does," Roddric agreed. "You got a plan, or you wanna sit back here and watch us?"

"We have a plan." Alex looked at Lena. He arched a brow at her.

Jackson made a noise of protest, but Lena grinned.

"I'm the plan," she murmured matter-of-factly. "I'm going to paralyze the guards. Then while all of you finish them, I'm going to deal with the collars."

"You're going to—" Roddric shifted. "You're like Rose."

"Rose is your girl out there?" Alex asked.

"Yeah. She can take any machine, no matter what, charge it up. Make it work. You like her?"

Lena made a more-or-less face. Of course, she meant more. Much more.

"You're going to take out all of those guards?" The man who'd been holding her spoke.

"I said that, yes," she answered, then looked at Alex. "I'm ready when you are."

She turned and picked her way to the wall of the canyon. She peered around and marked all four guards. The men fanned out around her. If the guards turned, they'd all be seen.

She slipped a breath in, eased it out, and let her vision blur, reaching to the Dust, sharing what she wanted. The Dust raced through the men's bodies, eager and quick.

Seconds later, she pulled back to herself and nodded at Alex and Roddric.

Roddric looked at her, then at Alex. He took a deep breath. Being told the men would be paralyzed and being willing to believe it and step out into the line of fire were apparently two different things.

She rolled her eyes, bent to scoop up a rock, and threw it at the back of one of the guards. She missed. The rock clattered past him and rolled away toward the river. Two of the girls nearest the guard looked up, startled and blinking as they shivered. The guards, of course, were still.

Alex and Jackson stepped out. She joined them, with Roddric only a step behind. His men moved in on the guards. The Council men collapsed to the ground in a flurry of metal glinting in the sunlight and four fanning sprays of blood.

Someone whooped in excitement. "She did it! She really did it!"

Lena ignored them. She had tunnel vision, moving straight to the smallest girl with her oddly canted chin. Lena smiled at her and made soft noises of comfort as she deactivated the collar. The girl's eyes went wide when Lena reached down and fumbled with the collar. She couldn't get the little hollow for a finger or thumb print to respond to her, so she wiggled her hand in the tight space between the collar and the girl's neck to protect her skin and instructed the Dust to part the collar. The heat released by the Dust as it complied went a step beyond merely painful, but Lena considered it a small price to pay. She pulled the broken collar apart and tossed it to the ground. Her arms went around the little girl.

"It's okay. It's okay now. You're safe."

The girl resisted for a moment, unable to keep from looking at the nearest guard, his blood reddening the rocks around him.

"No, no." Lena told her. "Look at me. Look at me."

The girl brought her enormous brown eyes up to Lena.

"I won't let them hurt you. I'm Lena. What's your name?"

The girl regarded her for a moment. She glanced away to take in the other girls sitting near them. When she looked back, she answered in a voice so breathlessly soft Lena wasn't sure she'd heard her.

"Missa?" Lena asked.

"No." The voice was soft, but stronger. "Marissa."

"Marissa. Okay. I'm going to put you down, now, Marissa. But I want you to stay right here with us, okay? We're going to take you away from these bad men, and keep you safe."

Marissa nodded.

Lena sank down. She knelt on the rocks and settled Marissa beside her, her back to the dying or dead man. A chestnut-haired girl was bold enough to dart forward. She looked at Marissa's collar on the ground and pulled at her own with one shaking hand.

Lena nodded and reached out, deactivating the collar a second before she slid her hand between the collar and the girl's skin. She separated the collar and pulled it from the girl's neck, wincing at the oozing blisters hidden beneath it.

"Oh, Dust." Tears sprang to her eyes, and she promised the girl, "I'm going to fix those for you as soon as everyone is free. I'm going to make sure you're okay."

The girl nodded and slid over to sit tight beside Marissa.

Lena turned to the next, and the next, pulling off collar after collar, ignoring the painful burns she inflicted on her own hands. She tried to place hoarse and whispered names to hollow-eyed faces as she winced at the injuries beneath and around the collars. Her rage grew.

She kept it buried deep, smiling reassuringly at the girls even as she wanted to rise and go to the guards to beat them, kick them, defile their bodies for what they'd done to these girls. For what cause? Because they were different? Because they had the audacity to be born?

Lena blinked away tears of anger and frustration to stare at the ring of solemn faces around her. The men, Alex, Jackson, Roddric, and the others, encircled Lena and the girls.

Rose stood in front of her, tall and proud before lowering herself into a squat. She stood the tallest and, with her appearance placing her near Lena's own twenty-four years, easily the oldest. She was the last of them.

Lena deactivated the collar and pulled it off.

Rose blinked. She sucked in a deep, cleansing breath to center herself. Had she been the newest addition? No wounds hid under her collar. Lena's gaze dropped down, noting the bruises on her chest, and what appeared to be the semi-circular imprint of teeth, disappearing under the 'V' of her prison shirt.

Lena looked up, meeting Rose's hard, angry eyes. "Do you have any wounds needing attention?"

Rose turned her lips down in a derisive snarl. "Nothing you can fix."

Before Lena could explain, Rose stood and looked around.

She found Roddric and went to him. They wrapped their arms around each other in silence.

Lena looked to Alex. "Do we have time for me to heal them? Some of their wounds are—"

The man closest to her grunted. A warm mist sprayed across her face. The little girl across from the man gasped wetly and slumped into the girl beside her.

The gunshot rang out and echoed off the cliffside.

Before Lena could catch her breath, a body forced her to the ground. She could hear shouts and shots.

"Where is he?" Alex demanded.

"The cliff, the cliff!" Unfamiliar voices.

"Where?"

It doesn't matter. She desperately scrabbled at the man on top of her. *It doesn't matter to me.* Jackson? "Jackson! Let me up!"

"No, Lena! Stay down!" His hand pushed on the back of her head, trying to force her down.

"Lena! Stay down, dammit!" Alex shouted at her. Then, to someone else, "Get those girls! Cover them!"

The hard squeals and whimpers of terrified girls finally did it. "Get off!"

Jackson flew back with a crackling pop. He thudded into the ground.

Lena pulled herself up to her hands and knees, spitting dirt from her mouth.

She flipped herself onto her back and crab-walked backward, scanning the cliff ahead of her. All she needed was a direction. Bolts and arrows arced up toward the right. Motion, a flicker behind a pocket of scrub leaning out from the edge.

Her hand, reaching beside her to pull herself back, landed on soft flesh. She glanced down. A thin arm, unmoving beneath her hand, led her up to a slack jaw, staring hazel eyes, wisps of rich chestnut hair being lifted by the gentle breeze still blowing across them. *Lydie.* A little girl who might have been ten beneath the grime and thinness of her captivity.

Breath hitched in Lena's throat. She turned back to the cliff and shrieked wordless rage up at the bastard on the cliff.

"Lena, no!"

The wave pulsing up and out from her slammed into the cliff below the scrub. The cliff side exploded with a roar of dust and flying rock. Lena curled into a ball over Lydie. The tiny sharp blows of pebbles on her back were brief, but the pattering of rocks sliding down the cliff went on longer.

It was quiet. Nearby, one of the girls made a frightened mewl. Quick footsteps responded. She lifted her head.

Rose leaned down and lifted Marissa into her arms, wiping the dirt from the terrified girl's eyes.

The other girls stirred.

Behind her, a man's rough voice asked, "Is he down?"

"He's in pieces," came the grim reply. The Neo-barb leader's voice. Roddric? "How about us?"

Lena counted small heads. All of the girls were moving. All but one.

She lifted herself to her knees and ran her hands down Lydie's small face to her chest, where bright red bloomed across the front of her shirt. She spread her shaking hands over Lydie's wound, trying. With a frustrated cry, she shoved one hand up to the girl's forehead, smearing bloody dust, searching.

She couldn't spark if there was nothing there. Death had come too fast.

Lena leaned over the girl until their foreheads met, her voice thick. "I'm sorry. I told you you'd be safe, and you weren't. I'm sorry."

A hand landed on her back. She refused to move.

"Lena." Mere seconds, and then the hand slid to her shoulder and pulled her up. "Lena, you can't help her. You can't. But you can help him." Alex leaned in, shook her slightly. "Lena. Look." He turned her.

One of Roddric's men splayed flat on the ground, coughing blood. His wound gaped high on his chest, blood bubbling. The bullet had gone through him and continued its trajectory down from the cliff into Lydie.

"We don't have much time. You need to help him now."

She wiped her cheeks with both hands, smearing Lydie's

blood into the tears and dust.

Roddric and another man were crouched beside the wounded Neo-barb. Wary, they watched her approach.

She knelt beside the man. "What's his name?" she asked Roddric.

"Trevor."

She nodded and leaned in. "This won't hurt, Trevor, but you'll feel heat." She barely recognized her own voice. She didn't know if the man even heard her.

He stared up at the sky and blinked slowly. Each breath sounded heavy and wet.

She pressed one hand to his chest and wormed the other beneath him to find the entrance wound on his back. She pulled in a deep centering breath.

A sweet half-smile in a pale, thin face beneath red brown hair flashed into her mind. Lydie had tried to smile at her as she'd pulled the collar free.

Lena's centering breath faltered and her eyes flooded. She gasped it back and drew in a second shaky breath.

She focused her will on the Dust within Trevor. It wouldn't be fast. Blood filled his pierced lung. The Dust would have to work a tandem job of healing the flesh and removing the blood that would otherwise drown him. She kept it focused, ignoring the sounds of movement and voices around her.

Trevor's chest rose then fell on a sharp, clear intake of breath. Her hand fell away from his chest. She struggled to free her other hand until Trevor felt her movements beneath his shoulder and rolled over. He sat up and ran one shaking hand up across the spot on his chest where there had been a hole moments before.

"Trev, can you stand?" Roddric asked the man, voice low. "Can you walk?"

Trevor nodded. "I think I could run."

"Good." Alex said grimly. He pulled Lena to her feet, his arms sliding around her, offering his strength.

She gratefully took it. She leaned into him, pressing her face against his chest. After a long moment, she lifted her head to look around, her vision hazy. They all stared at her. Even Jackson.

"I'm sorry I zapped you."

Jackson shook his head. "It's okay. I guess I got off easy. That was a really big boom." His attention swept along Alex's arms around her, and his jaw tightened.

"We've got to go now." Alex stepped away. He leaned over and picked up one of the smaller girls. "There's a boat coming around that bend any minute, and there's no way the prison didn't hear the fight."

Marissa was still tucked into Rose's arms. Lena wandered back over to Lydie. Were they going to leave her? They were *not* going to leave her.

She squatted down and scooped up the smaller girl. The little girl's limp body was heavy, but she managed to stand with her.

Alex sighed, the sound full of regret. "Lena, you can't."

"I can. I am." She raised her chin and held tighter to Lydie.

Jackson stood back, but he shook his head. At Alex's refusal, or at her desire to bring Lydie with them?

"You have to be practical," Jackson began.

Her resolve hardened. She shook her head. "I have to be practical? Like you're practical? If he told you to leave me behind, would you do it because it's practical?"

Jackson blanched. He turned away.

"I wouldn't leave you behind," Alex growled.

"And how is she different? She's not. I'm bringing her back to be buried. I will not leave her here so they can dispose of her like garbage, like she didn't matter. She mattered!"

Roddric pushed past Alex. The Neo-barb leaned down and gently pulled at Lydie.

Lena resisted, pulling away from him with a furious groan, nearly stumbling to wrest Lydie away.

Roddric shook his head at her, making soothing noises. "I'm going to carry her," he told her. His voice was soft. "There's a spot, along our way home. We lost one of ours." He nodded to the men behind him, solemn-faced. "He was snake-bit. We'll take her to him and put her down in the earth with him. She won't be alone."

Lena felt her chin quivering and sucked air in through her

nose. "Do you promise?" she asked him, not caring if she sounded like a child. She knew from personal experience that a Neo-barb oath wasn't given lightly. "Promise!"

"I promise." He reached out and took Lydie, draping her limp body across his chest and shoulder. As he turned and moved back through his men, he stopped first in front of Alex. "And you call us barbarians? We don't leave our dead behind. Not ever."

Alex's jaw tightened, but he nodded.

As one, they all turned and moved across the rocky ground to the south. Lena, standing in the midst of them, allowed herself to be swept along. Her feet moved automatically, but her mind was far away with an unknown, faceless woman in another Zone, a woman who had named a baby girl Lydie and who would never know her daughter was gone.

—⟋⟍—

They picked up the agent from the base camp along the way, Alex darting off to the side to order him out with them. The agent's knowledge of a series of lava tubes for them to use kept them ahead of their pursuers in spite of the extra weight of the girls. But staying ahead meant no stops. Even when Roddric set Lydie's body down briefly to pull a blanket from his pack, tuck it around her small body, and roll her in it, the others continued trotting. He settled her back in his arms again and caught up before the others were too far ahead.

They rested by slowing to a walk, but never for very long. By the time the sun lowered behind them and to their left, Lena was exhausted. She couldn't imagine how the girls felt, and Rose carried a double load in spite of her own condition. She admired the woman's strength, even as she was aware of Rose watching her with hooded eyes.

At some point in the late afternoon, Lena overheard Alex tell Roddric they'd be splitting up soon. Their way home lay to the west of the canyon. Though her feet were like lead, she increased her pace to catch up to them.

"We'll be taking the girls," she told Roddric, her voice uncompromising. "They need to be taught, and I'm the only one who can do it."

He looked over, tilting his head down at her. "You sure you don't wanna come with us? We could use a woman with your talents."

She smiled, but it felt dark.

Alex raised his head and opened his mouth to speak, but she waved him down.

"It's an intriguing offer," she finally told Rodddric, "but I'm…invested…in what Fort Nevada's trying to achieve now." She exchanged a long look with Alex. *There you go. Mission accomplished.* After a moment, she returned his small smile.

Roddric nodded. "I can appreciate that. You ever change your mind, you head out toward Tahoe. We'll find you."

Alex lost the smile he'd shared with Lena and swung his head around. He gave Roddric a long look. "Tahoe? You wouldn't be the group we hear about causing so much trouble for Canev, would you?"

"We're not in the business of causing trouble. We're in the business of surviving."

Lena waited, but Alex let the comment pass as they reached the edge of the canyon. They slid down into it, one by one.

At the bottom, Alex nodded up at the wall across from them, angling up and away. "Our way out is over there. The girls will make it fine," he told Roddric. "Safe journey. Long life."

Roddric nodded. "The same to you." He turned to Lena. "If you, any of you, ever need shelter, remember us."

"Thank you," she said. She placed her hand on the blanket over Lydie's back, then turned away to watch Alex lead Marissa, the smallest of the girls, from Rose.

Lena returned Rose's gaze. "Good luck," she told the other woman.

Rose said nothing.

Lena started up the canyon wall, helping Alex and Jackson herd the girls up the slope of the canyon. They slipped and slid, but made their way to the top.

At the top, she turned to look back. Rose and Roddric faced each other. Rose's hands moved emphatically in the air between them as they talked. She pointed at Lena and the others. Finally, Roddric closed his eyes and nodded once. Rose hugged him tight before turning away to trudge up the slope to join Lena and the others. Roddric didn't wait, and Rose didn't look back. Relieved of the extra weight of the girls, they jogged down the canyon.

Rose made it to the crest of the canyon. Alex growled surprise, but she ignored him. She stopped in front of Lena. "I'm coming with you."

"No, you're not," Alex said.

"I'm one of them." She nodded her head at the younger girls. She meant she was like them. Like Lena. Her focus never left Lena, as if only she mattered. "Are you going to teach them to do what you do?"

"I'm going to try. To control it. To explore it. As best I can, yes. I'm not very good yet." Lena admitted.

Rose laughed. "Well, then, I can't wait to see what I can learn from you when you are very good." Rose gave Alex a hard look. "I'm coming with you. I want to learn, just like them. I have as much right as they do. I'm like them. I was locked up like them. Treated like them."

Alex sighed and shook his head. "I understand. But you're also different."

Rose lifted her chin and she sneered, "Because I'm a *barbarian*?" Dismissing him, she turned back to Lena. They all looked at Lena.

Jackson spoke up, although he was clearly reluctant, not wanting to be the one to upset Lena again. "Councilor Five will never agree to this."

"He doesn't have a choice." Lena said. "She's right. She comes. Or I stay."

Alex closed his eyes. "This is a very bad idea."

"I'm full of bad ideas. You should be used to it by now."

He looked at her again. They stared at each other. Something had changed for Lena back there beside the Snake River. The men of Fort Nevada didn't know it yet, but it had changed for them, too.

Alex seemed to sense it. The muscle in his jaw jumped. He

backed away. "Let's go, then. Before they catch up and it's all academic anyway."

They ran on, moving across the plain, trying to beat both the night and the men pursuing them. Before they were halfway across the plain, it was clear they wouldn't make it. The distance to Mountain Home was further than the distance between them and the Council men pouring down into the canyon behind them. Lena looked back to see Alex and Jackson exchanging a look.

Only half the men behind them came up and out of the canyon. The other half must have followed the trail of Roddric and his men. Still, five well-trained Council guards were gaining on them, spurred on by the distance closing between them. Alex urged the girls on, passing Marissa back to Rose before pulling Lena and the agent from the camp aside as they ran.

"Why don't they shoot at us?" she gasped out.

"The girls." Alex answered. "They don't want to accidentally kill the girls. They're too valuable, too rare."

"That's good then, right? If we can beat them back to Mountain Home, we'll be good."

Alex shook his head. "We're going back," he told her, referring to himself and Jackson. "We're going to take out this group while the two of you get the girls back and down to the train."

"You're not serious?" She almost stopped running.

Alex dragged her on.

"Let me do this. You take the girls."

"Lena, don't argue!" Jackson had appeared at her other shoulder. He'd never raised his voice before. She stared at him.

"I can do this better than—"

"You can keep them safe better than we can." Alex interrupted.

"You wanted to rescue them," Jackson added, "so rescue them. Don't throw it all away. Let us do this."

As soon as Lena nodded tightly, lips compressed, the two men fell back, and she ran on with the silent agent from the camp beside her. She swept forward with arms out to gather the girls together and keep them moving. She and Rose both glanced back, but the men had disappeared into the tall grass behind them, waiting for those who pursued. She looked back again, and the prison men were closer.

The next time, the men were engaged, moving together in a brutal dance. One of the Council men was down, but it was still her two against their four. Lena slowed, staring back at the battle. Blades glinted in the last light of sunset as men slashed and circled, coming together and swinging around in each other's arms. Alex quickly disposed of one and immediately turned on another who had leaped in to take advantage of Alex's turned back. Alex sent him to the ground, as well.

Jackson took his prison guard to the ground, sinking below the grass. She strained up, searching the gloom. Breath whooshed into her lungs when Jackson rose up again, he and Alex moving together to finish the final man.

In the half-light, Jackson's man rose up behind them, wounded but not finished. He lifted a gun, lurching as he swung it toward the closest man—Alex. Lena gasped, a strangled cry half-caught in her throat.

She rose up on her toes and threw out her empty hands. The man froze, then slowly rose up on his own toes, gun falling to the ground as his back arched and mouth fell open, dark spittle frothing over his lips and chin.

"Is that you?" Fascination laced Rose's question. "Are you doing that?" The girls were behind her, aware in a way none of the men of Fort Nevada had ever been.

Jackson turned. He flinched away from the man for only a second, glancing over the guard's shoulder to the cluster of girls across the plain with Lena at their center and an agent hovering behind. Jackson shook his head, grim, and slipped across the short distance between them to finish the man himself.

He was angry. But Alex was alive to snap at him, as he was doing now.

The two men caught up with them before they'd reached the skeletons of the buildings. None of the adults mentioned what had happened out on the plain. Once they reached the scant cover of the ruined buildings, Alex stopped to crouch down.

"Okay, ladies. We're going down to a safe place, but there's scary stuff along the way. I need you to wear these blindfolds over your eyes, so you won't be scared. And we'll all hold hands as we go down. Once we're clear, we'll uncover you, okay?"

He reached into his pack and pulled out his blanket, flipping out a knife and cutting the blanket into strips. He called each girl to him and gently tied a strip of blanket around her eyes. When he finished with each, he set her next to the previous one and placed their small hands together until he had a chain of quiet little girls and two nervous teens sitting around him with clasped hands and blindfolds on their heads.

He took up the wide cloth and folded it double. He looked up then, his face set and uncompromising. He gestured for Rose to come closer.

She hung back, not trusting him. "I'm not a frightened little girl."

"You want to come with us, fine. But you're coming blind, or you're never leaving. And I don't mean just downstairs like the girls, either. You'll keep it on all the way to the fort." The tension in his voice told them he was dead serious. He cocked a finger at Rose.

Lena nodded, though she didn't understand why he was being so hard on the Neo-Barb. She *was* a strong power, just like the rest of them. Most Council citizens had prejudices against Neo-Barbs based on fear and misunderstanding, and Lena had to imagine that the agents who'd have to be on guard against them would be no different. She'd somehow expected better of Alex, though. The suspicion left her disappointed.

"It's okay, Rose." The least she could do would be soothe the woman's understandable offense and anger. It would take time they didn't have for Lena to try to convince Alex he was being a fool. "As soon as we get to safety, an hour at the most, it'll come off. I promise."

Rose straightened her shoulders, her distrustful gaze moving between them.

"Rose," Lena told her, "As soon as I saw you all, I promised you your freedom. You didn't know it. But I did. I promise you this now. I'm not going to let anything happen to you. And in spite of how he seems, neither is Alex."

He raised the strip. "Now or never. I'm not putting everyone else at risk for you."

Rose leaned in and allowed him to fasten it snugly around her head. It fit over the entire top of her head, from the tip of her nose to the back of her head. He double-checked it for gaps.

Relief flowed through Lena. She took a deep breath and reached to take Rose's hand.

Satisfied, Alex stood. He swung the blindfolded Marissa back up into his arms and took another little hand in his. The other girls held tight to each other as Alex led them along by the hand of his first small companion. "All right, soldiers. Now we march."

TWENTY-TWO

It bothered Lena that Rose sat back in her seat on the train, shoulders back, lips squeezed tightly. Her white-tipped fingers compressed the armrest of her chair, despite Lena's attempts to make her comfortable. Lena understood, though. Rose was more cooperative than Lena would have been had Alex tied a blanket around her head. Even if she was almost angry enough to rip the seat arms off.

Rose would have none of Lena's concern, so Lena decided to minister to the younger girls, instead. She couldn't do much for their psychological wounds. She couldn't even fix her own, after all. But the cuts and welts? The infected blistering? Those she could heal.

The girls huddled together. Alex had removed the blindfolds from all but Rose as they stepped on the train, and they tracked Lena's movements as she returned from checking on Rose. Two of them, little brunettes who looked to be the same age, sat together on one chair, their arms wrapped tight around each other and heads touching as they warily watched Alex, Jackson, Herrons, and the other agent instead. The others also huddled close together in adjacent seats. One, a dark-skinned girl with hollow eyes, sat apart, unmoving.

And Marissa, the smallest of them, had scooted all the way back in a chair that seemed to swallow her small body. The backs of her ankles barely tipped over the edge of the seat.

She'd start with Marissa.

She knelt in front of Marissa's seat. "How are you doing, Marissa?" she asked, and winced internally. *What a stupid question.*

The little girl shrank back against the chair.

"Remember when I said I could help your neck feel better?"

Marissa seemed to consider the question. She nodded.

"Can I do it now?"

Lena received another hesitant nod.

"Can you scoot forward a little?"

The little girl moved slightly forward. Lena smiled and gently pulled her a little closer. Marissa stiffened. Lena turned as the dusty hand of one of the teenagers reached past her to rub Marissa's shoulder with reassuring fingertips.

A pair of dark, steady doe-eyes met Lena's. Like Jackson, the teen girl's caramel-colored skin and full lips spoke of a multicultural heritage. Under the matted hair, dust, scratches, and sharp angles of hunger, Lena could see she'd be beautiful. Now she was wary.

"It's okay, Marissa," the girl said, her voice trying for confident but veering into false bravado. "She wants to help us."

Lena nodded. "Right. That's right..." Her voice faded. She'd forgotten the girl's name.

"Phoebe." Her tone said she wasn't surprised her name had been forgotten.

"I'm sorry," Lena murmured. She turned back to Marissa, acutely aware now that they were all attuned to her actions. "Phoebe is right, Marissa. I want to help. Will you let me?"

The little girl didn't answer, but she scooted forward a little more.

Lena might have started to believe she couldn't speak if she hadn't told Lena her name back at the Snake River. She raised her hands and settled them on the little girl's neck.

Marissa's body trembled as she fought not to pull away.

Anger spiked again at the jailers who had put the collars around these girls and at the Council who had ordered it. She added it to her list of acts requiring vengeance.

"It's going to get warm," she told Marissa, "but it shouldn't hurt. I'm going to tell the Dust where to go and how to fix your cuts. It will burn the infection away and knit your skin back together."

"Using your mind?" The little girl finally spoke. Her voice remained as faint and hoarse as it had been at the riverside.

Lena nodded. "Yep. Like you can do?" She guessed.

The girl frowned. She darted another look at Phoebe. "We're not allowed."

"You are now." Lena was matter-of-fact and firm. "And I'm going to teach you." She smiled. Then she focused, taking a breath and pushing out with the exhale. As she worked with the Dust, she could feel Marissa's mind poking at it, too, tentative and furtive.

She eased back. "Okay, Marissa. Now it's your turn."

Marissa frowned again.

"I could feel you," she whispered to the small girl, winking. "Did you understand what I was doing? Would you like to try? There's one blister left."

Marissa took a little breath. She gave Lena a searching look, then reached up and hooked her small fingers around Lena's hand. She squeezed tight and another breath hiccupped in.

Lena felt when she let go of her fear and reached out. Not only could she feel the girl's mind, stronger than any sense she got from the men, but she recognized the way her eyes glazed as she pushed away from herself and out to the Dust. Marissa was doing it.

Moments later, Marissa's face brightened as she popped back into her own mind. "I did it?" She breathed the question.

Lena could hear relief and happiness in her own laughter. "You did it!"

"Just like that?" Jackson asked from the front of the train.

Lena nodded. "Just like that." She snapped her fingers for emphasis, and then leaned in and stage-whispered, "Don't mind him. He's a little jealous. It took him two weeks to learn to heal." She looked in Alex's direction from the corner of her eyes, the smile playing over her lips answered by his own, "And *he* hasn't learned to do it well, at all."

"Yeah, yeah," Jackson said, but he smiled again, finally.

Alex guffawed, but his gaze was intent. She could feel his warmth and pride from across the car. It felt good.

Marissa tittered. The small sound seemed to surprise even her. She bit her lip to contain her broad, proud smile.

Lena ran a hand over the hair of her first precocious pupil and grinned. She turned to the other girls. "Can anybody else do that yet?" Lena asked them.

Rose's blindfolded face turned toward them as she listened intently. Heads shook.

The teenager next to Phoebe cleared her throat. A redhead with hair that shone a brilliant shade of orange, she didn't share Lena's freckles. Her pale skin was mottled and peeling from sunburn. "I think I might be able to now?"

"Okay." Lena patted Marissa's hand and stood. She crossed to the redhead. "Mmmm…." The girl's name started with "M".

"Marin," Rose supplied from beside her. The woman had risen and crossed to stand beside Lena with her blindfold still in place. She reached out with a searching hand for the arm of Marin's chair. When she found it, she crouched low, like Lena had before. "I'd like to try," she told Lena brusquely, "so do I have to see to do this?"

"I don't know," Lena told her. "But there's only one way to find out."

She knelt beside her. The rest of the girls scooted to the edge of their seats, peering around Lena and Rose, stretching to see.

"So, I just—" Rose stopped, at a loss.

"Breathe. And when you're ready, push your thoughts out to the Dust with your breath. I like to take it easy, a nice long exhale so I can reach out. But instead of feeling the space for the charge I'm going to leave in an object, I feel for the energy inside. The Dust in a body is warm and it…kind of pulses. Once I feel it, I show it what I want."

"Show it?" Rose was doubtful. "Like, pictures?"

"Pictures, if I don't have the words. Words, if I don't have the pictures." She smiled and put a reassuring hand on Rose's shoulder. "The Dust *wants* to help us. It was made to talk to us.

It'll meet you halfway, I promise." She glanced up and over Marin's shoulders at Alex, watchful and silent.

Rose thought for a moment. "Like…with a new machine? I might not have seen it before, but it's like my mind can sink down into it. And then I can see how it works."

"Yes! Exactly." Lena smiled. The smile faded when she remembered Rose wouldn't see it because of the blindfold. "I push out and into it. You sink down and settle in." She looked around at the girls. "Anyone else?"

One of the two hugging brunettes glanced at the other. "We see it as a reflection, like a mirror, and we …recognize it. But we've never talked to it."

Lena noted the tiny trio of moles like a constellation on the right cheek of one and the left of the other. They were twins, no more than twelve or thirteen years old. Had they first learned to recognize the Dust in each other?

Rose nodded again. She reached her hands out to Marin, searching without seeing.

Marin took Rose's hands and guided them up toward her neck. "I want to try, too," the girl reminded Rose.

Rose nodded again. Rose's fingers skimmed Marin's neck in a touch both feather-light and thorough. When she was sure she'd found all of the broken skin, her fingers stilled. Her breathing didn't shift.

Somehow Lena knew when Rose sank down, just as she felt the Neo-barb woman struggle.

"Rose," Lena reassured her, "she's just a machine. A living machine. And so is the Dust."

The other woman hesitated. She began again. Marin's skin knit together, healthy skin rippling across the wounds.

"Leave some for me!" Marin demanded.

Rose withdrew, both mentally and physically. Her hands dropped to her lap, and she took a shaky breath.

"Did she do it?" Alex's gaze was sharp on the Neo-barb woman.

Rose's chin lifted. "She did," she told him with pride. She stood in one smooth, fluid motion and moved back to her seat.

Even blind, she found it without stumbling.

"And so is Marin," Lena reported, focused on the girl in front of her. Patience was not Marin's strong suit, but healing was.

Marin healed the wounds on her own neck and moved on to her face and arms. Her sun-reddened, cracking, blistered skin smoothed. It became pink and shiny and then faded to her natural creamy paleness.

Phoebe made a low note of amazement deep in her throat. "Help me, Marin." She tugged on Marin's arm. "I can't figure it out."

Marin turned to her, and the two girls started working together. After a moment, she made it clear she not only understood how to do it, but she excelled at sharing how to do it, as well.

Lena settled back onto her heels and looked around. The twins had already turned to face each other, whispering and nodding in excitement. All four of the men watched with bemused expressions.

Their base camp agent, whose name Lena had never learned, looked a little shell-shocked. He asked Alex, "Is it supposed to be that easy for us, too?"

Jackson shook his head in small back and forth movements, chin tucked in his palm, elbow on his armrest as the girls easily practiced the skill he'd sweated and lost sleep over to master.

Alex chuckled. "No, I'm pretty sure they're special."

I'm not alone. Not ever again.

The dark place inside Lena felt warm and honeyed with pride for the damaged, amazing, fast-learning girls, and she felt a little generous. "Not necessarily special," she told them with a light shrug of one shoulder. "Just different."

"No," Alex replied, his voice soft as his gaze moved over her face. "You're definitely special."

Wh—?

Lena ducked her head, heat flaring across her cheeks and through her chest. She could feel her wide grin as she turned again to her girls.

Marissa had pulled her legs up to her chest and rocked, one

dirty thumb tucked into her mouth.

Lena reclaimed her focus and scanned the girls. She'd forgotten the quiet, dark girl with hollow eyes who couldn't be more than nine. She was overly thin with the coltish legs of a girl making the slow segue into womanhood but the still-round cheeks of childhood. She sat alone. The sense of loneliness radiating off of her miserable little person, though, had more to it than simply sitting alone. Lena searched her memory for the girl's name. Hania.

She crossed the four steps to her. "Your turn," she told the girl. She dipped down to squat before Hania and touched the girl's arm with her fingertips.

Hania shook her head solemnly. Her irises were as black as her pupils, making her eyes seem both bottomless and full of grief.

"She can't get better," she said. "I shouldn't get better, either."

Lena glanced around. "Everyone's getting better, Hania."

Hania shook her head again.

"Lydie was her match." The twin who spoke, either Constance or Charity, held tight to her sister's hand.

A knot twisted in Lena's stomach. "Her match?"

Rose turned her head toward them, her blindfolded face eerie with the streak of tunnel lights behind her. "They paired off girls they found," she explained, her voice flat. "I don't know why, or why we matched. The girls say we weren't alone. They got rid of any who didn't fit well, with each other, or with these girls. Supposed to be the same age, same power. Lydie was Hania's match. They did everything together. The exercises. The...." She stopped and swallowed. "Everything. For however long they were there before you came."

Her heart wanted to beat its way out of Lena's chest. "You don't have a match," she pointed out.

Rose's lips curved up in a dark smile below the blindfold. The movement held neither warmth nor mirth. "They talked about finding my other half," she said. "Some girl in the desert. But she got away. Did they mean you? They were saying there'll be hell to pay at the Council Meet this year." Her next words were sing-song and malicious, although the malice wasn't directed at Lena. "Someone's in trouble."

Lena's heart stuttered. Lucas and the Councilor had strapped her to the table. What was it Lucas had said? They wanted to know her limits?

They wanted to know if she was a match for Rose.

The memories of that day in the room flooded back. Air on her naked skin. Pain and shame at her helplessness. The look on her mother's face. The smell of the dust, thick in her nostrils.

They had been testing her, the same way they would have done if her parents hadn't hidden her as a child. Lena's stomach heaved, the spasms fighting against her tight throat. The same way they tested every high-powered girl Spark? The same way they'd tested all of these girls?

She gulped away the nausea. She looked at the girls, at Marin and Phoebe, holding hands without even seeming to be aware of the contact. The twins clutched at each other. She noticed Marissa, sitting alone, too. She shook her head to clear it of memories and fear.

"Look, Hania," she told the thin girl before her, somehow even more desperate to make the girl let Lena help her, "Marissa doesn't have a match, and she's better now."

Hania shook her head a third time. "She does. She got left behind."

The bud of horror taking root inside of Lena bloomed, each petal unfolding, consuming the space in her chest her lungs needed to expand. She couldn't catch her breath.

"What?"

"Jubilee got left behind." Phoebe was too sadly matter-of-fact to be lying.

"What? No!" Lena shook her head at Marissa. "I counted. When you all came out, I counted!"

Marissa pulled her thumb out of her mouth. "She wasn't with us. Her collar was breaking. They had to fix it." The little girl's eyes were too big, too wise in her toddler face. "She's okay now. I can feel her still. She's just sad to be alone on the boat."

"Alex!" Lena whirled.

He had already lunged to his feet. His look of horror mirrored her own, but more than fury and desperation lurked behind his emotion. She could feel his regret.

"No, Alex!" She could hear her voice crack, but she didn't care. "We have to go back. She's a child!"

He held up his hands. "We can't turn around. That's not how the train works. But I can, and I will, send agents back to watch and wait as soon as we get back."

"To watch and wait?" What was he saying? "For what? She's a child. Being sent who knows where by monsters. If we don't go back right now, she'll be gone up that river, and we'll never find her."

Alex took a deep breath. He swept a glance over the girls. "If we go back to get her now, we'd have to take an army."

"Then take a damn army."

"We don't have an army. Not yet. We're moving forward using stealth, not force. We're taking Zones from the top, not the bottom. And we're spread out. We don't have the men available at Fort Nevada. It looks like we do, I know. But we don't." He ran his hands through his hair in frustration. "And they'll be ready for a return force, anyway. We won't accomplish anything. Until we have something, some way to fight that's stronger than their bullets and numbers, we can't."

"We have me."

"Until one sniper makes his mark. And then we don't." He nodded at the girls. "And neither do they."

He was fighting dirty, and she could tell he knew it. They wanted her to train them all, and now they had her motivation.

"She's a little girl. And she's alone." How could he not *see*?

"I know." The thick emotion in his voice answered her own. He did see. The little boy who had refused to cry still lived behind Alex's eyes. But the man he'd become could open up a compartment deep inside and put away the grief and rage and guilt. Once he closed the drawer, it was all gone. His face had simply emptied of it. In its place was Thomas's perfect automaton agent, willing to do anything to further their cause.

When he spoke again, his voice reflected that brisk efficiency, and brooked no argument. "We cannot go back right now."

All of the warmth Lena had felt moments before fled. It left behind a cold void in her chest.

Remember this, Lena. This is why you cannot develop feelings for him. He's not capable of feeling them back. Remember this.

He waited for a moment, but she had nothing to say to him. It surprised her when he spoke again.

"We'll watch." He promised, his voice soothing but his single firm nod conveying the intensity behind the words. "As soon as an opportunity comes to follow those supply barges, we'll track her. We will find her."

Perhaps he wasn't quite the automaton she'd thought? It would have to do. She didn't have any choice.

It's about time to start creating my own choices.

"We're going to find Jubilee, Marissa," Lena said.

The little girl nodded. Why shouldn't she believe? They'd gotten her out, hadn't they? Lena turned to Hania and laid a hand upon the girl's heavy black waves of hair, snarled with neglect.

"I'm going to make you better now, Hania." Her voice trembled, and she cleared her throat as she knelt before Hania. When she spoke again, she was stronger. "I'm sorry I couldn't save her. I'm sorry. But Lydie would have wanted you to be better."

TWENTY-THREE

Lena prowled from room to room, checking on the girls, pacing the hall to keep them safe. She couldn't sleep, so she patrolled.

They'd put Marissa and Hania together. She'd spent much of her time looking in on the two girls. Marissa had climbed into bed with the older girl and curled into Hania's side. She slept.

Hania did not. Each time Lena cracked the door to look in, Hania's wide eyes turned to her in silent regard. Lena didn't say anything. Her own loss had taught her there wasn't anything to make it better, especially words. The twins had told her that Hania and Lydie had been there together longer than any of the rest of them, including Marin and Phoebe, who had been shipped in separately from other places. It was no wonder Hania was shell-shocked.

Finally, shortly after her fifth restless patrol in the hours before dawn, Lena peeked in, and Hania had fallen asleep. Her thick lashes curled down over the dark hollows under her eyes, emphasizing her poor health. Lena had asked about their condition. It made no sense—if the Council had use for them, why the starvation and abuse? Rose had taken the blame for that. She'd refused to eat. The other girls, especially the older girls, had followed her lead. The guards had tried to force feed them. When that didn't stop the small rebellion, they'd resorted to abuse.

Lena stood for a long time in the dark and the silence, watching the two girls sleep. She had lost so much. It had never occurred to her she should consider herself lucky.

The Councilors who were responsible would pay for it all. They'd caused too much pain. The only way she could see to purge it was with blood.

The blood rage kept her up. Every time she settled her head on her pillow, images flooded her mind: her mother, Lydie's chestnut hair blowing softly across her still little girl face, and a child who searched for her, calling out and running toward her, but getting lost in a mist too thick to see through. When she did manage to push them all away, other unwelcome thoughts came boiling up.

Why had she brought the girls back here? Yes, they would be protected from the Council, but she wasn't naïve enough to think Fort Nevada didn't hold any dangers for them. They had tried to keep the arrival of the powered girls as quiet as possible, for the girls' sakes. But Lena could feel the male energy she had learned to differentiate. It pulsed and curled expectantly, mimicking the excitement of the men and boys behind it as word of their arrival spread.

How could she keep them safe, even from the people who intended to provide the protection they all needed? How would she help them heal the wounds the Dust couldn't knit back together?

She threw off the blankets and rose to dress, rubbing grit from burning eyes. Her mind refused to let go of the fears and images tumbling through it. She left her room thinking of the cafeteria and maple syrup.

"What do you think you're doing?" The words were a low and menacing growl echoing down the hallway.

Lena jumped and spun. *Alex?* If it was, she'd never heard so much fury in his voice before. And that was saying something.

She strode down to the next intersection of corridors and looked both ways. Alex stood at the end of one hall. Between him and Lena in the junction, two teenaged boys were staring at him in frozen terror. From the guilt written plain on their faces, they were up to no good. Had they been sneaking toward the girls' rooms? Lena's vision flared red.

Enough.

Alex stalked toward the boys, chin down, eyes narrowed, and repeated his question, his normally husky voice grating and hard.

The boys exchanged a quick look. The shorter one told him, "We heard about girls, sir. Like us. We wanted to meet them...." He drifted off as Alex's brows lowered further.

"Before dawn? Sneaking, like criminals? What, you were planning to break into their rooms?"

Another look passed between them. "It was a dare," the taller one supplied.

"A dare? To harass little girls who were rescued from a prison where they were being tortured just yesterday?"

The boys exchanged another miserable look.

"Since you like choosing so much, I'll give you a choice," Alex continued. "You can come with me now, and we'll go upstairs where *you* will wake the Councilor to tell him what you were doing and why. Or you can go with *her* right now and take whatever she chooses to dish out." Alex pointed past them to Lena, standing silently in the hallway behind them, head lowered and lips compressed.

The boys turned and stared, wide-eyed. One of them swallowed. "Sir," the shorter whispered hoarsely. "She's—"

"Glowing." Alex's own attention was glued to her now, though he spoke to the boys. "Yes. She does that when she's very, very angry. Right around the time the energy she can channel blows things into tiny pieces."

Well, the truth was a little different. But it might happen this time.

"We'd like to talk to the Councilor, sir."

Alex held out his arm for the boys to walk past him to the elevators. They scurried up the hall, heads down. He came forward another few steps to ask her in a low voice, "Are you okay?"

She stared into the backs of the fleeing young men. She liked angry Alex. She even liked intimidating Alex. She couldn't deal with compassionate Alex right now. She shrugged.

"You haven't slept," he said. It wasn't a question, and the

words were laced with concern.

"No. I've been…patrolling."

He cocked his head at her. "You should have known I'd have it covered. They've been through enough. They don't need to be harassed, even if it is in curiosity and not—"

"It doesn't matter why." Her words were quick and cutting.

He nodded his agreement. Those dark eyes were still filled with concern. One hand lifted to touch her cheek, but she flinched away. She didn't know what his game was, but Jackson's rejection had hurt more than she'd let on. And she'd let on quite a bit. She didn't need another tall, dark, handsome asshole, even if he did kiss like lightning. And even if he looked like Alex.

Remember. He won't ever feel anything back. Not really.

But he wasn't accepting her rejection. He waited, hand still lifted, until she turned her face back to him. And then he slowly and gently brought his hand to her cheek until his long fingers curved around it, feather light and comforting. She tried to fight the calm spreading through her, although she didn't know why.

"Lena," his voice became husky again, and not hard at all, "it will be okay. We'll figure it all out."

She stepped back, two quick steps, breaking the contact between his hand and her cheek. "Tell that to Jubilee," she whispered, holding onto her anger and disappointment. "Tell that to Hania."

He nodded to himself and stepped away to go. He'd probably report the glow to Thomas as soon as the boys had been dismissed. Maybe before.

All of her worries and nightmares coalesced. She had to do it now. "Alex."

He turned back.

"Is there a space big enough for everyone to gather? Guardians and Wards?"

He nodded. "Yes, of course. The north gymnasium, where we have convocations."

"Please tell the Councilor I'd like everyone gathered there this morning at eight. There are some things that need to be cleared up."

His brows rose. "I—okay. If you want a general address, we should probably have a conversation about it first. Maybe later in the morn—"

"I'm not Jackson. I don't clear everything I do with either of you." She lifted her chin. "Eight will be fine. You can tell Thomas I said so when you report I'm glowing again." She held his gaze for a moment longer, then turned on her heel and marched back down to her hallway. After a moment, she could hear the sound of his brisk footsteps moving away down the hall to the waiting boys.

She made it halfway up her own corridor before a door opened behind her. She looked over her shoulder, ready with a word of comfort, but it was Rose. She didn't want comforting.

Rose joined her. Awake and alert, she inspected Lena minutely.

"Couldn't sleep?" Lena asked her. She wasn't going to bring up the glow herself. What would she say? She had no idea why or how it worked.

Rose shrugged. "We have long days back home. They start early."

"The Kewa are the same." Lena told her with a nod. "My days started earlier when I lived on my own outside the city, too."

Rose's brows rose. "You lived with Natives? And on your own?"

Amused and flattered by the newly appreciative light in Rose's eyes, Lena lifted her chin with pride. "After I decided to leave Azcon, I found an old gas station on the edge of Kewa lands. I cleaned it up, converted it, and built a life for myself out there. Spent time with the Kewa."

"By yourself?"

"Yes." She laughed, but the sound she heard coming from her throat was more than a little sad. Why did it seem so long ago? "It was good."

"You should come with me when I go," Rose blurted. Her lips turned up. "You belong with us, not here. There's nothing to challenge you or hold you here, not if you have it in you to carve your own place out there."

"I would have believed that not so long ago." She would have, before her mother, and Lydie, and a little girl named Jubilee, alone and haunting her dreams. Before the girls sleeping behind the doors of the hallway. "I don't anymore."

Rose made a small noise somewhere between frustration and understanding. "You're going to teach them, too?" From the way Rose voiced the word 'them,' she referenced the men of Fort Nevada.

"Maybe." Lena lowered her head, thinking of the meeting she'd called for a few hours from now. "Depends on how the, um, convocation I just demanded goes."

"What are you going to say to them?"

Lena rubbed her hands together. She reached up and tucked her hair behind her ears. "I don't know yet."

"But it's about us?"

"About all of us, yes. You, the girls, me. The rules have changed now. I won't have them do to you all what they've done to me."

Rose's face went cold and her lips curled back.

"No, no. They haven't abused me. It's…an issue of access. No." She shook her head. That wasn't it, either. "An issue of expectations."

"If they've treated you badly, then why stay? Why not come back with me?"

Lena took her time answering. "Because they're right," she finally said with a sigh. "They're right. The Council has to pay. And this place is…they…*we* are the best bet."

"Am I allowed to ask about that?" Apparently deciding to move on, she eyed the light Lena's skin gave off.

Lena shrugged and huffed a laugh. "You can ask anything you like. In this case, I don't happen to have an answer. Don't know what it is. Don't know why it happens."

"Don't know if it'll happen to the rest of us?"

She shook her head. "Nope."

"It seems like it'd be a distinct disadvantage outside, especially at night." She stopped and turned in front of Lena. "But it is arresting. Beautiful. Terrifying." She grinned. "How long does it last?"

"Little more than a couple of hours?" Lena wanted it to fade before she had to walk in front of the collected men of Fort Nevada.

"Hmmm. Should be long enough." It seemed Rose had a different idea. "If I were you, I'd use it to my advantage. A big meeting requires a big impression. We, men and women both, have ceremonial gowns we wear to address our people. Do you have anything like that?"

She didn't, and it took them some time to agree on what she should wear. Ultimately, Lena was out-voted. After the girls woke, they'd brought them back to her room. Eventually, all of them were gathered there.

She looked around at the girls in their borrowed clothes. Thomas had provided Ward uniforms for the girls after their baths the night before. They were all so thin that their bodies were swallowed up in folds of material. They'd belted and folded where they could. The girls would need clothes made to fit them, Lena told Thomas before he'd left for the night, and soon: just the first of her demands on behalf of the girls.

She hoped she wasn't making a huge mistake. She stood before the girls, the glow emanating from her skin magnified by the buff-colored clothing she wore. Rose had wrapped her in a long length of natural linen and tied it around Lena's hips. She'd then wound a long shawl of pale, raw wool around Lena, crisscrossing it behind her to knot at her waist.

The girls looked at her in awed silence, the light of her reflected in their wide eyes.

She felt ridiculous. She moved her shoulders restlessly.

"Stop fidgeting," Rose told her. She made a final adjustment to the crisscrossing section over Lena's breasts and stepped back. She wore a satisfied smirk. "Now, you *glow*. You're a vision. Intimidating from the moment you walk in."

Lena took a deep breath. "Thanks." She hoped she could pull it off. She looked at the ring of expectant faces. She had to make it work. "Before we go, you have to prepare yourselves. There's going to be…a lot of energy in there. And it will all be directed at us. It's going to be—"

"We know," Phoebe told her. "We can feel it."

"We're used to it," Marin added. "Our guards were Sparks. They liked the way we felt." She shrugged and looked down at her hands.

Constance and Charity shifted, moving closer together.

Lena's stomach turned over. Her furious gaze snapped to Rose. The woman stared back at her in silent confirmation. Her shoulders were back, tight and squared, and her hands fisted at her sides.

Hania had been looking off into space, her upper teeth scraping over her lower lip again and again. Now she brought her gaze directly to Lena. "Will they do that to us here?"

She felt a fire burning in her chest, white and pure as the root of a Sparked flame. "No." She answered Hania's hoarse, plaintive question. She wanted to say more, to reassure them all, but her gaze moved over them. Their treatment had been depraved. Words would mean so little. Even Marissa, the youngest of them, watched the other girls with knowing, pained eyes. Perhaps she hadn't been touched herself yet, but she knew.

A knock made them jump. After a polite pause, the door pushed open, revealing Alex. He searched the room, counting the girls. When he reached Lena, he stopped. Everything about him became still.

"Well," he finally said, "that's an effective look."

Rose snorted her agreement.

"Are they ready for us?" Lena's words were clipped. It was all she could do to remember that this man, this Spark, had not been to blame for what had been done to her girls. She had to remind herself he was one of the good guys, fighting for their safety.

He held onto the knob, twisting it. "I doubt it, but they are all in there waiting."

She nodded. The girls picked themselves up off the floor where they'd settled. She moved through them, touching hands with each of them as she went. When she stood before Alex, she ignored his weighing, cautious look and told him, "Lead the way."

They followed him out and through the warren of halls. Lena could feel the heaviness of male energy growing as they got close.

As they approached the filled hall, the buzz of voices augmented the energy. The energy rippled through the walls, pushing at them. Lena glanced over her shoulder at the now-alarmed faces of the girls and gave an angry push back at the male energy. The sound through the walls muted immediately. Her push had been felt.

Alex hesitated before opening the wide doors.

He opened his mouth to speak, but before he could, she reached out, grabbed the handle nearest her and pulled back. The muted sound became a total hush. She strode in ahead of Alex and lifted her chin.

Thomas stood toward the center of the open floor area, but forward. He'd been talking to a group of Guardians seated above him in the raised seating. His eyes widened as he took in her light.

She wished she hadn't brought the girls. It was too much energy. Even as she focused her will and pushed back, she knew she couldn't handle it. She didn't know if she'd be overwhelmed or intoxicated, but her time in this space would have to be limited.

Lena looked back over her shoulder and held out a hand, motioning for the girls to stay back.

Rose nodded her agreement, and she reached out to Hania's shoulder to reinforce the twins' hold on the fragile girl. They filed back along the wall beside the doors.

Jackson appeared beside them. He'd been standing at the back of the big room, but he moved into a protective posture now so they wouldn't have to stand alone.

Thomas walked across to meet her in the middle and greeted her with a solemn nod. She could see he, like Alex, was worried over what she was about to do. Still, they had honored her wishes and gathered everyone anyway.

Alex touched her on the arm, holding the contact. "Lena." His face was serious and his voice low. "Thomas and I worked a very long time to build what you see. We don't begrudge you the need to do this. Please don't tear it all down when you do. Remember there are only two of us—four damn hands—holding it all together."

"It's a delicate job," Thomas agreed softly, "and there's only so much damage control we can do at a time."

She shook her head at him. "No. There are six damn hands now. And honestly, I'm surprised the two of you didn't spend the last couple of hours figuring that out for yourselves."

The men exchanged a look. Thomas took a deep breath.

She wished they'd hurry. She felt battered. She stood straight and tall before them all. Mentally, she felt as if she leaned against a broad barrier of energy she had to make herself, her arms extended, palms pressed flat to keep it in place, back and legs braced. And she was slipping back.

The men parted, each moving to stand to either side.

She faced a thousand people alone. Thomas and Alex were still there with her, lending their support and, in effect, their agreement. But what she was about to do, she did alone. Could she?

Someone toward the back, high up above her, coughed. The sound echoed down to her. Her vision swam as she swept a look over them all. She blinked to clear them, and her eyes fell on a familiar face in the front. Guardian Wils.

He wasn't looking at her, though. He had reserved his calculating interest for her girls. The avaricious gleam was unmistakable.

She cleared her throat and projected as much as she could, straining with the pressure both to make herself heard and keep herself upright. "I know word travels fast," she said. "You all know I have joined you. And by now, you all know we have retrieved others like me. We—" she indicated the men beside her, drawing unexpected strength from them "—have gathered you here so there are no misunderstandings."

She turned and indicated her girls, wincing as she felt the energy pulse away from herself as attention shifted. She spoke quickly, drawing it back to herself to spare them. "We all feel the Spark within us. There's a pressure, a reaction that builds upon so many of us living and working together. The stronger we are, the stronger the weight. The stronger the pull on our attention and focus. But there are more of you than there are of us, at least for the time being. We need you to be mindful of that. I'm here now asking you to help us deal with the pressure and curb the demands on our time and attention as we settle into a routine."

"And how long exactly," Guardian Wils's voice rang out, "are we expected to wait to have...access?"

"These are my students, Guardian. *My Wards*. And as such, they will be left alone to learn. There will be no sneaking around to catch a glimpse or dares to get their attention." She let her stare strafe across the students. "There will be no...dinners to get to know them. No whining about access. It's simple: there will be none."

Now she had Wils's attention, but only for a moment. He snapped a look back to the girls. To one girl. She couldn't see which he'd selected, but it was clear that he'd already made a decision to have one of the girls she'd sworn to protect.

"You will not touch them, attempt to influence them, or act inappropriately in any way." Lena's glare bored into Wils's face, demanding that he turn his attention to her, that he hear her words. "You will leave us alone. We don't owe you anything, any more than you owe the unpowered the use of *your* bodies and skill. We are all working toward a new world where Sparks are more than tools to be used and discarded. We will achieve that vision. Do not presume to define our place in that world for us. The key to success is mutual respect."

A derisive snort came from the front row. She looked at the man who'd made it. She'd been waiting.

"Or what?" Wils turned his attention from her girls to Thomas. "Are you going to allow this—" he swept an ugly look over Lena "—little girl to stand before us and talk to all of us like this? Our end goal requires one thing and one thing only from all of them."

She could feel the flash of heat from Alex.

Before he could erupt, Thomas held up a hand. When Wils continued for a moment, Thomas's voice lashed out like a whip. "That's enough!"

Wils stopped talking, but he stood up, snugging down his

shirt and curling his lip in disdain.

"We brought Lena here to learn and to see what we could offer her, not the other way around. She is an ally—a powerful ally." Thomas stopped to spear Wils with a look of disgust. "Instead of treating her with honor, you made demands of her, whispered and plotted to gain access and favors. And then you have the audacity to be offended when she puts an end to it?" He shook his head. "Perhaps they require a demonstration, Lena."

Her lips curved into a smile. "Guardian Wils," she all but purred, "perhaps you'll help me?"

A faint ripple of laughter, more expectant than amused, rolled across the Guardians and Wards. They wanted to finally see what she could do. They'd been waiting. The anticipation pulsed against her.

Wils crossed his arms across his chest.

"You teach the Wards control, do you not? So I invite you to do what you've wanted from the beginning. Control me."

His brows bunched together. He had a moment of cockiness, both annoyed and confident for a moment longer before his sureness became concern. Concern flowed into panic. He reached out a hand and batted at the railing in front of himself, finally gripping it with failing strength as she took his breath.

"Stop me, Guardian Wils," she invited, "whenever you're ready."

He fell to his knees, eyes bulging. His face had purpled.

"Lena," Alex murmured.

But she wasn't done. She waited until his eyes rolled back into his head before she allowed him to collapse to the floor. The sound of his sudden breath wheezing in and out of his lungs filled the otherwise silent auditorium.

She lifted her chin. "We are meant to work together. We are *made* to work together. I am your ally." She tilted her head and regarded them, gaze moving over them, touching as many individually as she could before her focus snapped. She didn't have long. "Until the moment you decide I am not. Please don't make that decision."

She stepped back. The barrier she had erected in her mind

sagged, melted, and left her with nothing to use as a bar to the invading energy. She strode away, her heels cracking across the floor of the auditorium.

Rose's grin of triumph turned into narrow-eyed alarm at Lena's face. Jackson got the door open and Rose ushered the girls out ahead of Lena.

When Lena entered the hallway, she kept going, moving through and past them. She had to get as far away from the combined angry, confused, and excited male energy in the room behind her as she could.

She could feel Alex behind her, moving up fast. "Lena, stop."

"I can't," she gasped out, "I have to get away. It's too much energy."

"Let me help you!"

Her feet couldn't get her away fast enough. She'd cut it too close. The energy was inside of her now, building, burning into her own Dust, and she didn't know what to do. How did she get it out? Not even grounding could make this go away. She'd be fried, if she even made it all the way to the Grounding Pad. Her heart throbbed in her chest, the panicked beat of it hard and fast in her ears as she built to overload. Heat flared across her cheeks. Cold sweat ran down her spine.

She couldn't make sense of the sound of a scuffle behind her.

"Get back with them, dammit," Rose shouted. "You're part of the problem!"

The other woman appeared beside her.

Lena cringed away, hitting the wall. She didn't know what would happen to Rose if she touched her.

"Look at me." Rose stood before her, calm and certain. "You are my match. Remember? We were meant to be paired. You don't know what it means, but I do. Let me help you." The woman reached out for her.

Lena focused on her hands. Rose's hands shook.

"You have to share it, Rose, like you've seen us do in the lab." Phoebe's urgent voice floated down the hall. "But don't try to take it all. Hers is too much."

Rose grasped Lena's hands. "Let me help. Let it go." Rose

said more, indistinct noise.

Lena gasped for air. The small, ineffectual breaths sounded like crashing in her ears but did nothing to feed her body oxygen. The energy spiraled around her, coursing in.

Rose's fingers, clamped onto hers, were intertwined and white with pressure. Rose dropped to her knees to get Lena's attention. She looked up into Lena's face, her mouth moving, eyes urgent.

If she released it, if she gave it to Rose, she'd kill her. Rose was strong, but she wasn't used to doing what Lena did. Could Lena control it? Could she let the excess energy bleed out into the other woman little by little, enough for Lena to regain control? Lena's head rocked back against the wall and she squeezed her eyelids shut, holding back with everything she had.

Control it. Control it.

She opened herself to the connection.

TWENTY-FOUR

Lena's head rested on her curled arms. She fought nausea and the mother of all headaches at a desk in the small room Alex had hurriedly opened for them. They'd told her Jackson stood guard outside as the Wards and Guardians leaving the auditorium streamed past. Lena could still feel their energy buffeting her like a wind through a canyon. It slowed as their massed numbers dropped.

She would never again allow herself to be trapped in an area with a large group of powerful Sparks. *Small groups*, she told herself. *Small groups only*.

Rose paced, back and forth, back and forth.

The girls and Alex were lined up against the wall, avoiding the static discharges still crackling between Lena and Rose. The girls giggled at Rose's manic energy.

"Is this what it feels like to be you, all the time?" Rose asked again.

It was possibly the tenth time. She waited for the corollary question.

"Is this what it will feel like to be me?"

And there it was. One of the twins murmured a number. It set off a cascade of muffled laughter.

Lena took a deep breath, coughed back the nausea, and lifted her head. She squinted across the room at them.

She was acutely aware of Alex's concern.

He shifted, watching her carefully. "How're you feeling?"

"Pretty shitty. How close did I come to blowing everything up?"

"Pretty close. Let's try to make sure that doesn't happen again, okay?"

She nodded. "Okay." She allowed her gaze to follow Rose for a few seconds before her stomach heaved at the constant motion. "Is she glowing?"

He frowned. "It's more like a corona. And it's fading fast." He assessed Lena. "You've stopped glowing."

She processed that. She couldn't make heads or tails of it right now. Her head felt like someone had driven a spike from the base of her neck up at an angle into her brain.

She squinted at the girls. "How are you all doing?"

Marissa, leaning comfortably against Alex's leg, popped her thumb out of her mouth long enough to smile at Lena. Charity and Constance grinned across at her for a moment, and then returned to tracking Rose's movements. Phoebe and Marin murmured that they were all fine.

Hania cleared her throat. "You shouldn't worry about us. You get better."

Lena's heart clenched. "Were you scared, Hania?"

The girl nodded, the movement so small Lena barely perceived it. Her hair, clean now, hung in a dark shining curtain around her face. It gave away the movement Lena might have missed otherwise.

"I'm sorry I frightened you, Hania. I'm better now." She received the barest flutter of a smile. She decided then she would wipe the men who'd hurt these girls from the face of the planet. Nothing would stop her.

She looked back to Alex. As usual, he seemed to read her mind.

"When you're ready, we should go. They're hungry, but they wouldn't leave you. And Thomas is waiting to talk to you."

She lifted her brows in one motion with her raising head.

He shrugged. "There're some things we need to discuss with our new partner."

She took another big breath. "I'm ready when she is," she

said, nodding toward Rose.

Everyone looked at Rose, who stopped pacing and looked back, making an attempt at her usual tough, controlled persona.

"I'm fine. Better than fine. I feel great."

"Wonderful," Lena told her. "Want some more?"

"No." Alex and Marin chorused together.

Rose laughed, the sound a little manic.

Lena looked at Marin and Phoebe. "She will be okay, right?"

"Yes." Marin answered.

"We don't know." Phoebe said. The two looked at each other and then shrugged at her. "If we had to guess, probably yes," Phoebe allowed. "But we've never seen anyone share anything that...." She shook her head.

"Big?" Lena suggested.

"Dangerous." Alex supplied.

Phoebe pointed at him.

"I'm pretty sure you were literally about to—" He made an exploding motion with his hands. The sight of it keyed something in Lena's mind, something she should remember. Trying to catch the elusive memory made her head throb, though, so she let it go.

Marissa, taking a cue from Phoebe, pointed at Alex in confirmation.

"We'll work in more control exercises, for your Spark and your temper."

"With Wils?" she asked, then she smirked. The Guardian she'd humiliated taught control to the incoming and primary year students.

He chuckled. "We'll think of something."

"If you're really okay," Lena checked with Rose. "We should go."

Rose clapped her hands.

Lena winced and tried to swallow the heave. She gingerly got to her feet and followed them out of the room. Alex was making arrangements with Jackson to take the girls to the cafeteria. With a worried look for Lena, Jackson led them away.

She shook her head. "You've got to stop using him as a babysitter."

Alex smiled. "No worries on that front. He has his new orders. It's safe to say he's happy with them."

"Oh. Something more than training me in reconnaissance techniques, I take it?" It wasn't quite a pang inside. Perhaps regret for what might have been? She swallowed and pushed it away. She didn't want Jackson. She was an assignment to him. He'd made it clear.

Alex shrugged and nodded. "Sorry."

He didn't sound sorry. He sounded pleased. The king of the sexy smirk and the intense, sidelong gazes when he thought she wasn't looking sounded pleased. Perhaps they needed to revisit their agreement not to talk about that kiss?

"C'mon," he said. "Thomas is waiting."

They moved through the halls, and Alex adjusted his usual brisk pace to her pained walk. Lena noted the halls were unusually empty and said so.

"Yeah, well, you made an impression. Wards are tucked away in class. Guardians are teaching...or behind closed doors plotting."

"Plotting?" She winced. "So you think I alienated them enough to betray you to the Council?"

He moved his shoulders and looked at her, his lips quirked up. "That's always been a possibility, from the very beginning. We watch. We listen. We keep close tabs on entrances and exits." He laughed. "We've always been of the opinion that any coup will come after we've rid them of the Council. We'll see if our opinion changes any over the next few weeks."

"I'm sorry if I've screwed it all up."

"You haven't screwed anything up, Lena." He paused in the hallway outside Thomas's office. A slow smile spread across his face. "You have made things measurably more interesting. I've definitely been enjoying myself."

She managed a low laugh. "It's been an adventure, hasn't it? I'd say we've had our moments. You conduct a hell of a reconnaissance training, Agent Reyes."

"I could say the same for your private lessons."

It seemed his own words had taken him by surprise. He

turned his head to his shoulder for a moment, then turned back to her with a broad, unrepentant smile.

"I thought we weren't going to talk about that?"

His gaze dropped to her lips, tracing them as she grinned up at him. "We're not." He shook his head. "We're not," he repeated.

He pushed open the door, shooing her in ahead of him. Behind her, he muttered something about talking being overrated. He led her past an unmanned desk and into an office.

"Well, that doesn't seem very efficient," she remarked breathlessly, tilting her head toward the empty desk as they entered.

"I sent my assistant to get breakfast. I figured you might want to eat," Thomas told her, looking up from his desk. He dropped his pen and leaned back. "You need to eat. You look like hell."

"Thank you." That must be why she felt a little giddy. She needed to eat. She eased herself into a chair. She sat for a moment, uncomfortable and aware of them watching her. Finally, she cursed softly and pulled her legs up, tucking her knees under her chin.

Alex sprawled in the chair next to her.

Thomas leaned back in his chair. "That was quite the performance with Guardian Wils."

"You said they needed a demonstration."

He gave her a long look. She looked right back, completely unrepentant. He exhaled and frowned at Alex.

"She fits right in, doesn't she?" Alex deadpanned.

Thomas laughed, a quick burst of sound. He nodded agreement. "I guess she does. Except when we get mad at her, we can't work it out in the sparring ring."

"Oh, I don't know," she smirked, "I could probably take you—both."

They looked at her in startled silence, then both threw back their heads and roared with laughter.

"Yeah," Alex said, wiping tears away, "you probably could take Thomas. He could never hit a woman."

"And yet I hit you all the time, Alex."

"Are you two really going to sit there and use 'woman' as

code for being weak in front of the girl who could stop your heart in five seconds flat?"

"You're right," Thomas said, "We don't want you to get mad. You might, I don't know…" He looked at Alex for help.

"Explode?" Alex offered.

Thomas nodded. "There's the word I was looking for. Yeah, explode."

She made a face at them.

"What was that all about, Lena?" Suddenly all business, Thomas seemed worried. "The glow? The massive energy—" He gestured with his hands.

"I don't know. I really don't. It's only happened once before, and not like that. I have no idea why it happens."

"Except it happens when you're really angry?" He glanced at Alex, who was already shaking his head.

"No, she was healing me last time the glow happened."

Thomas digested that. "And you weren't angry?"

Lena shook her head.

"No strong emotions?"

She shook her head again.

"Nothing held back or—" He widened his eyes, clearly grasping at straws.

She started to shake her head again, but then stopped, considering.

"What? What did you think of?"

She could feel her face getting warm. She shook her head. "No…."

Thomas leaned forward. "Lena, this is important. We have big plans. We want to include you. But there are motivators that may upset you. We won't share them if we think you'll be a risk to yourself or anyone else as a result. So if there's something, spill it."

She took a big breath. "When I healed Alex, there may have been a strong reaction. To touching him. One I suppressed." She refused at look at Alex. Like the man didn't already have a huge ego? "Not anger."

Thomas flicked a glance at him.

She would not look over.

"I see." Thomas rubbed his lips. Was he trying not to laugh?

She closed her eyes in mortification.

"No, really, it's fine," Thomas continued drily. "That happens a lot with him. Happens to me sometimes when I hit him."

She did laugh at that. She shook her head and looked at Alex. He wore a small smile, but he didn't have anything to add.

The three of them fell silent. Lena cleared her throat. "So.... Big plans?" She prompted.

Thomas made a gesture for Alex to go ahead.

"You remember that we started all of this after noticing certain discrepancies?" Alex asked.

She nodded.

"After we made the decision to move, to make a change, we decided the one advantage we have that the Council does not is our longevity."

Lena frowned. "But the Council uses Sparks?"

"They use them, yes. But no Councilor is a Spark. Never has been. And under current traditions, there never will be."

She looked at Thomas, questioning. He was a Spark.

"They don't know I'm a Spark," he told her. "I'm very careful to maintain that side of the role when I'm outside of these walls. I only travel after a thorough grounding. And I never use the Spark, ever, anywhere but here."

She nodded her understanding.

Alex continued, "Our lifespans allow us the luxury of taking the long view."

"We moved quickly at first." Thomas interjected. "We had to consolidate our base here and put me in position on the Council. But since then, we've waited and watched. Until you. Things seem to be accelerating now. You have them in quite a state. We've decided to take advantage."

Alex leaned in, elbows on his knees. "Because of the distances involved and the autonomy of each Zone, each Councilor is responsible for naming his own successor. The successor is named within the first year, and the name is submitted in secret to the Council at the annual meeting. No one but the Councilor and the Council knows. Until now. At the Council meeting several years ago, long enough to not arouse suspicion, mixed in with Three's various reports and requests, he unknowingly submitted a change to his successor. A new name went in."

Thomas smiled. "It's time for Three's heir to take his place. With him, we will have two strategically critical Zones in our control. We can put in motion our plans to acquire the third."

"So…you're removing Three." She remembered the man in his garish clothes. She remembered his eyes on her body.

They nodded.

"The annual Council Meet is coming up. Three leaves via caravan in two weeks." Alex told her. "He's going to die on the way. When the caravan arrives at the Meet, the first order of business will be announcing the successor's name and installing him."

"Okay. So what's my role? You said you wanted to take advantage of the situation. I assume you have something reserved for me?" She did a terrible job of keeping the eagerness out of her voice. It wasn't merely what the Council had done to her. It was what they'd done to the girls.

Thomas nodded.

Alex exchanged a look with him and told her in a steady voice, "We want you to take revenge."

"Revenge?"

"On the man who ordered your torture and allowed the death of your mother." He looked at Thomas.

"On the man who killed your father," Thomas said.

Her breath caught. "Three?" She'd always suspected it.

They nodded.

"But my father was his aide." The cold sweat down her back returned. She had to know. "Was it because of me?"

"No. His security caught your father looking for information about something no one was to know about."

"The prison?" Lena breathed.

"The prison." Alex confirmed. "We didn't understand why until now. Everyone within the Council upper echelon knows about the prison. Even the citizens have some idea. But not about the secret program. Not about the girls."

"For the record," Thomas said, "I didn't know about the program. Either I'm too junior to be brought in on the conspiracy, or, as we suspect, not every Councilor is involved. We're hoping to get an answer on that after this strike." He grimaced.

Three was one of the Councilors involved in the imprisonment of powered girls. Her father had figured it out, and it had gotten him killed.

"So I'm to kill Three?"

The nonchalance of the question should have bothered her. It didn't. She had waited for this. Her family had earned it.

Alex nodded. "We'll insert you into the caravan as one of the workers. When the time comes, I'll bring you to Three. Courtesy of your power, he'll suffer a heart attack. He'll suffer his heart attack over and over until we have all the information about the Council conspiracy he can give us."

"Alex has been named as his Security Chief." Thomas said. "He can create a distraction and get you in."

"Won't that be dangerous? I mean, it's kind of obvious. New Security Chief? Death on the road?"

"We've got it covered." Alex told her. "It will look like a heart attack brought on by betrayal. After he's dead, there will be a strike by a well-trained force hunting the Councilor. They'll drag him off, leave his body in the woods. We'll find him after a search. And hopefully the seeds of suggestion we plant about agents coming for the Councilor will sow mistrust and confusion among his collaborators." He smiled. "It's a risk. They could close ranks. But self-preservation is a double-edged sword—we plan to work the angle that would bring some to abandon the cause, and work it hard. After all, we have a hysterical junior Councilor to demand investigations."

The first of the blood-price would be paid soon. Her answering smile, like the eagerness swirling inside her, was close to feral. "And we start in two weeks? I'm ready. I'm ready now."

TWENTY-FIVE

Lena yawned while she pushed Sam down the hall. It was late, and she'd discovered in the last week that there wasn't enough time in any day to complete everything she had to accomplish. Not only did she have her own lessons with Thomas to help her learn control, but she had to teach the girls, help them acclimate, and ensure they were safe, happy, and healthy. She gave daily lessons to a group of hand-picked Senior Wards. And she met with Thomas and Alex in debriefing meetings held late at night due to Alex's schedule.

She also carved out time to see Sam. It wasn't simply because he offered clarity about their history and where they might be headed. She liked spending time with him. He was her respite, the quiet part of her day.

They reached his room. She parked his chair beside the bed and put the brake on, but he waved her off again when she came around to lift him onto the bed. An aide would come and ready him for bed.

"It was beautiful, Sam." She smiled at him in the darkness, referring to the night sky they'd both enjoyed as they talked. "Thank you for bringing me." Never mind that she had pushed his chair. It had been his idea. He'd told her to come for him the night before she ran off to save the world from the Council.

Sam returned her smile, though his eyes were tired now. "Thank you. And Lena...."

She waited. He liked to send her off with a bit of wisdom he believed she needed to hear. She liked hearing them.

"Pay attention to the voice inside your head. I ignored mine for too many years, chasing after what I thought I needed to put things right. I was wrong. That voice knows exactly what you need. Listen to it."

"Yes, sir," she said. She leaned in to kiss the softness of his cheek. He held her hand for a moment, nodded at her, then let her go. She went, not saying good-bye. Sam didn't like good-byes.

She made her way back out to the private elevator, moving up and down the stairs and through the halls in a tired shuffle. As she turned the last corner, deep male voices echoed in the hall ahead of her, moving toward the elevator as well. She slowed, not willing to risk being trapped in an elevator with Guardians who resented her little display and did nothing to tamp down the lust or resentment threading through their energy. They weren't all like that, but a dedicated core—

Her head lifted at the sound of her name.

"—because of Lena. He says we'd all be better off once she's out of the picture."

She didn't recognize the voice, but the words froze her breath inside her.

"You shouldn't be listening to him. The man's a silver-tongued, two-faced snake—"

"And *no one* would ever suspect him. That's why it's beautiful. Think about it. Think about the army we could create if we had unlimited access to those girls." The first man's voice dropped, as if even he knew how foul the concept behind the words was and didn't want to say them fully aloud.

"When?" Reluctant agreement.

"Spring. We want them comfortable and recovered before—" The heavy security door closed behind them, closing Lena off from the rest of the hateful words. She leaned against the wall, staring at nothing, swallowing back disgust and rage and disappointment.

Some mystery Guardian wanted her out of the picture so they could have free reign with the powered girls? Not freaking likely. She didn't know how, but she'd make sure she and her girls were long gone by Spring.

—ᨍ—

Lena turned the corner, rage swirling with exhaustion in a mix guaranteed to keep her up. Ahead of her, Rose pulled Lena's door closed behind her. Lena frowned. Rose wasn't one of the girls to be tucked into bed, but she would take responsibility for them in Lena's absence. She'd mentioned heading to bed to be ready for the early risers. Charity and Constance were notorious for waking everyone well before dawn, ready to go.

"Hey," Rose greeted her with a yawn. "Alex is looking for you. Last minute details. I left you a note."

Alex, Jackson, and Lena would leave before dawn, hiding their movements through the city in pre-dawn murk. She'd hoped to get some rest before it was time to go. Better to be up with a purpose. The words she'd overheard would echo in her head all night anyway. She'd go find Alex.

Rose blinked and tensed. "What's wrong?"

"Nothing." She shook her head. "Just anticipation." She couldn't share what she'd heard with Rose. Not yet. The Neo-barb woman would gather up their charges like chicks and take off, and Lena wouldn't be available to protect them. She would come back after she'd finished Councilor Three, and she'd tell Rose then. They'd all go together.

"Are you sure?"

"Yep. Get some sleep. You'll need it."

Rose snorted a response, muttering about doing exercises, not taking over all of the other crap Lena did in a day.

"Rose. Thank you," she said. "Just keep them together and keep them close, away from the Guardians."

Rose nodded, wariness overcoming sleepiness. "Of course. Now, go find Alex. The world will be a different place for you once you've avenged your family, Lena. You'll make it right."

She hoped Rose was right. The things she needed to make right were piling up on her. Sometimes she wanted to push them away for a minute so she could breathe.

She checked Alex's office first. Next, she tried his rarely used personal quarters. As she raised her arm to knock, the door was pulled open from the inside.

Alex blinked in surprise, a huge reaction for the man. "There you are."

"Rose told me you were looking for me."

"I was. We wanted to bump up our departure, if you're ready."

A breath slipped out, long and slow. "I'm ready." Did she really sound that listless?

He frowned. "What's wrong? You're supposed to be excited."

"Nothing. I am."

"Uh huh." He leaned out and looked up and down the hallway, then backed into his room. "C'mon. Get in here. Spill it."

Lena arched a brow at him. "Afraid to be seen with me in your private quarters, Reyes?"

He grimaced. "It's not that. Someone might make assumptions."

She rolled her eyes as she walked past him. "We can't have anyone figuring out the real me, can we?" Of course, it'd been so long since she'd had sex, she could hardly say that anymore. It wasn't like she had what she considered viable candidates for a meaningless romp to relieve tension at Fort Nevada, anyway. Jackson had made himself as clear as day. And Alex had distanced himself from her over the last week. He was all business. No more flirtations. No more stolen kisses. She was so frustrated she could scream.

He closed the door behind her then stepped past to stand in the middle of the seating area, hands on hips. He glanced around as he waited for her to approach. The further she moved into his private space, the less comfortable he looked. She stopped a foot short of him.

He crossed his arms and focused on her. "Okay. So tell me. What's wrong? Heightened emotions are bad, remember? I can't have you start glowing as we trot through Azcon in the middle of the night, and I'd rather not go boom. So, where've you been? What happened? How can we fix it?"

Lena swallowed. She rubbed her forehead and smoothed her hair back, clasping her hands behind her neck. "I was with Sam. On the way back, I overheard some Guardians talking. And I'll fix it myself." There. She'd answered his questions. Could she go now?

"Sam?" Now concern colored his voice, although whether it was for her or for his ancient mentor, she wasn't sure. Sam always brought out the humanity in Alex. "Were they bothering him?"

"No. As if I'd allow that," she said.

"So what did you hear?"

She shrugged. "Some stuff." No big deal. A plot to get rid of her in nine or ten months so they could have full access to the wounded children Lena had brought to Fort Nevada for protection.

She'd put them in danger. Wasn't that how it worked? Tears of frustration sprang to her eyes. She blinked them back as fast as she could. She would not cry in front of him again, no matter how good it would feel to have him put his arms around her in comfort.

She caught the flare of panic that bloomed on his face, and he stepped back, easing over to a chair to sit. Was he putting more distance between them? He really didn't want to be alone with her. So much for that amazing kiss she hadn't put out of her head.

"So tell me this stuff," he said.

"I'd rather not."

Alex rubbed his chin. "Well then, how am I supposed to help you?"

You want to help, do you? Screw it.

She stalked over to stand directly in front of him. "You can help me by letting me feel human for fifteen minutes. I want to feel good for fifteen minutes. I want to not think, or plan, or worry for fifteen freaking minutes. I want to feel like a normal woman for *fifteen minutes*. Not someone who's *special*." She twisted the word.

"But you are special, Lena." The muscle in his jaw jumped.

"I want to be touched like a regular woman—no implications or expectations. Is that so much to ask?"

He was silent.

"I know you want me."

He growled and narrowed his dark eyes. "We all want you, because you're special."

"Then give me fifteen minutes. You want to fix it. That will. Give me that."

"Fifteen minutes of tension relief? That's what you're asking for?"

This isn't about feelings, she told herself. *No feelings.*

Lena lifted her chin. She wouldn't play by anyone else's rules. "Yes."

"Yes?" Alex nodded. "It's not me, then. Not personal." He looked past her, his eyes hooded. When he brought them back to her again, she could see the decision he'd made. "Sounds like something I can live with."

She leaned in as he reached to slide his hand up her jaw.

His palm cupped her face, fingers tangling in her hair as it slid forward. His thumb moved across her lips. Lena slid her knees up onto the seat to either side of him, straddling him as he pulled her mouth to his.

Like the first time, the contact was more than lips meeting, the electric flare deeper and brighter than it had been with Jackson. But this time, the only thing soft about his kiss was his lips.

Energy surged between them. As his tongue traced the inside of her lips, a blazing trail of shocks flared in her skin and exploded like bright lights behind her eyelids. He sucked at her lips, first one and then the other, and energy welled up from her. As he pulled and coaxed, the rising flow felt like fingers stroking deep inside. Each time he drew her lip into his mouth to suckle at the energy, those fingers of power slid up inside of her, moving toward him, leaving a quivering, electrified trail behind. He drew her power into himself.

Lena pulled away, and the electricity crackled white energy between their wet mouths. It hurt, little sparks popping against nerve endings. Alex's eyes were glazed. He wanted more. But it was her turn.

She lowered her mouth again, pulling the energy from him this time as she darted her tongue between his lips. She framed his face with her small hands and tapped the energy deep within him to draw it up into her through his nerves, his skin, his lips, and tongue.

Alex groaned and wrapped his hands around the backs of her legs. He slid them up, cupping the curve of her bottom, fingers caressing the crease that led him to her inner thighs. He drew her to him.

She allowed it, pressing against his body. She wanted more of him. More pressure. More skin against skin. Her hands sank down from his face to slip between them, pulling on his shirt. She pulled it up and off, tearing her mouth from his for an instant to yank the shirt over his head.

He worked the buttons of her shirt, fumbling at them in his hurry. He freed the last of them, spreading her shirt open and back and pushing it off her shoulders. He sat back to look at her.

She followed his gaze to his hands. They spread wide across her ribcage, his sun-darkened brown skin stark against her pale freckles. Above his fingers, her skin curved into the slight swell of paler skin and peaked nipples. He slid his palms up to her sensitive breasts, and she pressed into him, sliding her hands up to cover his. His thumb circled her nipple then slid away as he pulled her up.

He drew her into his mouth, the power slicking electric hot up her nerves. She arched her back, melting into him, already shuddering with the force of the energy surging through her as he licked at her. He slid his hands around her back, pulled her closer, holding tight. Everywhere their skin met, the searing flux of energy wove between them. Each time their skin parted, a white arc of heat spanned the distance and danced along their skin, joining them.

Lena sank lower, pushing her hand between his waistband and his skin. She slid her fingertips along his lower belly before dipping lower. The soft, almost delicate skin she found was a contrast to the rigid flesh it covered. She wrapped her hand around him and pulled energy along the length of him.

Alex's hands and mouth stilled and his eyes closed.

Like that, do you?

She danced her fingers down. She waited a beat, giving him a second of anticipation. She tightened her hand and drew up again, this time reaching further to pull more coursing energy through him as she drew her hand up in one smooth motion.

He growled deep in his throat, hiked her up on his body, and surged to his feet. He carried her to the rear of the room. She tipped back, falling onto her back on the bed, even as he held onto her waist. His fingers worked the buttons on her pants, and he pulled them from her, turning them inside out. She scooted herself back, watching him.

He shed his own pants, kicking them away. She traced his broad shoulders and chest with a heated gaze, down to his waist and the prominent line of hard-muscled lower belly arrowing down from the edges of his hips in a vee. He held himself, stroking where her gaze touched and she lifted it back up to his. He grinned at her in anticipation.

A breathless laugh escaped her. "You are such a jackass, Reyes."

His grin turned into a low, satisfied laugh, and he crawled onto the bed. As he moved, he slid his fingers up her skin, leaving a cascade of tiny sparks dancing along her skin.

He lowered his head to nip at her left calf, drawing electricity up through her and into himself. He did it again above her right knee, pulling up and igniting the Dust within and then letting it go to spark away. He smirked at her and winked before he lowered his head again, running the tip of his tongue along the inside of her thigh. His mouth slid inward, his lips and teeth nipping at her, drawing delicate skin and flaring power gently up before releasing it, again and again. His hands slid up around her hips so his fingertips could trace swirls of sparking, heated trails over the skin of her lower belly.

Power bubbled within her. It wanted out. She shivered, fevered, reaching for him and pulling him up her body. Lena wrapped him in her arms and legs, drew him down to her and inside of her. The energy battered at her for release as his mouth covered hers. Alex stared down into her eyes, moving with her, frenzied.

Unable to fight the heat welling up, she opened herself, her energy boiling out to merge with his. With every move, he devoured the energy her body poured into his and fed it back into her, a loop going on and on until she lost herself in it. He was electric heat that obliterated everything but the ecstasy of being. Finally, she lost even that to the crescendo of power and release.

She came back to herself slowly. Blood pounded in her ears, the sound of soldiers marching, thump, thump, thump. The lust and Dust fueled energy had already curled back into her. How long ago?

She opened her eyes. A ceiling above her. She didn't think there would be a ceiling if they had exploded. They must still be alive. She recognized the weight of one of Alex's legs across hers.

Lena turned her head. He was awake. His dark eyes traced the lines of her profile. Her breath hitched. Did he have any idea how clearly the yearning for connection shone across his face? Not any connection. Her. And she could feel the answer to his yearning inside her chest.

They stared at each other, into each other, shared energy nestled inside each of them. Alex swallowed. He pulled back from her, drawing his leg away and rolling onto his back. He closed his eyes and shook his head.

"Dammit, Lena."

"What?"

"Don't look at me like that."

Her chest clenched. In the long beat of silence, she decided whether or not to respond. She figured it wouldn't matter either way, so, a little defensively, she said, "I'm looking at you the same way you were looking at me."

He sat up, swinging his legs over the edge of the bed. He shook his head. "No. I wasn't. You were mistaken." He ran his hands through his hair, slicking it back, before turning to face her, except he didn't look at her. "I thought you understood. You said it was just fifteen minutes."

It was supposed to be.

He ran his hands through his hair again. "This was a bad idea." His throat worked as he swallowed hard. "Look." Long silence. "I've done a lot of shitty things in my life, and in the past three months, most of them have been to you. Making you feel like I have more to offer you than I do…would only be one more thing to add to the list. I can't do it." Alex reached out, as if he couldn't help himself, and ran a finger from the delicate point of her collarbone across to her shoulder. He pulled back at her shiver. When he raised his gaze to hers, she could almost watch the regret filling it. "I thought I could. I can't. I'm sorry."

She felt sick. A few minutes ago, she'd felt the same way. She didn't want this. She didn't need impossible feelings for a beautiful, broken man.

He jumped out of the bed, gathering up his clothes. He hopped on one leg, trying to shove the other leg into his pants.

"Alex." She wanted him to come back, to touch her again. That wouldn't happen. And she'd be damned if she'd ask.

He shook his head. He went in search of his shirt, muttering to himself about being a fucking idiot.

"Alex!" She could make this okay. She could bury it deep, cover it with all the other crap she carried inside her, and never look at it again.

He finally looked back and hesitated. She rolled out of the bed, moving toward him and scooping up her own clothes as she went. She stopped in front of him.

You can do this, Lena.

"I asked you for fifteen minutes, so I could feel better. And that's all I asked for. It's all I needed." *Liar.* She managed a chuckle. "I don't think you quite managed a full fifteen, but you get bonus points for style."

He stared down at her, face shifting like he was trying to decide whether to be relieved or insulted. She leaned in and rose up on her toes, pulling his head down so she could place a final soft kiss on his lips.

It was her signature move, the good-bye kiss she'd used on plenty of Azcon boys when she'd taken what she needed and never intended to see them again. Why did it make her throat tighten this time? Apparently Jackson had more in common with his mentor than any of them could have guessed. She somehow wanted them both, and neither of them seemed capable of giving love back.

Stupid girl. Congratulations. You're a freaking cliché.

She swallowed the lump away as she stepped back from him. "We can still leave early," she said, making her voice as light and free as a bird winging away. "I'll be ready in a flash."

TWENTY-SIX

A lex pushed himself away from the wall as Lena exited the elevator before him, reminding himself again to get his head back where it belonged.

She stopped and looked over her shoulder. "We're loading at the regular platform, right?"

He nodded, and she was off, a bounce in her step as she left him behind.

She glanced back at him. "Jackson is already here."

Lena boarded ahead of him, calling out a greeting to Jackson. If the young agent responded, Alex didn't hear. As soon as Alex stepped aboard, the train rose from the rails. He glanced up in surprise. He hadn't lost his balance, but a little warning would have been nice.

Jackson stood at the controls glowering at his reflection in the glass. Apparently, he'd said something to Lena before Alex had boarded, because she stared at Jackson now, twin spots of color on her cheeks and her lips compressed with anger.

Alex raised his brows in question.

"Apparently Jackson went looking for me tonight. And he found me. Or he *heard* me," she told Alex before she turned her furious attention back to Jackson. "You had your chance. You passed. *You* rejected *me.* You don't get to be pissed now."

Jackson's mouth opened in a little 'o' of shock. His mouth snapped shut, and he cast a look at Alex then compressed his lips.

Shit. Alex didn't need this, not right before the most crucial operation of the last twenty years.

Maybe you should have thought about the mission before you indulged yourself, dumbass.

Alex looked at Lena. He tried to tell himself she wasn't worth it, but it was a lie. If she gave him the opportunity, he'd do it again in a heartbeat, even after everything he'd told her. That pissed him off more than anything.

"Ward, get over here." Technically, Jackson had been promoted to agent. Alex wouldn't give him the honorific if he was going to behave like a student. Alex stalked over to stand beside Lena. She dropped into a chair to curl around herself, arms wrapped around her legs.

Jackson set the train to auto-drive and came directly over, focusing on Alex.

Alex met his stare. "Do you have a problem?"

Jackson shook his head. "No problem, sir. I am already over it. Mastering yourself is critical, right, sir? Isn't that what you told me after you ordered me to back off?"

Did the kid really throw my own words back at me? Before Alex could respond, though, Lena jumped in.

"You call this mastering yourself?" She shoved her hair behind her right ear in agitation and glared at Jackson, waiting until he met her gaze. "It's his fault for giving you an order. It's my fault for liking sex. At what point will you actually master yourself enough to take on the responsibility for walking away?"

"I was being respectful of the stature of someone I developed feelings for in spite of my training."

"No, you weren't. You didn't have feelings for me," she told him with quiet disdain. "If you had feelings for me, any kind of real feelings, you'd have done what you wanted and damn what anyone else thought. You didn't, Jackson Lee. But he did."

Jackson and Lena stared at each other.

Alex sighed. He really didn't want to pull Jackson, but he doubted the kid could get over this, not after that. She was brutal. Honest, but brutal.

As if reminded of Alex's presence, Jackson yanked his stare from Lena to look at him. "Sir—"

"I am not discussing this with you. All I need to know, Lee, is if you can put aside your personal issues."

They needed Lena. They wanted her. The plan would work, and it would make the pieces of future operations fall neatly into place. Jackson was the expendable one. He could choose another eager young agent. He might not be as good as Jackson, but he'd do.

Wouldn't have anything to do with removing a rival, now would it, Alex? He squelched the voice in his head mercilessly. He didn't have any rivals, because he damn well wasn't pursuing anyone.

Alex crossed his arms and stood still, waiting for Jackson to realize his status. Alex knew when he had. The realization washed over his face like a wave of water. Alex imagined it was icy cold. He gave the kid a minute to deal with reality.

"You understand?"

Jackson nodded once in response to Alex's question.

"We have one Lena. We will not risk her. If you cannot work with her, if you cannot overcome this, then you need to tell me now so we can get someone who can." He waited a moment while Jackson processed. "You've got to make your decision by the time we get to Azcon. We need to be able to make an exchange for a new agent. Lena will have to get started training him immediately. And," Alex added with a grimace, "We'll have to hope he's as quick as you are."

Jackson raised both brows. "There isn't anyone in my class as quick as I am. And there won't be an exchange. I understand." No apology came, but Alex was satisfied. The men looked at Lena.

She shrugged with one shoulder. Her next words told him what he needed to know: she could pretend all was well if it meant they could move forward. "Can we actually work now? Because I had an idea about why it's been such a struggle for you men to learn."

Alex sat on the arm of the chair behind him, one eye out the window at the front of the train. Jackson wasn't ready to pretend, but he sat stiffly and gave Lena his attention.

"It comes down to how we talk to the Dust. I think the Dust

responds to affection."

Alex could feel his brows lowering. Jackson stared at her with a look halfway to 'what are you babbling about?'

She rolled her eyes at their faces. "I know how it sounds, I do. But it occurred to me—" she glanced at Alex and then away "—recently, that Alex had significant success getting the Dust to do what he wanted when he was focused on…feeling…affection."

She rubbed her hands through her hair, mussing it in frustration. He could see the very direct Lena was both frustrated by and not particularly good at being circumspect. Alex had to assume she wanted to spare Jackson the details behind her theory, because it certainly wasn't because she was remotely shy about sex. Either way, it didn't matter to him.

"That is the most ridiculous thing I've ever heard in my life." He squinted at her. "What happened was related to you and me, not how I was talking to the Dust. They're machines. You think it was because I was whispering them sweet nothings?" Alex lowered his voice to a husky murmur. "'Dust, when I put my lips here, you spark out over there.' Is that what you think?"

Jackson stopped nodding agreement, going still and stoic beside him.

"Well, if that's how you were going to do it, I'd think your bedroom manner needs work."

"There's nothing wrong with my bedroom manner, as you damn well know."

"Exactly!" She tossed a look at Jackson and held up a finger to keep him from walking away. Her face flushed with frustration and temper under the freckles. "Alex, when you were…using your bedroom manner, were you ordering the Dust to respond? Or were you focused and…seductive? Because whatever you were doing, it was successful."

He smirked.

"Stop it. That's not the point."

"What is the point?" Jackson demanded.

Was he not enjoying the conversation as much as Alex?

"The point is you don't go around thinking about the Dust affectionately. But I do." She held up her hands and shrugged. "I think it's a male-female thing," she continued. "We express ourselves differently. And yes, I know, intellectually, they are machines. But I don't get how you cannot feel affection for something that is always *there*, waiting to do what you want. It's so eager to please. How can you not respond to the constant comfort of knowing—?"

"What do you mean by 'always there'?" Jackson interrupted.

"Always there. Waiting. You know, at the back of your mind. Can't you feel them, even kind of hear them, all the time?"

And suddenly Alex understood. He rolled his eyes and rocked forward, burying his face in his hands as he let loose a string of curses.

Jackson, who must have understood a moment behind him, tried to explain Alex's frustration to the mystified Lena. "The first lesson we get when we get to the Ward School is how to keep from accessing the Dust when we don't mean to, so we can keep ourselves and everyone else safe."

Alex looked up. It made absolute sense. "We learn how to block it off. They teach us to silence it except when it's needed for charging. It's the first series of lessons for every powered child, whether they rate the Ward School or not. Except for you. You didn't stay in school long enough to shut it out. You learned to listen. And I'm guessing it liked being heard."

—⁂—

Alex bent over the lockbox at the door, not in any particular hurry. Jackson and Lena laughed as they came up the street arm-in-arm behind him, posing as a young couple out too late. Alex wasn't worried about this stretch of their journey. They'd already made it through the worst of the public streets without any attention. Fortunately, the "new prosperity" Councilor Three bandied about in his speeches meant it was no longer uncommon for young people to be out at obscene hours.

They turned into the alley. He waited inside the entry. As soon as they joined him, Jackson dropped her hand like it had burned him. She rolled her eyes as she passed Alex, leaving the two men together in the small space. He was tempted to comment, but Jackson had done the job. Anyone who had been paying attention would have believed they were a young couple drunk on love.

"Let me get her settled in then I'll take you around through the gates so you can check in proper."

Jackson gave him a restrained nod. No more babysitting. Jackson was now Agent Lee.

Alex entered the small living area as Lena returned from the tiny hallway at the back which held the entrances to the three tiny sleeping areas and one bathroom. He gave her a grimace of apology, knowing she'd be stuck here for the week. "It's small."

She laughed. "It's positively palatial compared to the last one. And the kitchen is 'wow.'"

He nodded and looked over at the kitchen opening on the left of the living area. Bigger than the main area, it had broad counters, a wide, energy-sucking refrigerator, and an old-style stove. Even the sink was wide and roomy.

"The kitchen is the point," he told her. "You're going to be spending most of the next week learning how to cook Three's favorite meals from memory."

"I—what? Why?"

"Because that's your cover."

"I'm a cook?"

He wasn't sure her face could be any more doubtful. He wished he'd bothered to ask if she could cook. He'd assumed, since she lived alone, she could. She'd have to be a fast learner. Done was done.

Instead of voicing his concerns, he nodded. "You are a cook. It was the easiest placement and the best way to keep you out of Three's sight. He has very specific tastes. He takes a chef and one assistant from his favorite restaurant for himself and his senior staff. You are the sous chef. This keeps you out of view, for the most part. Three is the only one who can ID you concretely— Hernandez is dead, Lucas is gone, and no one else got significant face time."

"What about the guards who were in the room? The ones who brought my Mom? They left, but they were in there for a little while."

"They're not an issue."

She raised her brows at the stern certainty, but she let it stand. "And the chef? He's okay with this?"

He felt satisfaction and knew it reflected in his smile. "The chef is absolutely okay with this. In fact, I'd say he's eager to start."

Her eyes narrowed in suspicion. "What did you do?"

Alex shrugged. "I didn't do anything." He changed the subject, gesturing down the small hallway. "You have your pick of the bedrooms. Jackson will be in temporary Agent housing because he's official now. My people will be drifting in to leave status updates. Use them to give you feedback on the cooking." He grinned. "We'll have your official papers by Thursday, and you'll show up for inspection and placement on Friday with everyone else. It'll be a madhouse. Three doesn't travel to Council small."

She had all the information she needed. He should go. Instead, he paced into the kitchen and opened and closed the pantry and the refrigerator doors, inspecting the contents. Everything was in its place and fully stocked. Of course it was.

Her recipe book rested on the counter. He slid it toward himself to flip through it. "I don't have to tell you to stay put and work your ass off to learn these recipes, do I?"

"No." She laughed. "Other than Ace, there's no reason for me to want to leave."

"Ace is gone." He closed the book and handed it to her. "I checked to see if he could keep you company, but he was prepping for his own trip out. He left this morning with the trade caravan. They head in early to be set up and ready for all the Council households and their C-notes. It's quite the experience."

She nodded, obviously not surprised. She flipped the pages of the book, but seemed distracted.

Alex waited.

She opened her mouth to speak, and then closed it.

"What? Lena, speak up. I need to be confident we have everything dealt with before I leave you alone."

"I would like to see Danny, if it's possible?"

Her brother. Alex's heart fell. He'd been afraid she'd ask for him. "It's not," he told her. "In fact, it would be a very bad idea."

She looked up at him, eyes enormous and ridiculously green, and she shook her head imploringly.

He made himself go on. "He's not interested in seeing you." He wanted to be as gentle as possible, but he needed to be thorough.

"Danny was always supportive. He put himself at risk just to be sure I—"

"I know. But after everything happened, he was under a lot of pressure. He was investigated, and then he had your sister to cope with and your mother's funeral." Alex sighed. The sister alone would turn anyone sour. He rubbed his mouth. "I've been working up in Council Central," he said, referring to the upper floors where Council business was conducted in a warren of offices by cutthroat aides. "Danny was a rising star. His rise is on hold, and he's pissed. He's blaming you. I don't know how much of that is trying to salvage his career or his life, but I can't risk you seeing him. A betrayal now would be catastrophic on a number of levels."

"He would never turn me in." At Alex's questioning look, she insisted, "He wouldn't betray me!"

"I'm not so sure."

Lena looked at the floor. She picked at one fingernail, shoving her thumbnail into the edge of it over and over until the tip tore away. She made a soft sound and brought the finger to her mouth, sucking the blood away. Her lowered lids and lashes hid her wounded eyes.

It was clear that she wanted to pretend the tears in them were from the nail she'd torn past the quick, but Alex wasn't fooled. He took a minute to berate himself for feeling sick he'd been the one to hurt her. He couldn't afford to care. But he did.

He slid his hand along the counter and stepped closer, taking her hand away from her mouth. He looked down at her finger. Blood welled up from the torn nail. He curled his hand around the finger and took a deep breath, focusing his intent.

Nothing happened. The Dust didn't even swirl in acknowledgment. Alex huffed a nervous laugh and tried again.

"Dust. This should be easy, but I suck at healing. I'm sorry."

At least he'd made her smile.

"It's okay. I've got it." The bleeding slowed, and her torn skin grew back together. "See? All better."

"Not quite." He drew her hand up to his own mouth and settled his lips on her fingertip, pressing a kiss onto the new skin. He held the kiss for a long moment. Her pupils dilated, and her lips parted, drawing him down deeper.

Let her hand go. Back away. Right now.

Behind him, Jackson exited the bathroom and entered the living space. Alex lifted his head, glancing back at Jackson standing awkwardly behind them, keeping his focus everywhere but on them. Alex returned her hand to her, but waited a long beat before he stepped back.

She sighed, glanced at Jackson, and then refocused on Alex. "So," she said, her voice almost normal, "do you guys have time to practice dropping that shield you have before you leave? I want to know if I'm right about the Dust. Again."

TWENTY-SEVEN

"She wants to see Danny." Alex scrubbed his hands over his face as he brought up the last issue he had to discuss with Thomas tonight before he could head back to Azcon on the train. Just thinking of her face, her vulnerability when she'd asked for her brother, made something inside him tighten. It had been eating at him since the night before.

That wasn't true. The deception had been eating at him for months.

"She can't. It's too dangerous at this point. It's not possible."

"I know. That's what I told her. But with everything she's been through… He's essentially the last of her family. I think she needs it."

"And if he slips? If he tells her what's really going on? You know how volatile she is. At best, she'd walk away. At worst? She guilts Danny into going with her, and everything we've built that hinges on him falls apart. She goes to Ace and shares with him then *he* somehow shows our hand to the wrong people—"

"I told you months ago we should groom him, bring him on board—"

"I won't trust anyone associated with Dragonfly House. Ever." Thomas reached up to run his index finger over the smooth, scarred skin under his eye where the slaver's brand had burned Thomas's face as a child.

It was an unconscious movement. Thomas had been doing it since they were boys, and always at the mention of anything to do with his childhood captivity. Alex should have called him on his dislike of Ace at the beginning. A current-day entry-level trade house dealer had nothing to do with the decisions and backroom deals of the trade house thirty-odd years ago. Ace shouldn't pay for what had been done to Thomas before Lena's friend was even born. And Lena shouldn't pay by extension.

But the emotional investment in decades of hatred made Thomas intractable. Perhaps if Alex appealed to his friend's emotions, he could win a small victory for Lena—a private meet-up with her brother?

"You haven't spent as much time with her as I have." Alex had to tread carefully. Thomas hated it when he thought Alex was trying to finesse him. "She's hurting. This would help."

Thomas shook his head and tapped a finger on the desk in front of him. "There's more at stake here than her pain and you know it. So you're going to have to put your dalliance behind you—"

Alex narrowed his eyes and met Thomas's hard gaze with one of his own.

"—until it's time for us to use it, and *focus*."

"There's nothing wrong with my focus. And we're not using what happened between me and Lena. Period."

Thomas arched a brow and smiled, though the expression seemed on the sad side to Alex. Perhaps his friend wasn't as comfortable with his own decisions as he seemed.

"Unless she turns up pregnant."

Alex shook his head. "That's not a possibility."

"Alex. It's always a—"

"Not with Lena. She's got her reproductive system on lockdown." At Thomas's expression, Alex laughed. "I don't know why either of us would be remotely surprised. She's not one to be pushed around by fate or circumstances. Of course she's using her abilities to maintain her own health, with everything that implies."

"Well, that's damned inconvenient."

"Inconvenient? It's her life."

"It's our future. I was never going to force anyone on her, Alex, but we need this. We need the children she could produce.

We need her—"

"Happy. We need her happy, Thom. And she's damn well earned it."

Thomas leaned forward and steepled his hands in front of him. He met Alex's gaze and took a careful breath. "She is happy. Happier than she has been. You could convince her—"

"No. That's not going to happen. Leave it be."

Thomas shook his head. "This isn't about feelings."

"I said leave it. It's not negotiable. I'll deal with Danny, and all the repercussions that will bring when she finds out. I'll take all of that. But you will let this go, Thom." Alex willed his friend to feel how deadly serious he was about this. He wouldn't have her, have any of them, used like that. Not ever. "Not just for Lena. For all of them. Whatever will happen with the future, with children...leave it be. Let it happen naturally. Or we're no better than the Council, and we have no right to keep going."

Thomas tilted his head back and looked up at the ceiling. When he turned back to Alex, it was clear he'd made a decision. "Fine. But she stays in the dark. And so does Danny. Until it's a done deal, mission accomplished, risk averted, and you're all heading home, neither of them will know the other's role."

Alex nodded. It wasn't the answer he'd hoped for. It wasn't what she needed. But it bought her a larger freedom. He hoped it would be enough.

—✲—

Alex's hand paused above the lock plate. He shouldn't be here. He didn't know why he'd told Jackson that morning that he would conduct Lena's daily check-in himself. Yes, he had to share the chef's critique of her progress with her, but he'd already written his comments and planned to hand them off to Jackson to take to her.

He had no reason to be hovering outside the safe house door, except for the itch that had been keeping him up, distracting him every day, pricking at his awareness. He'd planned to stay away. It wasn't only logistically smart, but it was emotionally best, too, especially after his deal with Thomas. He didn't want to deal with the soft, wounded sound of her voice if she asked for her brother again.

He'd managed to hold out four days before he mentally slapped himself for being so obtuse. You didn't get rid of an itch by ignoring it. There was only one way to settle it down.

You scratched it, good and hard.

He keyed the lock and went in. Even here in the foyer, the layered spicy and savory aromas of what was cooking made his mouth water. And the chef claimed she couldn't cook?

When he turned around, Lena was framed in the light from the sunny living room, eyes wide.

"Alex? What are you doing here? Is everything okay?"

Her feet were bare, and she had on a summer dress for relief against the heat in the little house. The dress billowed light as a breeze around her small body, two thin straps all that held it on her shoulders. A riot of blues and greens swirled together across it. Flour dusted her chin and nose, and coated both hands, and her face was puzzled.

The night he'd left her here, he'd told her she wouldn't see him again until they were on the caravan and it was her time to take out the Councilor.

He came down the hall. The pressure inside eased at the sight of her, even as his heart rate increased. This was a bad idea. He smiled anyway. "Chef Domenico had some issues with his latest evaluation of your skills. I thought I should come over and talk them out with you."

Her eyes narrowed. "Chef Domenico is a pompous ass." She turned and went back into the kitchen.

Alex laughed as he followed her in. "He is. But he's also your cover, so we need to work smart. We need to keep him happy."

"Uh huh," she responded. "Work smart. Got it. I guess you came to tell me how to do that?" She leaned against the kitchen counter between them, waiting for him to answer her.

"Where did you get that dress?" he asked instead. The colors did amazing things to her eyes.

Where'd you get that dress? His inner voice howled with laughter.

He cleared his throat, a stern warning as he settled into one of the kitchen chairs across the counter from her, and added, "You didn't leave the house, did you?"

"Of course I didn't." She paused and tilted her head. "Jackson brought it for me."

"Did he?" Alex worked hard for that neutral tone.

She shrugged, looking down now to fiddle with dough in a bowl to the side of her. "I think it was kind of an apology. I'd been complaining how hot it was in here with the oven going all day—it is summer. He said it looked cool." She twisted a smile and peeked up at Alex through her lashes. "He said the color reminded him of my eyes, if you must know."

Alex gritted his teeth. *Oh, hello, Jealousy, you bastard. Get the hell out of my head.* She was manipulating him. He knew it. It didn't mean it wasn't effective.

He leaned back in the chair, crossing his arms.

She seemed put out when she didn't get any other reaction from him. She raised her brows. "Were you going to impart any 'work smarter' wisdom? Or was the stare supposed to cow me into behaving?"

"Pay attention. Don't be careless. If chef says presentation matters...then *present* the food on the plate. C'mon, you know this makes a difference."

She lowered her gaze again, and nodded. "Got it. Guess I can get back to work then." When Alex didn't move she looked back at him. This time, she only raised one brow. "Was there something else I screwed up? Or did you want a sample of my shitty cooking? Because the chicken won't be done baking for another fifteen minutes."

She turned away, dismissing him and busying herself at the side counter, fingers pulling off bits of dough, rolling them into small logs between her palms, and then shaping them into crescents on the wide, flat pan in front of her. Her posture told him that not only had she been bored, but now she was pissed, too.

Fifteen minutes, huh?

It was probably best that her back was turned so she didn't

see the wide, predatory grin he felt spreading across his face.

He rose and padded into the kitchen to ease up to her. Her body stiffened when she felt him close in behind her. He pressed his palms to the counter on either side of her working space and lowered his mouth to her ear.

"Fifteen minutes sounds perfect," he growled into her ear. "I think that's what you asked for when you were stressed out and in need of distraction, wasn't it? Fifteen minutes? Well, now it's my turn."

He closed his mouth around her earlobe, his lips gentle while the tip of his tongue ran along the soft curve of flesh, leaving a trail of popping sparks behind.

She shivered but pulled her head away and turned her face to him, angled down so she didn't have to meet his eyes.

"You're the one who said I had to work smarter to make the chef happy. Well, I'm working…" As if to prove her point, she showed him the curved crescent in her hand before settling it onto the pan.

The sugary, nutty scent of the dough rose up and swirled in his nostrils, mixing with the heady, heated fragrance of Lena herself. The scent cued the memory of her taste, and his blood pounded lower.

Dust, I need this.

He dipped his head down to press his lips to the curve where her neck joined her shoulder. When he ran his teeth along her skin, she shuddered in response.

"Stop it." Her voice was husky in his ears. "You're distracting me. This is hard."

A low chuckle bubbled up and hummed against his lips on her skin. "That's not the only thing that's hard." He pressed closer, rubbing himself against her back. "And I promise, I've been far more distracted by you than you know."

She leaned away. He could hear her swallow and then suck in a breath. She shook her head. "You said this was a bad idea. You said you didn't want—"

"I know what I said, dammit. But I can't stop thinking about you." He moved his arms in, wrapping them around her and tucking her in against his body. Her small back curved against his front, and the Dust started swirling, moving in where they were in contact. His voice dropped to a hoarse whisper.

"I can't stop thinking about you," he repeated, and kissed the spot low on her neck that had made her shudder for him, his tongue flicking out to taste her skin.

"About kissing you." He feathered light kisses across her shoulder and the back of her neck.

"Holding you," he murmured against the curve of her neck on the other side. His left hand slid up and across her to tug the thin strap of material off her shoulder. He moved his face down to the edge of her shoulder and licked little sparking explosions back up toward her neck again. He finished at her right ear.

"I can't stop thinking about how amazing it was," he whispered in her ear, "to slide inside you. Do you remember?"

She had the tightest, sweetest little—

Her head tipped back, opening her neck to give him access to the sensitive skin.

He pounced, licking and kissing, drawing up the Dust then releasing it. Her breath came in little pants now, and the sound of it made him crazy. He pulled her tighter against him, lifting her onto her toes so that he could feel the curve of her round ass.

She gulped air. "Fifteen minutes, huh?"

He reached one arm up, supporting her weight easily with the other as he tilted her face toward him. "Fifteen," he answered, voice just as breathless. "Say 'yes.'"

"Yes."

He captured her mouth with his, not gentle and not caring. She matched him heat for heat, pressure for pressure, electric and hard. His hand slid down, drawing down the other strap until both breasts were bare. He palmed one, using his thumb to play with her nipple until it pebbled before moving to the other. He toyed with them, loving how her body responded to his touch, before dipping his hand lower.

He pulled at the dress, gathering it up until he had access to the vee between her legs. She was naked under the dress. His blood pounded even harder. Though he ravaged her mouth with his, he kept his fingers gentle, easing between her legs to stroke at her most sensitive skin, dipping his fingers lower to draw up her wetness.

Her lips fell away from his, and she dropped both hands to wrap around his wrist and arm. Her eyes were closed as she focused on what his hand was doing. She rose up even higher onto her toes, leaning back into him for support, and spread her legs a little to offer him easier access.

He increased the friction and the pressure of the tight, swirling motions he made, and she responded. Her fingers tightened and released around his arm. The sounds she made were deeper, primal. Her brows drew down, and her eyelids squeezed shut.

He wanted to take her higher. He wanted her to scream for him.

Alex bore down, with more than just his finger. The Dust that had been swirling within them, surging between them like tides called by two moons, exploded toward the pressure.

She didn't scream. She went silent as her body spasmed, even the sound of her breathing stopped. It didn't matter. He couldn't stop watching her face transformed by the bliss that rolled over her in waves as the current rolled through her and he brought it back again and again.

She made no sound until she had finished. Then little moans caught in the back of her throat, slowly shifting to soft hiccupping breaths.

His head was going to explode. He needed to be inside her.
Now.

He slid his hand from between her legs so he could ease her back onto her own feet again, but her knees were jelly. With a proud grin, he scooped her up and moved around the counter to the table, kicking aside the chair and sitting her down on the table top. The dress he'd pulled from her arms had pooled at her waist. He slid his hand up her side and curved in to her breast, dipping his head down again to lick at her nipples while he eased her back. He wanted her bright-eyed again before he finished. He wanted full participation, but he was so hard he ached, and he couldn't wait.

Alex chuckled with anticipation as he worked at his pants with his free hand, but the sound that huffed against her skin came closer to a deranged cackle.

It must have got her attention. She threaded her fingers in his hair and pulled his head back. She wasn't gentle. And he hadn't thought he could get any harder than he was.

"What are you laughing at, Reyes?" Her smile was a little crooked, a little woozy, just a little drunken.

He laughed again. "Just thinking about what I'm going to do to you right now, Gracey."

Her lips curved up at his answer, and she leaned back and gave a little shimmy with her shoulders, making the rest of her undulate in a way that stopped his heart. It took some effort, but he brought his gaze back to her face.

She grinned back at him, orgasm-drunk no more. She was back, and clearly ready for more. He gave it to her, gripping her hips to pull her to him and thrusting inside. The wet friction and electric heat sizzled along him, over and over and over. His head fell back as his face contorted. He held on as long as he could, tendons straining, back tense. Her soft voice chanted his name in rhythm to his thrusts, and she let him have the charge she'd been building inside. He reared back, a shout exploding from him as he released.

He came back to himself slowly. The blood pounded in his temples still, and his breath sawed in his ears. He moved his head and discovered it was cradled on her chest, a small breast and small hand to either side. A smile flitted over his face, and he lifted his head to carefully rest his chin instead of his forehead on her chest.

She stared up at the ceiling, her smug smile answering his own. He laughed, and lifted himself up onto one arm.

"I think," she said between soft pants as her breath equalized, "that was even better," and she swallowed, "than the first time."

"I think," he said and closed one eye as he focused to think, "we may well get better every time."

She gasped a laugh. "You mean you're not running away this

time?"

Alex shook his head. "Nobody's allowed to run away. Deal?"

"Deal." She shrugged. "It makes the most sense, after all."

He struggled to stand, pushing himself up with both arms now. "What does?"

"Not running away. I mean, this revolution stuff is pretty intense. I have to imagine that's a lot of fifteen-minute increments of stress relief between the two of us."

Alex laughed, the sound rumbling up from deep in his chest. "I think you're right." He took a step back, glanced down, and then groaned as he reached down to pull his pants from around his ankles.

Lena sat up, watching him. A look that fell somewhere between curiosity and confusion played over face. "I thought you said no running away."

"I'm not." He leaned in to plant a kiss on her mouth to wipe away any concerns she had. "I'm *not*. But I stole away to come see you, and as much as I'd like to stay and spend the afternoon with you, I can't. We leave in three days."

She nodded. "Wow. So slam, bam—"

"*Lena.*"

She arched a brow at him.

"We'll have more time soon. When Three's gone. There's always a lull between missions." He leaned back in for a slower kiss. "But right now it's stolen moments. I'd like us to handle this." He searched her face. "Are you sorry I came?"

She met his eyes. A wicked light gleamed in hers. "I'd have been pissed if you didn't."

"That's not what I meant." He nipped at her lip.

"I know. But it's all the answer you need."

He answered her smile with his own, and dressed himself while she watched. Her head tilted to the side, and the dress still bunched around her waist. It was a great look on her.

When he'd finished, she finally reached down and found the straps to the dress, hopping off the table and pulling them up over her arms again. As she pulled the fabric up, she did that little shimmy that had made him lose his mind earlier, a mischievous smile on her face.

Alex barked a laugh at the provocation and pulled her into a kiss. When he let her go, he lightly smacked her ass and backed away. If he didn't leave right then, he wouldn't leave at all.

"Be sure and pass my regards to Jackson on his taste in women's clothing," he told her. "Unparalleled access."

She laughed loud and long, head thrown back. He couldn't help but grin. Happy sounded good on her.

"You tell him," she called out as he walked down the hall.

"I will," he shouted back. *Little fucker. Bringing gifts to my woman.*

Alex's hand paused above the lock plate. He leaned his forehead on the door. *My woman, huh?*

Yep. It had been a terrible idea coming here. And when he stopped smiling he might be able to make himself believe it.

TWENTY-EIGHT

Lena turned the small folder with her papers in it around and around in her hands. Alex had warned her against being late the morning before, but she'd still moved slowly this morning. She hadn't wanted to be among the first in line to gain final clearance to enter the caravan area.

Being first wouldn't be a problem. She'd arrived at mid-morning to find the line snaked up the alley beside the Council building and then curled around down the walkway bordering the street in front of the building. The sun had long since heated the top of her head and the shorter hair at the nape of her neck dripped beads of sweat. They ran down the curve of her spine, not chilling but itching her skin. She should have heeded Alex's warning.

Lena distracted herself with the memory of his last visit the morning before. He'd slipped into the safe house in the dark of the early morning hours, so they'd have more time for that last visit before heading out. They'd made good use of the time.

A sharp finger jabbed into her shoulder. She jumped, nearly dropping her papers.

"Why are you standing in this line with all of these...people?" Chef Domenico's disdain for those around her was palpable. His lip curled, and his nostrils pinched as if he'd smelled something foul. His expression made it clear what most displeased him was herself.

He pinched her blouse away from her shoulder with his index

finger and thumb and drew her out of the line to sweep her along beside him as he strode past those who'd been waiting in the hot sun since early morning.

"Excuse me," he drawled, giving a couple in front of him the once over as he pushed through the line. On the other side was another, far shorter line. Domenico marched over and stood in it, his thin lips still quivering with outrage. He waited four back from the desk manned by a Council official.

After a moment, he turned on Lena and growled in her face, "I do not wait in line with the *peones,* and neither do my people. It is simply not done. Anyone who knows me, knows this. What are you trying to do?"

Taken aback, she stared at the man. His face was florid. Did he care more about discovery or his reputation? She remembered her role as a new sous chef and dropped her gaze seconds before she would have responded to the man in like outrage. "I'm sorry, Chef," she murmured for any who might be listening. "I forgot. I was just so excited."

He pulled himself up to his full, impressive height. "Remember your place from here on. I am doing your…father…a favor by hiring you on. But my generosity does have limits. It would be a shame for you both if you exceeded them."

She kept her head bowed in what might appear to be crimson-faced shame to anyone looking. In reality, the threat left her shaking with rage.

"Papers?" The official snapped at her, and she realized it was the second time he'd spoken.

"Pay attention, you idiot girl," Domenico hissed at her.

She fumbled her papers out of the folder and handed them over.

"Mina Gardin?"

She nodded, acutely aware of the sweat beaded on her upper lip and across her brow.

The man dribbled a tiny amount of wax from a candle burning beside him across the first of four boxes and neatly pressed a small square seal into it. While the wax dried, he found her name in a ledger before him and initialed beside it. "You'll present your papers again upon arrival at the Meet, and then again when you rejoin the caravan to leave, and upon arrival home."

He refolded the papers and handed them back, watching as she tried and failed twice to slide them back into her folder.

Domenico sighed his impatience.

"Keep them with you at all times." The official smiled, but his lips barely perked. His face remained bored, and he had already focused on the VIP behind her as he extended his arm out and at an angle to be seen around Lena. "Papers?"

Domenico gripped her shirt between his fingers again and tugged her away toward the lines of steam-powered trucks, each with its attached car or trailer. The trucks and refitted train cars filled the cordoned-off parking area behind the Council building.

The converted trucks themselves were large, former industrial trucks retrofitted with fireboxes and boilers in the rear cargo area. Some of them had trailers attached to carry supplies or goods in large cargo boxes, or to carry the wood and water needed to fuel the trucks. Some pulled closed, adapted train cars where the caravaners would travel.

Their car was near the front of the second line of trucks. The position meant they'd be mid-way back from the head of the caravan, several cars down from the luxurious double-car carrying the Councilor. It was also many cars up from the regular kitchen cars and the supply trucks.

How efficient. She'd be spending a good portion of her day trotting back and forth, bringing up the non-specialty supplies they needed to feed Three and his elite staff, including Alex. Unfortunately, she wouldn't actually be seeing him at all until he came for her in two days.

Domenico released her shirt once they arrived at their car. He marched up the two metal steps to the door, slid it open, and entered. Lena followed.

The train wasn't what she expected. It was all kitchen, long, sleek, metal, and electric. As the sous chef, one of her responsibilities would be to keep it all powered. A narrow aisle ran the length of it. Stove and ovens were on one side, sinks and counter prep space on the other. At the far end of the aisle, each side had a narrow ladder leading up to curtained privacy areas: their beds. The aisle ended in a door she assumed was the bathroom they'd be sharing. Two flip-down stools at the head of the kitchen across from the entry were the only seating.

It was gleaming, clean, sophisticated, and practical. It only served to underscore that the next forty-eight hours would be hell. If she'd had any doubts, Domenico put them to rest when he walked immediately down the narrow aisle, climbed up the rungs on the wall to the right, and slid his duffel onto the mattress of that bunk.

"I always sleep above the sinks," he told her with a sniff as he climbed back down and came back.

Of course he did. The hellish residual heat rising up from the stove and ovens would be reserved for the sous. She didn't even bother rolling her eyes as she slid past him to climb the rungs on the left and put her own bag away.

"Hurry up," Domenico snapped when she pulled back the curtain to look at her meager sleep space. "We need to complete our inspection and be sure nothing is missing."

She dutifully hopped back down. The next five hours proceeded exactly as she expected. Domenico was furious with Alex for putting him in this position, but too frightened of the Agent to refuse. The fear, however, did not extend to her. He'd obviously decided to make her life as difficult as possible.

It didn't take her long to conclude Domenico fluttered from shelf to shelf noting the items he had deliberately forgotten to stock. The realization did not help her disposition as she ran back and forth from his car to the rear of the column where the supply trucks were in various stages of being loaded. Searching manifests for specific items and then sorting through the crates themselves, over and over, was exhausting in the full heat of the day. The embarrassment of returning to the foreman again and again added to her foul mood.

By the time Domenico pronounced everything in its place, she wore a gritty coating of dust. Her eyes burned from salty sweat and from smoke billowing from the rear kitchen area. An hour before, as dusk had fallen, the fires had blazed as cooks prepped dinner for the masses. She ran through the area with every trip, eyes tearing and stomach growling.

As soon as Domenico made his proclamation, she turned and slid the door open. Domenico's rapid footsteps chased her as she swung down from the car. The raucous voices and laughter from gathered workers sharing their first meal in the open sounded like freedom.

"Where do you think you're going?" He sounded offended again. "We take all of our meals in here."

The smoky fragrant breeze flowing outside the car raised gooseflesh on her sweat-dampened skin. She looked past him to the hot, closed space of the car. She could only imagine how much more miserable it would be once the boiler to power the steam engine was lit. She refused to spend every hour hiding in this car, even if it meant she spent the next days on constant alert.

"No," she told him firmly, "*we* don't." She strode away, weaving through the trucks and trailers she'd spent the afternoon darting between, and was gone before Domenico had even managed an exit.

Once she was sure Domenico wouldn't be pursuing her to pinch at her shirt in distaste and drag her back, she relaxed. She wandered through the gathered caravaners, lost in the crowd and the gathering dark. Were Alex and Jackson settled into their places within the caravan yet? Hoping to see Alex was pointless. Even if she caught a glimpse as he went about his duties as a senior member of the retinue, he'd pretend not to notice her. She understood that, and why, but it didn't help her mood now.

She hadn't expected there would be so many workers, although it did make sense. Scouts roved ahead and behind in the wild lands they'd move through. The caravan also needed drivers, and loaders, and techs in case equipment went wrong. While the trucks themselves were steam-powered and not electric, people still depended upon the old power. There had to be Sparks. And someone had to cook for all of them.

Even more than an hour after they'd started serving, a short line waited for food. Once she had her food, she went to hide in the shadows cast by a bonfire. She balanced her wooden plate on her lap and leaned back against the big wheel of a cargo truck to watch the others as she ate.

Although she'd come to look forward to Alex's all-too-brief visits, to laughing and talking and touching, neither the darkness nor the lack of company tonight bothered her much. She'd spent so much of her childhood alone, trapped in the house, that the solitude of her existence out in the desert had been calming. The constant light and movement and mental presence of so many others at Fort Nevada was overwhelming. Here, she wasn't a part of the hum of voices and laughter and the occasional shout. She curled around her plate in the darkness and went unnoticed by those around her. Or so she wished.

"What are you doing out here?" Jackson appeared out of the dark and squatted down beside her, keeping his voice low. He had clearly been taking inscrutable stare lessons from Alex. She gestured at her plate, to indicate the obvious. Jackson waited for a verbal response.

"Avoiding my boss so I don't kill him." Her voice was low, but she didn't bother to keep the agitation from it. "The man is insufferable."

"Don't you like insufferable men?"

She could see that Jackson immediately regretted the words.

"I'm sorry," he said to the ground. "That was unnecessary."

"I'm sorry, too." She waited until he lifted his face to her. "Not for—I'm happy now. I really am." She couldn't help the smile that tugged at her lips. "He may be insufferable, but he makes me happy. I am sorry you were hurt. I thought you'd made your choice, Jackson, and it wasn't me."

Jackson shrugged. "Guess I should've been more like Alex." A world of resentment welled up in the tight words.

She snorted and shook her head. "I fell for you because you weren't like him. Which is ironic now...."

A flash of something crossed his face. Disgust? Regret? Lena wasn't sure, and she wasn't sure whether it was aimed at her or at himself.

"Mmmm," he agreed. He swiped his finger over the dust on his boot. "And then I lost you for the same reason." He took a deep breath then swallowed. He met her gaze for a second before his swerved away. "It's fine. I understand. I just hope you know what you're doing."

"I always know what I'm doing."

"Like running away from your boss and jeopardizing everything?" He shook his head in disapproval. "I get that he's obnoxious. My understanding is he's also vain, egotistical, and stupid. That's why Alex was able to finagle you a spot. It would be a shame if everyone's hard work came to nothing because you couldn't deal with a difficult personality for a few hours." Jackson bounced twice on the balls of his feet, working his knees, before he rose to continue his patrol.

She picked at her dinner. Why had he bothered to say he understood, to apologize for Dust's sake, if he was just going to swipe at her?

What the Dust did Jackson know anyway, she seethed. He had the job he'd always wanted, and he'd used her to get it. He had no idea how much it had hurt. That she'd gotten over it and found unexpected feelings and happiness was irrelevant. He had no idea what she'd been through in the last few hours, either, and he felt perfectly free to criticize her for wanting a harassment-free dinner.

What really infuriated her, though, was that he was right. She shoved the last of the stewed pork into her mouth, even though it had lost its flavor, then hauled herself to her feet to carry her plate back to the kitchen. She grabbed her fry bread, scraped the rest of her dinner into the bins, and then stacked her plate for washing.

She trudged back through the darkness to Domenico's kitchen car. *Tomorrow, tomorrow night, the next day*, she told herself, counting down to her actual escape and the revenge she'd waited for so long. *You can do this.* She finished the last of the fry bread and wiped her hands on the back of her pants. One last deep breath of cool night air fortified her before she slid the door open.

"Oh! Has my wayward charge actually returned?" Domenico's voice, dark and still angry, twisted its way down the aisle to her. "I should make you sleep outside with the bugs for your disrespect!"

You can do this.

—⁓—

The Councilor always slept through breakfast, so they were officially off-duty for the morning meal. Three's senior staff had to eat with the rest of the rabble or go without. Lena and Domenico made their own light breakfast, as they had the day before on the road. In spite of the uncomfortable night, she found she had energy to spare as she buzzed with secret excitement. By that night, she'd have an accomplishment to show the memory of her parents.

In the afternoon, Fort Nevada agents would flow down over the caravan, creating a distraction while Lena went for the Councilor. By the evening, there would be no more Three. There would be one less corrupt Councilor ordering behind-the-scenes torture and death. Her girls would be one step closer to safe. As they got back underway, she lost herself in fantasies of how she'd do it. Suffocation? Little heart attacks? Stroke?

First they had to make it around the wastelands. She had been to Albuquerque and seen the charred areas where the pipeline still smoldered beneath the city. But nothing had prepared her for the Black Lands of Colorado.

The caravan made its way past what had been Denver, the caravaners tense and ready for attacks by Neo-barbs or Scavengers. The annual caravan made too attractive a target, and the rocky forests of Colorado were ideal for ambush staging.

The smell struck her first, an acrid, choking burn sneaking into the cars through cracks in windows and doors and catching in the back of the throat and nose. Domenico, a veteran of many Council trips, had already dampened a cloth and wrapped it around his face. She followed suit. Of course, where Domenico had a beautiful custom square of fabric, Lena had a dishcloth.

They stopped for lunch immediately north of Denver. It wasn't ideal, but they wouldn't be clear of the stink for hours anyway. The sooner they served, cleaned, and packed back up, the sooner they could leave again. Once Domenico took Three's luncheon out to the main cars, Lena leaned out to peer away from the caravan.

To the east, broken, black ground stretched as far as the eye could see. In a few places, steam still rose from the cracks, curling and toxic. The damage extended through what had been Kansas and Oklahoma and down into central and east Texas—the no man's lands which had borne the brunt of the immediate, fiery death that erupted over two hundred years before.

Sobered, she climbed back up into the car and began the clean-up. She tried to push away the imagined horror of the deaths of those trapped by the fumes but not incinerated by the flames. And then, of course, millions died afterward, of poisoning, of thirst, of starvation or disease once everything had collapsed. She couldn't shake the feeling of darkness and despair that seemed to creep in with the bad air.

What would she have done, if she'd been alive then? Would she have tried to flee?

I'd do whatever it took to find Alex.

It wasn't because the Alex she imagined from that time would be able to save them. At the root of the longing was the simple acknowledgment that she'd want to see him again, to hold him before death claimed them.

She pressed a hand to her chest, where an ache grew at the thought. She had always been about the physical. If she didn't care, it couldn't hurt. Where had this maudlin woman come from? Yes, they'd been through so much together, come so far since the day he'd walked into her home in the desert and changed everything. But this? She didn't love him, did she? No. They were friends, partners in revolution.

She swallowed back the ache in her throat and chest.

When the Dust had that happened?

A motion out the window to her right caught her eye. She moved closer and peered through the curtains. Alex stalked toward her car, his face set in grim lines. A huge, bald man with a bushy blond mustache paced him. Behind them, she could make out the legs of a smaller, slighter man, but the rest of him remained hidden.

Her glance strafed the area around her, recognizing

movement everywhere as people were moved away. Agents, some of whom she recognized as Alex's who'd slipped in to leave reports at the safe house for Jackson to pick up, slipped into positions around the car. Around her.

Around her? But it was too early. The attack hadn't started. They weren't in position. She caught another glimpse of his face as he moved in. It was dark, set, and not with anger alone. She recognized the expression. He had closed off, exactly as he had the day he'd stepped up and looked down at her strapped to the table in the Council building.

Her heart caught, twisted, and then began again, the slow, loud thumping a contrast to the panicked skittering of her thoughts. She stood, clearly visible through the window, as still as a rabbit that hoped it wasn't the prey being sought.

Alex moved around the front of the truck, out of view for a moment. When he appeared again, he roughly shoved the third man to the side, out of her view. Alex and the bald man moved into position on either side of the door.

He reached and slid it open. Alex called out as he met her frightened stare, "Magdalena Gracey?"

It isn't time. This isn't the plan.

Lena swallowed. "No. No. There must be a mistake. My name is Mina Gardin. I have papers."

He nodded at her, a small, comforting movement. It was a move designed to placate and disarm a suspect.

What was going on?

"Miss," he told her firmly, as if they hadn't spent as many stolen moments together over the past few days as they could manage, as if the whispered endearments that had made her feel like glowing Dust filled her chest hadn't come from his lips. His eyes were blank, like he'd never seen her before in his life. "If you could please step out of the car now, I'm sure we can clear this up."

It wasn't time yet, but he played his role so well.

It's a role. It's just a role....

She looked again out the window to peer through the gap in the curtains. Nothing moved. The agents had disappeared, and the caravaners were hiding. Was Jackson out there, too?

His words from her first night in the caravan came back to her. He would do whatever he had to do to ensure the plan went forward. He had made it clear that so should she.

She stepped one foot forward and reached up to pull the damp dishtowel from around her lower face. It fell to the floor beside her. Alex reached in, extending a helping hand.

She should go with him, shouldn't she? If this was all a part of the plan, or a contingency? Her heart thudded in her ears. She trusted him. It must be a change in plans.

She remembered his arm reaching out to her before—to shoot her with the electric barbs of a Taser. In the end, he'd made it right. He'd made his decision, but he'd done whatever it took to get her free.

"My name is Mina Gardin," she repeated. She couldn't read his eyes.

They looked nothing like they had two days before when he kissed her goodbye, fingers framing her face, forehead pressed to hers, reminding her to be careful. She couldn't read him at all.

It's a role.

She stopped and started to turn back. "I can get my papers."

They'd said to keep them on her at all times, hadn't they?

"No," Alex said. "We can get them in a minute, miss. You come on down, please."

She couldn't read his eyes.

Lean swallowed and stepped forward. She took the first step down and reached for his offered hand.

His fingers closed on hers like a vice, and he yanked her from the car.

She stumbled, caught herself, and then fell off balance again as he spun her around by her arm and pressed her against the hot metal side of the car.

He pinned her, one hand holding her wrist to the middle of her back, his knee pressing into the small of her back.

"Stop! What are you doing?" Terror filled her voice. Shame flooded through her, and she didn't know if it was because she couldn't make herself trust Alex or because she had ever trusted him at all. "Please, stop! You're making a mistake!" She tried to push against him but he was immovable.

"Shut up." A voice growled in her ear. Not Alex.

A hand fumbled at the back of her neck.

"Stop! Stop! This isn't what I wanted!" Another voice shouted at them. Danny's voice?

Lena tried to turn her head and look, but Alex held her fast. Another hand came up to push the side of her face against the car. Not Alex's hand. Why did it matter?

"You should have thought of that before," Alex snapped. The rage in his voice wasn't directed at her, and it wasn't an act. This was real. "What you want is irrelevant now, Mr. Gracey."

Danny did this? Her body sagged as her knees went loose. Her brother had seen her. He had reported her. She had been wrong. Her brother had done this, and Alex had no choice.

The hand fumbled against her neck again, pushing her hair up and away.

She felt the icy prick of awareness a moment before she heard the snick of connection. She bucked against them, desperate, wild for only a second. The Dust gathered within her chest, ready to burst out—

And then it scattered as the collar powered up, and the current surged through her.

TWENTY-NINE

As soon as the collar snapped into place, Alex stepped away. He forced himself not to avert his eyes as Lena fell into a boneless heap. Boneless, but not unconscious.

She stared at him, even as she blinked uncontrollably.

It didn't matter that he hadn't had a choice from the instant Merritt appeared at his shoulder just as Danny was asking why his sister was in camp, working with the Councilor's chef. At that point, her arrest wasn't in doubt. Alex made the decision to use her arrest to get her in front of Three instead of sneaking her in later. He'd be damned if he'd allow himself to look away from what he'd done.

His stomach heaved. His well-trained mind might be racing, picking through available choices and making strategic decisions, but his body fought his control. Even his chest felt hollow. He swallowed back the bile and tried to control the trembling of arms that wanted nothing more than to rip the collar from her now.

It's temporary. Ah, Dust, Lena, it's temporary, I promise!

He pulled the gloves from his belt and shoved his hands inside of them. When he knelt and reached out to touch her, intending to lift her to take her to the main car where Three waited, he could feel the charge surrounding her.

"Are you trying to give her a heart attack?" He reached his fingers around to adjust the current himself.

"If necessary." Merritt's response was even and satisfied. "And don't touch that collar, Reyes. This little bitch is the strongest Spark ever born. I saw what she did to the Council building. She gets max volts or she gets a bullet in the brain."

Alex looked up and sneered at the man. "Scared, Merritt? I've faced her twice now and lived to talk about it."

"Yes, you have." Merritt made it clear the fact made his skills, or him, suspect.

Merritt had responded to Three's selection of Alex as Security Chief by making the transition as difficult and tedious as he possibly could. Alex's original plan had been to simply wait the man out, until he'd discovered Merritt had been in charge of the long-ago interrogation and disposal of Lena's father. It wasn't shocking in itself, nor was it something he hadn't had to do himself in the past, but the mere fact of what it had done to *Lena* made him lean toward simply ridding himself of the man responsible.

It factored into his decision to bring the man on the trip. It had been widely assumed that Alex planned to leave Merritt as his Interim Chief while Alex was gone. Any Senior Agent could hold down the city, he told Merritt, but he needed the man who'd been responsible for the creation of the security plans to travel with them. Who better to deal with any lapses of security if they occurred?

Who better to take the fall? The lapse, and Merritt's subsequent fall, was already planned.

Alex held Merritt's cold stare as he adjusted the current. If Merritt's hand so much as twitched toward his gun, he would drop the man where he stood, even if he had to hunt down every witness watching the scene from in and behind the cars around them.

The big man was clearly unhappy, but he didn't make a move.

Alex lowered his attention to Lena. Her lids stopped spasming, but current still raged through her, rendering her powerless. He hoped somewhere in her was a kernel of trust big enough to know he'd get her out of the collar and safe. She might forgive him if he could get her to understand why he'd made the choice, a combination of tactics and knowing her resilience. The collar was a means to an end. He only had to make her see it.

She has to see. His mind tried to spin away to what would happen if she didn't, and his chest clenched, panic taking his breath. *Focus, Alex.*

He stood, watching Daniel Gracey now from the corner of his eye as he dusted off his knees. The young man was quite an adroit actor, although his emotions were probably real this time.

Lena's brother stood behind Merritt looking down at his sister in horror. He sobbed in great silent heaves, tears and snot flowing freely down his face.

That's right, he urged the young man's emotions on silently, *think about how you've betrayed your sister and the memory of your father. You betrayed your dead mother, too, and everything they ever asked of you.*

Instead of giving voice to his thoughts, he simply growled, "Get over here, Gracey, and make yourself useful."

Danny looked up and took the few shuddering steps over. He managed to get out, "This isn't what I wanted."

"I don't give a shit." He waited for it to sink in. It was the truth. "Now, pick her up. You can carry her back to the Councilor. We'll see what he wants us to do with her."

It was needlessly cruel, especially considering the true circumstances. He had no intention of allowing the Councilor to decide to do anything with her, but his people knew he couldn't abide stupidity. Danny approaching Alex directly about his sister qualified.

The kid stared at him. He looked down at his sister and then back up. He made a feeble gesture with his hand. "But...the current. I don't have any of those gloves."

"And you barely rate as a Spark." Merritt moved closer, threatening. "It'll hurt, but you won't be incapacitated. Pick her up. Now."

The muted sound of rapid footsteps falling on packed earth had both Alex and Merritt straightening. Alex had sent a message to Jackson before he and Merritt had taken Danny to see Three. He'd hoped Jackson might beat them here, so Lena would at least have notice of what was coming and steel herself for it. It hadn't happened. Jackson had been too slow. There'd been no warning for her.

Jackson rounded the edge of the car now and skidded to a stop, his focus going immediately to Lena on the ground. He froze. Panic and fear flared across his face. His blurted words, a shocked, "What are you doing?" made Alex silently curse him.

"Agent Lee," he snapped, "pull yourself together."

Jackson managed to recover, dragging his shocked stare from the collar around her neck. "Did you need me to transport her, sir?" he managed.

"No," Merritt answered for Alex. "Her brother was about to do that for us. Since he's the one who brought her to our attention, it's his privilege to carry her into custody. Isn't it, Mr. Gracey?"

Jackson glared at Danny, an obvious flare of fury.

Merritt's face tightened. The man's speculative eyes met Alex's.

"Find her papers, Lee," Alex told him, gesturing up to the car. "Then meet us in the Councilor's car."

Jackson nodded, keeping his face down. His attention flickered between the ground and the collar.

Really, Jackson? You think you're the only one disgusted by the need for this? You're not even the one involved with her, but your inability to control yourself has put her at risk! He cursed Jackson as Danny lifted his sister. He and the young agent would have a few things to straighten out once Alex had pulled their asses out of the fire and this was all over.

—◊◊—

By the time they made it to the Councilor's car, Alex had already revised the spur-of-the-moment plan. Merritt would make his suspicions about Jackson known to Three as soon as he could, casting doubt on Alex himself, since he had lobbied for Jackson to be his second. Without Three's trust in his leadership, their route might be changed, the security plan might be tweaked. Any number of small but significant changes could be made which might jeopardize the entire operation. They'd have to move the op up. They'd have to make it happen now.

"Don't put her on my furniture!" The Councilor's baritone command set his teeth on edge. "She might lose control of her bowels and soil it." Three made outraged shooing motions at Danny, urging him to pick up his incapacitated sister. "Put her over there, on the floor, away from the carpets. The floor can be scrubbed."

Alex snapped his fingers at Danny when the man hesitated. He pointed down to the spot on the floor as he assessed the twilit room.

The Councilor suffered from migraines and kept his own quarters darkened. Heavy drapes on the forward and side windows blocked out the light and prying eyes. It was about as good as he could hope for.

Alex leaned on the arm of the couch as Danny lifted Lena and hauled his sister to the corner to ease her body down. Danny held onto her head for a moment, kissing her forehead before gently settling her back against the floor.

Alex wasn't surprised. Guilt was a powerful emotion. He should know. He had enough of it coursing through him right now to power all of Azcon.

Three seated himself and ran his hands through his grey hair, his fingers pausing on the patch of black at his hairline. He smoothed it, the motion almost a caress. After a moment, he dropped his hands, and his fingers drummed the cushioned armrest as he looked at Lena, a small, pleased smile quirking his lips. The smile didn't move the seamed lines of his face, and it didn't reach his mean eyes.

Beneath the meanness, relief thrummed through the man. Which Councilor was Three so happy not to have to face after losing Lena? It was an academic question. They would find out shortly. Three would tell them everything.

Danny stood in front of Three, his head bowed. "Councilor?" He waited.

Three's attention turned slowly to his junior aide. The Councilor's face didn't lose the smile.

"I know you've had doubts, but I have been loyal, sir." Danny flopped his hand in his sister's direction, indicating his evidence. "May I ask that you please not kill her?"

"Oh, I have no intention of killing her, Daniel." The Councilor's voice was resonant and generous. "We're simply going to question her, find out where she has been. Who has been hiding her? And then she will pass to the custody of the Council."

"But...." Danny looked at his sister.

"They won't kill her, either, Daniel," Three reassured him.

No, they'll throw her in prison to experiment on her. What's a little torture to a Spark, after all?

A quick two-note knock at the metal door sounded. The Councilor called out, "Enter."

Jackson stepped up into the car. He'd regained his equilibrium. His gaze moved over Lena on the floor with no reaction.

Before the young Agent could speak, the Councilor dismissed Danny. "You should return to your transport, Daniel. We'll send someone for you if we need your assistance again. And to discuss again what you knew about your sister. And when."

The young aide had effectively been confined to his bunk.

Danny managed a miserable nod. He stepped over his sister's leg and around Jackson to leave the car.

After the door slid closed behind Danny, Jackson nodded respectfully at the Councilor and then lifted the papers to show Alex. "Her falsified papers, sir."

"I'll take those." Merritt leaned over and snatched them from Jackson's hand. He looked them over, fingering the heavy paper and holding it up to a nearby candle to check its translucence. "These are quality forgeries. I can barely tell them apart from authentic ID papers."

That's because they are authentic. Alex sneered internally at the man's posturing.

"She had help. Experienced help." Merritt met the Councilor's questioning look and then turned a considering gaze to Alex.

"Thank you for stating the obvious," Alex murmured, his voice dry. He tapped his lip as if he was thinking. "Agent Lee, I'd like you to go immediately to the nearest scout position. Inform them they are to make contact with our forward agents and pull back to reinforce us here."

Jackson's single nod confirmed he understood what Alex really wanted.

"Do you think that's necessary?"

"You're going to send *him*?"

Councilor Three and Merritt spoke at the same time. Alex answered only the Councilor.

"Sir, we may have exposed a larger plot. I can't risk that she's part of a sophisticated group intent on removing you. We'll make camp here tonight to ensure we are off schedule. We don't want to be where we're expected to be." He returned his attention to Jackson. "Why are you still here, Agent Lee?"

Jackson slipped out, hurrying away to the front of the caravan and the electric vehicles meant for speed and tactical response.

Alex turned his gaze to Merritt. "At this point, Councilor, the entire security plan is suspect." And Merritt had been the one to create it.

Merritt blinked. "You're not pinning this on me."

"Oh, no?" Alex just needed to buy time as he focused on releasing his block.

It was time to disable the collar. Lena needed to be a part of this. She had earned it. He had to give her that, after taking so much from her.

"No."

Before Alex could do more than pull his attention back from the collar, Merritt turned and slammed the door back into its track and jumped from the car. As a Spark in security, albeit a homegrown, locally educated Spark, Merritt was rated for a weapon, if barely. The man jumped away, pulling his gun and shouting for Agent Lee to come back.

Alex brushed past the powerful frame of the Councilor, telling the man to stay inside. He unholstered his own weapon as he went after Merritt.

"Stop right there, Merritt, or I will shoot you." He threw his already deep voice so it could be heard clearly not only by Merritt, but by anyone in the surrounding cars.

Merritt stopped moving forward, but he kept his weapon in his hand as he turned. "You're making a big mistake, Reyes."

"No, you made the mistake. Where are they?"

"Where are who?"

"The assassins you've set up to take the Councilor."

"You are not pinning this on me!"

"It was your security plan."

"Plenty of people had access. You had access."

"But not motive. It was your security plan, Lew!" Alex shifted to the left so the agent crawling beneath the car behind Merritt was no longer in his line of fire. He could sense the hovering presence of the Councilor in the door of the car. "Drop your weapon."

"Fuck you."

"Drop your weapon so we can go back inside and discuss this. You can still salvage things."

Merritt's hand tightened around the grip of his gun.

C'mon, Merritt, do me a favor. Lift it.

"If you think I'm going to let that play out, you're a fool." Merritt swung the weapon up.

Alex sparked the round as he fired the gun. A red hole appeared in the center of the man's chest. He judged it a little high. A second red hole appeared, bigger, tearing out, making the first irrelevant. The bullet came from the agent on the ground who had slithered into position under the car behind Merritt.

He barely registered the few scattered screams from those hiding in the cars around them. In the silence afterward, he crossed to Merritt's body, kicked away his gun, and then bent to check the man's vitals. He looked back at the Councilor. When he shook his head, Three disappeared back into the car. The agent rolled out from under the car and trotted over to him. They were shortly joined by two more.

He gave them their grim instructions: stow the body. Instruct everyone to hunker down in their cars until told otherwise. Create a perimeter, and confine the Councilor's senior staff to the forward car. He and the Councilor needed to be free to discover what they could from their surviving prisoner. The men nodded.

He picked up Merritt's gun on his way back to the Councilor.

Lena still lay in her heap on the floor.

The Councilor had crossed the room to make himself a drink with shaking hands.

"Sir?"

Three slashed his shaking hand through the air. He wasn't ready to discuss it yet. He raised the glass of amber liquid to his mouth with his other hand and began drinking noisily. That was fine with Alex.

With the Councilor's back turned, Alex crouched by Lena, reached around her neck and released the Council collar. He pulled it open.

Her eyes cleared, and her body went rigid with rage.

From one moment to the next, with the first blink of those beautiful blue-green eyes, he felt fear. Cold gripped him at the base of his spine and squeezed. Would anything be the same between them? He'd made the choice he'd had to. If he believed the hurt and fury on her face, the answer was no.

Please, Lena....

The Councilor slammed the glass on the counter in front of him and poured more whiskey.

"So there really is a plot? There's a conspiracy to assassinate me? Me!" He turned, drink in hand. His resonant voice dropped in shock. "What are you doing?"

"Collaborating," he told Three. He pulled the collar from her and tossed it across the room to the couch.

She sat up, moving slowly. Her recovery would be too slow.

He pulled his focus, hoped for cooperation, and then asked for what he wanted.

The Councilor opened his mouth to shout, his brows contorted over his nose in a vee of fury. It was too late. Three choked on his words.

Alex lunged to grip the Councilor's arm and twist it back and straight behind his body. He removed the glass from the Councilor's other hand and forced the man to his knees with barely a sound. Couldn't have a man of the Councilor's impressive size thumping onto the floor.

"Stop," Lena gasped. "Stop it." She lurched to her feet. "He's mine."

He nodded at her and sent out a silent wish she would get what she needed from the man's death. She was strong. This would make her stronger. Then they could talk.

Once she's come to terms with who she is, we'll be unstoppable together. She had to forgive him.

"He always was." He glanced at the door to her left in caution. "But quietly, Lena."

She straightened. "I can be quiet." Her voice was a bare whisper, hardly louder than the hoarse, fruitless gurgles coming from the Councilor as she crossed to him.

THIRTY

Lena stood over the still Councilor, her head bowed. The smell of his urine filled the closed air of the car as the pool widened around his waist where he lay. The hole inside her still gaped, black and empty. If anything, it was deeper. Why wasn't this enough?

Because of Danny.

Alex sat behind her on the couch. He'd settled himself there after he'd gotten answers to the soft questions he'd asked the Councilor as she worked on the man. He had learned it was Councilor Four who was making a move against Sparks, and that a major trade house stood behind him. She tried to care.

She turned to him now, and the dark grief of betrayal welled up from that pit. She couldn't believe her brother had been the one to force his hand.

He leaned into the corner of the couch, legs splayed, arm propped up on the armrest and three fingers spread over his mouth and chin as he watched her. She could see her grief reflected in him.

She left Three where he was and crossed to stand in front of him. His body tensed, muscles contracting in a barely perceptible wave as she approached. She looked to the side, at the collar beside him, open where it had come to rest when he'd pulled it off of her and thrown it across the room.

"I wish Danny was here." She struggled to look away from the collar back to Alex. "Just so I could snap it around his neck.

So he could know what he did."

His eyes were very dark and, classic Alex, unreadable. "He didn't do it. I did."

"I know." She did know. And she felt a fair share of anger for him, too. But she understood why he'd done it. Alex flexed around a situation. He made it work, and it had. He wouldn't have had to if her brother hadn't turned on her. "But when Danny saw me, he didn't come to me. He turned me in. If not for you, they would have killed me. He didn't care."

He opened his mouth to deny it, but then closed it, opting instead to shake his head. Otherwise, he remained quiet, tense and waiting.

She reached out and picked up the thing. Like the collars she'd removed from the girls, the thick, hollow choker of metal had a hinge on one side and a powered clasp on the other. A tiny double row of buttons led to the clasp. It looked totally innocuous. Yet her skin crawled, and her stomach twisted with fear and revulsion. She swallowed and tightened her jaw so her chin wouldn't give away her emotions.

He leaned forward in a slow, deliberate motion. "I'm so sorry, Lena. I should have found another way." His hoarse voice filled with regret and self-loathing. "It was a tactical decision, always temporary. I made the decision because I know how strong you are. But it doesn't excuse what *I* did."

"It was Danny—"

"It was my choice. If we're going to get past this, I need you to face it. Stop focusing on your brother and—"

"I can't!" She didn't have much left, and she couldn't lose them both. "I can understand a tactical decision. But I can't forgive my brother turning me in. And nothing you can say will change that." She stared at him as he reached out and took the collar from her to bend it backward and snap it at the hinge. A new fear bloomed. "Unless there's something more? Something that would change what we had?"

"Don't say 'had.'" He lifted his hands as if to reach for her, and she danced back, out of reach. He let her go. "There's nothing more to it. It made the most sense at the time. I wish I'd found another way. It was wrong."

She nodded her agreement.

"I won't collar you again. Not ever."

She nodded again. "Not me. Not my girls, either." If he tried, she'd drop him before he could raise his defenses. It didn't matter how she felt about him.

Alex took a deep breath and shook his head as if to clear it. "Look, we need to talk about this. But first I have to go reassure everyone that we're dealing with things, that we're questioning you, that we'll have answers soon. Are you okay for now?"

"Sure." She took a deep breath. "I'm fine. Go do what you need to do." She turned back to the Councilor.

This time when Alex approached her, she didn't pull away. His hands were gentle on her arms as he pressed a kiss to the top of her head.

"I'll be back. And Jackson will be here soon. You won't be alone."

She nodded, but said nothing.

He left.

She hoped Jackson wouldn't be back too soon. Contrary to Alex's assumption about the Councilor's still form, the man wasn't dead. Alex wasn't the only one who'd improvised as needed.

She had paralyzed Three while she tried to figure out how to make his passing enough to ease the pain inside her. As long as she had more pain welling up from inside, she had more pain to share with him. And the pain still formed a thick, untouched pool deep in her belly.

She squatted beside his head. "Open his eyes," she commanded.

His eyelids peeled back. The horror and desperation in them was real, but fading. Although she'd made sure the Dust still pumped his heart, the lack of oxygen from his paralyzed lungs slowly starved his brain. That would never do.

"Let him breathe."

Air wheezed in and out of his narrowed windpipe. The lights began to come back on. Terror bloomed again.

She smiled. "Hello again, Councilor Three," she said. "You do remember me still, yes?"

She could see he did, and it was good. She needed to feed off the fear and pain that didn't sate her. She hadn't decided yet what a just retribution would be. She should decide soon, though. He was fading fast, and she could only do so much to keep him around before she'd have to heal some of the damage in order to prolong his suffering. She reached out, considering how best to heal so he still felt the pain.

Her hands were shaking. She frowned. Why? She wanted this. She'd waited and worked toward this. She needed it to show her parents—

Your parents would be horrified by you.

No. No, they'd be proud. Wouldn't they?

The door behind her slid open and closed. She tensed and turned, still crouched beside Three.

A look of shock and revulsion crossed Jackson's face.

"Lena." His voice was strangled. "What are you doing?" He came closer, moving like a man approaching a feral animal.

"Making him pay," she said. She didn't sound like herself.

He crept close enough to see the Councilor's face over her head. His mouth fell open.

"Close his eyes," she told the Dust.

If it bothered him, she'd wait until he'd left again.

"Oh, Lena, no," Jackson breathed. "You don't want to do this."

She laughed at him. She didn't recognize the dark and ugly sound. "What do you mean, I don't want to do this? I do. Very much."

He stared down at her for a long moment, then he knelt in front of her. "No. You don't. This will hurt you more than him."

She blinked. "You have no idea what this man did to my family! To me!"

He reached out and took her hands from the Councilor's chest. She tried to pull her hands away, but he held tight, gentle but firm.

"Look at him."

She turned back to the Councilor, her gaze jerking over his chest in tiny, rapid movements. He wheezed with every labored breath.

You did that.

She clenched her jaw and looked down at her hands so she wouldn't have to look back at Jackson. "I know what you see. But I see my parents, too. And it's not enough."

"Do you think your parents would want this for you? The people who spent their lives hiding you to keep you safe?"

They didn't hide you just to keep you alive, Lena, they hid you to keep you from being corrupted.

He gripped her chin with gentle but firm pressure, pulling her face up. "I get it. And I understand wanting to make him pay. I do. But it will never be enough. You can't fill yourself with pain and expect it to heal you. It has to be mercy."

But Three hadn't paid. She still had a well of pain inside. The debt wouldn't be paid until it was gone.

In front of her, Jackson waited, face full of fear. He wanted her to believe that being merciful to a man who had no mercy would make it better?

"I can't," she whispered.

"You can." His voice was gentle, and implacable.

"I *can't*." The wail of frustration and pain and anger bubbled up from the darkness inside. The pain was bigger than she was.

"You can, Lena."

She stared at Jackson's bleak face. He'd kill Three if he had to. He'd do it so she wouldn't have to. She almost allowed him to take the burden for her. But she didn't want this for him any more than he wanted it for her.

No more than her parents had wanted it for her. She'd been so focused on her pain, on revenge, that she'd never stopped to ask herself what they'd want. They'd want her to use Three. They'd want her to discover everything she could about her girls, about any other girls, and use that knowledge to keep them all safe. She had that information. Alex had gotten everything they needed from the man. It was time to let him go.

She reached out with her mind. She turned her face away as

she spoke to the Dust—lungs, heart, brain, done. Councilor Three felt no more pain.

But she did.

Jackson sat with her for several long moments. He slid his hands up from her chin to cup her cheeks, thumbs stroking the eyelids she had squeezed shut. With the barest of pressure, light prismed beneath her lids, melted together, and spread across her face. Her Dust responded to his touch, not with explosions but with comfort. Warmth. Peace.

"Thank you, I guess," she finally mumbled, "for being here. Stopping me."

"I'm sorry."

"He was a really bad person." It was the only defense she could offer, in very small voice.

She almost didn't hear his response.

"Turns out he's not the only one."

Shock hitched her breath in her throat. The rainbow light flashed away, replaced by a void. She pulled her face from his grasp and got up, moving around him to sit on the couch.

"I didn't—I didn't mean you." He breathed out a heavy breath and ran his hands over his short hair. He stood in one smooth motion and came to the couch to crouch in front of her and take her cold hands in his.

When he spoke, urgency threaded through his words. "Alex has us sitting here, waiting for the others."

His voice sounded far away and distorted. She frowned. So what if they waited? It was the plan, unspooling now as they'd planned it.

Behind him, the door opened again. Alex climbed up and pulled it closed behind him.

Jackson rose and crossed to him. All she could hear of their whispered conversation was Jackson's angry, biting consonants.

Alex held up his hand, his head down, but staring at Jackson. "The plan has not changed significantly from the original—"

"We were supposed to be moving. They were supposed to have a fighting chance to get away."

His words ran up against the immovable object of Alex, and

Alex's expression never changed.

Jackson pulled back. "This isn't right."

"You have your orders, Agent Lee. Unless ensuring Lena's safety is a problem?" He gestured the younger man out.

Jackson straightened his shoulders and nodded with a jerk of his head. He didn't slam the door after himself. It closed with a barely audible click.

Alex shook his head and crossed to the Councilor. He leaned down and felt for a pulse.

Jackson had told him.

Her voice still sounded hollow. "He's really dead this time."

He looked up. "Why didn't you tell me?"

"I guess you're not the only one who can make decisions on the fly."

He blinked then barked a short laugh, more tense than amused. "I deserved that." He crossed the room to crouch in front of her. "Did you get what you needed?"

"What I needed?"

His voice was quiet and his eyes bleak. "From his death. From revenge. Did you get what you needed?"

Did she? She shook her head. "Was I supposed to?"

A long breath eased out of his lips. "I never have. But I hoped it might be different for you. I hoped his death might serve you somehow. It might make liking it a little easier on you."

He knew she'd liked it. He wasn't judging her for it. Jackson's horrified face flashed into her mind.

"We're not supposed to like it, are we?"

"Apparently not. I do. I wanted it to be different for you."

She slid forward to rest her head against his chest.

His slid his arms around her.

"It's okay, Alex. I got something." She leaned into him, drawing strength from his acceptance. "And that's enough."

THIRTY-ONE

Lena curled on the couch, staring at the wall opposite her, thinking about her parents. What would they make of her journey? What would they think of her choices? Of Alex? She looked at him now.

He had settled her back on the couch, telling her it was time for him to do his part in gathering information. He moved around to the far side of Three's desk and went through the drawers, lifting out leather binders and envelopes. He set them in front of him on the desk and pried them open, carefully preserving the wax seals of each. He didn't say anything. He went through the papers with methodical efficiency.

She turned to stare again at Councilor Three. In spite of what Alex had done, she couldn't deny how good it had felt to sit beside him earlier, working together to get the answers they needed from the Councilor to keep their movement, and Sparks themselves, safe. Somehow it made it easier to know that they were the same. Perhaps that's why she understood the choices he'd made all along? They were the same decisions she'd have made.

Confronting Alex head-on, his actions seemed not far removed from those of the Council. But from the side, from the angle she had on his motives and their truth, was he wrong? She didn't think so. He didn't care about consolidating power. He only wanted to reserve a place for people like them. If his methods were similar, so be it. Sometimes fire wasn't fought with water.

She leaned forward and scrubbed her face with her hands. A moment later, her head popped back up.

Was that a scream?

As if her movement had reminded him again of her presence, he started to speak. "Lena—"

She held her hand up for silence and listened. Her heart thumped in her ears, and she focused to hear above it. Yes, outside the silence in the room, faraway shrieks and shouting came closer.

He listened, too, then nodded and returned his attention to the paper in front of him.

She stared at the wall, focused on the sounds filtering in from the outside. "What's happening out there?"

He turned a glance up to her and then back down. "The attack."

She frowned. "Wait. Our attack?"

"Mm-hmm." He set the slip of paper to the side and shuffled the other papers back together. He began slipping them back into binders and envelopes.

"I don't understand. I thought it was a focused strike to come for the Councilor. Who is that screaming?"

"The caravaners."

The caravaners? The people who worked the caravan? "But—are they being attacked?"

"It's a necessary component of the larger strategy."

"A necessary component? What strategy? And when did you throw that in there?"

"It was always a part of the plan." He was matter-of-fact. "It's collateral damage. But there will be very few actual casualties, and those who die were chosen for specific reasons." He held her shocked stare, his own face utterly calm. "There has to be terror. They have to be in *fear* for their lives, Lena, or when they're questioned at the Meet, the stories won't support the evidence. But despite what you're hearing, it isn't indiscriminate killing out there. They just think it is."

Before she could respond, the door opened and Jackson slipped in.

"We need to move her. Now." He marched across to the couch and grabbed her hand.

Alex stood up. "What's happened?"

Jackson pointed to the side of the car, indicating the sounds coming from outside. "All of that? It isn't just us. There's another group out there, in black and grey. Not us." He yanked her up from the couch. "Their leader is tall and thin. He came in with them, blew right past me and told his men to focus on finding the Councilor and kill anyone who got in the way. They're coming here, too."

Alex cursed. He stood and gathered up all of the papers and little wax seals. As he shoved them together in a folio and stuck it under his arm, he told Lena, "Light him up."

"What?"

"Light. Him. Up. Burn the car. It needs to burn hot and fast. This group may really be from the Council, and we can't have the truth reported back to them."

She turned to the Councilor. *The man she tortured to death.* She gritted her teeth. She would not feel guilt for what she'd done, nor for the darkness in which she'd reveled. He had earned it, and more. Now, the easiest solution would be to ignite the carpets beneath him.

She looked at Alex, shoving the last of the drawers closed and moving quickly to join them.

"Ready?"

"Ready."

Alex stood in the entry. "Agents dressed in green and brown are ours. Black and grey," he looked to Jackson for confirmation. At Jackson's tense nod, he continued, "Black and grey are not. You follow Jackson, Lena." He nodded at Jackson. "I'm clearing the way to the rendezvous point. Stay close." Alex darted off into the twilit grey.

She turned back for just a second, sending out her wishes. The fire whooshed up, hot and pale, running up the man-shaped bulk on the floor in a bright wave that crested at the top and ran together in a bright twisting column. It threw off sparks that nestled in folds of the garish fabric covering the ceiling and walls and couch. The embers burrowed in, glowing, smoking, and then lighting. It was beautiful. It was just.

By the time Jackson pulled her away, pulling on her hand held tight in his own, little fires were already burning merrily. She looked back once. Orange light danced behind the curtained windows. One of the curtains went up, peeling away in a cascade of orange.

With her attention on the car behind them, she ran into Jackson.

"Pay attention," he grunted. He had stopped beside one of the caravan cars. He leaned out, looking around the front of the car next to them. They slipped between the car and the truck it was tethered to, high-stepping over the joint. Ahead, she could see Alex in a similar position between a car and truck about twenty feet away, hidden in shadow. He leaned back against the car, nodding at Jackson when they appeared. The half-light of dusk colored his face grim before he darted away again.

They followed, racing across the opening, avoiding fleeing people who had realized too late there was no safety in following orders and remaining in their cars.

In front of her, a man wearing black and grey lunged to grapple with a fleeing caravaner, likely a truck tech from his rough, stained clothing. He gripped the back of the man's collar and dragged him screaming back. The tech got in a kick and two blows before his attacker's knife took him across the throat. The man gurgled and flopped over to try and crawl away, arterial blood spraying out before him into the dirt.

The agent, face set and focused in a familiar expression, already rose. He went in search of his next victim, even as Jackson pulled her away behind the attacker.

Was this the same horror Jackson felt earlier?

"Lena, come on!" He jerked at her hand again, pulling her with him toward the shelter of another car. They moved along the side of it, fast, before he pulled up shy of the end. He released her hand to grip her shoulder, exerting pressure to force her down behind a tire. She leaned her face out around the tire, trying to catch some glimpse of Alex ahead of them. Why were they stopping?

A movement from beneath the car flashed in her peripheral vision.

A boy cowered beneath it. Dirt clung to the silent tears and mucous flowing down his muddy, contorted face. He looked frantically around, trying to figure out which way to go. His enormous eyes reminded her of Marissa.

Lena dropped to her belly and squeezed under the car, reaching for the boy. He scrambled away, back and sideways.

"It's okay, it's okay."

The boy scrambled back farther, terrified.

"No, no, it's okay. You can come with us. You'll be safe." She lunged forward to grip his wrist before he could reveal himself by crawling back out of the shelter of the car on the other side. His thin, muddy wrist slipped through her fingers. Hissing with frustration and fear, she went after him.

He rolled out, stopped, stared up for a second, and then scrambled to his feet and ran away. Lena crawled to the edge to run after him. She froze when a pair of men's boots stepped from behind the tire on the other side of the car.

A man dropped down to look under the car. He wore black and grey.

He lashed out with the club in his hand, smashing it into her forehead.

Darkness and pain warred with blurred vision. She tried to focus through a wash of involuntary tears as he grabbed her under the arms and pulled her from beneath the car.

He slid his hand into her hair, gripping it and holding her head firmly in place.

Did he have a collar in his free hand?

She had to focus, to talk to the Dust. *Stop him. End him!* Her brain tried to swim to black, but she fought it. She reached up, clawed at his face, his eyes. As soon as her fingers made contact, the Dust responded. He fell, heart stopped, dead already. She didn't even know what had happened to him.

The Dust had chosen.

She fell to one knee and slumped against the side of the car.

Through the darkness, as if from very far away, she could hear Jackson call out, searching for her on the other side.

"I'm here." The words were almost inaudible even to her own ears. She pressed her hand to her forehead. Pain seared at her touch. The torn skin peeled away from a lump already firming. Her hand came away bloody. She pushed herself to a stand. She had to get back to Jackson.

Movement in the tree line a hundred feet away caught her attention. A blond man, tall and thin, hurried into the trees. Recognition zinged through her. Rage roared after it.

Lucas.

Her legs jerked into motion, running after the man who'd tortured her. She didn't even look back until she made the trees herself.

She wasn't sure if the falling night or the pain spreading from within her head made the caravan darken behind her. Cars burned bright in the closing black, brilliant points that made her eyes swim. She blinked. No pain. *No pain.*

Jackson tore through the center of the caravan after her.

A faint shout sounded behind him. Alex pursued them, as well, shooting every man in grey and black along the way, leaving splashes of blood behind him. Apparently subterfuge wasn't a priority anymore.

Was that croaking sound her voice? It didn't matter whether they heard her calling them. The dark beneath the trees would hide her from them if she went in after Lucas.

Lena turned and ran on.

Find him. Find him and then—then what? A plan. I need a plan. Every thought slipped away. The injury to her head acted like a collar, destroying her focus.

An image of the man she'd killed back in the caravan flashed. She still had touch. It had to be touch. She had to get close enough to lay hands on Lucas.

Ahead, he'd stopped to meet up with another man in black and grey. At the sound of her crashing through the underbrush, they turned together. She slid to a stop, reaching one hand out to use a rough tree trunk as a support.

Lucas took a sliding step back, warily watching her. Was he waiting for the attack on his body? It didn't come. He paused.

"Is that—" the other man said.

"Yes." Lucas stared, assessing.

She shoved at the darkness that threatened to overtake her. Her head throbbed in time to the blood pumping in her veins. She couldn't focus. She couldn't reach out.

It has to be touch.

Lucas curved his lips into a smile. "She has a head injury. She can't do anything. Kill her."

The other soldier crouched, moving in cautiously. He feinted at her and pulled away.

Her fingers curled into the bark. *It'll be brain bleeds for you both. Vessels bursting. Blood flowing. Vessels bursting....*

The soldier lunged in, grabbed her arm, and pulled her from the tree.

With the contact, the desire she couldn't project sang through him to the Dust.

He froze. Stiffened. His hands jumped up to paw at the sides of his head until a long breath gasped out of his lungs. He fell.

Lucas stared at them in horror.

She gave him a little smile, just a quick flash of teeth. "A brain bleed," she whispered. "A massive bleed for you both. Just like my mother. Remember?" She lifted her hand and wiggled her fingers, urging him to come closer.

Lucas lunged to the side and came up with a long, thick fallen branch, deadweight from a tree. "No. You're damaged. You have to touch me, don't you?" He laughed, lifting the branch between them. "That's not going to happen, demon bitch."

Lena moved toward him. Her fingers curled.

Vessels bursting. Blood flowing. Vessels bursting. Blood flowing.

He waved the branch between them, as if he could hear the chant she kept up in her head in anticipation of the moment she made contact with his skin. He glanced behind her, and new panic bloomed.

Dimly, above the throbbing of blood and her private chant,

she could hear crashing behind her as someone came toward them through the woods. Jackson? Or Alex?

Lucas didn't wait for the new threat to arrive. Desperate, he lunged forward, swinging the branch back and around.

She curled away from it. It cracked into her side and shoulder.

New hurt bloomed and then faded to join the pain already crashing through her blood. She scrambled away as he swung again, the branch passing short of her. She dove in, arms outstretched, hands reaching.

He scrambled back, then stumbled in the undergrowth.

Even as he regained his footing and swung the branch back, she rushed to take advantage of the opening. The branch swung around, but she had poured her body into the breach, fingers outstretched for his face.

The branch cracked into her chin and nose. Her head snapped back. Her lower jaw smashed up. She was weightless, flying away for a terrible, stomach-twisting second before landing facedown in a heap.

Her vision went dark. The must of leaves and the metallic tang of her own blood filled her nose. A rhythmic thumping came closer and closer, and something thrashed near her. Pain engulfed her face and neck like flames racing along her nerves, fire that consumed, leaving behind char with a glowing core.

Noise coming. Danger?

She got her arms under her, her push feeble with shock but enough to roll her over. Movement flashed by her feet, and a body came toward her with the sound of crashing leaves.

Her legs automatically kicked out and caught him, one foot low in the belly and the other in the thigh, sweeping his leg out from beneath him. She closed her eyes, braced for an impact on her body that didn't come. The thumping behind her stopped and became air pressure shifting above.

Air rushed from a man's lungs with a hoarse groan and the dull thud of bodies colliding. They crashed to earth beside her.

Even as she reopened her eyes, Lena scooted back away from them. She tasted metal. Blood bubbled as it flowed from her nose.

She panted through her open mouth.

Jackson and Lucas both rolled to their feet. No longer worried about keeping her touch at bay, Lucas discarded the branch for a knife from his belt. Jackson bent forward, ready, and his own blade glinted. The men circled and then came together, grunting. They slashed and grappled, each searching for an advantage. They didn't speak. No words, just thick groans of effort echoed through the clearing.

Lucas's hand broke free to slash at Jackson's face. Jackson feinted back. The blade cut him across the bridge of his nose and skimmed both cheeks. Blood spattered out and ran in fast rivulets like dark tear tracks. Lucas laughed hoarsely, an ugly sound. The men closed again, each holding the other's knife hand away while kicking at his enemy in an obscene dance.

She focused, reaching for the Dust. Communication wavered away like a heat wave with every attempt.

You want to help. I know you want to help. Help me now.

One of them groaned in pain. Lucas tore away, spinning and landing on his belly before her.

He lifted his face, contorted with pain and rage. He brought his knife hand around.

Lena dragged up a handful of dirt and broken bark and leaves from beside her. She threw it in his face, hoping bits of it would catch in his hateful eyes.

He roared in pain.

Jackson pounced from behind, gripping Lucas by the hair and dragging him back. He smashed his foot down on Lucas's wrist once, twice, then kicked the knife away. He flipped Lucas, pulled him to his feet, and then rocked Lucas's head back with his fist.

Lucas staggered, gasping around a nose as bloodied now as Jackson's. His glazed stare at Jackson shifted, looking behind him.

Footsteps pounded closer, dull impacts in the silence of the forest broken only by the labored sounds of the three of them breathing through blood.

Was it Alex? Or Lucas's soldiers? She reached back, grabbed the rough bark of the tree, and pulled herself up. She didn't know what she could do. She'd manage something.

Jackson didn't turn. He didn't wait. He smashed his fists again into Lucas, striking his jaw and cheek on the left and his temple on the right.

Lucas staggered to the left after the second impact, bent double, before falling sideways and rolling down a slope. A moment later, a splash echoed up as he hit water somewhere below.

Alex slid to a stop before her. His left hand pressed a long wet tear in his shirt. The leather binder was gone. He stared at her, chest heaving.

Her chin and lip pulsed, heat beneath the cold wet of torn flesh. Her face must be a bloody mess.

He reached out his hand to her face, as if his first thought was to heal.

"Lucas," she gasped out, spattering droplets of blood on his chest and face as she tried to explain. She collapsed to the side, gasping for air.

Alex scrambled for her, holding her up, pulling her in to his chest. "Lena," he said. And then again, and again. His voice was heavy with fear and something else she couldn't name. He caught her to his chest, his arms like vises around her.

She tilted her head back to look up at him. Her blood smeared across his chest.

He lifted a shaking hand to her face. His lips compressed with tension and focus. Nothing happened. He gasped, his face contorted with disappointment and fear for her.

"Come on!" Alex bore down again, gaze trained on her torn face. A moment later a groaned sob tore from him before he snarled over his shoulder at Jackson, "Get over here."

Jackson moved closer, but not fast enough for Alex. One arm uncurled from around Lena, shooting out to grab the front of Jackson's shirt and drag him to them.

"Heal her. Heal her now!"

He scooted backward, pushing Jackson into his place before Lena. He rose, then, and scrambled away down the slope. His head dipped below her line of sight.

She blinked, fingers curling into loose soil and crushed leaves beside her.

Jackson reached out his hands to her face, as if to heal.

It took a few long, metallic-tinged wet breaths before the panic faded and she came back to herself.

Jackson nodded, little movements meant to soothe.

And Alex?

He was somewhere else, with a man who had almost gouged Jackson's eyes out with a knife. He had gone over the slope.

She pushed Jackson away and struggled to rise. He leaned in to pull her back, and she batted him off.

"No, get off. Alex!"

He was still in danger. She surged away and staggered to the edge of the hillside. She managed two shaky steps over the edge before falling to her hip and sliding through the moldering remains of last winter's leaves caught in the underbrush of the steep slope. She came to a rest halfway to the bottom, her fingers caught in the branches of a fragrant honeysuckle.

Below, barely discernible through the failing light, Alex straddled Lucas, his hands around the man's neck. Water half-submerged Lucas's head. His body stretched out into the deepening river where he'd fallen.

She used the bush to pull herself to a stand. She half-slid and half-walked down the slope, until the forms of the two men became clear.

Lucas's arms flailed. He tried to beat at Alex's sides, but the impacts, and the arcs of his arms, grew smaller and smaller as his strength failed. His hands clutched at Alex's shirt in a final grip before falling to the side. Lucas's legs kicked out, splashing twice in the deeper water before they stilled and bobbed as they were tugged at by a swift current.

Alex leaned away from Lucas, pulling his shaking hands from the man's throat. "No. It isn't enough," he growled down at the still man below him. "Not for what you did." He stared down at Lucas, his features twisted.

She didn't think it was just fury. What did he have to be ashamed of?

"It's okay, Alex," she called out to him. Her voice sounded wet and hoarse. Hearing it hurt as much as the effort of speaking.

He lifted his head to stare across the stream at her on the hillside.

"It's okay. It's okay to like it. Remember?"

His head fell to the side and grief twisted his face. He shook his head, rubbed his face, and muttered under his breath. "You did that, Reyes. Proud of yourself?"

She started to descend toward him.

"No," he shouted. He waved her back. "I'm coming." Alex swung his leg over Lucas. He slid on his backside through water and leaves and mud until he pulled clear of Lucas, kicking the man's side as he pushed away.

The kick had enough force to dislodge Lucas's head and shoulders from the hold of the muddy shore. Lucas slid out, spun as the current caught his lower body and then flowed loosely away in the water.

Alex started, then scrambled to his feet and waded in, following a few steps as if to retrieve Lucas's body. When he stopped, he stared after his former partner for a long moment before turning back to her.

His beautiful face was a study in rage and shame. He splashed across the shallow water to the hillside then climbed to her. He moved as if in pain, but it wasn't physical pain slowing him.

He stopped in front of her. "It's not okay, Lena. It's not."

She stared back into his face. His expression was as haunted as that of the boy under the train car and filled with pain. The bloody slash showing through his torn shirt flashed her to a man crawling away, a gaping wound across his throat. *It's not okay. It's not. But he does.*

Alex cupped her cheek away from her wounds. He shook his head in small movements back and forth as he searched her eyes above her mangled face.

It's not okay to like it. But I do, too.

"I just—I almost lost you." His voice broke, and he swallowed.

She nodded. That made it okay? It didn't. "It's not okay to like it," she whispered. "But we do. We do."

He picked small bits of forest detritus from the blood thick on her face. His hand fell to her shoulder, and he pulled her close, wrapping his arms around her, not a vise this time, but a cradle.

Lena's hands went up automatically, wrapping around his sides.

Alex bent into the embrace, lowering his face into the space between her head and neck. His voice was muffled, meant only for her, "We do what we have to. And I almost lost you."

"Hey." Jackson called down to them from the top of the hill. How long had he been there?

Alex's arms tightened around her for a second before he pressed his lips to her temple. The warmth of his breath curled on her skin. When he pulled away, her blood coated his cheek and lips.

Jackson said something above, but Lena lost the words to the look on Alex's face. Grief and guilt mingled with rage—darkness. But something else pushed at the darkness like light oil spreading through wine.

He ignored Jackson. He kept his focus on her. He swiped the back of his hand across his face, smearing her blood into his skin.

"Thought I told you to heal her, Lee?"

"She ran to you." Irritation flared in Jackson's voice. "Was he done? You want me to head downstream to find and finish him?"

Alex still didn't raise his face. Instead, he looked back down the river as if he could see Lucas's body, long gone like a log fallen in the night.

"He's done enough. Let him drown." The words throbbed with hatred, different from his usual agent cool. He pressed his hand to his side. "It's going to be full dark soon. We need to get Lena to the rendezvous. Let him rot."

"Yes, sir." Jackson said.

She looked up at him. Jackson nodded, his expression as empty and implacable as that of the man he looked down on from above.

THIRTY-TWO

A lex took Lena's hand and helped her up the hill. If he thought she'd let him, he'd carry her. When they reached the top, he could feel her resist, but he tightened his grip. He pulled her the last few feet to where he stood. The sharp twist of fear and guilt and anger at the ruin of her face eclipsed the burning throb of his wound. Somehow the smell of bruised honeysuckle that clung to her made the torn skin that much more devastating.

"It's going to be okay," he told her. "As soon as we get you healed."

But would it?

She glanced back over her shoulder.

His eyes followed hers to where Jackson still stood behind them on the crest of the hill, gazing down. Alex wanted nothing more than to peel away the skin of the young agent's face in retribution. He had one job. How could he have lost her?

Alex led her back to the tree and pressed her down in front of it, kneeling before her. He examined her face in the half-light and winced. Glancing back at Jackson, he growled again for the younger man to get over to them.

"Can you heal this?" He demanded of Jackson. "Really heal it this time?"

Jackson nodded without hesitation. "I'd have healed it last time if she hadn't gone after you."

Alex turned back to Lena. "I'd do it myself if I could." The fact that he couldn't bothered him more than he'd say. The way she tangled her fingers in his for a moment made it evident that his voice reflected his disappointment. The self-recrimination made his next comment come out as a rasp. "Hopefully Jackson won't fuck this up, too."

She shook her head. "I saw Lucas. I came after him. It wasn't Jackson's fault," she managed to speak with a minimum of movement.

"No, just his responsibility."

Alex rose, pressing his hand to the knife wound on his lower abdomen again. Jackson wouldn't meet his gaze.

Guilty conscience, kid? He should feel guilty. He should feel damned lucky, too. If Lena had died, Alex would have carved his loss out of the Agent and left him to bleed out on the forest floor while trying to gather up his scattered body parts.

"Much as I hate to leave you in his care again, I've got to make sure our route to the rendezvous is secure and that there aren't any more surprises in these woods."

"Alex," she protested, "you're wounded, too."

He looked back at her. The torn skin of her lower face oozed blood, and she had an enormous broken goose egg across her forehead where she'd been hit. Except for her eyes, her face was painted with dried and drying blood filled with debris. He shook his head.

"You have priority. I'll be fine. I'll be back soon and we can get you to the rendezvous. Once you're there, you can take care of me yourself, if you want to." Alex stalked away, moving through the darkening forest.

He moved back and forth, quickly and quietly. Their area of the forest secured, he headed back in a straight line. He swallowed, trying to push back the remains of the acrid near-panic in his throat. He couldn't believe he'd nearly lost her.

He'd done everything right, even to the point of risking the loss of her affection. He had adapted to every change in circumstances, worked every scenario, before and after they'd set out. He had kept her protected from things he didn't think she could handle yet, urged her to take on the things she needed to in order to grow into the powerful woman she could be. He'd achieved everything they'd set out to accomplish.

Except he hadn't gotten to her first after *Jackson* lost her. Alex had managed to catch up to Jackson at the edge of the woods. It was Alex who had covered his back, pulling a knife after he'd run out of bullets to engage all three of Lucas's soldiers who'd pursued them from the caravan. It was Alex who had urged Jackson on after Lucas and Lena, the distraction costing him the slash across the belly. Once he'd disposed of the soldiers, Alex had hauled ass to make it to her. And he'd been too late.

Watching from a distance as Lucas slammed her in the face and sent her in a crumpled heap across the clearing had nearly been his undoing. Too far away to do anything. Too far away to even make it there in time to engage Lucas. All he could do was run to her, mind blank and savage.

And now as he silently approached the clearing where he'd left them, Jackson's voice snaked through the trees.

"—and I could go with you, help you build your own school, help you find more girls. There are more. There have to be. If they could discard some, there are more. And they need to be found. We can do it together. Stop listening to Alex. Don't give him another opportunity to betray you. Everything out of his mouth is a lie. Everything."

Alex felt a low throb of rage pulse at the base of his skull. Red washed forward and colored the forest in front of him. He might have charged forward, but for Lena's response.

"No, he hasn't lied to me. It's hard for you to see, to understand, because you're not like him. You can't do whatever it takes and justify it and feed off of it. I can. I *do*. I know where I belong and what my role is."

Alex enjoyed the exultant surge of emotion as she denied Jackson so much he almost missed her next quiet words.

"Even if it destroys me." The calm certainty in her voice stopped him in his tracks.

Alex stood frozen in the dark murk beyond their vision. Is that what she thought would happen?

I almost lost her already.

"It doesn't have to be like that. Get away from him. Step out

of his shadow. Stay away from the dark. Lena, there's light in
you. I helped you find it back in that car. I can do it again. That's
what you *need*."

A wave of relief flowed through Alex at the low, impatient
sound she made.

"I need to make a difference for those girls. I *need* to make
sure they have the chance to decide who and what they'll be for
themselves. This path is the way to do it. We've cleared the
Council from one city. There are seven more."

*Seven more cities to stalk and clear. Seven more chances for
the Council to strike at Lena.*

Alex's eyes closed for less than a second, but the weight of
the truth pulled at him. When he opened them, the red haze
dissipated. He had done what he did so well. He'd made a
decision.

He glanced down at the forest floor and deliberately stepped
on a branch. The crack echoed through the clearing, and he
stepped out to their faces turning toward him. Except for the
smears of dried blood on their cheeks, they'd both been healed.
After Jackson had worked on her, she'd evidently been well
enough to fix his face. Maybe it was the stark newness of the skin
beneath the smears, but his face seemed livid with guilt to Alex.

Jackson dropped his gaze.

Lena didn't. She watched him come, eyes wide, and
scrambled to her feet to meet him.

He wanted to go to her and reassure her, give her soft words
and a soothing touch like the idiot in front of her, lay it out for her
and make the choice so easy Jackson would never be able to make
her doubt it. But Jackson was right about one thing.

And it had Alex's stomach churning.

The anxiety made him stride forward, keeping his voice
business-like instead of offering her comfort.

"Are we good? Everybody healed up and ready to go?"

Her reaching hands caught at the bottom of his shirt, tried to
lift it to get to the bloody slash beneath. He caught her hand and
forced a small, tough-nut smirk. "Once we're at the rendezvous
point. I want to get you out of here. Now."

She opened her mouth to protest, but he turned away, gesturing Jackson ahead of him with his head. They marched through the forest, the last of the light from dusk falling outside the dense foliage barely penetrating.

With Jackson and Lena healed, they made good time. His mind roamed ahead to what was coming—not just the conversation he'd need to have with her, but the decisions he'd have to make for his men. Unable to predict the outcome of the former, he focused instead on the latter.

How many men had they lost? They couldn't afford any. It took too long to train their young agents, and the available pool of candidates was limited to Sparks strong enough to be sent off to the Ward School.

Alex had been telling Thomas for years they needed to expand their reach and begin drawing in mid-ranges to the cause. Erika had been an example of what a talented, dedicated mid-range could achieve. It wouldn't take much to plant some of their Ward School Guardians in the Relo-city schools to keep an eye out for likely candidates. He'd even made the strategic move himself at Azcon a decade before, grooming a sympathetic young Azcon student he'd overheard making impolitic statements against the Council to his mother as they shopped. That the relationship had eventually revealed secrets that led to complications didn't lessen the young man's overall usefulness.

He glanced down at one of those complications now as she marched beside him. Judging from Jackson's stiff back as he moved through the underbrush ahead of them, he was none too pleased with her loyalty, even if she had been angry and disappointed with Alex before.

In spite of her apparent choice, Alex didn't doubt the decision he'd made. This time, he'd rather stay the course and let events play out as they should, even if they led to danger. Even if the danger was emotional, and not physical.

They came over the next rise, leaving the tree line, and a line of electric vehicles spread out as dark shadows below them on the back road. His men moved around them, wearing their headlamps, stowing gear and weapons. A group of five of his most senior

Agents gathered around a map one of them had spread over the hood of a vehicle.

"Lena, can you wait for us?" He nodded to indicate the middle cars. "You know where the water is if you want to clean up." They carried a supply in the back of every vehicle. "Jackson and I need to check on what we know about Lucas and his soldiers."

"Wait," she protested, "you said you'd let me take care of you."

He flashed her a smile. "I can keep five more minutes. They need orders. Go get cleaned up. I'll be done before you know it."

He didn't look back when he turned. He stalked away, moving through the dark to his men, expecting Jackson to follow.

They turned at his approach and made room for him before the map. One of them produced a headlamp for him.

"Tell me you have something good," he told them as he slipped it onto his head, "because someone needs to pay for that clusterfuck."

"We have their camp, sir." Derion, one of his top Agents, pointed to a spot marked on the map. Derion had been a possible replacement for Lucas before he'd met the multi-talented, and ultimately disappointing, Jackson. He'd just become the prime candidate again. "Three of our men followed their retreat. Instead of pulling out, they went in, set a perimeter, and hunkered down. We figured it may be a trap."

Derion's finger moved over the landscape features that led Alex to agree it could indeed be a deliberate attempt to draw his men in.

"But the way they packed up everything but the essentials and made the effort to hide their trail," he shook his head, "it seems more like they're waiting for someone before pulling out."

Alex grinned. The bastards knew they couldn't go back without Councilor Four's grandson.

"They are. And it's going to be a long wait." He laughed softly.

"Really, sir?" Derion's grin mirrored his.

"Yeah. Really." He nodded with satisfaction and then leaned

in, hands spread wide as he studied the map. He chewed his lip. "Work up a northern approach for me."

"Over the bluff?"

He nodded. His attention briefly turned to Jackson, who hovered at the outskirts of the circle of men. Field maneuvers, maps, navigation, and ambushes were the young Agent's specialty, but he had barely engaged. He wasn't interested in their plans. Jackson really was already gone, and he planned to convince Lena to join him. Alex's lips thinned.

Instead of dwelling on it, he outlined what he wanted from his men, pointing at positions on the map. "I want a clean sweep," he concluded. "We're taking out everyone but two."

"Two, sir? Which two?"

"Any two. They're going to be messengers." He tapped the map. "Work it up." Alex backed away. It was time to give the kid *his* new orders.

Derion nodded. He and his men closed back in around the map, talking fast and low.

Alex moved in close to Jackson, close enough to make the younger man feel threatened. He should feel threatened.

"You, with me, now." Alex took Jackson's arm and walked south along the road. He kept his voice low and clipped, telling Jackson what he expected in a tone that brooked no arguments.

Jackson threw him one startled look before he tucked his chin to his chest and listened.

Alex had to give him his due. When Jackson realized that not only did Alex know what he'd been attempting, but that the senior agent had twisted it for his own purposes, the kid didn't react more than tightening his jaw.

You want to walk away from your duty post with me? You want to be by her side, keeping her safe, helping her carve out a place of her own for her girls at Fort Nevada? Okay. Done.

When Alex finished, he leaned in close, using his body as a threat again, to ensure Jackson had a full grasp of what he expected to get from the younger man.

"Do you understand? What you *will* do, now and until I give you direct orders otherwise, and what the stakes are for you if you don't?"

Jackson finally looked at him then.

Alex had expected the resentment. He hadn't expected to see a grudging respect from the kid after he'd outmaneuvered him.

"Yes, sir."

"And you understand that you will keep her safe this time, and you will keep your fucking hands off of her?" At Jackson's affirmative nod, Alex gave him a curt nod of his own. "I don't give second chances often, Lee. Believe me when I say I'm not giving this one because I think you've earned it. I'm giving it to you for her. Now take a walk."

He left the kid there, knowing the younger man would stay close enough to be ready to go when it was time. He'd do his job. He'd been conditioned his whole life to do it.

Alex glanced into each car as he passed, looking for Lena. He found her five cars back.

The water tank was out and open, and a wide puddle of dark water ran off to the side of the road. Lena, scrubbed clean of the bloody smears, leaned back against the rear tire looking up at the sky. At his approach, she turned to look at him, watching him walk. Even exhausted and probably pissed off, her gaze still moved over him like a caress.

He felt his body responding and took a deep breath.

What comes next is going to suck.

She squinted when he drew up to her, covering her eyes with her hand. "You wanna tone that light down?"

Instead of turning it down, Alex pulled the lamp off and set it on the ground beside her. The light flared up, brightening the area but not shining in her face. She dropped her hand.

He pressed hard on his lower belly for support and started to lower himself down beside her.

"Stop."

He hesitated.

She picked herself up off the ground, shaking her head at him. She scooped the light up and tossed her head at the car. "Get in the back, Reyes."

He raised his brows and grinned at her. "When you want your

fifteen minutes, you really want it. Not sure I can perform like this, but I'll give it the Reyes effort."

"Enticing as the offer is...." She snorted and rolled her eyes. "It's time to heal you. No more excuses. Get in the car."

He eased himself back on the rear seat. He lost his grin when she lifted his shirt and her breath hissed out.

"Oh, Alex."

The slash stretched from hip to hip across his groin. He'd been able to function because it wasn't deep, but it was ugly. She lifted her hands to hover over his belly.

Alex couldn't resist a tease. "No scar, now. I'd hate to have a mark across one of your favorite places to lick."

She glanced up and arched a brow at him. The warmth spread under his skin as the Dust did her bidding and knit his skin back together. Like before, the warmth became a hot itch that faded a few moments later.

Lena darted down, her tongue leaving behind a wet, warm path of sparks as she licked up toward his navel.

His breath caught, and his hands went automatically to her hair.

She reached up and tugged them away with a laugh. "Just checking. No scar."

With the pain from his midsection gone, he had a good deal more ability to move. He flipped his hands around, caught her wrists, and pulled her in and up his body. She squirmed for a moment before he tightened his arms around her. She snuggled in to his chest. The Dust swirled lazily between them, warm and easy. It was home.

She rubbed her cheek against his chest, inhaling. "All right, Alex. I can tell your brain is working something over. Let me have it."

He didn't want to send her away, certainly not with Jackson. He'd rather keep her with him, fighting by his side. It just wasn't the right decision—not for her, not for the movement.

He wouldn't draw it out. She wouldn't let him get away with beating around the bush anyway. "Jackson's not going with the caravan. He's not going to be Azcon's new security chief. I don't know how aware you were, but I basically made Merritt confess to being part of a plot to take out the Councilor. It changed the strategy for this operation."

"I know," she answered. "With his confession, and all the witnesses, you don't have to 'die.' No one will be looking at you. You can keep your position, consolidate your hold on Zone Three, and deal with the assholes behind Lucas." She exhaled again, and the long, warm breath flowed across his skin, chased by Dust beneath it. "You don't need Jackson to stay. Don't need me to stay, either. I'm going back with him."

His breath eased out. The difficult scene he'd envisioned, her fighting to stay and him fighting against his desire to let her stay, winked away. She knew. Of course she did.

Now it became difficult for an entirely different reason. He didn't have to send her back. She was leaving. Was it the recognition of the greater strategy that had her returning to the Fort? Or was it something else? Jackson. Or the decisions Alex had made back at the caravan.

What about us? He hated how plaintive the question in his head sounded.

He waited. Not only did he not trust himself to say anything yet, but he could feel her gathering her breath. She wasn't finished.

"I want you to know that I'm not going because of the collar. I know why you made that choice. I understand all of your choices. And I want to stay with you. But you don't need me here, not like those girls need me."

He couldn't stay silent. "I want you to stay, too—"

She nodded as she talked over him, needing to get the words out. "And I know that in the same way you can stay now, I could too. Mina Gardin could go on."

He could feel her cheek move against his chest as she smiled at her code name. He could also feel the hesitation at the end of the sentence. "Except?"

"Except Mina Gardin, sous chef, serves absolutely zero tactical purpose at the Meet. I don't offer what we're doing enough value in that role to offset the danger of me being there."

Alex felt a smile tug at his lips. His heart swelled. The smile grew into a grin. Just as he hadn't been preparing to send her away as a means to end what they had, she wasn't going away to abandon him. She was going back to fulfill a more important role. She believed in what they were doing. She was with them. She was with him.

Apparently unnerved by his silence, she finally lifted her head from his chest to rear up and peer down at him. "Wow. That relieved, huh? I guess maybe I underestimated the effect of all that darkness I soaked up."

"Nope. That proud. I want you to come. I want you by my side, where I can keep an eye on you myself. And there's nothing about you—certainly not any darkness—that could make me relieved to see you go." He held up a finger when she started to talk again, silencing her. He couldn't send her away not knowing exactly what had drawn him to her. "I want all of you, not just the pretty sparkly bits that shine in the light."

"You think light inside is bad," she interrupted, probably parroting something Jackson had told her. "You think kindness is weakness."

"No, I don't. I know your kindness is what makes you care enough to fight. It's what made you take on the responsibility of those girls without a second thought. But you need to understand that it's your darkness that allows you to protect them. It's your darkness that gives me the confidence to send you off with Light Boy to teach those girls. I know that you can protect them. Not Jackson. You, Lena. Because of your darkness. You're the perfect balance of light and dark."

He settled his head back against the seat of the car. She was. And he had been prepared to send her away. Instead, he had to let her go as she went on her own. What a fucking idiot.

When he continued, it was as much to remind himself as to tell her, "I figured out way before now that my woman needs purpose, not safety. And you're right. Your purpose is waiting for you back at the fort."

She bit her lip. "Your woman, huh?"

Alex lifted his head and raised a hand to her cheek, rubbing his thumb across her lips. "Yeah. Mine."

"I thought you weren't interested in having your focus compromised."

"No, that's not what I said." He huffed a laugh when she raised her brows and started shaking her head. "I said I couldn't— that I had nothing to offer. I was wrong. I was scared."

"Alex Reyes, scared?"

He could hear the laughter catching in her throat, sweet and heady. He couldn't help the answering smile. "Woman, I don't scare easy, but damn if you don't terrify me."

"That's what I hear. I don't get it. What's so scary about me?"

His smile faded. Alex stared into her eyes. It came down to this. This moment. And even though she'd walked right up to it with him, ready and willing, he felt a hot flare of anxiety stab into his chest and then settle in, throbbing. They both recognized that her role in their war was best fulfilled at the Fort. She'd told him it wasn't to get away from him. Except for the distance, they'd go on.

Except for the distance? You won't be there.

If he sent her with Jackson, everything would change. Yes, they'd both be working to push through this revolution. But Lena would be wrapped up in her new world, building a life for her girls. She'd build a new life for herself. Would there be room in it for Alex each time he returned? Or would she turn to Jackson?

He was taking a huge risk. Perhaps he should follow the course his heart screamed for him to take: make her stay, keep her close, find another way for her to contribute to what they were doing. The moment stretched. Alex swallowed.

What was so scary, she wanted to know.

"The possibility of losing you," he said.

She shook her head. "You're not losing me." She narrowed her eyes teasingly and drawled, "You're sending me away with another man, sure, but you're not losing me."

He'd be damned if he would let her head off into the sunset with another man, even at his own insistence, without making good and sure she understood they were meant for each other.

"Prove it, then." He stroked his thumb back up her cheek. "Kiss me a promise, so neither of us forgets that this is home." He gestured with his chin to the small space between them. "Right here with us. Make it a good one."

Her mouth turned up. A small smile grew into a familiar naughty grin, her top teeth catching her bottom lip in a way that made his breath catch. She slid her legs around him and boosted herself further up him, then leaned down over his face. She hovered there, inches away.

"A promise, huh?"

The Spark between them already gathered into a glow he could feel just under his skin. He gave his head a tiny nod, and she smiled again. Her face softened as she leaned in and opened her mouth to his.

She made it a good one.

THIRTY-THREE

A lex moved through the caravan as those under his care moved around preparing for another post-attack night on the road. Much of the damage to the caravan was psychological, from the loss of caravaners and the Councilor and his senior staff. They'd waited as long as they could before leaving two days before. Most of those who'd run away had drifted back in over the day and a half they remained outside of old Denver. Alex and those few of Councilor Three's administrative staff who had survived managed to sop up the mess and organize the survivors. They buried the dead together near the tree line, a way to appease the living who didn't want to leave their loved ones behind in a Hell Zone.

Those of his agents who had posed as Council attackers had long since pulled back. Alex had thoroughly enjoyed the raid on Lucas's waiting mercenaries in the early morning hours after he'd seen Lena and Jackson off. He was happy to take out his frustration and fear on those who'd attacked his people. That he had also been responsible for an attack on them was irrelevant—his attack had been for the greater good, and his agents had only targeted known Council collaborators. It served a purpose other than the terrorizing of Zone Three's people. They didn't know it yet, but he was freeing them.

The bulk of Alex's Fort Nevada force had been sent back to the fort to await his and Thomas's return from the Council Meet.

Jackson and Lena were with them.

Alex savored the warmth that spread through his chest at the memory of their goodbye. Once they'd managed to pull themselves out of the car, they'd handled the final details of their group's pull-out together. He'd been right. They made an excellent team. She'd even smoothed Jackson's ruffled feathers as she took control of those who'd be returning with her, while Alex handed out final orders to the men who'd be staying with him.

As the men had scattered to their assigned exit points, she'd taken Alex's hand in hers and pulled him to the side. After running her hands up his sides, she'd risen to her toes to cup his face in her small hands.

"Tell me again," she'd demanded softly. "We will make this work."

He'd grinned down at her. "I'm Alex. You're Lena. It's what we do."

She'd returned his expression with a broad smile of her own. "Especially when we're highly motivated."

Alex had leaned down to press his lips to hers, to pull up on the Dust within her and feed on the energy that swirled between them. Feeling her doing the same had deepened the exchange. It had been about sharing who they were, and not just what they could do to each other.

When he'd caught his breath again, he whispered against her lips, "I'm about as motivated as a man can be."

She'd pressed her lips softly to his for barely a moment, then she'd gone, turning away and signaling the men who'd be heading back with her with a three-note whistle she must have heard him use before. Minutes later, they'd pulled out.

Alex had headed over to the ridge where his men were waiting to lead the raid on Lucas's men. He hadn't looked back. He didn't need to. Everything he needed he carried within him until he returned to his home or she came back to him.

He hadn't felt this focused and energized in a long time. It wasn't just the relationship, he told himself, because that was tucked away in its compartment. He only allowed that to affect him when he he were together.

Okay, Alex. Sure.

It wasn't that. It wasn't. It must be that he had the chance to return to what he did best. There were other villains afoot. Courtesy of Councilor Three, Alex had names. And courtesy of Lucas's ineffectual leadership, they had proof, too. The Meet would be even more of a spectacle than he had planned. He meant to flush his prey out of hiding. And once they were exposed, he and Lena could hunt them together.

Ya see? Lena again.

His growl at himself turned into an unrepentant grin. Whatever the source of the new enjoyment, he had a caravan to rebuild, people to inspire, and a new Councilor-elect to prep. He hoped the young man had the foresight to be out among the caravaners, now, cultivating their feelings for him. If they played it right, he would have a swollen wave of popularity to ride into Azcon after the Council Meet.

Alex stopped to watch a scene playing out at the end of a car two up from him. A small, satisfied smile played about his lips. Danny, the most senior survivor of the Councilor's staff other than Alex himself, had taken command and handed out evening assignments as the caravan tucked in for another post-raid night on the road. Tend to the wounded. Set a perimeter. Ensure everyone was fed. See to the equipment.

As the charismatic young man spoke to a mechanic and sent him off to check an engine, Danny caught Alex standing at the end of the car line. He strode over.

"Word about Lena?" He spoke her name in an undertone. Of course he'd take the first opportunity they'd had to speak alone to ask about her.

Alex shook his head. "She'll be making Fort Nevada in a day or two. It'll be fine."

"Tell me again that she doesn't hate me." He'd always feared her discovering the full truth.

After Danny had screwed up and caused her arrest, Alex had to imagine the feeling had multiplied. It had turned out all right, though.

It had turned out better than Alex could have imagined.

Alex hated that he'd had to keep this from her. He hated that Thomas had forced his hand, but he'd extracted a promise from Thomas in exchange that would guarantee her and her girls time and space. Still, there would be hell to pay when he was finally able to share the full arc of what they'd done with her. He just wasn't sure if he dreaded the fireworks, or looked forward to them. Lena did fiery like nobody else.

Alex shook his head again. "I'll make it right. Lena and I will work it out."

It's what we do.

He swallowed the smile that was threatening to break out and made his voice no-nonsense for the young man in front of him now. "Are you ready? We have a lot to get done tonight. We'll reach the Meet the day after tomorrow, and once we get there and they swear you in as Councilor Three, it's going to be meeting after crisis after intrigue."

Danny nodded, excitement written across his face.

Alex might not have found a successor in Jackson, but he'd found a kindred spirit in Lena's brother. He'd been training him for this for a long time.

"I'm ready."

ACKNOWLEDGMENTS

I've been telling stories since I could talk, some better than others. According to family legend, one of them got me expelled from preschool. Outside of that early experience, there have been many who encouraged me, especially my teachers.

In the ninth grade, I promised my English teacher that someday I would be thanking her in my first book. She grinned back and told me she had no doubt that I would, and I better not forget! It grieves me that it took me so long to accomplish this that she did not live to see it. I hope she knew how much her encouragement, lessons, and belief in my abilities meant to me. Thank you, Mary Adah Curbera. I never forgot.

Thank you also to my beta readers and critique partners, Charity, Anne Marie, Christi, Martin, Amy, Cathryn, Danny, Tammy, Jenn.

To Bryan Thomas Schmidt and Claire Ashgrove, my amazing editors, thank you for your hard work, dedication, and belief in this story. You made this story better. I am so grateful to the entire team at Finish the Story editing!

Thank you to Regina Wamba of MaeI Designs for my amazing cover. Your work is, as always, gorgeous!

I also offer a heart full of thanks to my family and all of the friends over the years who have also believed in me, urging me on, sometimes sweetly, sometimes with threats. Special thanks to my mother, who reads every word I write, and my sister, whose demands for more encourage me to keep going. My dad and oldest brother lit the fire by introducing me to sci fi so many years ago, and they've has been enthusiastic and honest champions since. I love you all...and look! I did it!

My younger brother, Tim, deserves a special mention. Not only does he read every word I write, but he is a patient and enthusiastic sounding board, confidante, imagination fire-er, cheerleader, and babysitter (when I absolutely have to get out of the house and go write in a coffee shop). Without his support, this book would not be what it is.

And to you, my readers, *thank you*. Without an audience, the stories that come would just be daydreams. You are what makes a writer. I'd love to hear from you, and I would be pleased and honored if you were moved to leave a review at your point of sale. Thank you for reading, and for going on the journey.

And finally, I finish the way the book began...with gratitude and love for my amazing husband for his support and the love story that rivals any romance novel reunion story. I am grateful for that first love in high school. I am grateful you never forgot. I am grateful we found each other again as adults. And I am so grateful that you've never stopped believing in me, not once, along that journey.

I raise a glass to all of you! Many, many thanks!

ABOUT THE AUTHOR

Kate Corcino is a reformed shy girl who found her voice (and uses it...a lot). She believes in magic, coffee, Starburst candies, genre fiction, descriptive profanity, and cackling over wine with good friends. A recovering Dr. Pepper addict, she knows the only addiction worth feeding is the one that comes with characters and dialogue.

Corcino also believes in the transformative power of second chances. Cheers to works-in-progress of the literary and lifelong variety!

She currently lives in her beloved desert Southwest with her family, three dogs, two cats, and a rotating cast of invisible friends (aka very demanding characters).

For more information, or to keep up-to-date on releases, free offerings, and general fun, feel free to follow the author on either her Facebook page https://www.facebook.com/AuthorKateCorcino or her web page www.KateCorcino.com